JUKIMA

Kathleen C. Arceneaux

Jukima
Copyright Kathleen C. Arceneaux
2010
ISBN: 978-0615554983
https://www.createspace.com/3831126

Acknowledgements

I would like to thank the Virginia Commission for the Arts for their Fellowship award, that gave me valuable time to work toward completing the novel. Thanks go to David Dugas for formatting the book and creating the cover-art. I would also like to acknowledge the friendship and encouragement of Elizabeth Fine and Robert Walker – both authors, themselves, and as such, they understand very well the creative process and the hard work required to complete a manuscript. I also would like to acknowledge Humberto Camilloni-Rodriguez, major professor for my Ph.D. The challenges of my dissertation helped my understanding of the process of weaving together the many components of a complex manuscript,

I would like to acknowledge the editors of the late *bananafish* literary journal. A Pushcart nomination for my short story, "Survivor," gave me encouragement to believe in the quality of my work, and to continue writing. Thanks, also, to the Heekin Group for a Tara Fellowship for short fiction. The encouragement from these and other awards gave me some measure of confidence to continue perfecting my craft, and to complete *Jukima*.

A special thanks goes to my daughter, Robin Dugas, for her astute editing of the manuscript. *Jukima* is a better book because of her input.

JUKIMA

Chapter One

In my memories of childhood, it's almost always raining. The rain slopped in gouts of gray water, or it drizzled, and sometimes it roared, or it surrounded in hisses, a seething, woven sound, and it drilled holes in the pale, weak lawn where the gutters compressed the water and forced it down strongly. I was amazed by the strength of that water. Often a puddle spread from where the water shot out of the drain at the west corner of the house where I lived for all of my early years, and the grass beneath the metal-colored water looked like a drowned forest. When the sky cleared, the grass stems were upright and lithe, magnified and swaying slightly beneath the thin skin of the water. The pool there, all the pools, filled and ebbed.

I was born into a house full of sisters and was second to the last one. There were six of us, and our parents, living together in the same house and following the same routines until we began to leave to take up our own lives, except for our parents of course, who remained behind and seemed as permanent as the geometry of the house. Gretta was first. Two years after Gretta had come Vernelle, and then another space of two years and Martha was born, and only eleven months after that came Amanda, so close to Martha in age that they moved about together as a unit and usually excluded me. And then I was born, and the family must have seemed finished. But it was not finished, because Doreen arrived to complete us. She looked very much like the rest of us, with eyes the color of lichens, and rough, almost blond hair.

When my little sister Doreen was born, I was seven. My childhood was unpunctuated except for Doreen's birth. There were no serious illnesses, no deaths. That there were so many of us seemed to be an unavoidable condition, as though we were rooted in a place that had certain qualities of land or weather that must be worked around, or coaxed, or humored. Because in my family we resemble each other so closely and because we had so little need for companionship outside of the cluster of us, we thought of everyone else as not completely real. That someone could have black hair, or dark, emotional eyes was a source of wonder, or pity, that they were not of our world.

Only when it was raining did I feel fulfilled, as though the water falling everywhere was a kind of inexhaustible nourishment. The concussions of rain on the roof in winter made me glad that there were so many of us, because it made me feel that together, we could withstand anything if we had to. As a child, I was almost never alone. On winter nights I lay in my bed in the room I shared with Doreen and I worried the fluff of the blanket and listened to the rain, and in its pauses, the little, feral sounds Doreen made as she slept. Mewling sounds, soft grunts, and the slurping as she sucked her thumb in moments of wakefulness. When the thunder bellowed and the room snapped into brightness it seemed to be full of fantastic shapes that moved in jerks. When that happened, I was grateful that Doreen climbed into my bed and attached herself to me like a limpet. She smelled both sugary and soured, like sweetened, turning milk. Her hair was damp against her face and she was mysterious and soft in her lack of knowledge about anything that I took for granted. I think of her as always being three years old, or four. Even if the adult Doreen were to stand before me at this moment, I would sense the small, rounded child ensnared somehow within her womanly flesh.

Outside of my parents' house, everything was so green, lush to the point of decadence. The vegetation grew madly and outlived its capabilities. In the spring, the new growth of the forsythia and azaleas was stretched and moist, in the way I think of all baby things as being slightly wet and not yet hardened to their lives. The fresh needles on the hemlocks were bendable, and their cones were tightly creased packages. The puddles of spring were clean, formed on the raw grass from barrages of rain that had no time to soak in.

My father began projects and then he veered off, while my mother was dogged and focused. When she began to sew a quilt, it might take ten years, but at the end of it, there would be a quilt, its fabrics already polished by the rub of her fingers. I like to think that I have absorbed some of both their natures: the optimism, and the stamina. I didn't understand then how tired my mother must have been; being only a child, I was unable to recognize the signs of her exhaustion. She said often that she was of Scottish extraction, which made genealogy sound clinical, and regulated. I felt that her being of Scottish extraction had nothing to do with me, although had I thought about it, I might have seen my future written in her face.

There was never any explanation offered for how many of us there were in our family. We were not Catholic, and we were not farmers who needed many children to work the land, to grow into an adulthood that was prearranged. My parents must have been stunned by the time that I joined them. I was born near to Christmas and was named Noelle, and when my parents described me to anyone, as differentiated from the others, they said I was "a winter child."

One of my strongest remembrances of childhood has to do with the attic room. The attic was unfinished and smelled wildly of the ooze of cedar. All the wood there was raw and blond, as though it had been freshly cut and was still as clean as the blade of the saw. The floor was of bare rafters, bridging the prickling, pink billows of the insulation. Boards had been laid in paths and so one could walk along them safely if one did not step off onto the thin flooring. In the attic were a few trunks and boxes, a dress-form like a dismembered witch, and deeply recessed dormer windows that drew planks of light out into the open spaces. This light, the transparent color of cider, was busy with motes and had edges as abrupt as those of the rafters. I had claimed a space in the attic as my own, in the narrow cleft of the westward dormer window. I had floored the space with scraps of plywood, had tacked up a shelf for whatever books I was reading that season, had even washed the window. My family knew that I went up into the attic often (they had no interest in it themselves), but did not question why, or bother me there. The house was so full that when I was elsewhere, I was one less body in it.

Something unusual happened in the attic, or at least it was unusual to my childish self, and it is my strongest memory. I think it was in late fall, although it could have been early spring -- some awkward time where the air has the scent of immanence, like the tang of approaching snow. Ours was a house replete with books of all sorts, some of them trashy, some classics, many of them hurriedly chosen from the book clubs my parents joined and then were baffled about how to cancel. I remember one of them in particular from that time -- *The Golden Bough* -- an anthropology text that I understand now was more of a catalog of the bizarre than it was rigorous scholarship of any kind that could be respected. Although I don't recall that it had illustrations, it seemed to me to be a book filled with colors, very vivid, smoldering impressions, and snips of information about customs that I had no idea existed in the same world where I lived so comfortably. These customs seemed unreal, peculiar to the point of provoking my complete fascination, although I assumed they were factual from the strict text and the somber cover of the book. The way we lived, in our family, had seemed to me to be the only way it was possible to be, and *The Golden Bough* showed me what else was available, hinted at choices.

It was amazing to me to realize how some people decorated themselves, drew or carved on their skins or wore fanciful headgear -- unwieldy, and splashily painted, sprouting feathers and fur and dangling thin, flashing slices of metal. And this book was ripe with sexuality, specifically, something else I had no idea about. It made of it a thing of feathers and paint and the odd, flickering dances that I imagined went along with the costuming, like the contortions of lusty birds. I had seen the way the squirrels went mad in the spring, flipping and leaping about, and now I felt I understood something of that.

And so it was spring, or it was the dregs of autumn, and I had discovered the *Golden Bough* and was on my way to the attic to read it, when my sister Gretta gave me a trinket. She handed me a palm-sized, faceted, pear-shaped crystal with a hole drilled through it for a string or cord. I don't know why she gave it to me at that time; it was just something she didn't want, and I had passed by her in the kitchen. If someone else had passed by then, it would have gone elsewhere. She asked, "Do you want this? Well, *do* you?" Impatient, trivializing whatever it was she offered, giving me a glimpse of it in her hand, like a wink, and then snatching it back.

I said, "Sure. I guess. What's it for?" She said, "An ornament, of course. Well, do you want it, or not? I'm sure the baby would like to play with it. I could give it to her?" At that, I took the crystal from her hand and it was as warm as if it generated its own energy. In my other hand was the book, and the two objects seemed to go together interestingly.

The attic was entered by a stair that swung down from the ceiling of the kitchen, and it was magical, like a stairway to a distant and slightly naughty part of the world. You would pull on the cord and a door would slide back and slowly the stair would extend, tongue-like, and then there it would be -- the cleated ramp and the dark, rectangular hole in the ceiling into which the stair vanished. I nurtured a hope that the house held other magical and clever things -- secret passages and walls that

4

swung out quietly on hidden gears -- but if they were there, they remained undiscovered. I waited until Gretta had gone on up the hall, and then I pulled the cord and climbed to the attic, which was several degrees warmer. It was an uncommonly luminous day, and the attic was gilded with light from the west windows. The wood of the rafters took in the light and held it awhile, and the walls soaked in what of it they could capture. The attic smelled clean and somewhat dangerous, like a recently felled tree that still has attached to it the violence of the blade.

The journey along the path of boards to my secret nook was made with careful attention, and then I curled into the space to read. But before I opened the book, I hung the crystal at the window, using a thread stripped from the hem of my jeans. And then I forgot it was there. I read for quite a long time, and the sun dropped down in increments. I could feel the warmth on my cheek and then on my shoulder, and then on my hip, like the body of a small child resting there. I could smell roasting onions and pork, and I heard, faintly, the buzz of voices below me. I was already entranced by the book. I was reading about masks, how the masks could transform not only appearance, but identity. The dancer in the butterfly mask, for instance, would become light and lighter, would flitter or float on slight puffs of breeze. The one who wore a mask was a god, or was butterfly incarnate, or a gazelle, a snake, or a hedgehog. Or something not wholly explainable? The one wearing the mask could become anything chosen and enacted, could participate in magic, or even cause it.

This book was like the discovery of a secret, or a giant step toward a maturity that could accommodate the ambiguous, even incorporate it. As a child, I sometimes wondered what anyone saw when they looked at me? One like all the others? In my family we all look so similar that when I was first viewed as an infant, I am sure that my features were expected and were regarded with the satisfaction that comes when the anticipated comes to pass. A little sign that all is regular in a world where surprise is rude. The masked and costumed dancers I was reading about *believed* that they had been transformed, and who was to say, for certain, that they had not been changed? I suddenly wanted to make masks and costumes, to clothe myself in a difference that gave me more power than I presently had, which, I felt, was none at all.

The rituals of the masks suggested genuine magic and brought up the possibility of my participation in it. It was then that something happened that seemed to affirm those thoughts.

On the page of the book, teasing the line I was reading, appeared a spot of light -- a mothy, flickering rainbow. I extended my finger to touch this spot, and it settled on the back of my hand. I gasped, then laughed. It was my idea, externalized purely and expressed in light. I moved my hand away and the spot floated again on the page, or on the invisible air above it, and then it spun away. When I jerked my head around to search for the spot, I saw that it had multiplied astoundingly. The walls of my little space, the inverted "V" of the ceiling, were swarming with these moths of colored light that twirled and bounced. I saw that they were also spangling my body, scurrying the cloth of jeans and shirt, alighting on the toe of my tennis shoe and bouncing away again. And then, of course I saw the crystal rotating on the end of its thread. The sky beyond it was molten with sunset. I was disappointed for only an instant and then I reconstructed the significance of what was happening. That the crystal facets were prisms in no way negated the magic. It was a display that was focused by a certain synchronicity with the lines I had just read, the ideas sparked by those lines, and the playful chips of light that were dancing across my limbs and body and all around me. There was an optimism in all of this, and a sense that the answers to the deeper questions did not reside within the confines of relics, but were elusive and gorgeous as butterflies made of light.

It was a discovery that I could not have articulated then, but I knew that I had to share it. I was alone in a lost corner of a house full of people. The sunset was beginning to leach out its colors, and so I hurried back along the path of planks and backed down the ladder. I felt with excruciating slowness for the next rung, planted my foot there, squared it under my weight and then located the next, and so on, and down. It was all taking such a long time. The kitchen into which I descended was empty, although the aromas there gave the room a heaviness, or a sogginess, as though I had descended again into the most mundane of earthly spaces. I decided that I would command the first person I saw to come up into the attic with me and I would reveal the colored lights. That the first person I saw was Doreen was problematic. She was only three years old at the time, and too heavy for me to carry, yet too small to negotiate the widely spaced rungs of the ladder.

"Do-Dee," I said, "there's something wonderful upstairs!" Her eyes bulged with greed as she looked up at the hole in the ceiling. Then she looked back at me.

"Candy?"

6

"No, but it's like candy. You can look at it."

Doreen placed a slimy corner of her shirt in her mouth and sucked noisily. Then she unplugged her mouth and stretched up her arms to me. I carried her up. I have no idea how I did that. I was nine years old. A very wiry nine, but I don't really remember the ascent. I must have drooped her from the crook of my arm, pushed her upwards with the lift of my alternating thighs. She was completely silent, as though the nudge caused by any sound might dislodge us. I am sure that she was impressed by my previously concealed powers, my heroic effort on the ladder, and also, she had never been in the attic before. How could she have? I saw it through her eyes. The space was huge. The white-blond wood glistened with beads of sap and the insulation padding the space between the rafters must have seemed like an angel's cloud. Doreen still said nothing. She still hung from my arms. I hurried along the path, but carefully, because I dared not drop her -- the voids between the rafters were only as solid as lath and plaster and paint. I had the thought, for an instant, that if I did drop her, someone in whatever room was below us would see the miracle of a cherub falling through the ceiling.

Of course the lights were gone by then. My elation crumpled. The sun had lowered until only a gold rim was showing at the horizon. I had set Doreen down on the plywood flooring of my little niche and she reached out, I assumed, to touch my row of books. I restrained her wrist to prevent her from pestering my books, and then saw the object of her attention. One spot of light remained, dangling from the wand of a tardy beam. It seemed to be hopping and Doreen was laughing and opening and closing her fist. Had she been able to snare it she would have crushed out all its juices, but I was simply relieved that she had seen it.

The sun's rim dropped away quickly. The sky was completely gray then, fading to ordinary as it retracted its light. The spot vanished, and Doreen yelped, "Give it!" and when I could not, she was outraged. The screech she let loose was directed at everything and at myself; she must have thought I had somehow produced the rainbowed spot of light, and then had withheld it from her. I grabbed her around the middle and hurried her to the hole in the attic floor, but her body was rigid now, jutting and braced. Her elbows bored into my ribs and her knees impeded me everywhere. I was unable to carry Doreen down the ladder. Just the thought of the reverse journey was terrifying. Doreen's squalls brought a crowd to the foot of the ladder. I stood there with Doreen captured by the waist, her face squirming and flushed, tears streaming down. The excitement had stripped her of language, which at her age was only tenuously held and must have seemed as magical as anything could have been to her, to be able to make herself clearly understood. The family stood below us, with expressions of consternation.

My father eventually carried Doreen down. I remember it as a trip full of contortions, cursings, and advice from his audience, which consisted of myself looking down at him and Doreen (who had gone self-protectively silent again) and my mother and sisters standing so close to the bottom of the stair that they would have been a living cushion had there been a misstep. The aftermath of that episode, I don't remember very well. I know that I was not punished, for that was not our habit, but there was a subtle difference in the way I was regarded. I had proven myself to be unpredictable and would bear watching. I took a certain pleasure in my family's uneasiness about me. Doreen followed me around slavishly after that, and could be counted upon as an unwavering audience for my little adventures. And I did become more adventurous, as though I were trying to live up to my family's altered perceptions of my character.

I explored, not only books, but all the territory within walking distance of my house. Although I sometimes took Doreen along with me, most of my wanderings were solitary, because when I was alone and exploring, I ceased to be exactly myself. I became absorbed into some larger idea -- I was neither child nor adult -- I simply *was*. When alone with no one but myself to speak to or to answer to, I could enter into fantasy, could play any role. Doreen babbled. She asked interminable questions, and the sound of my simple explanations, in my own childish voice, made invention difficult. She didn't understand that we were to be pioneers, for example, and by the time I had explained our respective roles, my scenarios had became hopelessly contrived.

I had a favorite place that I discovered not long after the event with Doreen and the attic. Some distance from my family's house was a place that seemed to me to be an unspoiled territory, although it was actually only a field of scruffy grasses. The field consisted of several adjacent vacant lots that have long since been gridded and tamed by pavement, houses, and orderly shrubs. At the time I discovered it, it was purely spacious, untroubled by human presence. I discovered this field one day when I decided to alter the usual route of my walk home from school. I walked until the pavement ended abruptly in brambles, their coils dredged with an ashy dust. I would later discover that in summers, the brambles there were heavy with blackberries, but I never brought berries home because I didn't want to reveal where I had found them. I guarded the secret of the field closely.

That first time, I edged my way through the brambles and then stood hesitating in the long, seed-drooped grass and looked up at the sky, which was very large over an openness that was prairie-like. Behind me were streets and houses and tended lawns, and before me I could see only the silvering grasses. The thought of crossing this untried territory was alluring, but the field did end eventually, and I found my way home without much difficulty. As I left it I glanced back and could see the trampled path I had made in the tall grass, as civilizing as tracks left in snow.

I returned to the field I had found as often as I could, because it had yielded a treasure -- a pond was there, held in a scoop in the earth and not visible from the field's borders. The bulges in the land were deceptive, and made of each quiet slope a horizon. The pond was murky with silt and algae, stirring slightly in a current that I discovered came from a rusting pipe that evacuated its contents into the water. I ignored the pipe as irrelevant. The pond was mine, and when I claimed it, it grew in importance. I was the discoverer of an ocean, although it couldn't have been more than thirty feet across at its widest, and had greenish gray water and a collar of sudsy scum ringing its banks. There were scrub willows next to the pond's edge. They were weak, in that the banks were shelved and hollowed and some of the trees had fallen, while others listed irrevocably. There were logs where I could sit, and there was a narrow, silty beach, iridescent with oil.

Once I had discovered that the field could be crossed and took me no more than three blocks out of my way, I usually walked home by that route. I remember that sometimes my mother would comment about the seeds and burrs that had hooked themselves onto the cloth of my skirt and onto my socks and shoelaces as opportunistic travelers. But, she was distracted and tired, and asked me no questions about where I had been or what I had been doing. I visited my pond in all kinds of weathers and seasons and came to know the birds that visited there, and I investigated the prints of animals pressed into the mud of the pond's banks. I knew of course that most of the prints had been made by transient dogs, but I imagined unseen wolves -- almost hoped for them. The pond stank in summers, steamed on cold mornings, and in deep winters it never froze completely but was glazed with plates of rime under which bubbles drifted and slid.

When alone in the field -- truly alone -- with no visible streets, sidewalks, or the rooflines of houses, I was unreachable by my family. No errands or chores could be tossed my way and I could belch comfortably or sit with legs spraddled with no one to rebuke my carelessness. It was much more emancipating than the attic room, where I could still hear the murmur of my family's voices. When alone at my pond, there was something else that I came to notice -- I felt a small but growing discomfort, like a generalized yearning, or an ache that spreads out from a small core of dissatisfaction. I could not name this yearning, except that I sensed it was a kind of sorrow. I think now that it was perhaps the beginning of an urge to go somewhere else other than where I had been born. Even to be someone else? I didn't really lack for anything, except that I was restless.

My daydreams ran rampant when I was alone. I imagined that the clusters of seed pods were a natural, unclaimed harvest and I gathered them in my skirt, and on a flat rock I pretended to pound the seeds into flour. I was patient as I did this, imagined that it was a simple and worthy contribution to some, unnamed, greater good. I dug for riches in the soft earth of the field, and sometimes I found petrified clamshells, which I welcomed as proof that the pond was an ocean. My fantasies about this new land eventually became repetitive until I was not satisfied with having discovered an ocean. I wanted to cross it. I became obsessed with that one idea.

One autumn afternoon I did cross the pond, on a raft I made of fallen saplings snugged together with rope I had pilfered from my parents' garage. I labored over this raft for a long time, struggling with the shaggy rope until my hands were abraded and sore. I worked in solitude. I was sometimes tempted to share these secrets with Doreen, although I was sensible enough to realize that a pond and a raft were too perilous for her. When the raft was finally finished, I paddled it across with a long switch of pine-branch, and my weight partially submerged the shelf of poles, and my shoes were swamped. It didn't matter, because the raft held, did not tip and roll me into the water, and did not sink completely. The water-bugs skated with ease around the raft, but to me the water was heavy and formidable as I dragged at it with the branch. I

10

labored forward, crossing the water under my own power. I remember that there were pewter-colored clouds that day and I was almost certain that a storm would break before I reached the safe harbor of the stand of reeds that approached, so slowly. As the raft threatened to come unstrung and the murky water swamped my shoes and the clouds glowered down, I realized that I did not know how deep the water was. Perhaps that was the point -- that I didn't know how deep the water was?

Chapter Two

When I left my childhood home, I didn't really comprehend that I would never go back there again as quite the person I had been. Now, I sense that there should have been something commemorative, some ceremony with its special words, actions, and music, to signify that transition. To me, college was a place of honor. The Douglas firs on the campus were very stern in their regimental rows. I chose to live alone, most likely because I had grown up in a house full of people and wanted to discover my own rhythms and preferences.

I thought of college as a kind of adventure. I studied diligently, passing through each level, impatient for the next. I saw myself as a scavenger, pinching up facts here and there and placing them next to one another to see how they could be made to fit together. When I studied anthropology, I became evermore captured by the different ways people were in their lives. I worked in the campus bookstore, and in summers I traveled. I was impressed by the languages people spoke. and I listened to how the words issued from their mouths in melodious garbles or were bitten off in splinters. I watched how words formed the shapes of people's mouths, wetted their lips, made their shoulders shrug or their hands wave about. When I traveled, I felt that I moved about in a strange kind of silence; I did not understand most of the languages I heard, but I connected closely with the worlds of things I saw.

The summer before I began my graduate studies, I went to Paris, to visit the Musee de l'Homme. I lurked there for days. There had been a sharply rotten smell in certain out-of-the-way corners; when I returned to my hotel room, my clothing smelled faintly of rancid tallow and I felt that I had been in the presence of something forbidden. The art I had seen had been so bold and lusty that it had made even the glitter of Paris dim in comparison. I had never seen such objects before, made by human hands. The carvings, the sculptures, had been given souls by their makers. Some of the carved things were huge and still had shreds of fabric or shells nailed onto the leather or the wood. Or, there were remnants of paint, mostly black, red, and white, but other colors too. They all seemed so large. Not only large in size, although some of the pieces were quite small -- the utensils, the baskets, and bowls. But everything seemed larger than reality. The sculptures loomed and were ominous and commanding. It was as though each had a space around it, like a magnetic field that couldn't be breached. And there was a feeling to them, that if I touched them they would be fleshy, heated, perhaps even pulsing slightly. It was the feeling that the art had been fabricated by human beings, yes, but also and simultaneously that the pieces had constructed themselves, turning imperceptibly this way and that in light and shadow as they were carved. I decided, in Paris, that I wanted to journey to some sultry and risky place and find the living art and the people who made it.

When I was a young woman of twenty-five, I went to live with the Tekhla Indians for the fieldwork that was required for the completion of my degree in anthropology. I don't know if this was a genuine decision, or if it was the way my life bent under the influences of that time, and in particular, the influence of my professor, George Ollieburton. It was something that had seemed inevitable. I couldn't know, then, that my journey would be much more than the fulfillment of a requirement.

In my later years at college, my life revolved around Professor Ollieburton. He had often used the Tekhla Indians to illustrate points he was making in the classroom, and it was understood that the Tekhla were *his* people, the people he studied with an alarming intensity. I respected that he had found a subject so compelling that a lifetime was not enough to dilute his fascination, although I didn't completely understand why he had selected them and not some other, more colorful culture in a friendlier, less swampy location? There was something that drew him to these people, again and again. His obsession painted them with mystery and elevated them to worthiness.

I don't know what Ollie thought of me, really. As his student, I was probably earnest to the point of absurdity, and malleable. I regarded Ollie with the deference that he must have thought he deserved. I remember one lecture in particular that captivated me. He had said, "Just suppose, for the sake of argument, that existing in the world are people who have never been contacted by anyone who belongs to modern life? Imagine that? People not yet studied, or categorized. Not diminished or diluted?" I had asked, "But is it possible there are people like that?"

Ollie raised his bushy eyebrows and said, "I think there are still places where such people could conceal themselves, if that's what they choose. Just imagine what they could tell us! And what they could tell us about ourselves, by contrast?" I wondered, then, could it be true that there still were such people, and if it were true, what would be the effects of contact with them? Would it seem like reciprocity of revealed magic? I spun away in a reverie, imagining that if I were the one to make the first contact, how would I explain to those people the contrails of jets in the sky, for example? Would I be tempted to self-aggrandizement, or would I simply tell the truth as I knew it? And just how could it be said with any authenticity that there are metal tubes in the sky and that those tubes are filled with people who do not understand, not really, how that is done, but yet they are there and they trust and are not gods at all.

Professor Ollieburton was not a calm man. He sizzled and sparked, but he seemed to have a core of compassion that gentled him. Primarily, his nature was one of continuous combustion. Teaching excited him still, although he had to be in his sixties when I began to work with him. His physical presence lent much to his authority. He was burly and impressive. He was also boyishly enthusiastic, always on the brink of emotional disarray. He seemed to be fueled by the insights of his students, and would ask in a resonant voice, "Yes, and you? What do you have to add? And you?" All the while he would be whisking his hands through his graying, yellow hair, a gesture that made him seem almost maniacal because his hair rose up wildly in tufts. He wore a snakeskin belt. Denim jeans, or more accurately, dungarees, not fashionable, but more as though he was a farm hand who relished brutal work.

During my first week in Ollie's seminar, he had mentioned the Tekhla, and I had immediately rushed to the library for more information. I was hoping, I suppose, to ingratiate myself to Ollie by displaying an interest in a topic so close to his heart? I read as many of Ollie's monographs as I could find, but was disappointed that they were largely unembellished by illustrations or photographs. There was little that had been written about the Tekhla by anyone else, and there was only one photograph that I could discover. It was on microfilm, from a newspaper clipping from the fifties, and it depicted a miserable group of Tekhla miners standing on a bluff with nothing but grainy, gray sky and rags of clouds behind them. The Indians looked flimsy. Their clothes hung loosely upon their bodies, and their stringy arms poked out of shirt sleeves. There were five men in the photograph, and they all had wide faces and stunned expressions; their faces had been emptied of all curiosity. They wore heavy-looking helmets too large for their heads, and bulky boots encumbered their feet. From my reading, I knew that these mines had closed soon after the picture had been taken. The Indians had not done well. They had sickened or broken down, and when the mines closed, the Indians who were still alive had been absorbed back into the forest.

A chapter in the Tekhla's story had closed and the ones who were left at the end of it had melted back into their former surroundings and except for Professor Ollieburton, no one had taken much interest in them since then. That the Tekhla were so pitiful in appearance was only a momentary disappointment, for in class Ollie conferred upon them a kind of splendor. I had the feeling that anyone, any subject, toward which he turned his fascination would be elevated in that way. It is rare, but it sometimes happens that into one's life steps such a teacher. When listening to Ollie's lectures, I sometimes could feel my own future approaching.

Professor Ollieburton took a sabbatical toward the end of my graduate studies; he went to live again with the Tekhla Indians, and his absence left drabness where formerly there had been vibrancy. Without the justification of Ollie's presence, the textbooks I read became stale and irrelevant. When he left, it rained and rained, and for once I was irritated by the monotonous prattling of the rain. I resented Ollie's absence. The gray pavement, the cars swishing by and lifting up fans of dirty spray, the dour buildings, the flooded sidewalks with their hopeless strings of worms, all suddenly became very average and local and restricting.

Almost nothing was heard from Ollie for months. I had become one of his teaching assistants during my last year of studies, and I was troubled by his silence, even though he had told everyone that he would be unreachable by any sort of modern communication for extended periods. He had told his students that he went to the Tekhla for renewal of spirit, and we could not argue with anything responsible for renewing Ollie's spirit. However, rumors spread among us and held the menace of dark premonitions. Ollie had died in the jungle of an esoteric, tropical illness, or he had succumbed to snake-bite? He had had some sort of accident? The most likely rumor was one that I almost believed, that Ollie had joined with the Tekhla as one of them and had no intention of returning to us. We didn't know what to make of his silence. I wondered, also, if some of the faculty knew much more than they were saying? And if that was true, why had no one gone to search for him? The faculty in the department were all accounted for and grinding away at their usual tasks. It was all very troubling.

And then Ollieburton did return, but quite uncharacteristically, he saw no one, spoke to no one on the telephone except for the department chair, who passed along the news that Ollie was indeed home, but that he would return to his academic responsibilities if and when he felt entirely up to the task. It was true, that Ollie had had an accident while in the jungle. No other information was offered, and I was terrified.

When I saw Ollie again, he was large, still, but now he seemed much older than his age -- almost doddering. He supported himself on a cane tipped by a straggle of parrot feathers. His flesh had sunk downward several notches and he belted his trousers high, nearly under his armpits, like the old men who sat, doing nothing, on the benches outside the residential hotel downtown. I grieved next for his voice, that his huge and roughly textured voice had been ground down to blandness.

Ollieburton did not return to teaching, but he maintained an office in the building. After some weeks had passed, I was summoned to visit him there. I was uncertain as to what was expected of me. He met me at the doorway, squinting from behind his gold, wire-rimmed glasses and then said, "I know you must be wondering about this." He shook his cane, swayed on his feet slightly, and then centered the cane again under his weight. We moved, so slowly, across the room to his desk and the two chairs there -- his, with its back facing the window, and mine, the plain wooden chair opposite, with the desk between them. Mine was the supplicant's chair.

As we moved slowly across the room, I must have said something encouraging, and Ollie continued.

"It was a sharpened stake. The Indians do that sometimes, sharpen a stake and hide it in the foliage, to discourage strangers. It's very effective.

"That's terrible! Was it poisoned?" I couldn't ask, specifically, but I wanted to know, had these Indians turned on Ollie, in the end -- had the stake been placed there to ambush him? Had they had enough of being the focus of his attention?

"It could have been poisoned, and I blundered into it accidentally?" Ollie tapped his leg with the cane, and almost lost his balance. He tapped, and the leg twanged, with the horrifying sound of metal being struck, muffled by the cloth of his trousers. As I feared he would, Ollie lifted the cuff of his trousers slightly, and I saw a stainless-steel rod, with a shoe attached. It looked like the purest, most efficient sort of bone. I felt ambushed by it.

"Could have been a frog," Ollie said. "Could have been, but it would take more than that to bring me down." He paused, expecting affirmation.

I said, "Obviously it would take more than that," not knowing how else to respond. Ollie was talking about frogs? He had seated himself by then, an elaborate process, and spread his hands flat on the table.

"The Tekhla tip their arrows in poison extracted from frogs, as you must know." I remembered, then, a mention of those poisonous frogs in one of Ollie's lectures. The winter day glowed softly outside the window, but the room was dark and stuffy and the radiators clanked, and there was a slightly noxious, unidentifiable scent. Ollie said, "They're blue. A sort of a turquoise, actually."

"The frogs? The frogs are blue?"

"Yes, yes. Blue. The Tekhla were kind. They were very kind to me. They applied their poultices and such. I insisted on using their medicines. It seemed like the courteous thing to do, or so I felt at the time." And then a thin, self-deprecating laugh. "My assistant went to fetch some help, finally. Frederick. My assistant. My good friend. He's an Indian, you know, but not a Tekhla. He is a Tuylo, and he is a linguist. A natural. A savant."

I had not heard of Frederick before, but Ollie seemed to think that I had. It diminished him further to me, that he had had someone with him, an expert, perhaps. I had thought he had been alone there, and it felt strangely like a betrayal.

Ollie said, "I had to be airlifted out, at great personal expense."

"Thank God you survived!" I said. What else could I say? Ollie's eyes sparkled with an almost lunatic brightness, and he said, abruptly, "There are 'others' out there." Others? I had no idea where this was leading. I asked, "Do you mean other researchers, or other Indians?"

"Other Indians, or at least that's what I assume. Other Indians who haven't been studied, assimilated, who haven't been contacted at all by modern life. They are prehistoric. They keep to the old ways, from prehistoric times. They sing the ancient songs. I thought they were fables, but then I saw them. They're like the ancestors of all people. They could be ancient enough to be the ancestors of all people, but yet, they're there and I saw them." There was a near-hysteria to Ollie's voice now, but thin and querulous, not at all commanding anymore. His mood broke. He closed his eyes. "And now, even the Tekhla are forgetting the old ways, forgetting who they are. There's not much time, or everything will be spoiled." In the shadowed light I could see a knot of pulse pounding at Ollie's forehead.

I asked, "Did you see these Indians? You saw them while you were living with the Tekhla?"

"Yes, of course I saw them. When I was ill, some of them came and sat vigil, and I could tell they were concerned. And they were magnificent, physically and in their ornaments. They had tattoos or drawings on their skins, of vines, or maybe they were just curves? Lines that curved around their bodies. They sang, and in the forest I could hear them playing instruments of some sort. Like flutes, but with incredible range, and they played eerie tunes that I'd never heard before. It could've simply been their own voices, in harmony. I don't know. The Tekhla have nothing like those instruments or songs."

"But can you be sure that they were genuinely there?" I knew I was being disrespectful, doubting Ollie's veracity and perceptions, but he said, "I admit I wasn't completely oriented to what was what. But I knew they were there. I saw them and heard them. Sometimes I fell into amazing dreams -- beautiful and terrifying dreams -- and they appeared in my dreams as well." Ollie reached out his hands as if he were imploring me. . . to what? To affirm what he had seen? I could understand how he might have had the need to invent these glorious Indians.

Ollie covered his eyes with his hands. Then he slid his hands down his face and stared at me for a moment, as though he didn't know who I was. Finally, he said, "I think these beings appear in the Tekhla legends as guardian souls. Or perhaps some sort of ancestral, collective conscience. Like angels, or how some people think of angels. Not cruel, but beings who are strong in the powers either of compassion or retribution. They are called by the Tekhla -- 'Jukima.' The Tekhla say it means 'others.' Sometimes the Tekhla just call them 'the people of the shadows.'"

I wondered, had Ollie stepped over some metaphysical edge? He was smiling to himself, then. "Or if not angels, then they're surely the previously unencountered. At least that. They played flutes. They had voices like flutes. Angelic voices, and they sang in a language I'd never heard before."

Around us, the room had darkened smoothly. Ollie didn't switch on the light and the room silvered gradually and was suffused with a tarnished light -- almost lunar. I had the digressive thought that it's so rare that anything spoken amounts to anything. People talk and talk, but I wondered, why is it so rare for anyone to make something from those words, to change something? I didn't know if I believed what Ollie was telling me. I closed my eyes. Surrendered to possibilities, in a way. I almost saw the Indians that Ollieburton spoke of, leafy shadows of Indians who might or might not have been there. In my fugue, they rustled, shifted their positions, had human, shadowy shapes and eyes that glowed golden and steady, like the eyes of panthers. The rustling could have been the rustling of wings.

Ollie began to paw through his desk, and the sudden activity broke the mood that had covered us. He shuffled through a desk drawer and then he switched on a lamp, peered into the drawer and took out a sheaf of photographs. He fanned them out on the table between us. I could recognize nearly nothing in them. Ollie was no photographer, and the images were fuzzy and off-center. I saw the forms of people, but they appeared dim. Ollie had used the wrong sort of camera, or the light had been too weak, or he had shaken the camera at the wrong moment.

Ollie shoved the photographs in front of me, smoothing the creased corners of the topmost image, leaving streaks of the oils of his fingerprints on the glossy surface. "That's Muffa, there." I could see a man-shaped blot, and it appeared that Muffa was broad-bodied and bow-legged. Ollie said, "He's a strange one, very reticent, but he was a brilliant tracker. He could tell you every sort of animal that had been nosing around the camp at night."

Ollie shuffled another photograph to the top of the stack. This one was light-struck to the point where it was almost entirely white. The white of the photograph looked sharded on its edges, like broken glass. "That's where the Tekhla fire their pottery. They build a bonfire and roll the pots around on the ends of sticks." I could see nothing in the photograph that resembled pottery, but I murmured encouragingly.

Ollie flipped through the photographs, placing each one on the top of the stack for my inspection. They were all very poor, blots of shapes where only occasionally an object or person could be identified clearly enough to be named. Muffa. A bonfire in the forest. Some vegetables laid out on a light-glazed mat. The back of a woman's head, her cap of hair as slick and glossy as patent leather. Ollie was smiling fondly, and it was clear that he didn't see the photographs as I did. To him they were perhaps reminders of events and people that were far more complicated than any, one, instant. I had the sense that when I left Ollie's office, he would riffle through these images again and again, and perhaps he would weep, and he would narrate them to no one, needing to repeat many times to himself the moments of his final trip.

Ollie placed a last photograph on top of the pile and gazed at me shrewdly. The image in this photograph was almost focused. It was the only one that was. "That's my proof," Ollie said. "My only proof." He ran his hands through his hair. He waited for my response. I studied the photograph.

I saw something, certainly, but it could have been an object fabricated by a contemporary artist. There was a moist haze of blue-green foliage, gauzy and soft, and in the foreground a tiny figure dangled from a twist of what appeared to be a thin, metallic cord. The figure was intricately carved of close-textured wood, although it was slightly blurred by the impatient hand that held the camera. The object I saw appeared to be a composite of forms -- both bird-like and human. It was exquisite. It was winged with feathers of subtle colors that looked like the colors of flesh, the flesh of various races. The limbs of the creature tapered and it had long-fingered hands, but wings grew along the length of the arms and had overlapped feathers that formed a supple wedge

The limbs of the little figure, the entirety of its form, were decorated in what appeared to be a continuous, spiraling line, as though the figure itself had been fabricated from annealed wire. I had never seen anything like it. It might have been decorated with paint, but it didn't look like paint. It could have been art transported backward from the future, from some culture that did not yet exist, with a technology that was as organic as it was magical. It was an amazing piece.

I said to Ollie, "This isn't Tekhla. Is it?" He said, softly, "Then you see what I mean?" I knew from my studies that the Tekhla could not possibly have made anything like it. Theirs was an art that had had few infusions of originality for generations. The Tekhla made simple pottery with rigid decorations scratched into the clay, of stick figures and animals and cross-hatched lines. The Tekhla wove mats. They embroidered with simply colored beads and they used motifs that were limited by the process of stringing beads on a thread. Chevrons and diamonds. Parallel lines. Simple grids.

When I saw the little figure, I was tempted to believe in Ollie's discovery of Indians who were isolated and whose culture had evolved differently from other known peoples. There had to be some explanation, and then I wondered if Ollie had somehow manufactured this artifact himself. As soon as I thought it could be a hoax, I rejected the possibility. Ollie had no skill as a photographer, and I doubted that he had the ability to make sculpture. I asked him, "Were you able to collect anything on this trip?" It was rude, of course. I was asking if he had brought back with him examples of the art made by the Indians he thought he had seen. As a further proof of his discovery.

"Of course! Of course I collected examples. Of course. I had several of those -- charms. I hid them in my tent because I didn't know how the Tekhla would react to them, and I didn't know what they were for. What sort of meaning they carried or what magic might be attached? But then when I was injured, well, I lost track of them when I was taken out of there. My things were packed up hurriedly. By others, of course. The sculptures were lost. I don't have them."

"I'm sorry," I said. Ollie said, "I'll never go back there. How could I, now?" His eyes were wet and bleary. Then he said, "You see how it is?" I saw how it was, but I wondered, did he? I wondered if the Tekhla had had enough of him, in the end?

Ollie swept the photographs back into the drawer, leaned forward and put his head in his hands. I stayed with him until he eventually made little, weak motions as if to rise from his chair. I was not surprised when he said, "Will you go, then? To continue my work?" I understood what he meant. I agreed, because it was impossible not to agree with him. I promised. I would continue his work.

When I stood to leave, Ollie succeeded in shoving himself up from his chair. He took a pen from his desktop, rotated it as if he had never seen such an implement before, and then he tucked it into his pocket. And then, I was walking home under a clear, winter evening arched over by stars. I sensed that there must be one, perfect word for that condition of sparkle, abundance, and untouchability. I was so young, then, but I felt that I understood how complicated Ollieburton was, how complicated anyone with intelligence was. Ollie was somehow a paradox of innocence and arrogance, and he was old, and not well, and grievously facing the end of his work, while mine was just then beginning.

That I would go to live among the Tekhla to continue Ollie's had seemed to be an inevitable decision. Yet, I was unprepared. The photograph I had seen in the old newspaper clipping worried me. It appeared that the Tekhla were a dour, introverted, passionless people. I thought that perhaps to Ollie, it was the idea of them and not their literal culture that he found compelling, or it was the rain-forest itself, where he said that there were places where direct sunlight never touched. I imagined a place where all the light was inflected by moisture and strained through foliage, filtered and scattered and weakened. In such a murky light, only the most adapted of things could thrive. I tried to prepare myself, but it was impossible to know, really, what I would face. I resolved to maintain an anthropologist's detachment. The idea of the "people of the shadows," as Ollie had referred to them, seemed like a fairy tale. I would study the Tekhla, and would remain open to possibilities. I felt invulnerable and my future stretched long and bright before me.

Chapter Three

I tried to prepare for my trip as best I could. I thought that my project was clear -- I would study the things the Tekhla made and the ways their beliefs were represented in their material production. I would fill in the blank spaces in Ollie's research. Ollie had given me the mildewed notebook he had compiled of the Tekhla language, and I studied it. The pronunciation was difficult because many of the sounds were liquid and slurred -- there were subtle differences that gave similar sounds entirely different meanings. The Tekhla grammar was complicated, and I struggled to make sense of the unusual ways of linking words together. Despite my efforts, I knew I would be going to these people with only the slightest ability to communicate. Mistakes were likely.

I knew that with the Tekhla I would live in a village of straw houses that were placed very near to one another, and I would see the patterned surfaces of the people's lives, and I supposed I would hear intimate noises and conversations, arguments, and seductions. I wasn't afraid of the differences I would encounter, or of the risks, because I was very young and possessed the security of energy and health.

By the time I left, Ollieburton had greatly deteriorated. His face had become a greasy gray, with spidery blotches on his cheeks. He sat in his office and stared out the window, and it was said that he had taken to drinking. However, on his good days he was able to help me obtain the necessary grants and he assisted in making arrangements to travel. Once begun, the process of departure was unstoppable. And finally, all had been done that could be done.

My mother and Doreen drove me to the airport. I had not seen them for a long time, and both of them looked slightly thickened and different from my most recent memories of them.

This confused me for an instant, and then they slipped into their identities as though no time had passed. My mother was wearing a plain, dark dress and a little linen jacket and a single, unassuming strand of pearls. Doreen had married over a year before this, and had her sleeping baby slung from her neck in a canvas pouch. Doreen, or the combination of Doreen and her baby, smelled like spoiling applesauce and rose petals. I had seen this infant, Joel, soon after his birth, but now he hung there as a significant weight and his head was plush with sprouting hair.

My mother's expression was hard to decipher. I had never seen her face arranged in quite that way before, stiff with concern or fear. I had the thought that she was memorizing me, the way I looked just then, in my khaki slacks, my hair swept up in a practical headband, my luggage in disarray around my feet. She softened her lips only for a kiss on my cheek. I thought her dark, understated but expensive clothing was brave, and that she was brave, and that her sealed, firm lips were pressing back all types of useless admonitions.

The flight took only a few hours, and I amused myself during that time. That the plane bored a self-sealing tunnel through the clouds didn't seem extraordinary to me. I read magazines, ate the food when it was offered, and worried, slightly, about the grubby look of the horizon, like oily dust soiling the collar of a shirt. My destination was the city of Riolapa, and I saw from the airplane that its buildings were pressed together in a bowl of a valley that trapped dirty fog . All around were the jags of mountains, snowy in swatches, but sooty-dark on the sunny ridges. The cab ride took me through a city that reeked of asphalt and citrus, although from my clothing I still caught whiffs of evergreen forest. Buses and trucks ejected gouts of soot. I blinked and blinked in a glare so intense that it was caustic. I had the kind of grainy headache that comes from too little sleep and unrelenting noise.

The cab driver was peevish, saying, "A rich lady would have that much stuff. You must be a rich lady." And then, "Too much stuff. My whole family altogether and their children's children do not have that much stuff." He was stating facts as he understood them. His eyes were wet and brown, and his eyelids drooped morosely. I thought his assumptions were insulting -- after all, he did not know me. The cab was humid and my clothing clung to the seat and peeled away rudely whenever I shifted to cross my legs. When we reached the hotel, I over-tipped and was angry with myself for doing so. I hissed at the driver, "Now go and buy some stuff." I was immediately ashamed of snapping at him, but he seemed not to have heard me and was gazing carefully at the money as if inspecting it for fleas.

The next few days I don't remember clearly. The anti-malarial pills I had begun to take made me woozy and swarmy and altered my perceptions until I stepped inelegantly from ledges that did not exist. I over-reached for objects, and was generally awkward. The pills made me feel quite unlike myself. It was as if I were lodged in a raucous daydream suffused with the spicy, high-voltage color of equatorial dawnings and dusks. My hotel room was too bright: a flamingo-colored spread on the bed, a turquoise, over-stuffed chair, and painfully white walls that appeared to have been dragged with the tines of a fork. The view from my hotel window was a privileged over-look, a very lofty perch -- a hot-colored room levitating on the fog of gritty exhaust. The buildings across from the hotel glittered a salty sparkle. The awnings that covered the sidewalks were juicy with color: turquoise and strawberry-red, lime-green, and there were flowering vines tumbling about in their containers close to the street. Night fell abruptly, and a paunchy, orange moon hung low in the sky.

When I called the airport, daily, I was told that my plane was not ready. Not ready? It was a charter flight, and I couldn't understand what was causing the delay. Not ready? Were they constructing an airplane from scratch out of wire and tin and rubber bands? I waited. I called the airport. I bought extra cans of insect spray and boxes of Band-Aids until I began to feel over-prepared, as an athlete loses a whetted edge if over-trained. During the nights, when I eventually slept, I dreamed of broad, cocoa-colored faces with inscrutable but probably hostile expressions. The faces were surrounded by coronas of feathers, dangerously hued.

I waited in my hotel room, but I had my plans, which actually didn't seem too complicated at that point. I would fly to the village of Bualati, where arrangements had been made for a driver, with a jeep, to meet me. It would be three days to Tuylo by jeep from Bualati, and then there would be a boat for the up-river journey, and then, if I were lucky, I would locate the Tekhla encampment quickly. Settle in very quickly.

In Riolapa, there was no one I could really speak with, and I felt the edges of my personality beginning to blur. It was a large enough place for anonymity to be nearly automatic, and my moods had been trampled flat by the heat. As I went about my errands, the streets seemed to be buckling and oozed beads of tar that fouled my shoes. At night, sirens cut slices in the night. The sirens were self-important and awful, as though all the city were in flames and the fire-engines were racing about ineffectually.

I had asked Ollieburton what I should take to the Indians, what sort of tokens might be appropriate? And he had said, "candy." I was appalled. Not that I presumed that they could be bought off by strings of plastic beads, but candy? It was fiendish. Ollie had said their teeth were unspoiled, tough and brilliantly white. They used their teeth like tools, shredding the bark from saplings with them -- saplings that were used for the struts of the larger baskets they wove and for the frames of their beds. Or, they chewed roots and tubers, spitting the wads of pulp into porridge. I could have brought them cloth, or flour, or tea -- but candy? Ollie had said that the candy was utterly strange to them and awakened in them something like lust. They were not a lusty people, he said, but the candy tweaked their imaginations and inspired the desire for more. It gave him the upper-hand, he said.

Ollie had not spoken to me of angels again, and it was as if that particular conversation had never happened. However, he had bestowed Frederick upon me, had passed him along as an interpreter. Frederick would remain with me during my stay with the Tekhla, which was planned to be a stint of about four months -- just long enough, I hoped, for me to complete Ollie's work. Frederick would without question be waiting for me, Ollie had said, at Tuylo, and he would be reliable because he had no other options, and he more or less understood his responsibilities.

I was finally informed that the plane had been readied. On my last day before the trek to Tuylo, I bought sacks of candy -- durable, enameled-looking candies in the shapes of ribbons, coils, and twists. The candies clicked together lightly in their sacks and from the sound, I could have been carrying sacks of teeth. And then another cab-ride to the airport through the sulfurous streets, and then finally, there was the plane. It was a delicate thing of starched canvas pulled taut by the wires that strung it together.

The flight was short and terrifying, dipping and bouncing through monstrous curds of clouds that were billowing into castles, into topiary, or decadent coifs. There were slim passages between the mountains and we passed shakily through these narrow clefts in the black, rocky walls that had smears of melting snow on the highest ridges. From the air, the land was raw, bitterly orange in scrapings of bare earth among the spongy trees. And then we made a jouncing descent to a runway that had been plucked bare of rock.

Amazingly, the jeep was parked at the terminal, which was a tin-roofed shed open on three sides, all the wood of it painted bright blue but liquefying with rot where it contacted the ground. The driver was sitting on the jeep's bumper pitching pebbles at weeds. The driver looked as though he had been waiting just so, in perpetuity, pitching the pebbles, smoking, and watching his shadow growing. He was a spidery, ageless man who wore his own sort of uniform: roomy, khaki pants and an olive green vest spotted with badges, home-made from soft-drink caps. He demanded what I thought was an outrageous payment, but I really had no choice because he was the only one there waiting for me.

The journey to Tuylo took three days and two nights, over roads that had been crumpled by downpours and then had hardened in the sun to a rippled surface, like a corroded washboard. The road coiled between cliffs of forest, so that it seemed we were being propelled down a green-walled chute. The driver was stoic and efficient, and almost completely silent. I wanted to ask him what was in his arsenal, what was at the ready for contingencies and how could I, also, acquire such knowledge and self-sufficiency?

The cliffs of vegetation that squeezed at the road were unbroken except for the rare offshoots of barely passable tracks leading to the remnants of rubber plantations. It was in those cul-de-sacs that we camped. The driver, whose name I never did discover, left me each night to set up a rough camp just off the road. I could see his fire twitching through the trees, and it brought small comfort. I didn't sleep well, contorted in the back seat of the jeep until my arms and legs tingled and numbed. The insect noise was outrageous.

At times during the drive to Tuylo, I was certain I had been foolish to place myself in such a situation. The driver had a rifle and a pistol, and I had only my camera. However, on the third and last day, I was optimistic in my nearness to my destination. And then, finally, the arrival at the village of Tuylo. In Tuylo, the farthest outpost that could be reached by road, the forest pressed at the crude buildings on the edges of the place. It all felt so fragile and uncomplicated, but a necessary, even a vital location for those who had the need to shelter there. I was installed without ceremony in the village's only hotel, a row of five cellular rooms strung along a red-clay street. I dropped my luggage from my slackening hands and barred the door and slept for twenty-four hours.

Chapter Four

Time almost stopped its forward motion. The rains of the past season had swollen the river -- the Tesoura -- and I waited in Tuylo for it to fall to a level where boat traffic could resume. I hadn't expected to wait there, and I felt marooned and trivial. I was drastically out of place, but I grooved certain routines. In my room during the siesta hours, the wall next to the bed became as familiar as anything had ever been to me, but I knew that the specific terrain of the wall's humid plaster would dim in my memory, perhaps condense to a single impression.

The heat of the afternoons seemed feverish, although the nights were cold. I lay on the squashy mattress that clung to my skin like an unwholesome companion when I rolled over to face the wall, where I saw mildew flourishing at the edges of a crack. The crack was shaped like a river pattern, fed by capillaries of finer cracks. I imagined that the mildew was vegetation seen from high above the earth.

I studied the wall's terrain as if it were a map. I bent it around, cleverly, I thought, to match the map I had memorized. There was the Tafairu River, and its twin, the Oncas, joining to make a "Y" -- thicker-stemmed below the confluence where the two rivers mingled to become the Tesoura. And further beyond that, the Bacuran Falls where a collar-shaped flake of plaster had lifted away from the wall and foamed with moisture on its edges. The finer cracks were the rambling water-channels of the riverine woodland. It was no use memorizing the patterns of the smaller streams. They flickered across the land during the rainy season, and then were sucked dry by the short season of drought, or they simply soaked into the land and vanished, sent down under the earth where, perhaps, they persisted in darkness.

In Tuylo, certain smells had already become customary. I smelled burnt coffee somewhere, and bread baking, the sour decay of the packed earth of the lanes, the starchy paint degenerating in bare sunlight, and I could smell the sweet rot of thatched roofs and the tang of rust as it devoured metals. It was a unique mixture and I supposed that I would remember it, and that at some future time if I caught an unexpected, familiar whiff I would be thrust back to Tuylo and its huddle of rough buildings, its patchy town square straggled by chickens and irrigated by the numerous and identical yellow dogs.

It was May, and the nights were pleasantly chilly. At night I had to use both of the two provided gray blankets. There was no source of heat in the room at all, other than the warmth of my own body and the simple warmth given off by the one electric light, a neon tube that roiled and fizzed. I awakened early each day at the first flush of dawn at the room's one window. The weather was reasonable in the mornings, with a blue sky, translucent and fresh. There were occasional, frantic bursts of wind, but it had not rained since my arrival. I washed, dressed in clean clothing, and then wrote in my journal until eight o'clock when the Urubus cantina opened.

At the Urubus I had coffee and bread, and when Frederick slouched in to join me, I fed him as well, for he had been on my payroll from the instant we met. "At your service, professor," he had said, and I thought it prudent not to correct him about my title. The rest of the morning, I devoted to language study, using Ollieburton's notes. I could have enlisted Frederick's help for this, but I didn't want to shift the balance between us by revealing too much ignorance. Then a lunch of fish, rice, and roasted corn at the Urubus. Following that, I would go to the telegraph office to visit Sparks and perhaps to borrow a book. I expected no word from Ollie, although it would have been gratefully received. Daily I took note of the condition of the river. According to Sparks, it was down three inches, then four, then six, and so on, laboriously.

The bracing gusts of the morning dwindled by afternoon and the heat settled in. After my visit to the telegraph office, I followed the trend of the rest of Tuylo's residents and took a siesta. The afternoon siesta was a sticky, protracted struggle with the swelter and the pestering flies. When I eventually slept, my dreams were dreams of futility, of beginning again and again some basic thing and then being thwarted in some way or making clumsy mistakes and being powerless to stop the pattern of foolish blundering. I squirmed, fought with the pillow, only awakening fully when the room had begun to darken and it was time to repair to the Urubus once again for another meal.

Evenings, I usually read or studied vocabulary from Ollieburton's notes or wrote in my journal, for there was little else to do and no one reasonable to speak with. It was a sort of noisy solitude, because the insects and small, unnamed creatures buzzed and churred. I found in the forest's noise a hint of desolation, a moody humming. It oscillated, but was always within boundaries, almost machine-like in the way its cogs notched together. And then I slept, but badly, always with the thought that I had left something important unfinished and that incompleteness would be a source of embarrassment, eventually. And so it went.

Or, sometimes, after dinner I would stroll to the dock to watch the river, which sucked at the pilings and spread its folding and unfolding surface almost to the dock's platform of boards. Across the river, nearly obscured by the spray, the trees closest to the shore were being drowned by the flood that pulled at their trunks and bared their roots like bent knees. While I had been waiting in Riolapa for the plane to be ready, somewhere it had been raining steadily. The river that I watched was not navigable, and it looked as though it had always been this way: sharp-crested, disheveled, and bossy.

I came to feel that Frederick was maddeningly sluggish. He promised that there were current maps of the region, including those indicating the Indian encampments, and he said that he could provide them, but there was no sign of progress in that regard. He sat at his favorite table at the Urubus and smiled brilliantly. He poured coffee into himself at an alarming rate, at my expense. However, there was really no one else I could use. I had to endure him, although he languished there at the cantina like a lord overseeing the serfs. His shorts were rotting off his body, but when he shook my hand I was amazed to feel that his hand was as smooth as if he were the privileged and idle rich. (Frederick jammed a dainty, pearly pistol into the waistband of his shorts. It was troubling.) Ollie had said that Frederick was gifted as a "word-smith," but Ollie was prone to over-statement and Frederick's skills had yet to be proven to me.

I know I glossed over Tuylo's poverty, or perhaps it was simply the surrounding forest that I admired, with its billows of orchids and the confetti birds sprinkling the sky with their colors: the iridescent plums, acid-greens, yellows, and carmines. The forest was a bottomless green and it squeezed all around the village, even though it was different from the forest I traveled through on my way there. The cliff of forest that began where the buildings finished was soiled with dust, scabbed with sooty, black molds, all of it sullied except for the tree-tops that waved high above the roofs, untouched and clean.

In contrast to the forest, Tuylo was a rut in the road, a place of vague personality, and it seemed sour to me. The very earth of it had soured from the dishwater that was thrown out the doorways, and from the overfull latrines, and there were small, smoky stinks from the generators that powered the cantina, the hotel, and the telegraph office. The church was at the center of the village, and was powered only by faith. It was painted pink, with a whitewash to which brick dust had been added. It was the cloying color of a disguised medicine. The church was perfumed by candles of rolled beeswax and was a place of garlands and statues. Except for the candles, its only light was admitted by windows so high that none of the rotten rooftops of Tuylo could be seen.

Two weeks in Tuylo became three, and three became four. The river was still swollen and was passing me by, but the weather had begun to shift, and the wind came in surges, nearly aggressive enough to snap feathers from the chickens and send the dogs bouncing along the lanes. I wrote a note to Ollie, telling him that I would try to be worthy of his trust, although it seemed pointless to send it.

The supplies waited in my room: the empty notebooks and sketchbooks, and I had my camera, wrapped in plastic as per suggestion, the foil-wrapped canisters of film, the sturdy Remington typewriter and extra ribbons. The two pairs of boots, the abundance of thick socks. The medicines for malaria and fevers, the jug of one thousand aspirin, and a mirror made of metal.

I sat opposite Frederick in the Urubus, my elbows drawing lazy ovals in the dust of the table. I asked, "Did you get the sugar yet? And the coffee?" Frederick put on his theatrically compliant face as he assembled his response. "Arrangements are in nearly completed progress. I will go around to fetch the coffee tomorrow. Or on the day following tomorrow. And the sugar."

"And tinned meat? Is there here that we could buy?"

Disgust rippled, unguarded, across the broad landscape of Frederick's face. "There are a few things gathering possibilities at the store, but I worry for the lids."

"The lids?"

"The lids." Frederick leaned forward conspiratorially, and

I nearly recoiled (but restrained myself) from the reek of rancid-sweet coffee on his breath. "The rust may be breaching on its traveling through them. Through some of them. And if so, then they are befouled."

"Befouled?" I heard an echo of Professor Ollieburton's vocabulary in the unlikely location of Frederick's speech. I imagined the poisoned contents of such breached cans.

Frederick brightened. "Dried meats superiorly better. Very superiorly appropriate."

"And dried beans, then? Also?"

"Yes, most assuredly. Dried beans can be done."

"And has there been progress in obtaining maps? Recent maps? Or even sketches will do, from someone recently returned?" Frederick's face closed in an expression he might have been rehearsing for a nagging wife. I knew, then, that he had not obtained the maps.

Frederick was an enigma. He was by his own admission and pride, a full-blooded Tuylo Indian. He boasted to me about his skills in tracking and other unwritten lore, so perhaps he felt that maps were extraneous. It didn't occur to me then that he might be unable to read a map. However, he seemed insouciantly at ease in what he must have regarded as urban surroundings. And, he had eyeglasses, for which I suspected there was no need other than the decorative. They distinguished him, those gold-wire ovals and their clear glass inserts that reflected his surroundings – including my own face, already somewhat haggard. I surmised that it was the eyeglasses themselves that provoked Frederick's condescending and stilted manner. Ollieburton wore similar glasses.

By the end of May, the river was down and nearly navigable, or so I was told. Sparks said that it would be at least a week before the motorboats could resume their traffic. I felt that my presence in Tuylo had made scarcely a dent. After the initial curiosity about an unaccompanied woman in a post made up almost entirely of men, I was ignored. I could have been a ghost whose passing was felt with only a shudder. The road ended there, and from there I would have to travel by boat until the place where the river was barricaded by the Bacuran Falls.

Other than Frederick, Sparks in the telegraph office was the only person I could speak with, and I visited him daily. On this day, I visited the telegraph office yet again, to inquire if there were news, any news, about anything, or if there had been forecasts about the river's condition in the coming week. The telegraph office had the mild but deathly odor of mildewed paper -- Spark's deteriorating collection of encyclopedias, compendiums of botany, entomology, herpetology, and medical texts. And, a bloated copy of the Boy Scout Handbook. It was enough reading material for a siege, or an imprisonment. Sparks himself was as bleached as a cave worm, but with startling golden hair on his arms, and he had a blond, crimped beard that nested around pink, babyish lips.

I was unreasonably drawn to the telegraph office, returning daily as one would visit a local newspaper stand. Sparks didn't seem to relish company, but he didn't reject it. He was animal-like in that regard. He twitched and sometimes made sudden, rude sounds. I remember collecting him, in a way, as an amusing anecdote with which I would decorate my stories of the trip.

All the windows of the little office gaped open and there was no difference between the mugginess of its tin-roofed space and the forest that was steaming and thriving very near to the small building. Sparks heard me come in; the door had a strand of rusted bells that looked and sounded incongruously like sleigh bells. He glanced up, saw me, and returned without comment to his project of the moment. He was making tea, and I watched fascinated as he dipped the tea-bag into the cup of tepid water, withdrew it, dipped it again, with the utmost deliberation. As he did this he seemed to be watching his hand, somewhat clinically, as though it were a clawed and hinged device ingeniously designed for just that purpose, the diligent raising and lowering of small objects. He watched his hand, and I watched him. I was fascinated by the exacting pinch of his thumb and forefinger precisely in the center of the little paper tag as he immersed the pouch of tea, withdrew it, immersed it again. I marveled at how the hinges of joints were perfectly fitted and how the fine cables of tendons functioned in smooth coordination. It was a little miracle -- the way a hand worked. Sparks' lips were moving silently, as if he were counting. He had taken the tea-bag from where it had been placed on a shelf, in a row with other, often-used tea-bags. They had the blotched, soiled appearance of wet cigarettes.

I was hesitant about interrupting Sparks, for he seemed to be conducting a ceremony involving the tea-bag, for reasons known only to himself -- Tuylo was a place were eccentricity was tolerated, if not indulged. Finally, I spoke, "They say at the Urubus that there are some Indians up-river, some cultures, that are as yet uncontacted. But how can that be, after so much time and with the protection of the Park?" Sparks said nothing, continued to raise and lower the pouch of tea. I waited.

As an entertainment following dinner, Frederick had been eavesdropping on the conversations around us, probably as a gesture to reassure me of his effectiveness as an interpreter. He would repeat back to me the gist of what was being said. At first it had been amusing, then annoying, because I thought he was unfairly intruding on private exchanges. However, the topic of the previous evening had been quite different, and it had rekindled my interest. Frederick had overheard and interpreted a conversation about uncontacted Indians. It had seemed as if their existence were common knowledge. As he recounted the conversation, Frederick had become restive. His voice had dwindled to a whisper and he seemed annoyed with me, although I had done nothing but listen.

Brackish water streamed from the pouch and Sparks' hand eventually stilled its raising and lowering of the tea-bag. The soggy bag gradually slowed its pendulous swing over the pale water in the cup. I was encouraged, until he commenced the winding, which was a tedious process with many corrections. He wrapped the string a single turn around the bag, drew it tight, wrapped it another turn, stopped and regarded his progress. Then he unwound the string, centered it around the bag, pulled it taut again, wrapped it again, and so forth. The bag was constricted so fiercely that I could hear the thin paper creaking. It was lunacy, but with just enough genuine conviction as to be believable as something greater than the making of an ordinary cup of tea. It almost seemed to be a ritual that Sparks had learned, rather than invented.

Sparks finally unwound his little package for the last time, straightened the creases, and then crossed the room to lay the tea bag on the shelf, its string and little tag hanging over the edge. He returned to his chair. He arose again patiently, approached the shelf, adjusted the string a fraction so that the tag hung infinitesimally straighter. All the little tags fluttered slightly in a humid draft. Sparks returned to his chair. Wiped the rim of his cup with a cloth, inspected it, wiped it again. If I had had somewhere else to go, if I had been hurried, I think I might have screamed. The insect noise, the nonsensical waving of the little tags, Sparks' focused silence, were maddening.

Sparks sipped his tea luxuriously, and then asked, "Would you like a cup of tea?"

"No, no thanks," I said, "No thank you."

"I doubt it," Sparks said.

"Doubt what?"

"What you said you heard at the Urubus."

"Then it isn't true?"

"I doubt that you heard it there. I didn't say it was true or not true. Perhaps you dreamed it."

I didn't know if I was being insulted, or not. I waited.

"All the Indians at the post believe it, but they rarely speak of it, especially to strangers," Sparks finally said.

"Believe what?"

That there are Indians out there who don't want to be seen. That they watch us. That they follow the old ways, and are people from when the old ways were stronger." The fine hairs on the back of my neck tingled. What I understood -- had thought I had understood about the possible and the extraordinary -- shifted. I felt a thrill that was only a hint of what Ollie must have experienced at finding the small, hand-made figures.

I asked, "They watch us here at Tuylo?"

"Maybe. And in the forest. They watch the others." And then Sparks yelped as if he had been stung by an insect. I ignored it, because it was just one of those usual interruptions that punctuated any exchange with Sparks.

I asked, "Do you mean they watch the other Indians? But why, and who are they? And do they speak to the other Indians out there? Is there communication?" I had asked too many questions consecutively without waiting for an answer. Sparks yelped again loudly and began tapping an accelerating rhythm with his fingers. This was particularly disconcerting, because the thumb on his left hand was missing. The thumb ended just beneath the second joint and was sealed with runic scars, like the waxen seal on a letter. He caught me staring, but did not cover or withdraw his hand. Although I hadn't asked, he said, "Snake bite. Fer de Lance. I had to be quick about it." At first I didn't understand, and then I did. He had cut off the thumb himself, without hesitation, before the poison could spread. I shuddered. Sparks' tapping accelerated. Then he said, "She believes it."

"What?" I was mesmerized by the tapping, which threatened to break free of Sparks' compulsive fingers and run away on its own.

"My wife. She believes it, that there are other Indians out there who keep to themselves completely." Sparks' wife was a Tuylo Indian whom I had seen often, crossing the square to the church or on the lane to the telegraph office, bringing him small packages of food. The woman wore modest calico shifts under which I imagined her plump, coppery skin shone in secrecy. She was an excellent cook, it was said. She greeted me pleasantly when we passed, and for that I was grateful.

"Your wife believes it? Has she seen them?"

"Only in dreams," Sparks said. At that he squawked three times, jerked his shoulder to his jawbone, also three times, and then gazed around himself as if awakening from a reverie. He began to focus, swinging his head this way and that until the motion awakened drafts of air and sent motes twirling. He gradually slowed the wagging of his head and then looked at me directly and with what seemed to be an instant of an ordinary sort of intelligence.

"I haven't seen them," he said. "But my wife says they paint their bodies, and they have quills through their noses, and crowns of feathers and capes of feathers, in layers. White on the surface. Foamy white, rainbowed underneath." And then another tangent while Sparks chanted, "rainbowed-underneath, rainbowed-underneath, rainbowed-underneath," enough times so that the sounds lost all meaning. When Sparks subsided, I said, "Like waterfall spray?" He said, "Yes, exactly, white and foamy, rainbowed-underneath."

I wanted to drag details from this odd man who couldn't evade his compulsions even here, at the absolute end of a road. He seemed to be staring incredulously at a spot just above my head. We sat quietly for a time, although perhaps not companionably. There was nothing further Sparks could tell me. He had not the resources. When I stood to leave, Sparks said, reasonably, "Be sure to get in and get out in four months or the rains will hold you there, or the Tekhla could decide to move camp, and then where would you be? Could be very tricky."

"But Frederick will be with me," I said, as if that solved it.

"Yes of course," Sparks said, and then squealed like a trodden-upon pig.

I made my way back to my room, side-stepping the puddles where dishwater had been tossed, nodding cordially to anyone I passed on the lane, although I expected little response because I had gone as invisible as furniture. By then I knew every corner of Tuylo with intimacy. The church loomed in the plaza and it was like a conscience -- a weary and disillusioned conscience. A road of sorts ran through Tuylo, passing by the church, the hotel, the Urubus, and then concluding at the dock. Intersecting this road were paths wide enough only for foot-traffic, of which there was very little. These paths led from the village into the forest, and to the gardens kept by the local Indian women. Every path entered the forest through a gateway of luscious, soiled green foliage. I was too wary to follow these paths, in part because I didn't know if I would be welcome, and in part because I didn't want to lose my way.

That night I had a ferocious dream. In this dream, I was already in the forest and was well accustomed to it. The forest was ominously silent, with the kind of sucked-back vacancy that portends extraordinary changes: eruptions, floods, subsidences of the earth, or powerful winds. A dry mist was rising so that I was unable to see even my feet or the bases of the trees, the knuckles of roots, and the rocks. There was water close. I could hear it, like a kettle boiling, and the ground sloped down and away from me, in the direction of the water-sounds.

As I looked toward where the water must be, the mist began to clear, tattering and lifting on a sudden breeze. I could see where the stream arose from a hole in the ground, and I understood that this was the beginning of a river. The source. And the beginning of oceans. It was a humble birth, but magnificently essential. I knew I must tell of this, must make someone else understand how such a beginning could be simple and yet worthy of reverence, as though I had discovered the center of the earth.

It was when I looked up from the stream that I saw them -- the Indians -- arranged in silence in their regalia. I knew who they were. The Jukima -- the people of the shadows -- the same ones mentioned in the Urubus. These were the same people that Ollie had spoken about, and that Sparks had mentioned, and in whose reality Sparks' wife believed in, more than she believed in the promises of the church.

There were seven Indians, or eight, or more. It was difficult to tell how many there were, because behind their colorful row on the stream's far bank, I saw thin, drifting patches of color that might or might not have been a phantom throng. I had the distinct sense that this was more than a dream. I knew, then, that they were not simply fabrications of Ollie's mind, and more than that, there was an eerie awareness that the Indians were dreaming of me even as I dreamed of them. There had been a convergence of our combined dreamings in an unavoidable hollow of the forest, and it was a convergence of significance.

When the fog burned away, I could see the Indians clearly, standing in sunlight. They looked more real than a dream. The Indians wore headdresses, magnificent sprays of frothy white plumage, and they wore capes of milky feathers that shifted and stirred around their lean bodies. I caught glimpses of color where the feathers parted and closed -- shocks of ember-red, azure, citrus-yellow and green, and a blue as brilliant as a luminous sky. The Indians had quills threaded through their noses, longer and shapelier than porcupine quills, ornamented with little snaps of light from inlaid, opalescent shell, catching the light and slinging it back in tiny splinters. The Indians' skins were of various colors, from ashy charcoal to the light coffee of turbid water. It was surprising, and I would not have thought them to be all of the same race, except for similarities in their features: broad, calm foreheads, aquiline noses, and curving, well-defined lips.

The Indians watched me, their collective gaze moving over me. They could have been carvings, motionless but for their flickering eyes and the stirring of their plumage. The plumage moved in the slight breeze and uncovered and covered their bodies. The most extraordinary thing was the ornament applied to their skins -- the juice of dark berries, or inky tattoos? Their skins were embellished with interlocking lines: geometric, aquatic, botanical. They looked as though they had been draped with fine nets of strung and knotted indigo lace. The Indians were regal, but they seemed starved to me, or starving, not only in the sparseness of flesh but in a kind of hunger that was somehow conveyed by attitude and expression. I knew that this was a dream, and more than a dream. I didn't know what they wanted of me, why they had presented themselves in this way. I didn't know what the proper response should be.

The mist rose again and slowly obscured the Indians, and then the forest beyond them. It rose up from the water and the ground, and covered the bases of the trees and the shafts of vines pushing up from the earth. The Indians vanished into the powdery whiteness. The forest vanished, and I could not see my hand in front of my face. A rooster crowed, and then gargled as if it had been choked. I awakened panting, in complete darkness. There were no seams of light edging the door or the window. The room was so directionless in its darkness that I felt as if I were on the brink of sliding off the edge of the world. I slept again, and awakened to Frederick's vigorous hammering on my door.

Frederick yelled at me through the closed door, "The river is fallen and we are transporting the cargo to the dock. Awaken in there. Are you awaken in there?" I rubbed crust from my eyes with my fists, dressed, shook out my shoes. An angry brown spider dropped out and crabbed away. I swept my few personal belongings into my canvas pack, hefted the metal box that contained my papers, money, and medicines, and then lifted up my journal from the table next to the bed and stowed it in the pack. On a whim, I wrote my initials next to the door-frame, digging deeply into the plaster with the tip of a ball-point pen. Then I stood back and regarded the little marks that were as insignificant as fly-specks on the wall.

When I arrived at the dock, Frederick had preceded me and was standing at attention before the crates and the jumble of smaller boxes containing the dried and canned goods and the other provisions. He had gathered a small collection of Indian boys to help in carrying the cargo. They shuffled and glanced anxiously at Frederick, who disdained to look at them at all. It seemed a very meager assembly, both of objects and of people, now that we were ready to depart. Frederick was posturing as if he were holding off an army of thieves, although except for the ragged group of Indian boys pressed into service, no one was taking more than a slight interest.

And then there was the motor-boat, shallow and wide, with a slosh of oily bilge underfoot. My final view of the settlement was from the stern of the boat. Church bells were ringing -- not genuine bells, but a scratchy recording amplified beyond its capacity. Sparks' Indian wife was gliding across the plaza in a pink calico shift. She was very small, already, as the settlement receded. By the shrinking dock, the usual chickens raked at the sand. Then the dock, the flashing tin roof of the cantina, and then the settlement, itself, vanished. The throb of the boat's motor was enormous as the boat bucked its way around a steep bend in the river. Frederick worried the stem of a damp, unlit cigar. When he turned in profile, I could see daylight through a tiny hole punched through his septum. I had not noticed that before, and then I wondered if I knew him even slightly, and if there were enough similarities between us to allow confidence to flourish under difficult conditions?

The boat toiled up the river, and in the tumbling water I saw the debris of the forest being carried away. A dead monkey, face up, made of its open mouth a water-filled bowl. The vase of a bromeliad, rouged in its center, spun in a whirlpool. A yellow-barked branch raced past, still squeezed by a vine although both had fallen and both were doomed. And there were leaves, twigs, petals, the swollen, khaki-colored corpses of snakes sloughing a litter of scales. Soapy foam flattened under the bow of the boat. At times, the bends in the river were so steep as to loop back on themselves and I saw that we were taking the opposite direction until the river straightened out its kink and swung us in another arabesque. The engine noise made conversation impossible, but I doubted if Frederick would have spoken, regardless. His eyes had taken on a filmed cast and he sat motionless. The four Indian boys squatted at the stern of the boat, so quietly that I soon forgot they were there.

The sun scorched the top of my head and I nearly dozed with the swaying of the boat and the sameness of the landscape, an unarticulated green as bright and hurtful as if all of the foliage had been boiled. Eventually I did sleep, lulled by the sway and vibration. I must have dozed for a long time, because when I looked up again the daylight was already disappearing. The sky had colored to lilac, and then it glowed burnt orange low over the trees, which were immense and looming close to the water's edge. Bats cut scallops against the orange sky. The boatman began to maneuver the boat closer to shore and I saw a spindly dock, its toothpick legs canted by the tug of the water. Just up ahead but hidden by a curve in the river, I could hear the roar of the Bacuran falls.

In our first camp, I sat cross-legged on the cot in my tent and wrote in my journal. I could see the nervous motion of the water in the moonlight, shards of light playing its surface. The river was there and moving each time I looked over at it -- black, with silver creases -- but the water I saw was not the same water, the same molecules, as a moment before. It was the same yet not the same, a paradox I could not resolve. Spouts of water thrust up, caught moonlight in their fists and ducked under again. The forest pressed close, and I knew the little clearing scratched out there on the bank would be quickly covered over again if not tended. I had the sense that all here wavered on the cusp of life or obliteration. All sorts of lives, all sorts of endings.

I thought of Ollieburton. It was a sharpened and concealed stake that he stumbled into and it may well have been poisoned. It concerned me. It was a trap designed specifically for him, I had come to believe. Had he inadvertently been disrespectful? Were the Indians unforgiving and hard, or lenient in certain cases? And if a man as wily and knowledgeable as Ollieburton couldn't avoid breaching courtesy, what chance did I have? And then I thought, my advantage is the sensitivity of a woman who came to learn and not to gloat or to dominate. I brought the manners I had learned as second nature with me, even though I felt that I had traveled to a different planet than the one I thought I knew well, a place so far from my origins that it did not share the same sky. The moon of this place shone differently -- fat and pocked, and very near. The forest was glowing with the health of a wilderness. It was ancient and hadn't been harnessed, yet, for human purposes.

The mosquitoes were a nuisance, and the malaria medication made me dizzy. Nauseated, or perhaps it was just that I continued to feel the echo of the rocking of the boat. Frederick had draped netting over my cot, but a few mosquitoes managed to penetrate nonetheless, and a few seemed like a hundred, or a thousand. The campfire sank down into its embers and it was a comfort, shushing gently, flaring, resting again. The moon was bright enough for me to see the page I was writing upon, to see the shadow of my hand moving across the page. The river was rushing noisily, but its pitch rose and fell. A baby in the womb might hear such a loudness from the mother's blood-flow and sloshing. I wrote in my journal, "I am an innocent here."

Chapter Five

In the morning, I realized that the bilge-water of the boat had slopped into my boots. My other boots were packed away in a crate. I would have to put on the same boots again, and they would be coldly slimed. When I climbed from my tent, I saw the form of Frederick, nearly erased by rising fog as he encouraged the campfire with a stick. He stirred and stirred at the embers and crept around the fire like an archetype of obligation. As he did so, he assumed an awesome importance to me. I was a child in the shape of a woman and I was pretending that all of this was acceptable, even reasonable, when surely it was not. I had the starkly realistic thought that I should not be alone here -- and by that I meant that I should have another with me who spoke my language unselfconsciously and who understood, or even shared, my assumptions.

Vapor was rising, first a chilly blue and then warming to pink, and the birds began to sing noisily. And then the Indians were toasting bread on saplings, and there was coffee boiling. Then the heated cup was in my hand, and the bread, even as Frederick was already dousing the fire with the dregs of the coffee. The fire steamed and died. The Indian boys shouldered the crates we had brought with us, and I shrugged my shoulders into the straps of my pack. Frederick motioned for us to follow, and we entered the forest behind him.

It was a sham. I was a pretender behaving suitably for my audience, in this instance, Frederick and the four Indians he had brought with us to carry the supplies. However, they didn't appear to have expectations that I would behave one way or another way; they didn't care who or what I was, particularly. I was a circumstance to them, I thought, a circumstance or a condition, but possibly not a person. The Indian boys didn't speak to me at all, and Frederick had become uncharacteristically silent. I felt prematurely exhausted, but I smiled tightly through my unreadiness, trying on the smile I would present to the Tekhla as a proof of my confidence and good sense.

This forest that we walked through was fresh and good and I realized that it had a different character than the forest at Tuylo. Tuylo's forest was soggy and stagnant, possibly even cruel. It had not rained here lately, but there were spatters and drips; the liquids of the atmosphere had settled lightly, had attached to one another, and were weeping down. The Indians were carrying the heavy boxes and parcels and were following a transformed Frederick, who had become a creature of fluid motion and caution. He swept at the foliage with a wide, flat knife. The vines and stalks severed wetly at the snicks of the blade. A path opened out to us where there had been no path before. I was ashamed of the noise my camera made, slung crosswise and bumping on my hip.

We moved ever more deeply into the forest, and I was relieved somewhat that there was still a visible path behind me, even though the boat had gone. I knew that the boat would push its way up the river until it reached the place where the river widened and was blocked by the falls. Then the boat would reverse itself and begin the easy slide down-river again, although I would not be there to see it.

The day grew warmer and warmer, and then almost hot. The earth underfoot yielded, slightly, at each footfall and then sprang back, thumping like a beaten drum. My legs were aching when Frederick finally stopped. We ate a simple lunch. Frederick and the Indians squatted comfortably and I tried to imitate their postures. My thighs quivered and jerked at holding the unfamiliar position. The difference in our postures was like an illustration of the separation I sensed between myself and these people. The very way the Indians bodies were positioned in space was different from what I had learned - - the way my joints and muscles had been conditioned.

I hoped that we would camp there, but we quickly moved on. The forest was not darker as we moved deeper into it, but instead there were open spaces, almost meadow-like but padded with juicy-looking foliage and feathery, melon colored flowers. I looked at my watch and saw that we had gone on for about an hour further. At that same instant, Frederick halted us with a spitting sort of word that I hadn't heard before. I assumed from the stiff backs and rigid necks before me that there was danger here; everyone was staring at a spot about three feet from the head of the path Frederick was hacking out for us. Frederick was grim and deliberate, with just his head turning, owl-like, and he said, "You come forward now but with not-sounding feet." The Indians were as motionless as the tree trunks. I tried to move forward soundlessly, but my clothing rustled and the camera thumped and I could hear the subtle failure of the squeak of my hiking boots.

I came nearly abreast of Frederick and he stopped me with a flick of his hand. He said, softly, "Look there." I saw nothing, and then looked as carefully as I could at Frederick's eyes and tried to follow the line of his gaze. I still saw nothing. No one moved or spoke. I had the thought that it was a test of sorts, or a little game. I saw nothing, and then there it was, a gleam of color, intensely red, like a small tongue of flame. The color slid just under a leaf and resolved itself as snake, although the word I nearly spoke was "serpent." It was a little thing, banded scarlet and yellow-white and black, and it was coiled around itself like an ornament fabricated by human hands.

"Do you know that one?" Frederick asked, as carelessly as if he had been asking, did I recognize the scene on a postcard? I said, "snake" and Frederick again spat out a word that I understood was the name of the little, fiery thing. He said, "That is a three-hour snake. Almost always a three-hour snake." And then he flipped it aside with the tip of his knife, so casually that I was appalled.

I said, "Like the little blue frogs?"

"What is there of little blue frogs that you could know?" Frederick was incredulous.

"Ollieburton told me. That they are poisonous."

Frederick's face split open in an unpleasant smile. "Ollie-burden talks very extremely much." And then he turned away from me and we went on.

The forest shifted horribly in that instant. Even its smell had shifted. It smelled meaty and slightly rotten, like something recently dead. I wondered, was a three-hour snake preferable to one whose toxins were more efficient, if death were certain? Was a one-hour snake a greater mercy? A philosophical exchange with Frederick on that subject seemed ludicrous. Insects rose up out of the undergrowth and I didn't know their capabilities, except now I breathed them in and they were an invasion, whereas moments before the insects had been like harmless cinders sparking in columns of light.

I was the last in the little line of us and the snakes surely would be frightened away by our footfalls, but there could be something terrible and stealthy behind me, awaiting the opportunity to snatch me up. Shadows that had been ordinary were now spectral. My disillusionment was complete. The trees jumped and jittered with my awkward, ignorant steps, and the vines swung their nooses. A snake, disturbed by our passage, could loosen and drop. I could feel it then, dry and tepid, a slather of snake heavy and muscular and sudden upon my shoulders. And what of Ollieburton and the little blue frogs and Frederick's derogatory tone? Ollie-burden? Could Frederick be as deft as that? I thought, in a brief and cowardly moment, that perhaps I should instruct Frederick to take me back to Tuylo. I could study the various Indians there, in relative luxury.

As we traveled through it, the forest lightened, and the trees were spread more widely apart. I could see the ground more clearly. The bark of these trees was like lacquered furniture, reddish-brown and varnished slick. With the openness, the sunlight became bland, buttery, coating everything so evenly that it could have been a genuine substance, like the chlorophyll that colored the leaves. The Indians began to talk and joke amongst themselves, although their laughter was private and excluded me. The Indians faced straight ahead, bobbing elegantly under the weight of their cargo, their knees rubbery. They marched so resolutely that their mission seemed no longer to include me.

And then we came to our campsite and halted, so abruptly that I assumed that Frederick had intended all along that we stop just there, although I had not known that. In a clearing on a knoll there was a crusty hearth dug into a depression in the ground. All the earth around it had been cleared in a small circle, raked clean. In contrast to the snaky forest, it was a normal place and I was grateful for it. The terror of before, that had been like a sudden descent into chaos, was passing. Frederick was jovial now, and he unfolded a canvas camp-chair for me, saying, "The Professor will sit here and all will be done," a pronouncement made with such self-assurance that it inspired confidence. There was activity around me, but I could scarcely follow it. Seated upon my canvas chair, I felt like a film director who has forgotten to bring the script.

Soon there was a tent for me, spread open at its front in welcome. Frederick hung mosquito netting to cover the opening, and he arranged the folds and drapes as though he were an interior decorator caught in a fit of perfectionism. There was a smaller, army-issue tent for Frederick, and the Indians put down the raffia mats that they had carried in snug rolls across their shoulders.

On a whim I took out my camera and said to Frederick, "Gather up the others. I'd like to record this." He looked quizzical until I raised the camera and then he understood. He punched and shoved the Indians into a tight row and they stood at attention, glowering and put-upon. I didn't care that they were put-upon. It was my trek and they were there at my service, or so I thought at that moment. I snapped a few pictures, lowered the camera and waved everyone away.

I said, "Frederick. This camera is worth more than all the village of Tuylo and everything in it." I don't know why I said that -- surely it wasn't so, but Frederick said, gravely, "I know it." He was wounded. Humbled. I knew instantly that I had made an arrogant and thoughtless mistake. Would he kill me for my camera and set off to purchase an entire town? But no, his defeated expression told me that he thought the camera unobtainable, somehow. He went about his business and soon wood had been gathered and the fire begun. We ate fruit and bread and gnawed at strips of dried meat. The day was blotted out rapidly, coloring to an icy-lavender and then there was that autumnal, orange sky above the crowns of the trees.

Gradually the sky darkened and the trees pasted themselves to it as darker shapes. The stars pricked through the material of the sky with their tiny lights and the noise of the forest rose up. I went into my tent and left the Indians, including Frederick, murmuring around the fire, its light distorting their faces so that they looked beaked, like predatory birds. I wondered, briefly, if serpents were nocturnal, but I was too tired for fear. I slept dreamlessly, with no sense of time passing.

On the following day, the forest pressed close again and the ground sloped downward. Blackish water, like poisonous broth, seeped in to fill my footprints. I felt again that I wanted to go back, but not to Tuylo or even back to the safety of the university. I wanted to go back to the camping site of the preceding evening because of its openness and sprightly breezes. I allowed myself to think back no farther than that, because the last night's camp was as far as I thought I could travel on my own.

There was no banter among the Indians on this day. They were sullen, and cautious. I took on their mood, also. We walked through a dank mud that oozed and bubbled fermented liquor, coating my boots and making them heavier with each step. We didn't stop for a meal, and by the time we made camp I was faint with hunger and saw little zips of light. I stared around myself dully, not really seeing anything but those active, jagged lights. We ate, and then I slept on my cot, leaving the others out in the open to sleep on the swampy ground. I dreamed that we were ringed by animals that then mutated to men, masked with the faces of almost comically ferocious creatures. The masks were painted with blunt colors, as if they had been painted by a child in a savage mood.

On the next day of our march, my head ached and my eyes burned. I was almost feverish, although it could have been only the feverish heat under the trees -- a thick, wet heat. On that day we saw monkeys, who squalled at us, outraged and self-important. I wanted to apologize to them, to everything around us, for disturbing an equilibrium that had been managing uninterrupted until we intruded. I looked everywhere for snakes, felt them squirming under my feet. I cringed at the idea of the sun-basked heat of them scraping past my limbs as I pushed vines and foliage aside, for the forest there was too dense for Frederick to make much impression with his knife. We climbed over spreading, thick-fingered roots, swished through moist foliage that soaked our legs. I had now been placed in the center of the line, deliberately, and I wondered, what was it that I didn't know that the Indians took as fact about this section of the forest?

It was four days, or perhaps five, when I realized that Frederick had no specific destination in mind. No map had ever materialized, and I understood that it had been impossible, that the markings on maps would have been meaningless to him. Frederick was looking for signs, and I respected him for that, for his awareness of things that to me were a blur of sameness. He was not sure of the location of the Tekhla encampment, but he would do his best to find it and he was at peace with that imprecision, a notion that carried a different kind of exactness. Perhaps he didn't know if he would ever reach a destination that was concealed from him, but he was secure in his command of the process of the search. I lost track of the date, despite my good intentions to be precise. Day piled onto day as shadow piled onto shadow. Tomorrow and tomorrow. Frederick assured me that we had reached the last camp we would make before reaching the Tekhla, but how could he know? We camped at another good place -- open and dry. It smelled of torn clover, of healthy decay. We were on the summit of a gentle hill and the trees were more widely spaced again, with scant undergrowth so that the gaps between the trees were uncluttered and had currents of air moving through.

There were strange flowers there, that I saw before the night fell. The flowers that daubed the trees had wizened faces, monkey-like, and were peppered with spots. The colors were quite alien to me in their combinations: olive-green, a dusky maroon, mustard, and a syrupy pink. At night, the lantern in Frederick's tent threw his shadow onto its wall and made me think about my own shadow as I worked on my notes by lantern-light. To anyone outside watching my image on the skin of the tent, I would have been an uncomplicated silhouette.

The Indians who were carrying the cargo had seemed childish to me when we first began this journey. I was ashamed, now, to have thought that. I realized it was because of the language they spoke in Tuylo, an expedient patois that was stitched together from pieces of many languages. I had thought it crude, with flamboyant, clownish gestures to fill in the vacancies where words were lacking. These Indians were adolescents, but they were actually adults in spirit, supple, uncomplaining, very strong, even though burdened by my absurd quantity of stuff. They did not acknowledge me. Frederick explained nearly nothing of the place, like a technician who has no expectations that a lay-person could appreciate the depth of his expertise. We set up our camp, ate, and then we slept, to begin again at dawn. Frederick said that tomorrow we would see the Tekhla, and I wondered, how did he know that?

I dreamed of snow the night of the last camp, and the dream flashed back at me as we walked during the day, of a snowy place that was the highest place in the world. The air was thin and bluish, and the snow squeaked underfoot as I marched up the steep incline. The wind lifted up fine crystals of snow, and molded the crusty snow into small dunes and ripples. I reached the summit, and below, the vista was primeval. The snow met the forest in dwindling slivers, and then there was no more snow and the forest was verdant with a healthy luster. I could see rivers, and other mountains poking up from the green. Some had snowy peaks, but none were as high as where I stood. Before me was a nearly vertical cliff of bluish snow.

The dream changed, first with a faraway wisp of smoke in the forest below, and then another, closer, and then there were gouts of smoke everywhere. Fires smoldered and flared. I saw that the forest had been peeled back in places in reddish, crusting scrapes. When I would look away from any place and then look back, it had changed. It was all changing. The lines of what must have been roads dropped down onto the forest like a confining net that pulled itself tighter with each blink of my eyes. I looked down to where my feet were securely planted in the snow and the snow had soiled, as if with black grease or ash. The song of the wind changed to the impersonal and robotic noise of engines. I awakened to a whining noise that was neither music nor machine, and realized that mosquitoes had slipped through a rent in the mosquito netting. I wondered why I had dreamed of snow when green was all around me, waiting in the dark to shine again?

At mid-day, the landscape changed interestingly. There were rocks now, plush with sculpted-looking moss, and there was a sound that rose and fell, a muffled, rapid sound that was different from the insect din and moist clash of leaves. The forest gave way to a rock-jumbled beach and a stream was before us, shallow and noisy. The stream was furred with mist, and as though they had been required to gather there, the Tekhla, a small group of them, stood on the far bank, their legs wrapped to the shins with fog. It was not a dream, and the Tekhla offered a tired display. Feathers hung limply from arm-bands. Their faces were smeared with black lines across their foreheads, like the furrows of frowns, and there were a few obligatory streaks of muddy red on their cheeks. Their noses were pierced and quills swung out. The quills looked like the waxed mustaches of pretentious artists. There were no women among them, and no children, but I had the impression that women and children were giggling at us from just behind blinds of ferns.

We stood on one bank and the Tekhla stood on the other. The stream gabbled and frothed between our groups. No one spoke, and I didn't know what greeting would be appropriate. I looked to Frederick for clues. The four Indians with us looked at him also, and Frederick seemed to wither under the pressure. He actually took a step backward. "Frederick?" I said, "What should we do?" He said nothing. "But don't you know them?" I asked incredulously, because it was my understanding that he and Ollieburton had lived with these Indians for months at a time, over a period of many years. "No," he answered. "These aren't the same ones. I don't recognize these ones."

"What do you mean, 'not the same ones?' Aren't they Tekhla?" I was confused, and rapidly growing alarmed. Frederick said, in a somewhat whiny voice, "Yes, they are surely for certain Tekhla. But not the same ones of them. They are different ones of them." As he said that, the impasse broke open and I had nearly no time to react, which was fortunate, because I might have done something irrevocably ignorant.

The Tekhla Indians, all six or seven of them, stormed toward us across the stream with such velocity and commotion that I was stunned. It couldn't have taken more than seconds for them to cross the stream, but my perception of their charge was slowed by terror and separated itself into discrete and luminous instants. I saw the face of one man distorted by the paint he wore on his cheeks, and I saw him as though his face had been raked by claws and was bleeding. Another man slipped on a wet rock, dipped to one knee, and sprang up again. The quills the Indians wore through their noses swayed and bobbed and were strangely graceful.

While I saw the Indians charging at us, I also heard disjointed sounds. There was the hollow rumble of the stones as they shifted under the Indians' feet. There was Frederick's expletive, "Oh hell," and it could have been Ollie's own voice I heard behind me. And there was the crashing of the wooden crates as they were thrown down. I whipped around in an instant to see the Indians from Tuylo dropping their crates. The Indians' elbows were pumping as they ran back into the forest, which accepted them and sealed after them like a hole in water. One of the crates had broken open and its contents spilled out interminably. I might have fled, too, then, but that would have been a dangerous mistake, because I would have lost my way immediately. Then the Tekhla were upon us, grinning ferociously with those immaculate white teeth.

It is to Frederick's credit that he held his ground, although it may simply have been that he was immobilized by fear. The Indians were grinning, or they were baring their teeth. They all were repeating a sound, or sounds, or words, that sounded like "chup-chup." And then Frederick was also making that sound. It was "chup-chup," or "kop-kop," or possibly "chomp-chomp." They all sounded like distraught chickens. It was outrageous, but I was calm to the point of serenity. Terror will do that sometimes? My mind was calm, but my heart was beating so rapidly and forcefully that I could feel the pulse of it throbbing in the root of my tongue. And then the Tekhla, incredibly, began shouldering the crates that the Tuylo Indians had left behind. Under their clayey paint, they wore expressions of peaceful resignation.

Frederick lurched toward me and reached out as though to take my arm, although he did not touch me. His gesture was oddly respectful, or he could have been halted by aversion, for his skin rarely touched mine, as though we were of different and incompatible species. He said, "chop-chop," and shook his head ruefully.

"And what is that?" I asked, "What is everyone saying?"

He said, "The little fish with teeth. Chop-chop," and he champed his teeth. "Many-many-many little fish with teeth in that stream." The Indians' charge immediately was altered in the way I would remember it, or it was doubled -- the way that the Indians had, all of a single mind, clattered and splashed toward us belligerently, and the way I now understood it. The Indians had tripped nimbly and mincingly across the water. They had run quicker than little, ravenous fish could swim. They had seen us there and had been concerned that we would wade into the water unsuspecting. I was encouraged, and felt that we had returned to a kind of civilization, one that was, in a way, of the finest kind, where the strong protected the weak or saved the ignorant from themselves. The Tekhla were human beings, of the finest, noblest sort. My relief that I had not been killed a moment before enhanced this impression, of course.

We began to march alongside the stream, the Tuylo Indians having been smoothly replaced by the Tekhla. I asked Frederick, almost apologetically, "What about the broken crate we left behind?" for the Tekhla had not scooped up its contents, nor had they attempted to reassemble the crate. "They say 'leave it,'" Frederick told me, and I accepted the loss of it immediately. Whatever had been in the crate was a small loss. I felt wonderfully alive.

Chapter Six

We walked for I don't know how long, always near enough to the stream so that it was an audible mumble. The sound of it was orienting as nothing had been since we left the river. The Tekhla were efficient in the pace of the march, not dawdling, not rushing. When we came upon the village it was so sudden -- there was no warning. The speckled light of the forest strengthened to a glare and the village was upon us, a crescent of bell-shaped, straw houses loosely clasped around a clearing with its outdoor hearth made of a ring of smooth river-stones. There was a smell of habitation to the place, the indefinable, familiar, slightly stale odor that accumulates in places where people live shoulder-to-shoulder. Or, I thought the village and its clearing smelled somewhat like a room where babies have been -- a milky, fertile, ammonia smell. The place looked urban to me. It was stable and ordered in comparison to the jumbled excess of the forest.

The village was located in a good place, but not entirely good. It was low and damp, and vines swung heavily from the trees and formed a moist perimeter around the incomplete circle of Tekhla houses. The encampment seemed to be located at the bottom of a deep, emerald-green pit. As we crossed the little clearing, the ground was soggy underfoot. It deflated and oozed pearls of moisture. Where the ground was not cleared completely of vegetation down to bare earth, the grass was trampled and yellowed and damaged. Clumps of prehistoric cycad ferns spewed from their woven trunks. They looked arranged and waxen -- not completely real.

When we arrived, the Indians rushed out of their houses as though our arrival were some sort of emergency. They were an undifferentiated seethe of people to me and I allowed myself to be led this way and that way. The women all wanted to touch me, my skin and hair, and rub pinches of the fabric of my clothes shrewdly between their fingers. Everyone talked at once and I smiled and smiled until my cheeks ached and twitched. Frederick had said that he didn't know these Indians, but he was a gregarious soul and immediately was comfortable and in his natural element. He was insatiable in his talking. He and the Indians all spoke in simultaneous or overlapping phrases that lifted and fell like the sound of water being poured into other water. My ears rang and I felt light, floating. I wanted to laugh nonsensically, in the way that any abrupt and unexpected change can spark a kind of protective laughter. However, I was rendered utterly silent, for once we had reached the village, Frederick took no notice of me. So this was how it would be, I thought? He was my interpreter, but when he glanced in my direction I could have been transparent. I was too intoxicated by fatigue to be worried about that, at the time.

Incredibly, the contents of the broken crate had preceded us. The things were laid out on a mat in straight rows, and I saw that it had been the crate of gifts I had purchased to hand out at prudent intervals to the Tekhla. I had not taken Ollie's advice and brought only candy. It was all there -- the pots and pans and spoons, bars of soap, glass beads, hairbrushes, citronella candles, tins of coffee, sacks of beans, and lengths of cloth. I felt that I had been stripped naked and was standing before the Tekhla chagrined, embarrassed, and at a loss about what I could possibly show them next. However, they carefully ignored the display, even though they had arranged it there. They stepped around it with courteous disinterest. Perhaps they understood that those things were intended for them, but that the time for their dispersal was not yet proper.

There were not many Tekhla in this group, perhaps a few more than thirty adults, but there seemed to be hundreds. I knew none of their names and could not tell them apart except for categories, young or not so young, men or women, boy or girl children -- for the children were luxuriously naked except for red cords looped around their waists. Their black caps of lacquered hair made them look like a scattering of exotic mushrooms. I was so very tired and my cheeks trembled from my grinning -- my face felt stretched. I wanted more than anything to find somewhere where I could lie down and be alone, in deep quiet.

I was led from house to house and I was shown many things. All the while the children's sticky fingers were picking at my skin, trailing web-like across my bare arms, legs, and face. I was startled again and again by their slithering touches. The dwellings looked from the outside like dry blisters on the land, tiny domes of grasses, reeds, and leaves. Inside they reeked of aging grease, mildew, and the yeasty-sweet warmth of many bodies jammed into stifling pockets of space. The houses were dim, smoky, and crammed with people shoving, prattling and peering at me, perhaps to assess my reactions to what they were showing me. They thrust baskets and utensils in my face, and handfuls of grains and fruits and vegetables, but I could see nothing very clearly in the dimness. There were objects from my world in the houses, as well as from theirs. A few polished cans hung from cords strung across the ceilings, and I was impressed by their sheen. The cans had been buffed and kept dry, and were not tainted by rust. They had been cared for. And I recognized the texture of one of the baskets that was placed in my hands -- it was plastic, woven from strips of thin plastic bags that had been twisted into hard strands.

After leaving each house, I was blinded again by the sunlight. I tried to open out to these experiences, but actually it was more of a surrender. I was bombarded by everything, allowing myself to be led and touched and discussed as though I were not present. I accepted all this because I knew a time would come when this day would close and these people would stop their incessant talking and they would sleep, and I would be left alone. Eventually and as time passed, I hoped to be incorporated into the rhythm of their daily lives. I hoped to become uninteresting to the Tekhla.

When the village tour was over and I was led to the center of the ring of houses, the Tekhla men were gone, and Frederick was gone. However, I heard their voices and their rumbling laughter. I looked around with questions pulling at the muscles of my face. Someone had noticed my discomfiture -- I became aware that all this time my arm had been firmly gripped with a dry, calloused, but motherly grasp. I saw her then, an individual woman, perhaps one more sensitive than the others, or more assertive, or even dictatorial. I knew it was far too early to identify an ally among the Tekhla. I had not yet seen this woman mirrored in the eyes of the Tekhla. The woman was not young in the way that the wand-thin girls of the village were young, but neither was she middle-aged. She was taller, somewhat, than the others, and she had a level, intelligent gaze. She pointed to herself with a finger and said, "Falatha." I said, "Falatha." I repeated her gesture, and said, "Noelle." She said,

"Nole?" I shook my head and repeated my name. She said, "Wella?" I shook my head, and Falatha looked disappointed, and did not try to pronounce my name again.

Falatha had been beside me and in firm contact all the while, even though I had not noticed. I risked a tentative smile, and then looked away, my gaze glancing off the shell of her difference. She was a stranger, with warm-bronze skin, almond-shaped, nearly lidless eyes and an interesting smell of camphor and cooked meat. When I looked back at her she was pointing, not with her finger but with her chin, which she jutted in the direction of the men's voices. She had understood my anxiety at the absence of Frederick, and I was relieved almost to tears that I had been comprehended, even in such a minor thing. The men, including Frederick, had repaired to a small structure, which was rectangular rather than domed. The men's house was shingled to the ground with overlapping dried leaves. The men's house. The men's gathering place, their clubhouse. I knew about that -- I had read all of Ollie's work and was armed with facts. I knew that the men's house was where stories were told and dreams recounted and examined. Where songs were invented and ceremonial objects fabricated. It was a secret place forbidden to women.

I thought that the day would not end in my lifetime. Following what had amounted to a tour of homes, Falatha took me to see the gardens, accompanied by an entourage of children. By the time we visited the gardens, I had recovered some of my poise. Falatha must have sensed my change of mood, for she released my arm, but she touched me lightly from time to time. Her touch was dry and hard, and it inspired confidence. The Tekhla at the river had rescued us from the little fish with teeth, and Falatha had rescued me from my confusion. I smiled at her from time to time, trying on an expression that I hoped was deferential without being weak.

Although these were not the same Tekhla with whom Ollie had stayed, their gardens were as he had described. I recognized corn. Beans. A serrated leaf that I didn't know, but one that when rubbed smelled sun-parched and pungently oily, somewhat like a tomato vine leaf. What was interesting about these gardens is that they were in all stages of growth simultaneously. The shoots of plants just pushing out looked succulent and promising. There was ripely swollen corn ready to harvest, and there were burnt, hollowed-looking plants that had gone prostrate on the ground. It didn't freeze in the forest, and there were no extremes in the seasons other than it rained daily or it did not rain.

The tour of gardens took a long time, because we saw them all, or the same few again and again. Had I had the presence of mind to notice, I might have seen my shoe-prints mingling with the marks of bare feet. As the sun sank lower and the light hazed to amber, I realized that I was being deliberately delayed. What I did not know was that while we were touring, the women were cooking a feast. Was their cooking of this feast the drudgery of obligation? Or an excuse for feasting? Or had we blundered into some sort of scheduled celebration and would have to be accommodated? My descending upon them seemed almost expected, or anticipated but awkwardly premature.

Upon our return from the gardens, the men, Frederick included, emerged from their clubhouse. They looked flushed and their expressions were somewhat slurred and unguarded. I realized that they had been drinking. They had the strong, winey scent of windfall apples. Frederick's eyes were bleary. It was twilight when we returned, and the light didn't so much fade as it thickened to a tarry darkness. A fire was begun in the central hearth and meat was put to roast. The men sat with the men and the women with the women. I nodded and smiled, but I felt vacant and dull. We feasted. I ate what was handed to me, wiped grease from my mouth with my hand, as everyone did. Falatha watched over me as though I were an honored guest, a captive, or an idiot. Speeches were given. Toward the end of it I was woozy and stared at the lively bonfire, completely entranced by its squirming flames.

Frederick had proven thus far to be nearly useless to me here, but Falatha didn't leave me, and for that I was grateful. Otherwise, I felt like an outsider at a party given in my honor. Frederick sat with the men and ignored me completely. I don't know how the Tekhla saw him. He was either a preposterous misfit, or cosmopolitan and lordly? The speeches pealed out in voices that grew and trembled with the sing-song vibrato of orators. There was no obvious chief or leader, and phrases ricocheted from one man to another. It must have been very late, but the children scurried until near to collapsing, renewed themselves on their mothers' laps and began revolving again around one another, wrestling, playing, imitating their elders with impromptu, shrilly quavering speeches of their own. All the while I sat as silently but intrusively as a stone that curls water noisily around itself.

I wondered, "Do these people ever sleep?" A lull would overtake us and I would droop gratefully and then another log would be fed to the fire and the fire would swell and crackle, and sparks flew up. The evening eventually ended, or at least it ended for me. I scarcely remember being guided away through a forest energized by the firelight that seemed to mark the only habitable place anywhere in the world. At some point, Frederick had set up our camp, and I was led to my tent where I fell asleep immediately.

It was my fourth night among the Tekhla, and I finally had the time to write in my journal. I sat on the canvas chair outside my tent and the privacy at that moment was overwhelming, the first I had had, it seemed, since leaving Tuylo. Frederick's tent was some distance from mine, visible as a dark, wedge-shaped blot against the darker forest. He had been instructed to pitch our tents just off a track, one of several fanning out from the village. It was a location set apart from the crescent of Indian dwellings, and our placement seemed like a kind of ostracism. After the excesses of the night of feasting which might or might not have been in our honor, the Indians were cautiously, dutifully hospitable. On that night, I had listened to speeches I didn't understand. I had kissed so many babies that I felt like a jaded politician. I had thought of Ollie with a pang as I was feasting, because I didn't feel what he would have felt among these Indians. I was a tolerated stranger and I imagined Ollie, ostentatiously at ease with these people, fluent in the Tekhla language, smoking a pipe and forcing his voice into the men's conversations and jamming in his opinions until the group had no choice but to widen to include him. Ollie would have relished being where I was, but I, myself, was a time-traveler just learning how this new world was constructed.

I had eaten roast monkey, and had watched with a feigned dispassion the monkey carcasses blackening over the fire like the shriveling forms of infants. I had eaten foods I couldn't identify, although Ollie once assured me that the Tekhla were not cannibals and had never been cannibals. Even so, it wasn't comfortable chewing stringy or rubbery wads of things that could have been meat or vegetable, or even insect or arachnid. I told myself that I must believe that everything was fine. Everyone was intrinsically good and honorable and everyone was adhering to a structure of principles that was much stouter than the soft, limber vegetation that was merely a mushy backdrop for the rules that ordered the Indians' lives. And I wondered, "Who am I to intrude on any of this? To insert myself into this and make judgments?"

I had recorded particulars in my field notebook, those facts that are usually recorded because they can be managed. Counted. Compared. How many dwellings there were (there were thirteen), the layout of the dwellings relative to one another, diagrams, rough measurements, those sorts of things. But what does that tell one about personality, or character, or deficiencies in insight, or wisdom? Of a group, of an individual? I was at a loss about what to do with my facts. They were not a deep enough accounting.

I took an inventory of what I had at the moment. My typewriter and my kerosene lantern. The canvas folding chair, already beginning to spoil with the creeping flowers of mildew. The flimsy tent that smelled of mold and chemical water-proofing. Beside the tent, the crates of my things covered with a tarp. In the crates were stores of food, a few pieces of clean clothing, two blankets, and an extra length of mosquito netting. There were the baskets that the women gave me to hold the gifts I had brought. My metal box was close beside me, the one in which I stored those most precious of things: my medicines, my money, my tickets, my passport, and my unbreakable, metal mirror. I realized as I wrote in my journal that it was a kind of assessment that I felt compelled to make, as though my definition resided primarily within those few objects.

I had noticed that nothing in the village was old. There seemed to be no hoarding, because the gardens were productive in all seasons and the forest was crowded with game. I thought, how strange, that nothing was old. The trees may have been old, but there was not much sense of that, because the flowers that decorated them were youthful. Even though some flowers were beginning to bruise and wilt, there were new buds opening in what seemed to be a perpetual and rapid display. The vines were slick as new skin. The composting forest detritus smelled sweet and busy in its integral work of decomposing and regenerating its substance. Not many of the Indians were old, except for a very few of the women and one elderly man, gummy, rheumy-eyed, scrawny, but with whittled muscle hard and necessary as bone. It was impossible to figure his age -- he could have been a devastated forty, or a spry one hundred.

I had my language notebook, which was fortunate because of Frederick's unhelpfulness. If pressed, he sometimes would repeat what had been said and he would translate my words, but I had no way of verifying accuracy. He had the upper-hand. He sat in the men's house and smoked a pipe. He guffawed, swaggered, posed and preened, and then at night he returned to his private campsite. He would sit on a log by his campfire, his head bowed, looking at nothing, doing nothing. I saw the sad, sparking ovals of his nonfunctional eyeglasses in the firelight. He muttered to himself in a language that might have been no language at all. As for the Indians, it was impossible to read their thoughts from the flexible clay of their features.

In the morning, everything was tinted with a salmon-colored light; the delicacy of that light was a special kind of luxury. Just as dawn awakened the forest and heightened its clamor, a building party arrived with Frederick in the lead. He was looking princely in a clean white shirt. I had been sitting in my chair, intensely savoring my first cup of coffee and thinking that it was almost possible that I could feel at ease here and could find peace in these sorts of moments. I had not known that Frederick was not in his tent. The morning before, he had joined me at dawn and drunk my coffee at will, sugaring it heavily and slurping.

Frederick and the building party came upon me so quietly that I was alarmed. They, or anyone, could have been watching me for a long time and I wouldn't have known. When Frederick spoke to me, explaining, the Indians took no notice of us but began scraping at the ground, clearing, leveling, digging out gnarly roots and tugging at clumps of grass, lifting them free and clotted with loamy mud so that they looked like human heads held aloft by the hair, and then tossed aside.

"The people will now grow you a house," Frederick said magnanimously, as though he himself would accomplish this work, but without expending actual, physical effort. I wondered if the Tekhla found him to be as tiresome as I did, but I was intrigued by the choice of words -- "to grow a house," which seemed to place the Tekhla at the center of their universe as directors of its processes.

It was only the men who worked at this. The women were not there. Frederick explained the process of this "growing a house" with a solicitous unctuousness and in a resonant whisper, like the over-voice of the narrator of a nature-film. "The materials are separated from the earth." He made tugging motions with his hands as though pulling up a sapling by its roots. "Things are rearranged." I saw what he meant. The Indians cleared the forest site, racing through the work, chopping the stems of bushes with their knives, tugging away roots and tufts and burls, scraping at the ground, filling in the small excavations where grasses had been uprooted, leveling, smoothing, stamping the earth hard with bare feet as one would press moisture from washed cloth.

I was fascinated and impressed, but couldn't help feeling a pang that I was not to be located closer to the village. I suspected that Frederick was a failure as a diplomat, and perhaps the choice of a site for my house was an insult. When the ground had been cleared, the Indians -- the men -- centered a ring of poles. They laced saplings between the struts, weaving a slight and buoyant container and chinking the interstices with mosses and leaves stuffed in tightly. They worked hastily. I could only deduce a mood or motive in their hastiness, which felt more like an assault than a favor. They had other and more compelling business that they had been taken from in order to attend to this duty. Frederick didn't lift a finger to help them. He stood statuesquely apart from the busy Indians, arms folded -- a conquering warlord regarding his subjects. I knew that he would have to be dealt with before he subverted the entire project.

As if on cue, the women strode out of the forest, carrying bushy bundles of foliage -- monstrously huge, flappy leaves with veins as thick as pencils. Each leaf was large enough to wrap for a skirt. They laid these bundles in a heap and began constructing the roof out of the remainder of the saplings the men had cleared away. These slender poles were bound together with vines until they belled to a soft peak. This roof-building was done on the ground, while I hovered around the fringes of the activity, superfluous, probably making useless, hand-wringing gestures?

I tried to participate, to assist by copying the women's work, but they took the materials from my hands. There was a certain order to things, apparently, that could not be violated, or at least I hoped that was why I was pushed aside. Whatever the reason, I was brushed away and that caused me to question my competence. Was I actually clumsy, in comparison to the Indians? Was I insincere? I watched as the women bound the leaf stems together with a raffia-like cord, clothing the roof in a banana-leaf hoop-skirt. All together, they lifted the roof on top of the structure. It settled gracefully. I noticed that the door was facing the village, so perhaps that was a conciliatory gesture.

Frederick sprang into action when it was time to organize the interior. The women had pounded the earthen floor smooth and firm with palm-sized river rocks. They had set up a hearth in the center, a microcosmic version of the central hearth in the village, and they fabricated a raised bed-frame of saplings lashed together and topped with a nest of leaves and grasses, strewn loosely. The smell of leaking, sappy juice was as welcome as a new coat of paint. When this was done, the women tittered behind their hands as Frederick shouldered me aside and began placing my belongings in the house, adjusting, tinkering, and aligning things. He was muttering to himself, almost crooning. He had a proprietary air that angered me, because he claimed my few possessions by stroking them with his hands. It was a gesture that was not lost on me. It was a crass caressing and I found it inappropriate. These were the things that linked us to the realm of the town -- the stores of packaged food, the mosquito netting, the sleeping bag, typewriter, and the camera. It wasn't so much that Frederick was covetous, although he may have been. It was a statement of allegiance, not to me specifically, but to the largesse to which I had access through no particular virtue on my part. It was faintly derogatory, and somewhat pathetic.

When Frederick had strutted out to his tent, the women put things right, appropriating my belongings yet again, but not so offensively. They strung vine cords across the rafters and when they knotted this webbing -- it could have been my imagination -- it seemed that they shielded their work from my sight by hunching their shoulders or adding extraneous motions as though they were performing sleight of hand. I assumed that they didn't want me to learn the knots. I knew from the visits to the village huts on the first day that the webbing was where the valuables should hang, and I had a surplus of them, apparently. It looked like a shanty strung with laundry. The women had accomplished a crowdedness, a closeness that was both slum-like and homey in the midst of the relatively open clearing. But if it was slum-like, it was a natural sort of poverty. When the women were finished, I handed them some of the gifts that I had brought with me. The women seemed genuinely pleased with the spoons, but murmured with faint politeness over the beads, the soap, the cloth, and the other things. I worried over any mistakes I might have made in courtesy.

My first night in my new house, it rained. The rain soothed me, and I marveled at how dry and snug I was in a home as suitable as any the Tekhla enjoyed. I was warm under my blanket, cushioned by my mattress that smelled tenderly of alfalfa. Over my head, my worldly belongings were slung from ropes of fiber. It was a moment of rightness and a private confidence -- a centeredness -- inspired by the thin but firm horizon of the continuous, round wall that I sensed rather than saw. I slept to the lilting percussion of the rain. In the morning, the rain was still falling and I could see its silvery, little multiplied lights through the arch of my doorway. I was at peace and did not feel vulnerable or trapped by my silence.

The rain ended quickly, and I swung my legs over the edge of my low bed, put my bare feet on the floor thoughtlessly. I immediately felt a tickle on my foot, like the stroke of a feather. A glossy black ant was crawling across the arch of my foot. The ant was gigantic, and its body segments were large enough to look heavy, like glazed ceramic beads attached to a wire. It's mandibles were some sort of awful contraption, roughly serrated and obvious in their purpose. I leaped back on the bed. The floor was in motion with ants, beetles, cockroaches, and centipedes, like burnished threads gliding on delicate waves as their many legs worked in ripples.

This was outrageous! I thought I could hear the ticking of insect legs on the reeds of my wall, and the floor seethed. I minced briskly on my toes to the pack and scrabbled for the can of insect spray. I sprayed and sprayed until the toxic fog drove me, choking, out of my house. Later, Frederick asked me, "What is that smell?" When I explained, he laughed until he cried. "Your house is full of holes! You have no door! More bugs will always come! Anything could come in." Frederick was writhing with laughter, at my expense. He was right, of course. There was nothing I could do, and I would have to accept a constant crowd of bugs, somehow.

Frederick continued to be territorial and miserly about translating. I said to him, "You tell me nothing of importance." He was unperturbed by my comment, as if I had told an indolent husband that he didn't take out the trash often enough. Frederick brushed it off. He said, "What the men say is private. And the women speak about babies. Foods. They gossip and criticize."

"But I am a professor," I said, not quite accurately, but it was how Frederick had referred to me.

"Ollie was a professor," Frederick said.

"And I am," I told him. Confusion swarmed, momentarily undefended, across his face.

"Ollie is a *man*," he said, as if that fact held a core of superiority that was beyond argument. It was impossible.

"Frederick," I said, "I can't do my work if you don't tell me, at least, what the women say."

"I have not a tiniest interest in babies. One baby, two babies, who has which baby, who they resemble. That is women's talk."

"I am not here to study babies," I said, resolving to be

patient, to appeal to logic. "I understand that what the men make in the clubhouse is private. But the women also make many things. I'm here to learn about the things the Tekhla make."

"The women make babies!" Frederick said and then broke into a broadly masculine laugh, casting about disappointedly for an audience to appreciate his witticism. There was no one else with us at the time, and the laugh faltered, arose again slightly, and then ended.

"It's the men who tell the stories about the ancestors and the stories given to them in dreams," Frederick said, finally, and I nearly scrambled for my notebook. Frederick wasn't a Tekhla, but he was the only conduit I had at the moment.

"Well, then that's what you must tell me," I said, as assertively as I could.

"But you are a woman." Frederick was becoming bored with our conversation, and shifted like a restless child.

"The women know the legends," I said. Of course they did. By day, when they were not hunting, the men mostly slept, lounged, smoked, drank, chatted, and at night they repaired to the men's house in the village center, where they also lounged, smoked, drank and chatted, but at a louder, grittier, more rollicking pitch. Their words were fully audible and the women heard secrets nightly, secrets that were not secrets. The children heard them. All the forest heard them. Sometimes the men sang in monotonous, nasal voices, rising in volume as time passed. It was not so much secrecy as it was discretion. The women couldn't repeat what they heard. They knew, but could not say.

Chapter Seven

A muddy mood sat down upon us whenever Frederick and I were alone together. I realized I would have to learn the Tekhla language on my own, and I knew that immersion was how language was most efficiently acquired. I began to consider sending Frederick away. It would be risky for me to send him back to Tuylo, but I didn't think it would be overwhelmingly dangerous to be alone with the Tekhla. The Indians were self-consciously cordial to me. I was physically fit, not ill. My supplies were abundant and even if they had not been, the forest teemed with potential food. If a genuine emergency arose, what good would Frederick be? What could he do that someone else here could not, if I could communicate, that is? This wasn't an evil place and Frederick would be as ineffectual as anyone, if I were bitten by a five-hour snake.

I decided to send Frederick back to Tuylo for a time, but with instructions. He would see if there were mail for me, or telegrams, and he would take my outgoing mail. He would discover any problems of which I should be made aware. I would give him some money to replenish our stockpile of coffee and other staples, but not enough money for him to squander. If necessary, I would promise to give him my camera when we both arrived intact at Tuylo at the end of my stay with the Tekhla.

When I told Frederick I would like him to return to Tuylo, he was at first incredulous, then miffed, then agitated with nervous excitement. In hindsight, I perhaps should have seen that he wanted this too much and agreed too enthusiastically. Yes, he would return to Tuylo to do these errands, and most assuredly he would return within a month, which was the longest span of time I dared risk. I told him of my plan concerning his eventual ownership of my camera. His eyes glistened and he smacked his lips, so I had been wrong -- he had considered what I had said about the worth of the camera. I wondered then, had I been safe with him? Was I safe with him even now? He didn't respect me as he should, that was clear. It would be incredibly easy for him to arrange some sort of accident for me and then abscond with the camera.

The night before Frederick left I was vigilant. I could see his smoldering campfire through a slot I had picked in the fronds of my wall. Frederick didn't sleep. He arose occasionally from his seat on the log, stoked the fire, and sparks rose up toward the tree-tops. I turned loudly on my rustling mattress, flicked on and off my flashlight as if searching for something, so that he would know that I was awake, also.

In the morning, I gave Frederick my small sheaf of letters and an adequate, but hopefully not liberating, amount of money. When I handed him these things, he kept inquiring, did I have enough of everything, was I well, would I manage? His attitude was so different from the usual that I thought he was concerned about the prospect of his own personal failure if something should happen to me. Or, he was concerned that if I managed to survive without him, then I might not need him anymore?

I wrote a note for Frederick to deliver to Sparks, the only person I knew in Tuylo. Frederick was illiterate and so I wasn't constrained, but I wrote simply, "I have sent Frederick back to take care of some errands. I am fine. He has instructions to return here in three, or at most, four weeks. If you should see him still in Tuylo after one month, please remind him of his responsibilities and send him back to me. Thanks, Noelle." I wanted to give my location, then, but was unsure of just where we were. I added a post-script. "Have Frederick explain to you the location of the Tekhla camp. We are close to a stream, and to the east of it." And then that seemed absurd. Of course we were close to a stream. Streams came and went, and in this land were as numerous and unpredictable as the yellow dogs in Tuylo. It was nonsense, but I sealed the note into an envelope and handed it to Frederick. He took this note and made me watch him as he theatrically folded it to the size of a pill and slid it into the pocket of his shredded shorts.

I stayed to myself for a few days, appearing in the Tekhla village just enough for courtesy. When I was alone, I invented specific conversations from the fund of vocabulary in Ollie's notebook, and then I practiced these conversations. I memorized the Tekhla words for "Please speak more slowly," and, "What is that called?" I memorized other terms, such as the words for mother, daughter, son, wife -- all those words that denoted connections. I memorized everything that I thought would be suitable for building upon. The obvious nouns, the simplest, stoutest verbs. My goal was to learn the living words in their combinations.

Five days had passed since Frederick's departure, and there had been a tragedy in the village. Because of the tragedy, I had managed to speak directly to the Tekhla for the first time and they had understood me. It's amazing what nerve one can summon if absolutely necessary? It had been morning, after my coffee and biscuits and after the washing up and the tidying of my house, when I had walked the short path to the village. I shuffled noisily, swishing through the leaves, not wanting to startle anyone with my sudden appearance. Also, with Frederick's departure my concern about snakes had resurfaced.

There was an uncharacteristic desolation to the village -- a place that was, after all, only an arc of buildings that were as inconsequential as warts on the land. The hearth looked like a crater made by a bomb blast, rubbled with charred bones and the dull nuggets of coals. A complicated smell hung over the hearth, like the smell of burnt wool, rancid grease and the resinous perfumes that had boiled out of the firewood. The village seemed hollow -- a sense of vacancy that was accentuated by the absence of Frederick. I realized that the men weren't there, and I assumed that they were in the forest hunting. The forest was full of prey.

The women also seemed to be gone, but then I heard their voices and laughter coming from somewhere not visible from where I stood. As I hesitated near the hearth, Falatha came around hastily from between two of the huts, a drooping leather sack in her hand. When she saw me, I was encouraged by her smile. I looked pointedly at her sack and raised my eyebrows in a question. Falatha made digging, scooping motions with her hand.

I recognized the type of sack that Falatha carried, and understood that it was used to gather the tubers the Tekhla used as the staple in their diet. This was a ubiquitous food, so common that it was not cultivated. The tubers were roasted and eaten unsalted, or they were cut into chunks for stews, or mashed into a porridge that was disagreeably slimed and gray. Falatha smiled at me again and motioned for me to follow her. She led me to her house, which was crammed with women and small children -- so full of people that some had spilled out into the clearing in front of the house. Each woman held a similar leather sack. Falatha rummaged, found another sack next to a basket of squash. She handed me this empty sack, and I nodded gratefully. I would be included in the adventure. We didn't all go on this expedition -- some of the older women and the adolescent girls stayed behind with the children. Babies were carried with us in slings on their mother's backs.

Soon after we entered the forest, the group split into two parties and went different ways. I followed Falatha submissively. The morning was warm but not yet hot; the bird-song was pleasant, and colored scraps of butterflies flickered up from the moist hollows. As we walked, I inspected the sack I carried and found it to be disappointingly plain -- simply an unembellished leather sack with a musty odor and a broad leather strap for a handle. The terrain around us was very understandable compared to the forest I had traversed with Frederick. There were paths here already, worn nearly smooth from frequent use. The women's strides were long and elegant and they talked and laughed strongly, which was unlike the way the Tekhla women behaved when the men were present. The Tekhla men were taciturn and seemed annoyed by the chatter of women. In the company of men, the women giggled quietly behind their hands and hushed their babies. I walked along with these women, smiling when they laughed, but was as silent as the babies that were slumbering on the mother's backs, lulled by their rocking steps.

We walked for perhaps an hour and then stopped at a low place where the ground became soggy, although the water that seeped around our feet was clear. There were sword-shaped fronds growing there, on the slightly higher ground, and the women began to dig at the earth with sticks they had brought with them. These sticks had been whittled flat on the tips, and the women used them to lift away the soft soil at the bases of the fronds, exposing the tubers. This was not difficult work, and I picked up a stick from the ground and managed to collect many of these tubers and put them in my sack. I was feeling useful at last, and was quite satisfied with myself. The insects droned peacefully and somewhere close a bird was gracing us with an ascending melody. When the sacks were full, the women straightened, almost as one, and we left that place.

It was at the honey-tree that tragedy struck us, and it was there that I finally dared to speak. I had thought that we would return to the village, but instead we went deeper into the forest, to where the light was feeble and gave our flesh an olive-green cast. We walked until we could hear the excited voices of women ahead of us. The forest became more open and there was the enormous, fissured trunk of a tree at the end of the path. Clustered at its base were the women who had split off from our party. I looked up the spire of this tree and saw what had excited the women, for in the tree was a small figure, climbing.

The person in the tree had climbed so high that I couldn't make out her features. The women below were speaking all at once to one another, or calling out what must have been instructions or warnings to the woman in the tree. I strained to listen -- urgently wanting to know who she was and why she was climbing. However, I couldn't understand anything in the torrent of words. Exasperated, I tapped at Falatha's shoulder and spoke my first phrases in Tekhla that were not common greetings. I asked, "Who is that? What is happening here?" Falatha wheeled about to face me and from the expression on her face, I felt I had assumed the sudden importance of a boulder falling on her head. I had spoken like a *person*. Like a Tekhla. Falatha uttered a string of words all in a rush, and I understood nothing. However, I said, "Please speak more slowly." Falatha spoke to me more deliberately, leaving a little space around each word. I didn't understand everything she told me, but this time, I understood enough. She said, "Luaka is in the tree. There is tyilili" -- a word I didn't know -- "in the tree and Luaka is" -- and here I assumed the word was "climbing" -- "to get it."

I asked, "What is 'tyilili?'"

Falatha said, "It is what" -- and another word I didn't know -- "are making."

I must have still looked quizzical, so Falatha made a buzzing noise with her lips and I said, "Honey! Tyilili is honey!" Luaka was climbing to get the honey! The Tekhla didn't have sugar, and honey must have been a very coveted thing. I wondered, had Luaka been appointed by these women to climb the tree for the honey, or had greed overcome her? Luaka was a chubby young woman with a broad, brown face and her widely spaced eyes gave her a placid, bovine expression, although she was not placid. She was capricious and loud, with an adolescent sort of giddiness. About her, I only knew that she was married to a much older man and that she had a plump baby. I looked around for the baby, then, and thought I recognized her in the arms of Rupaki. The baby was involved with an exploration of the waggling fingers of her outstretched hand, oblivious to the drama of her mother's climb.

I then turned my attention back to the tree. Luaka was so high above us that she was only a silhouette moving along the tapering branch where the bees' nest was lodged. I could see the bees' nest as a dark lump secured to a fork at the end of the branch. Luaka was straddling the branch -- hugging it closely with her arms and legs. She seemed to be making careful progress and there was no wind, but the branch was limber and dipped slightly each time she inched forward. I was fearful for her. The branch grew horizontally from the tree trunk, and Luaka was a stout girl. I turned again to Falatha, a sentence already forming on my lips. I didn't have the time to say, "Luaka is in danger of falling," because just then there was an awful, prolonged, popping-rending sound. The branch was tearing away noisily, close to where it joined the tree and behind where Luaka clung. It was ripping loose and beginning to sag. For an instant, the noise of its tearing eased and I thought, perhaps if Luaka could retreat slowly along the branch, she would be safe. But no, the branch ripped free of the tree entirely and began to fall.

Luaka still clung and didn't roll from the falling limb at first. Then the branch struck another, and she tipped forward and fell. The branch tumbled interminably, bouncing and crashing and stripping loose great wads of foliage. In the midst of this welter, Luaka also plummeted, her body striking branches, her hands scrabbling at leaves that shredded loose. I saw with horror that a clump of her hair caught on a twig and slowed her fall for a brief instant, until the hair tore from her head and she continued her descent. But even then, I didn't believe in what I was seeing in those long instants. I thought, still, that there could be salvation here? A fork in the branches below could break Luaka's fall? She could survive, and we would joke about this incident in the future. That did not happen. Luaka struck the ground with such a profoundly sodden impact that I released any hope for her. I turned away, only to see Rupaki shielding the face of Luaka's baby. Luaka struck the ground brutally and did not move at all. The fallen branch crashed down on top of her.

We all stepped back a pace and averted our eyes, making room for this certain death. I looked back, then -- I had to -- and saw Luaka's body displayed on the ground grotesquely, her neck twisted at an angle impossible in life. Her open eyes were already dulling. The bald patch on her head was bleeding slightly, and a thin ooze of blood was slipping from her mouth. And then another, smaller, almost ridiculous mishap. On my arm just above the elbow I felt a sharp, fiery pain, like a stabbing with a pointed twig, and then another on my cheek, and then all of us were running, waving our arms about our heads, batting away the bees that were pouring from the ruptured bees' nest and stinging us again and again. When we were out of sight of the tree, the bees abandoned the chase and we were free of them.

We stopped, and stood together stunned, rubbing our smarting arms and legs and faces. The babies were whimpering and the mothers rubbed their arms and legs as well. And then Neemba began to chant. It was a moaning sound that I hadn't heard before anywhere, although I understood it completely. She was chanting the word "Luaka," but the sound was drawn out and morbidly peculiar -- "Looo-aaah-kaa! Looo-aaah-kaa!" Luaka's infant began to cry desperately. The other women took up the dirge. Tears were stinging my eyes and I also chanted, "Looo-aah-kaa! Looo-aah-kaa!" I chanted this until the chant became a continuous drone in my throat, and at the same time, I was conscious of adding my own voice to this howl of grief. I hadn't seen a dead body before this, and I had never seen anyone die.

Although the forest was relatively dim where we were, the sunlight was too bright and it seared my eyes. I wiped at my eyes with my hands and discovered tears. I hadn't realized that I'd been crying. Falatha was standing next to me and I gripped her arm in a steadying, comforting gesture as she had gripped mine on my first day with the Tekhla. Falatha accepted the touch, leaned toward me slightly and must have seen the moisture in my eyes as she chanted in unison with me and all the others. I was honestly devastated by what had happened, but my emotions were divided. I had the deplorable and selfish thought that I had been lucky that day. Someone had died. Luaka had died, and her passing had evoked the most basic of female responses -- to participate in grief, and to comfort. My participation had been noted and I could use it to my advantage. I was immediately ashamed of myself, but it was done; the thought had come into my mind and it was true and disgustingly selfish. I had been lucky that day.

After a few minutes, the chanting dwindled and ceased. There were decisions to be made, and work to be done. This calamity had been pivotal for me. The intensity of the emotions had cleared my mind. I already knew how to speak. I knew the words; I hadn't been trying hard enough. I had been embarrassed about my mistakes, but now I would let that embarrassment go. I asked Neemba, "What is happening now? What do we do?"

Neemba seemed not to notice that I was speaking, whereas

before I had been unable. She said, "We must get the body. Take the body from the forest. It is necessary to prepare the body for the funeral." I understood this. Then I asked, "But there are bees there. We cannot go back."

Luaka's baby had stopped crying when the chanting ended, and now Rupaki shifted her from one hip to the other. Rupaki said, "We will wait, then. Perhaps the bees will not be angry soon." I thought her wrong about that, but didn't contradict. And then, impulsively, I said, "Let me carry her," and I reached for Luaka's baby. Rupaki handed her to me without saying anything. I was grateful for the solid, humid warmth of the baby in my arms. Holding the baby gave me a task that I understood. Because I had cared for my sister Doreen so often, I knew well how to hold a baby, how to cuddle and rock it so that it conformed its body to mine. The baby gazed up at my face and I was touched by how closely she resembled Luaka. Her cheeks were firm and round, her mouth interestingly peaked, and her shoulders were squarish and unusually broad for an infant. I wondered if she would have more sense than Luaka, when she matured?

The women shifted uneasily and some began to gather damp earth in their hands and apply the cool poultices to the swellings on their bodies. I stooped and gathered some earth, molded it in my hands and pressed it to the angry-looking welts on the baby's skin. Then I pressed poultices to my arms and legs and face. Our faces were soon spotted with mud and we looked foolish. Not far up the trail, Luaka lay dead and unattended.

"Perhaps the men have returned to the village, now," Hlisi offered.

"Yes, that is possible," said Falatha.

"Perhaps the men could get Luaka?" I suggested.

"We should wait here longer, and then try to get Luaka," said Neemba firmly. "She should not be alone under that tree."

Falatha said, "Someone could go to the village for the men, and we could wait here."

Rupaki had been stung more seriously than any of us, and she shuffled her feet uncomfortably. She said, "I will go." Although I didn't know her well, somehow Rupaki's handing Luaka's baby to me so willingly had made me feel an allegiance to her, and so I said, "I will go with you." And with that decided, I began to pass the baby to Neemba, who had no infant with her. I was surprised when she refused by folding her arms tightly across her chest. She said, "You take the child to the village. She should not be here." I cradled the baby close again and said,

"Yes. You are right. She should not be here."

Rupaki was a small, densely built woman with eyes that squinted as though perpetually irritated by smoke. Although she usually wore a rather sour expression, I had assumed that she would appreciate company on the walk back to the village. The Tekhla women seemed never to be alone. Apparently I was mistaken, because she frowned at me quite rudely and said, "The baby will slow you. You have no sling for your back to carry the baby."

I said, "My arms will carry the baby." Rupaki just snorted and shrugged and turned on her heel. I followed, carrying the heavy bundle of Luaka's infant. Rupaki moved quickly and didn't speak to me. Soon I was struggling and nearly running to keep pace. The poultices of mud were drying and cracking away from my skin, and my arms were aching already from the baby's weight. However, this was such an extraordinary day that I was full of words, and if there was only Rupaki to speak with, well then I would tolerate her rudeness and speak. I said, "Who will care for this baby now?"

Rupaki was silent for such a long time that I thought she hadn't heard me, but then she said, "Luaka has no family with us. Just Tadu. And Tadu will not stay here." Tadu, Luaka's husband, was a minor presence among us, a small, bow-legged, light skinned Indian who most usually glowered and said very little.

"Why will Tadu not stay?" I asked.

Rupaki said, "Tadu is not a Tekhla. He is a Hlang. From the place of the Bacaran Falls."

I asked her, "Hlang are not Tekhla? They are like Tekhla?"

She answered, "Many generations past, Hlang and Tekhla were the same. Not now."

I continued my questioning. "Why do you say that Luaka has no family?"

Rupaki snorted again and said, "Luaka's mother and father and brother were all killed by a fever. Everyone knows that." But I hadn't known, and wondered, was it malaria that had killed them, or some pestilence that I had no medicines to prevent?

I pressed on. "But who will care for the baby?"

Rupaki said, "No Tekhla will take it. The baby is not very much one of us. Tadu has a sister. Someone in the village will take it to her and perhaps she will care for it." And then she had had enough of me, apparently, for she said, "You are too slow. I will hurry now."

Rupaki increased the length of her strides and soon it was impossible for me to keep pace with her. She vanished up the trail without looking back at me. The baby had become squirmy and twisted in my arms until I was so unbalanced I thought I would fall. As I staggered up the trail, pestilence and snakes began to darken my thoughts. However, the path here was wide and obvious, and I hurried as rapidly as I could. Despite my soreness, the weight of the baby, and the tragedy that was the nucleus of this day, I was strangely elated, almost euphoric. I had begun to communicate, authentically.

I was nearly to the village when I met a small party of men on the trail, coming toward me. Rupaki wasn't with them. Their expressions looked more annoyed than grim. They barely acknowledged me as we passed, and didn't seem curious as to why I was carrying an infant in my arms. Shortly after that, I arrived at the village, my eyes aching from the strong sunlight in the clearing. The baby was flushed and dug at her eyes with her fists. I brought the baby into Falatha's house where some of the women waited. If Rupaki was there, I didn't see her, but I had to assume that these women had been told of the disaster because they didn't question why I had brought this infant to them. I handed the baby to the closest person -- Sheoni, a young girl who already had a baby of her own. When I relinquished Luaka's infant to Sheoni, I said, "I have nothing to feed her." Sheoni had not heard me speak before, and she looked at me oddly, as though she could not quite identify what was different about me on this day. She said nothing, but took the baby brusquely and laid it on the bed of leaves. I didn't attempt conversation again. I was overwhelmed by my tiredness and went to my own house to think.

Luaka's fall from the tree had been terrible, but I hadn't really known her. She had seemed superficial to me, an opinionated, portly girl playing at marriage and motherhood rather than digging into her responsibilities with commitment. That her cooking was bad was common knowledge, even to me. I knew that in reality I wouldn't miss Luaka very much, but the fate of the baby still concerned me. I soothed my conscience by imagining the sister-in-law to be a good-hearted and generous woman. There was a need, and she would surely meet it. And then a thought struck me. If these women would not take in and care for a baby that was the child of a friend and a member of their group, who would care for me, if necessary? What chance did I have if I were to become ill or injured? It was disturbing, and I wondered, where was goodness to be found here? In

74

which of the personalities of these women was strength of character at the ready? How could one know for certain who would step forward if there was a need? Would anyone?

Chapter Eight

The Tekhla often speak of the timing of events by position, as one would describe scenery on a trek as in front of, in back of, to the side of, and so on. On the night in front of the day that Luaka died, I was ambushed by a powerful dream, so terrifying that for months after, I was fearful of the coming of the dark. It was horrifyingly to think of night with all its hungry vacancies both ahead of and behind me. The dream must have been burgeoning in secrecy and the shock of Luaka's death brought it to the forefront. I dreamed first of the people's houses -- the Tekhla houses -- and I saw something I had not noticed before, that they were capped by circlets of little, blackened skulls laid like wreaths around the dome of each house. They were monkey skulls; they were the charred skulls of children. I didn't know which they were. I saw these wreaths of skulls in an inkily shadowed daylight. The shadows made dark pits of the skull's cavities.

The dream folded itself inside-out and it was night. I was dreaming that Frederick had gone and with him any connection to the ordinariness that had been suggested by Tuylo and its conveniences and protections. The telegraph office and an occasional jeep. Food more or less preserved in cans. A solid building with cinder-block walls, and a road that would eventually lead me home. I was dreaming that Frederick was gone and I knew that it was actually so, in a kind of awareness of dream and not dream. I was dreaming that I was awake, because when I looked out the peep-hole in the wall toward where Frederick's tent had been, there was nothing but the moon-bathed hunk of log where he had sat, the tree-trunks that were like the torsos of giants, and the alien splendor of moonlight slicking the philodendron leaves. There was nothing between me and the forest except for my pathetic screen of reeds and thatch that was so insubstantial that it quaked in breezes. A giant's foot-step could squash my hut and the giant would feel nothing but irritation at a bump on the ground.

At first, I had the orienting realization that I was noting the data of the dream, even as I was caught up in its imagery and sensations. And then the dream deepened and seemed to be a reality more genuine than the perceptions of my censored and regulated wakeful self. The dream became terrifying. As I looked out through the crack in the wall and toward where Frederick had once served as my unappreciated protector, I saw eyes shining among the trees and dark foliage. They were at human height and spaced the same as human, forward-looking eyes. They were a luminous, reflective green with centered dots of blood-red, similar to the almost malignant strangeness of eyes in a photograph taken with a flash-camera.

I was being watched, and I sensed that this was a kind of vision that could cut through the darkness and the flimsy walls and could see me clearly. They were like animal-eyes, but they were human and because of that were more terrible than any animal. They belonged to the most terrible of creatures, those who could be coldly dangerous because they could differentiate evil and goodness, and could deliberately choose evil. I didn't know who or what they were, or if they were real. This dream placed me in familiar surroundings, and had a more or less average sequence. The imagery of the dream wasn't distorted nor impossible. These were actual people watching me in a dream, or they were spirits, or ancestors, or something unknown, some force that I had not the words to name. They were prying even more deeply than I desired to pry into the souls of the Tekhla.

I thought I knew who they were. The eyes belonged to the ones Ollie had called the people of the shadows. The watchers. The Jukima. They were very close, beyond the reach of an arm, but moving closer. I could begin to detect motion as figures separated themselves from the dark shapes of foliage and trunks and vines. They were advancing toward me and my house, inexorably. When I understood that they were approaching, I tried to cry out, but no sound escaped from my throat except for the croak of a scream attempted while dreaming.

I struggled, but I couldn't awaken. I also feared to awaken only to discover that I was indeed being watched. Inspected. Evaluated. Hunted? And then I did awaken, with a colossal effort that left my teeth chattering and my muscles fluttering with twitches. I managed to sit up. I was conscious and lucid, and was almost entirely certain that I was awake. I noticed immediately that the forest had gone silent. It was the kind of pause in the insect drone that is like the nervous quiet before a tempest.

The world had vanished in the darkness except for my tiny compartment of a house and the things in it -- surroundings that I felt rather than saw. I heard the texture of the forest noise more clearly in its absence. I wished fervently for it to resume. I heard its echo in the bumping of my pulse, in my rasping breaths, and in the creaking of the mattress. And then the noise did resume, and I hoped that perhaps I hadn't been awake at all during that moment of silence, that it had been a final swatch of the dream. But yet, I knew I'd been awake, and that something abnormal had startled the creatures of the forest into silence.

I dared not look out through a chink in the wall of reeds, although I could have parted the reeds anywhere with my fingers. I lay rigid and panting and that frightened me further, for the sound of my rapid breathing seemed to be made by another person there with me. My fear was nearly boundless. It was a horrible emotion, as though a premonition were on the cusp of proving the veracity of its hint. I hadn't imagined that such a consuming fear was possible.

I fumbled through a meager fund of options. There really were only two possibilities. To lie there unmoving and utterly vulnerable, or to sprint through the night to the Tekhla encampment where there were people whom I more or less knew. The Tekhla village seemed impossibly far from where I was. The dark path that led to it was a horrible gauntlet that I thought I might not survive. I knew how brainless and hysterical I would seem if I fled to the village. I imagined myself running, the darting cone of light from my flashlight tipping and wobbling and fashioning every root and shadow into a snake. If I was not set upon by the Indians who might or might not have been there and approaching, there were predatory animals that were real, and there were snakes. I was weaponless and ignorant.

One can't sustain terror at the same level for a long time. Terror is a disability, but one that ebbs and surges. I found myself thinking of my younger sister. The thought of Doreen calmed me, because I imagined what she might be doing, not at that moment necessarily, but what she did customarily in her life. I thought of Doreen driving, perhaps to the supermarket, and I imagined myself beside her in a car and secure with the smoothness of her shifting its gears, slowing or accelerating, depending on the circumstances. Or, I saw her watering her plants, tipping the watering can at a habitual and graceful angle, frowning slightly at a small spill on the floor. I tried to think about the most mundane and harmless of things. I even imagined that Doreen was with me now and we were discussing, in whispers, what it all meant and what we could do about our situation.

I was thinking of Doreen when the silence descended again, more startling than any outpouring of sound. I willed, or tried to will, the night birds to warble and hoot and the insects and frogs to drone as was their custom. The silence broke once more and the commotion of the forest scrambled in. The resurgence of noise was proper and safe. I allowed myself to feel a slightly victorious thrill at the resumption of sound, as though I had caused it personally. It was very much like having a phobia about flying and focusing acutely on every slight change in pitch of the engines -- every small hitch in their rumble would bring a catch in the throat. In such a situation, I would try to command through force of will and attention that the tone of the engines not alter in any way, because it was only my undeviating concentration that kept the plane aloft. My concentration on the noise of the forest would keep it humming.

I continued to sit rigid and attentive until I felt the night lifting. The interior of my house slipped back into its details, gradually. My familiar things strung from the ceiling looked more homey than any surroundings ever had to me. I could begin to see the textured weave of the basket hanging over my head. The strict lacing of my boots on the earthen floor. That often-seen but unremarkable arch of the low doorway over which I had hung a cloth. The dilution of night by the faint glow of pre-dawn was allowing me to regain my sight and something of my composure. I watched as the curve of the doorway lightened, in increments, and I watched its graying as one would watch a clock. The birds of daylight began chorusing and their songs were joyously unconcerned.

When the dawn was well established, I risked prying apart the reeds of the wall. I saw the bare smudge on the ground where Frederick's tent had been, and the scars left in the dirt when he pulled up its stakes. The dirty gouge his camp-fire had left was still there. The flaps of philodendron leaves were nodding and lifting as they shed the night's moisture. A light rain of flower petals sifted down from the forest canopy. I stood, walked stiffly to my doorway, shook out my boots, then tugged them on, stooped, and went out. The forest glistened with dew and the babbles and calls of the day-creatures were reasonable. I laid wood on my campfire and sat on my canvas chair and shaved peelings from sticks until there was enough tinder to start a fire. I boiled water for coffee. The terror of the night was a distant passage that I had navigated and the dream became, almost, a nightmare that was merely a creative illusion.

On the morning after my nightmare, I couldn't wait for the sounds of the village in its awakenings. The thump of mortar and pestle, and the occasional squeals of children. I was too shaken to stay alone in my house and I was angry with myself, because there was enough to fear in the jungle if one studied the pitfalls, without having to fear one's own nightmares. As soon as I'd been fortified by coffee and the sun had burned away the chill of the night, I went up the path to the village. I saw no snakes, and there was nothing different about the path than on the previous day.

In the village, I sat on a stone near the central hearth to wait until someone came out to discover me there. I was fortunate that the first person to emerge from his house, sticky-eyed and wobbling, was Neethu. The old man. The oldest man, whom I had discovered was the village leader and patriarch and who was so brimmed with confidence that he had no need for any distinguishing trappings of his office. He strolled about bravely toothless and nearly naked, wearing his stringy arms and legs as the only insignia that he had survived for as long as he had. I had misunderstood and discounted him, at first.

Neethu wobbled out of his house, legs threatening to buckle under his negligible weight, his head bobbing with some sort of palsy, like a heavy ball nodding on a weak stem. I was speaking to him even as he crossed the narrow space of tamped ground between us. So much had happened in a short time, and my resolve to speak, regardless of errors, was strong. I said, "I was dreaming of looking. Of watching. In the forest there was watching." And then I added, "on the night in back of this day." I hugged my sides and rolled my eyes theatrically. I felt ridiculous at once, sharing my dream like that, like some neurotic woman whose need is so great that she humbles herself by laying out her fears openly. The terror of the night was rapidly fading because the sunlight was so benign and friendly, its coins of light shimmering on the ground.

The sounds of the stirring village were the same as on any other day, in any century. However, Neethu imitated my gestures, hugging his sides and rolling his eyes. He said, "Dreaming too much is continuing again." Or something like that. I thought he was saying that I had been dreaming strongly and unhealthily, but the "continuing again" didn't make sense to me. I hadn't mentioned the private substance of my dreams to any of the Tekhla before this, and how could Neethu know how often I dreamed? But then he said, "Dreaming too much is continuing night in back of day." Neethu had said dreaming "too much," which in this case simply meant "very," and I still didn't understand the significance of that. However, Neethu then asked, "What did you see in your dream?" This struck me as uncharacteristically gracious, because usually he paid not the slightest attention to me. I could have been the village pet.

I said, "I saw eyes coming closer. The eyes of people, not animals. I could not awaken."

Neethu grunted, apparently unsatisfied with my explanation. At that, I risked telling him what I really thought, because as the village leader, he was its caretaker and its pivot, and the anthropologist in me hinted that I could gain much by being frank. I could gain knowledge, or I could endanger myself. I didn't know which it would be. I said, "I think I saw the eyes of the shadow people." And then I awaited his response. I expected him to recoil, or deny, or even affirm in wonderment that I knew of this secret, but he only nodded and patted his gums together, as if I were repeating common knowledge. He said, "Jukima. They are Jukima."

I asked, "Are they related to the Tekhla?"

Neethu seemed not to understand my question, and said only, "They are Jukima." And then he asked, "In your dream, were they speaking to you? Were they saying messages to you?" At this, I felt that he didn't particularly care that I had had a terrifying dream. He was gathering news, and wanted to inspect the limits of my understanding.

I said, "They did not speak."

Then Neethu said something incredible. He said, "In my dream, they were speaking to me." He rocked back on his heels and folded his arms across his chest in an attitude that I found smug. I asked, "In your dream they were speaking to you? You dreamed the same thing?" This was impossible, and for an instant, I thought the nightmare had not ended, but Neethu continued. "Perhaps not completely the same thing. But the eyes watching, yes, I dreamed of them. And the Jukima spoke to me." I began to ask, "And what . . . " but he raised his palm to block my words. "It is not for you to know," he said. And then he relented, somewhat, and said, "They sometimes come to warn of dangers."

I asked, "Are they dangerous themselves? Are they dangerous to us?" I deliberately used the word "us" to fortify the idea that I should be included with the Tekhla in any of Neethu's considerations. Neethu looked incredibly strange to me then; he was a nearly naked, toothless, alien being. The small, domed huts suddenly didn't look at all like houses should be. The rocky hearth was severe and foreign. Nothing was normal anymore. "I shouldn't be here, now," I thought. It was too much.

Neethu said, "I do not know if they are dangerous. We do not really understand them." And then he paused, and said, "I think that perhaps your house is too far from the rest of the houses."

I nodded enthusiastically, and said, "Yes. I think that, too." It was perhaps that I showed signs of humanity in my attempts to learn their language that Neethu might allow the Tekhla to absorb me, rather than banish me. There were other questions I wanted to ask, but my audience with Neethu was over. The rest of the village was beginning to awaken, and when three or four men came out of their houses and saw us conversing there, Neethu brushed me away as one would brush away an annoying insect.

On the afternoon of the same day, some of the Tekhla women moved my belongings into Luaka's house. They didn't ask permission to enter my house and remove my things, but I accepted it without protest. Spending another night in my isolated house was unthinkable. I followed along behind them carrying my pack and my metal box, my lantern, and the coffee pot, its handle hooked over my finger. The women didn't arrange my things as they had done before, in the house that had been built for me. They hastily dropped everything in a heap on the floor, and left me to sort it and place it as I would. I had been told that Luaka's widowed husband had gone already to his village of origin somewhere near the Bacaran Falls, and the house was empty of any sign of him. Of the baby, there was no trace at all. All of the aging materials were tainted by gray mold, and I missed, already, the mellowing fragrance of my own house. I was surrounded by the straggles of Luaka's belongings and by the pestering, sourish odor of the reed walls, the thatch, the straw-like bedding. Cockroaches of all sizes waved their antennae in unhealthy greetings, and I shuddered. There was a slovenly, used odor, like the unclean aura of a sadness that made me think it had not been a happy marriage -- Luaka and Tadu. I was both frightened and busy and did not dwell very much on

Luaka's death or the location of the baby. I assumed that the infant had been taken, as Rupaki had said, to Tadu's sister.

Whether or not the Jukima were malevolent, I didn't know. I didn't know if they were real. They had left nothing of themselves behind except for my memories of them, which could have been only the remnants of a dream. There was no proof that they had been present in the flesh. I recorded all that happened, including my dreams and speculations. I had the thought that if someone should happen to read my journal -- if through some misfortune I didn't return -- then I didn't know what they would possibly make of it. After the night of dreaming, things became almost intolerably strange.

What happened was this -- the Tekhla all seemed to have had similar dreams, with variations, but similar to mine and on the same night. They had dreamed in unison of nearly identical imagery. I had no explanation for this. Through careful questioning and eavesdropping, I discovered that the Tekhla's dreams were far more detailed than my own, but then, they had more material with which to work. I was able to gather that they saw the Jukima in full regalia standing like phantoms in the moonlight, and it was as if they had an urgent message or command, or possibly they even came bearing threats. Threats, or warnings, possibly of an unbalancing pressure that was growing in our surroundings. They seemed to be warning us of some evil that had not yet been named. I felt that I had been loosened by uncertainty. My personality required some scraping together so that I could think more clearly. I hadn't spoken my own language since Frederick left.

Before I learned enough of the language to be functional, I had a measure of innocent security. Perhaps I had assumed that the Tekhla were simple and their language crude? The technologies of the Tekhla were primitive, but they were not a simple people, and their language was not. It was as complicated as any language, or more so than most, because past and present were often scrambled and they referred conversationally to ancestors long-vanished or to contemporary peers. It was confusing. And then the "night of dreaming" was another confusion. I didn't have the resources to understand it, and found myself confronted by something that was like a slippage of natural laws.

Chapter Nine

A change had come over the village. One of the small group of Tekhla had suffered a violent death, and there had been strange dreams carrying a threat or warning. The Tekhla houses were now so close to mine that I could hear the Indians' murmuring in the night, and their snoring, their arguments, the moist, practiced slaps of their love-making. A heaviness had come upon us, a strain of anxiety with occasional angry outbursts. There were quarrels where I had not noticed quarrels before. The teenaged girls squabbled over the young men, and I was shocked to see Sheoni slap Meezak across the face smartly. At the central hearth in the evenings, the men pushed spaces around themselves with their shoulders and elbows. Domestic spats burst out at night, and at one such disturbance I spread apart the thatch of my house to see Rupaki running across the clearing naked, then vanishing into Falatha's house.

The Tekhla knew that I understood enough of their language now to follow their conversations, and they dealt with me accordingly. They hushed their voices when I approached. I had thought that the Tekhla were not intense. They had appeared almost lethargic to me, but now their eyes seemed to blaze. More alarming than these things was the warning that Neemba gave me. I had begun to walk up one of the paths that led from the village, intending to collect firewood. Neemba called out to me, "You -- wait a moment." I had thought that she was going to offer to go with me, but that was not the case. Instead, she said, "Do not go that way. Take another path."

"Why should I take another path?" Neemba had approached me by then. She glanced around, and then said, " It is because of Piptcha and Dguu. They are feuding."

"Are they up ahead on this trail? And they are angry?"

Neemba pressed her lips together, paused, and finally said, "They may have set accidents for one another. Go another way."

I was appalled, and wondered what she had seen or heard. I asked, "Do you mean with poisons? The little blue frogs?" Neemba wheeled about and marched away, raising puffs of dust as she went. I could hear her muttering, "I have said too much." I rarely ventured out of the village alone after that, and then only nervously and for short distances.

A week passed since the night of dreaming, and then one week became two. I didn't dream of the Jukima again during that time. The tension in the village began to lift, and I became more at ease in my surroundings. The insects in my house did not worry me quite as much. I asked Falatha, "What of Luaka's funeral?" She said, "There is no hurry." I did not understand why there was no hurry, but she offered no explanation.

My thoughts turned more and more to Frederick. It had been about three weeks since I had sent him away and I anticipated his return at any moment. I expected to see him saunter out of the forest, perhaps brandishing a sheaf of letters for me. When the sun was overhead, I still had some hope that he would appear on that day, but later, when night came, my mind would turn to other things. There was always tomorrow.

During the days, I joined the women as they worked at the communal tasks of weaving or preparing porridge in a large pot nested in the coals of the central hearth. Falatha poked out her lips and pressed them together, an expression she put on while concentrating -- a mannerism I had come to know well. She took up a bundle of raffia strands that had been dyed blue and began to weave them over and under the spokes that extended from a knot of reeds that formed the base of a basket. I watched her hands as she worked. My mother's hands had the same quick authority. Falatha's hands were the color of parchment stained with darker oils -- darker in the creases where the skin bunched and stretched over the hinges of joints as her fingers worked with the fibers. Her nails were notched and torn. I imagined her hands snagging and catching if they were ever to stroke silk.

I asked Falatha, "Is there a meaning to blue?"

Falatha answered, "Blue is bleeding from berries."

I said, somewhat curtly, "I am not asking 'how' blue is made. I am asking, is there any meaning to blue? Is blue the water in a pool?"

Falatha said, "Water is not blue. Water is green, or water is no color. Blue is far."

I asked, "Do you mean 'distance?'"

Falatha said, "Yes. Blue is far. And, it is the feathers of parrots."

Of course water was not blue to Falatha. The sky and water were so widely separated by the height and substance of the forest as to be strangers, and the sky was not often reflected in water that was deeply shaded. The sky was the only distance she could see. Everything surrounding us was close enough to rub up against until it bruised and leaked its smell.

I bounced my pencil above my notebook, and Falatha sighed. Surely she was annoyed with my constant pestering. She asked, then, "Are you wanting to know yellow?" Without pausing for my response, she said, "Yellow is straw and moon and jaguar. Straw of homes, and yellow-circle moon, yellow of jaguar -- peace and danger. You see?" The punching motions of her fingers as she worked suggested irritation. I had noticed that she no longer smiled at me very much. However, she elaborated, "The old woman who is moon wears colors of yellow and her hair is straw-yellow. And the jaguar is the greatest, most courageous, most dangerous beast." I scribbled all this down, then poised the pen again. Falatha sighed again and said, "Next I am doing black."

As I typed my notes each day, I imagined the papers I would write. Ollieburton hadn't had access to this -- to the women's version. I allowed myself to gloat, momentarily, and then came a twinge of sorrow -- Ollie might not even be alive when I returned. I sat crouched, folded as the Tekhla often sat, with knees tucked near my armpits. I was balancing on the balls of my feet almost effortlessly, for my thighs had strengthened and my joints were more limber from imitating the postures of the Indians.

When I first joined the women when they worked, Falatha had put materials in my hands and had tried to instruct me. I didn't want to be rude, but I told her, "I am here to learn about the stories you tell," and I gently laid the materials aside and took up my notebook and pen. Falatha seemed mildly curious about my writing, but when she could make no sense of the scrawls on the paper, she apparently discounted my activity as trivial, or even wasteful of my time. She soon ignored my writing completely, as though it were merely a nervous habit or compulsive tic, which left me free to note in shorthand everything she said.

From Falatha, I learned that the stars were seeds. She told me about this one evening as we sat in her dark and smoky house, following the evening meal she and her husband had shared with me. Falatha stirred the embers of the hearth and a scattering of sparks sizzled over the fire briefly, and then extinguished. Falatha said, "You should know this," somewhat tersely, as though I had been lazy and had neglected gaps in my knowledge. She said, "A falling star is planting an ancestor. From that seed, a tribe grows. That is how we are here." Diama, her husband, said, "Of *course* that is how we are here!" Falatha ignored him and said, "Stars are as small and numerous as seeds and there is no end to them, but it is rare that they fall. The Tekhla -- the people -- are few and all are able to trace themselves to the full night sky."

Falatha's husband sniffed wetly, bored by what must have seemed to be an obvious lesson for a child, and he repaired to the men's house. Falatha continued, "And also, the stars are the lights on the scales of a snake that rolls in the sky with its tail in its mouth." And then she asked, "You have seen this, of course?" I nodded, although I had not seen constellations as serpents before Falatha told me it was so. I would try, in the future, to see the stars that way. Falatha spat into the fire, something she would not have done if her husband had been present. The fire hissed briefly.

Falatha went on, "Stars are also the campfire sparks that take with them the Tekhla prayers." I had heard these prayers, and they were usually in the form of practical and sincere requests. The Tekhla were not alone in a verdant wasteland that both provided for them and took their lives. They were governed by a large family of spirits, each with his or her responsibilities toward the world of the living. The Tekhla beliefs were solidified in their campfire stories, and Falatha had told me with some pride, that these stories had remained unchanged for uncountable generations.

Later that night, I recorded Falatha's fable in my journal. Stars were all of the things that Falatha had spoken about, and she had not seemed to think that these meanings were contradictory. Stars were the ancestors of the past; they were the ones who had not yet fallen. They were the scales on a mythical snake, and they were prayers. Falatha had said, "If we do things in the proper ways, and if we remember our ancestors, they will guide us when we die and help us take our places in the other world. And if our living families remember us when we die, they will honor us with songs and the ancestors will know our importance."

I had asked, "And what if there is no family to sing the songs?"

"If we are not accepted into the sky, then we are taken in by the forest. Everything has a spirit, you know. The trees have spirits, and everything under them, too." Then Falatha looked at me pointedly and said, "If there is a woman with no family, no husband, no child, then she is a lonely spirit." I wondered if Luaka's husband would sing for her?

I had asked Falatha, "What do you mean, 'everything has a spirit?'"

She paused, and said, "The way Neethu is, is one way to be. And, some of the men are diligent hunters, and some do less than they should."

"Some are lazy," I said.

Falatha said, "I won't tell you the names."

At that, I laughed. "I know the names."

I had wanted to question Falatha further, but she began to sweep her floor as though she wanted to sweep me out of her house. Later, in my own house, I looked at the mold that was beginning to fur the containers strung from my ceiling, and I thought about how all things changed. And yet, the Tekhla had no questions that were not answered by their stories. And then I thought, "Falatha doesn't know everything." I took a rag and began to wipe the baskets clean.

I recorded everything in my notebook. There was a plague of fleas and everyone was testy, and then the fleas abated. A serpent hanging in a swag from Rupaki's doorway was killed with a flourish and then discussed until the occasion became an abstraction. One night, Matta's sons ate spiders, cooked on a campfire near to the men's house, out in the open like an imitation of a ceremonial feast. The spiders were huge and hairy and stiffened on the blaze like wiry hands drawing into fists. This would have been an average happening if I hadn't reacted to it by scribbling in my notebook and asking questions. And so it went, with my thrusting sticks into the spokes of the turning days.

Luaka's odors in the house had become my own, like a soured, borrowed cloak that I wore. Those subtle whiffs had, perhaps subliminally, put the Tekhla more at ease about me. Perhaps they could smell me and I smelled like a Tekhla -- sweaty, flowery, smoky, and mildewed. I was becoming more normal to the Tekhla, which was a good thing, because Frederick was on the brink of being late. The rainy season, when the Tekhla would move their camp, was weeks away, and I tried not to worry.

Four weeks passed and then five, and Frederick had not

returned. He was late now, and it was with great effort that I suppressed panic. Not only was Frederick decidedly late, but the Jukima had made themselves known again. Yutta, Hlisi's toddler son, had found a doll-like figure dangling from a bush.

I watched Yutta's bouncy stagger across the clearing, his black hair bluing with sun-gleam as he passed through each patch of sunlight, and then he chortled happily and reached up - - I hadn't seen the figure until he reached for it. Yutta batted the doll down and it fell to the ground with the springy impact of a living thing. He grasped it up, and I saw it in his dusty fist as he toddled past me. It was a carved figure with silky-beige wings, and it was exquisitely painted with the touch of a tiny brush. Yutta vanished into his house with the prize, and I waited. I don't know for what -- a shriek? I waited to see his mother emerge brandishing the doll and shouting, like a town crier, that the Jukima were among us again. Nothing happened. The little doll vanished into Hlisi's house. But I knew what it was, and later that day, on the pretext of bringing Hlisi some dried beans, I asked if I could see the thing that Yutta had found. Hlisi narrowed her eyes so that her pupils shrank to dots against the brown of her eyes and she said only, "Jukima." For whatever reason, she didn't want me to see it.

I glanced at the most obvious places, but there was no trace of the doll in Hlisi's house. Hlisi squatted on the floor, turning her back to me and involving herself with plucking the stems from some berries laid out on a mat. Yutta ignored me, pushed a coal around the hearth with a stick and yipped in amazement when the tip of the stick ignited. I wanted to search for the doll, but the woven sacks, lidded baskets, and skin pouches dangling from the rafters were like closed mouths. I never saw the little figure again.

At night when I was alone with my notes, I speculated, could the Tekhla have made the thing and hung it from a bush to delight the children? I thought not, and Hlisi had said, "Jukima." I thought I knew the women's crafts by then, and there was nothing like it. But the men, in the men's house, where they were said to make the masks I had yet to see, and the crowns of feathers, the bands for arms and ankles -- could they have made the little figure? I somehow doubted it. I thought, then, that my nightmare had not been a dream at all.

I was absorbed, now, by thoughts of Frederick. I wondered if he had become distracted in Tuylo and had postponed his return to the Tekhla and to me? I didn't yet admit that he could have had an accident that prevented his return. He had been traveling to Tuylo alone, and I could not tolerate the thought that he could have died. I nearly hated him for not protesting against my sending him away.

I didn't know whether or not the discovery of the Jukima charm was the cause, but a brittle temper had permeated the village again. The thought that I was inconveniencing the Tekhla was horrible, really, although Falatha remained more or less friendly. I couldn't tell if she liked me genuinely, or was interested in me for some personal reason that I didn't understand. I perhaps ascribed more complexity to her than she deserved?

I had my gifts for the Tekhla, those that I hadn't already handed out, but they'd seen them. It was likely that they had considered all of my belongings and there was nothing that they particularly needed or wanted. The glass beads I brought for them were too bulky. They usually drank tea, not coffee. The children had sucked all of the candy to sweet memories in a day. The cloth discolored with mildew and rotted. The pots and pans were interesting to the women, but they let it be known that they were too heavy to carry when they moved their camp. It was a criticism, and I knew that.

The Indians had begun to be brusque with me, as one would be short with a distant relative whose opinion doesn't matter very much. I desired to identify a true generosity of feeling, a genuine caring for a stranger, but I wasn't able to separate the manners required by rules, from concern. I had felt much more independent and sure in the crowds of Riolapa, where I was competent, even agile in negotiating all types of impersonal, modern transactions. I realized, of course, that I had been very foolish in sending Fredrick away.

Chapter Ten

When I had been with the Tekhla for a little over five weeks, there was an event that distracted me from my fear that Frederick had abandoned me. The funeral for Luaka was held. Among the Tekhla, funerals happen when convenient, or when there is other pressing business that can be incorporated into the occasion. In the weeks before the funeral, Luaka was spoken of less and less, and Tadu was scarcely mentioned. Of the baby, I knew only that she had been taken to Tadu's sister. Tadu had been of low stature and there was no one in the village who was specifically responsible for him, or to him. He was a grumpy and tight-lipped man, and an unproductive hunter. Apparently the lines of obligation that connected Luaka to the group had been pitifully weak. There had been little to be gained from her. She had been dithering and careless, with spongy edges to her personality. That thought restored confidence, somewhat, because I wasn't that way. I was more significant than she had been?

On the day of the funeral, the normally stodgy Tekhla were frantic, in the same way that animals and birds are excited by coming changes in weather. The children played crazily and chased one another, or pasted feathers onto their skins with wet ashes, mixed water with the dust and drew upon their faces with a rust-colored slurry. I assumed that the children's play was a mimicry of what was to come that evening.

All through the day, an unusual sound strummed at the poles of the men's house -- a sound like a throaty whirring, or an eerie gale of wind pushed past tight wires. It had the vigor and strangeness of myth being born. The men's voices escaped through the thin walls of their clubhouse as they sang in a loud, monotonous chant that seemed to have only four or five notes that they repeated in all their possible combinations. They sang, and as they sang their rhythm became ever more propulsive and richer. When they were not singing, they gossiped, or they argued, sometimes so violently that I was worried.

I knew that the men's house was the staging for the performance to come that evening, and I knew that there would be songs, dancing, and speeches. I would note every aspect of the ceremony. Although it would be a condensed picture of what I had come to record, it would be *something*. I had by then resolved that I would return to Tuylo as soon as Frederick arrived and could guide me back to the river and the boat. I vowed not to attempt fieldwork alone again. I would record every instant of the funeral and it would have to be sufficient.

The evening of the funeral was cooperative. It was cool, somewhat windy. The sunset was like melodramatic stage-lighting in its hues of coral and a bilious, pale green. Bats made daintily sinister loops overhead. The fire was stoked and the flames bent and twisted as gusts passed through them. When dusk had gathered its last light into the hearth's fire, the women and children began to assemble and the men's house fell silent. The night was a bowl inverted over us, and we were together inside this container.

I was shaky and queasy, probably because of the whining, droning sound that had filled the village all through the day. Some of the women brought out leaking, leaf-wrapped packages of food and lounged just outside of their doorways to eat and feed the children. Neemba invited me to stand with her in front of her doorway and share her food. I was encouraged by that, by not being excluded.

When the thatch parted and the men emerged all in a group, it was a thrilling moment. The men stepped in unison from their club house in a dance that was as strict as a military march. They danced to a beat of drums that was resonant and slow. The drums were made from hollowed logs with leather stretched thinly over them, and the pulse of those drums awakened something like the deepest memories. It was music that was not quite earthly; it energized the small clearing in the forest.

Bringing up the rear of the group was Neethu, who swung a flat, lozenge-shaped instrument from a cord -- it was a type of bull-roarer. It was this that had made the vibrating, mesmerizing sound heard throughout the day. It was a sound capable of conjuring ghosts. The firelight played across the bodies and the painted faces and masks of the dancers and distorted them. For just a moment, the Tekhla men looked to me like fashion models preening down a ramp, with those same hollow eyed and fierce expressions; they were not quite inhabiting their bodies.

Some of the men had colored their faces with red and black slashes and concentric circles and spirals. Others were masked and wore the faces of beasts, and some wore colossal, teetering diadems of lattice woven with feathers and hung with bones, shells, swatches of fur, and little, star-burst discs of metal with sharp flanges. I realized that the discs were made from flattened and polished tin cans that had been shaped into prongs --a little like children's drawings of a rayed sun. The metal clanked like wind-chimes. I wondered about the cans -- had they been gleaned from some other visitor in some other time? Had these people dug up my garbage, and had I been remiss for not offering my leavings to them?

The dance was, at first, hypnotically slow. The dancers advanced, then retreated, advanced slightly more, toward the fire and the arc of houses beyond it and toward the women waiting in their doorways. The measured push of the dance was like a force of nature. The women stood in their doorways and urged the men forward with trilling sounds, and they began to tread in place as if caught by the same tidal force that pulled the men toward them and away from them. On either side of me, Meezak and Neemba had begun to move their feet and bodies to the rhythm. I copied them, lifting and setting down my feet, shrugging my shoulders, moving my hips. The music was so compelling that I couldn't be still, but I tried to be unobtrusive. This was their ceremony, and not mine.

I was still standing next to Neemba when she was gripped by a sudden jerk that thrust her head back and rolled her eyes up into her skull, as though a platform had given way and she were being hanged by the neck. She began chanting in a huge, strangely altered voice, using words that were not from any language I recognized. I took an involuntary and stumbling step away from her, because she had ceased at that moment to be entirely human. The hair tingled and lifted at the back of my neck.

Meezak snagged my shoulder and drew me toward her so closely that I could smell her armpits. She said in a gruff stage-whisper, "She is being Luaka, now." I understood that this was not meant metaphorically. Instead, it was a declaration that at that moment Luaka was actually, physically present in the skin of Neemba.

"But what is she saying?" I asked, and Meezak answered, "How could I know? It is the language spoken by the dead." Neemba's chanting emerged in angry blurts from her mouth. The performance was so extraordinary, that for a moment I believed wholly that Luaka's soul was speaking; the words emerging from Neemba's mouth were delivering Luaka's last statement, and Luaka was angry to the point of outrage. I didn't know if she was angry at her untimely death, or if she was angry at all of us for not being more respectful when she was with us? Neemba's outpouring axed through the drumming and halted it. She slumped and slid to the ground. Her voice was silenced, and the drumming resumed.

The men took up again their advancing, stomping dance, but it was now more rapid, staccato, and inevitable. Everything slid toward collision -- the men dancing strongly, perhaps menacingly, toward the women, stamping at the ground as if to crush it with their feet. The women took up the rhythm through their feet, their legs, taking it into their bodies. The space between the men and women was rapidly closing. Around us was the spirit-inhabited forest, the same forest that nourished and sheltered and provided unexpected gifts, and also had engineered Luaka's death.

Neemba's lay still for a short time, and then she stiffened her limbs, propped herself on all fours and shook herself, shaking off the invasion that had been Luaka. She stood upright again and took up the steps of the dance. With the resumption of the drumming, the dance became frenetic with leaps and lunges. Meezak was dancing next to me. Her face was distorted, her eyes wide and glassy, and her mouth stretched wide in a grimace. Her elbows and knees pumped with the beat of the drums. It had been my plan to stand apart and watch the Tekhla as they performed this rite. Instead, I danced with them. What else could I do? The drumming caught all of us up in its frenzy. I felt the tug of the rhythm powerfully and was nearly wild with it.

The slashes of paint on the men's skins jumped and leaped with the workings of their muscles. The antennae-quills the men wore through their noses flexed as their line pressed forward, retreated, pressed forward again, closer each time. They danced like an advancing army whose strategy was to overwhelm their opponents with a show of color and serious, physical potential. The women also advanced and fell back, but their strength was more of grace than it was of force. These differences both repelled and attracted.

94

The void between the lines of dancers was compressed until it vanished, and now was filled with a dense mass of sweating, writhing people. The firelight stained skins dusky orange, equally. I felt that I understood Ollie completely, then. He had been driven to return again and again to something here that was genuine and powerful. The Indians were not dancing for Luaka, but for themselves. I think what I heard and saw that night was strength -- strength in the face of the capricious and cruel directions that life can take. The Tekhla were not going to surrender without a struggle.

We danced for hours, until the colors of the costumes and the sounds of the drums merged into a kinetic chaos from which I had to protect myself. My muscles ached and the throbbing of my heartbeats was almost painful. My dancing slowed until I stopped dancing altogether and shrank back into the shadows of a doorway to watch.

As the evening deepened, the dancing became more disorderly, even vulgar, more athletic display than ritual. And then suddenly, it ended. The drums were stilled, although their pulse still echoed in my ears. The dancing slowed and faltered until the dancers stood idle, grinning sheepishly or readjusting their costumes. The dancers literally wandered off. Men strolled away and began to squat before the doorways of the houses and the women fed them, handing them the leaf-wrapped packages of food, and gourds of the fermented drink that had the thick, almost rancid smell of curing mulch.

This exhausted and necessary pause continued for perhaps half an hour, and then the people regrouped, but differently this time. The men squatted in a loose circle near to the fire. The women brought out mats and sat some distance from the fire, but close enough to it so that the flames reflected in their eyes and glossed their hair. I brought out a mat of my own, or rather, one that had belonged to Luaka, and I spread it near where Neemba, Meezak, and Falatha were sitting.

There was one final act that recalled Luaka and also situated her permanently in her death. It was both appalling and tender -- it was the handing out of her bones. I struggled not to find it grotesque. Neethu had re-entered the men's house while the others were relaxing, and now he emerged carrying a large but plain basket. He began to pass out its contents to everyone present. When he approached me, he paused only infinitesimally, and then handed a bone to me also. I was beyond revulsion or astonishment. This was the distribution of the bones of a human-being.

The bone I was given was surprisingly light in my hand, with plain, functional knobs and gristled whorls on its tips. It looked like one of the lesser bones of a chicken. It had been from Luaka's hand, or perhaps her foot, but probably the hand, the same hand that had waved flies away from her baby's face or had dithered at crafts or had reached greedily for the honey in the tree. I was touched, with a sentimental longing to have clasped her hand in life and to have made more of an effort.

I asked Falatha, "How did the bones come from Luaka?" It sounded crass, but I wanted to know the facts of it, the mechanics. She said, "From the stream, the little fish with teeth. The 'chop-chop.'" I shuddered, because I could imagine it vividly. It would have been quick, thorough, and efficient. Falatha said, "Luaka's body was placed in cage and the little fish swam through," and then a word I did not understand -- lattice? "and Luaka became many little fish with teeth, and sometimes the larger fish eat the smaller fish." At that, Meezak said, "And if the jaguar eats the larger fish. . . . "

Neemba laughed rudely, for she had been eavesdropping, and Falatha made a snorting sound and said, "Not too much possibility that Luaka would become jaguar. Hah! Jaguar!" She snorted again, and I dropped the subject. Falatha pointed to the tiny bone that I was negligently rolling around in the palm of my hand, and said, "You could make beads out of that."

Luaka had been left behind permanently, and no one had stepped forward to sing for her. When the memories of her carried by these few people were snuffed out by their own deaths, Luaka would be gone, as permanently as an extinct species. Whereas just a short time ago, these people had been stricken with a rhythm that belonged to both culture and wilderness, they now were utterly tamed, in comparison. What followed the handing out of the bones can best be described as a town meeting.

A man I recognized as Tchilhu stood, seeming to rise above his short, stocky limitations. He began to speak. Incredibly, he was speaking about pigs. I bent to a page of my notebook, to record what he was saying. My eyes were scorched from the resinous campfire smoke and from my tiredness, and I blinked and squinted, teary-eyed, as I bent to a page of my notebook. Tchilhu was aggrieved about something, and his oration was delivered with a kind of spunky bravado. He was speaking of a hunting expedition with Rodomo, a rather ineffectual and overweight Indian whose wife often drove him from her house with streams of rude complaints that he shouldered as his life's work.

Apparently, Tchilhu and Rodomo had gone to hunt as a team; they had been a rather awkward team. A wild boar had been flushed from a thorn bush. Wild boar could be savage, and had caused far more deaths among the Indians than jaguars or snakes. Both Tchilhu and Rodomo had shot their arrows, but Rodomo had been sluggish in his reactions and his arrow had snagged in the quiver, while Tchilhu's arrow had hit its mark. His arrow had pierced the skull of the boar, between the eyes. I was impressed, and dutifully recorded this.

Immediately following the fatal arrow-strike, Rodomo fumbled free his arrow, notched it to the bow. While the boar flipped and struggled -- I could only imagine the shrieking and confusion -- Rodomo quite unnecessarily released his own arrow, which struck the animal broadside, in the flank. The boar dropped just then as though it had been bludgeoned with a mallet. Rodomo had thereupon claimed the kill as his own, and as a further insult, had offered to share a large portion of the meat with Tchilhu and his family. As he spoke, Tchilhu went through the most amazing contortions, first as himself, the shrewd, sophisticated hunter, then as Rodomo, the blundering fool who hadn't learned the most rudimentary technique of extracting an arrow from his quiver without bobbling it, and then finally as the wild boar in its dramatic thrashings. I recorded all of this, and impressed myself with how much of the story I understood.

It was then Rodomo's turn, and the story began to warp until it had deformed significantly. Rodomo's recounting was even more florid than Tchilhu's had been. It was comical to see such a rotund man mimic the choreography of the consummate hunter. His rendition of the death throes of the wild pig was particularly apt, and by then his performance was interrupted by the hooting comments of the other men who reclined, smoked, and nibbled on succulent morsels of wild boar. In Rodomo's version, it was Tchilhu who fumbled the extraction of the arrow, and it was Rodomo himself who smoothly and with timely expertise brought down the animal. Rodomo had slipped into the role of court jester, which was both entertaining and pathetic, for he seemed to be completely convinced of the truthfulness of his version of the incident. His face writhed with effort and a spray of perspiration flew from his forehead.

Rodomo said, "My arrow was then and always first, and Tchilhu himself was telling you that his arrow was sent second-position after aiming more slowly." I scribbled that down, but noted the inconsistency. Tchilhu had not said his arrow was second. He had asserted and demonstrated that his arrow had been the first to be released.

An argument flared immediately. Tchilhu stood again -- for he had reclined on a mat companionably with his wife. He flailed his arms as if to attack Rodomo, but it was a feigned assault and he was easily subdued by his cronies. There was much posturing and garbling of what had been said, and by whom. The evening was coming unraveled as the argument escalated. Neethu squatted and sucked on his pipe. His head wobbled with palsy, and his hand jiggled with tremors as he lifted and lowered the pipe. The women burst in on the argument at that point, and were nearly as vociferous as the men. It seemed as though violence were immanent.

And then a most surprising thing, and the thing that made all the difference to me and to my future with the Tekhla. Falatha said, with a strong, clear voice, "Pressa is knowing." Falatha habitually called me Pressa, that word being her own contraction of "professor," Frederick's somewhat ironic term for me. She said, "Pressa knows." The quarreling dampened and all looked quizzically in my direction. Falatha said, almost smugly, "It is here in the tracks of the speaking," and she pointed with her chin to my notebook. I hadn't realized that she had understood, much less valued, what I had been doing. She said, "Like a knowing of the sense of the tracks of snakes or the pads of animals with claws in or out, she is able to give back what was said."

I said, "It is true. It is in these tracks," and I flourished the notebook. Neethu levered himself to standing, almost elegantly, in an unfolding of his authority which had been waiting for its precise moment. He extended his right hand toward me, and then drew it tremblingly back toward his chest. He wanted my notebook.

I was daring, and perhaps impolite, but I couldn't afford to embarrass this influential man. I said, "I do not track animals," and then I ventured a macabre humor, "and I do not locate the honey-trees. I track the speeches and the doings of people. It is here," and I waved the notebook about in the air but out of reach of Neethu. And then I said, "I would be honored to do this for you." Neethu was not a stupid man, and he chose discretion. He gave a wobbling but authoritative nod in my direction, and sat down again. I stood like a school-girl and read back my transcription, minus my asides about the lewd gestures and humor of the quarreling hunters.

The Tekhla were incredulous. There seemed to be no arguing with the accuracy of the transcription I read back to them. To a tracker, the paw-print of a jaguar is not to be confused with the ropy groove of a snake, and perhaps the Indians respected that aspect of my performance, or perhaps it was the certainty with which I read back the facts as I had heard them? Rodomo glowered and stirred at the dust with his toe, but was ignored as the controversy snuffed out. When I had finished reading, Neethu rendered his verdict, which was that Tchilhu was to receive proper credit and thanks for his contribution of the boar-meat, and that was to be the end of it.

The rest of the evening was very difficult work, for on the agenda there were many dissatisfactions to be reviewed. I wearily transcribed complaints of wives about indolent husbands, and husbands about slovenly wives. Long chains of gift-giving and obligations were recounted, and infractions of reciprocity were dealt with. After each long oration, I was required to stand and read back my notes, tilting the notebook toward the firelight, which flickered across the words and warped them. My eyes burned and my voice grew croaky. However, I was elated by the turn of events. I had become Neethu's scribe.

The meeting droned on until dawn. The clearing gradually revealed a tawdriness that was as grubby and repulsive as a theater in daylight. The ground was dented with scuff-marks and strewn with bones and gristle and the limp, greasy leaves in which the food had been wrapped. Flies had begun to drone. There was no formal adjournment; the Indians began to yawn and stroll away individually. I crept to my own little house and dropped onto the mattress, falling asleep immediately.

I hadn't expected to dream anything of significance, particularly in daylight, but I did dream, very strongly. I dreamed once more of the Jukima, and again I had the sense that I was not awake but yet was conscious of my dreaming as it occurred. I saw the Jukima standing on the banks of a stream. I realized that it was the same stream and the same slightly sloping, foggy ground where they had first appeared to me, and it was also the same as the stream across which I had first seen the Tekhla. These images slipped into alignment and became one thing, one place. There was the heightened detail of an extraordinary encounter, and was an encounter whose purpose was to warn.

The Indians were positioned on the far bank, and their

finery didn't look so fine as it once had. The feathers they wore were ravaged, dusty and unstrung by the passage of time or travel. Their faces were whittled to a leanness that suggested starvation. Their eyes gleamed, star-bright in the hollow cups of their sockets. And then the dream advanced and became somewhat frightening, in that I was frightened for them, but not of them. The Jukima began to press forward, drawn toward me by a connection that I didn't understand, as though their dreaming of me had caused them to appear in my own dream.

The Indians began to wade into the water like somnambulists. I tried to cry out, to warn them about the hordes of little, razor-toothed fish, but my rising voice was covered by the thrashing of the stream. They waded in to shin-deep, then to their knees. The current pulled at their feathered capes and spread them on the water, and feathers were plucked loose and twirled down-stream like the heartbreaking corpses of birds. The water snagged at the Indians' legs and then it boiled up and frothed as I had expected it would. I covered my eyes with my hands, but I still saw them coming toward me. The little fish arched, glinting and slim, up out of the water and pelted down in a squirming mass. The Indians reached the bank on which I was standing. I was transfixed and horrified. I expected to witness them tottering from the water on the stilts of their own bones.

It was a dream, or some sort of dreamlike threshold, and the Indians were not harmed. Their flesh was not torn at all by the teeth of the fish. It was supernatural in the way that a dream is not quite of this world -- it was like a barrier-shield the Indians themselves radiated. As the last one of the Indians stepped free of the water, the stream ceased its agitation and settled again into a monotonous purling.

The Indians approached me until they were very close, so near that I could see their wan faces and details of the convoluted, blue netting of designs on their skins. I sensed that they had a message intended for me, specifically, although I had no idea why I had been selected to receive it. They enveloped me somehow with an understanding, one that was as personally felt as their warm, sweet breaths on my face. Their message was collectively given, and it had to do with rain, and water -- something about a perilous and extreme rain and about water breaching channels and spreading.

In the dream, I saw disjointed vignettes of inundations of water, water sweeping over places that were familiar and meaningful to me. One by one these places were flooded and leveled by the sameness of water. The path to the Tekhla gardens vanished under a silvery glide of liquid. My bell of a house floated free of the ground, bobbing and deflating into a debris of straw. Then the dock at Tuylo slipped under. Water sealed the land with its membrane and made it different.

As I watched the rising flood, the sound of the stream became muffled. The Indians receded into the kind of haze that I assumed was the stuff -- like protoplasm -- that they were made of. And then they vanished. And one more thing; when the Indians had crossed the stream and stood before me so closely that I could smell the exotic spiciness of their skins and breaths, one of them stretched out his hand to me. He offered me a small figure, a material sign of their presence. I reached to take the figure from his hand, and saw that it was of the same class as the figure in Ollie's photograph -- a winged figure vined all around with a silvery strand. It was the same as the doll that Yutta had plucked from a bush. As I reached for the figure, it was withdrawn, not by meanness, but because of the illusory substance of dreams. I knew that even if I had taken the gift that was offered, the Indian's hand would have slid through mine and there would be no sensation, other than numbness or the faintest chill where our hands had passed through one another but had failed to make contact, in a dream-space where different realms coexist.

Chapter Eleven

I awakened gradually to the light ticking of rain on the straw roof. There was a hot smell of rain in the air, as vegetable-steamy as if someone had thrown spinach into boiling water. The earth smelled freshly tilled. The dream of the Jukima was rapidly fading, but before its mood left me, I had the self-protective thought, "That's all it was; I heard the rain and I dreamed of water." But that was not all it was, and I must have known it was not.

I came out of my house and saw that the Tekhla, too, were only just then awakening and coming out of their houses. Their eyes were swollen with sleep, and they were grumbling at having been disturbed. Some of the men were beginning to stir on their mats by the hearth, where they had reclined because they were too spent to return to their wives' houses or to their club house. They squirmed themselves awake and stood blinking and stretching, their skins slick with rain. The forest all around was transformed, and I found it lovely in its gentleness. Its acid greens had been softened and were misted by the steam that rose from the ground. There was an overwhelming aroma of freshening growth as the earth slackened and opened to welcome the rain.

At first, the rain drizzled, and then it became more forceful. The droplets multiplied and filled in the spaces among them with more rain. The foliage all around the clearing bent low, and then it went nearly prostrate under the barrage of rain. The water poured down in strings and fashioned thick, rainbowed chains of beads that hung trembling from the thatch of the huts. The beads detached singly and splashed down. Steam rose from the domed roofs as though the thatch were burning. It was like a fairy-land, as transformative as snow --

everything now gleamed on its simplified surfaces. The pale daylight was bottle-green, and a greenish vapor was swirling around the trees. Puddles were forming and widening, for the earth in the village was too hardened and densely packed, to absorb all of the water and so the ground repelled what it could not drink up, and it spread the water out flatly.

And then the children came pouring out of their houses, flushed out into the open by the noisy novelty of the rain. They scrambled about with upturned faces and unhinged, opened mouths. Rain-water sluiced down their chins, cluttered their eyelashes. The children stomped and splashed, and their naked legs mottled with the churned, reddish water. I stood outside my doorway, still swarmy with sleep, and the remainder of my dream melted as the rain pattered on my head, roped my hair and slid from my nose, my fingertips, soaked through my clothing. I realized that I was barefoot. The mud that squashed up between my toes had a healthful, almost medicinal warmth to it. I wanted to stomp and play as the children were doing. I told myself it was only a brief, heavy rainstorm, a squall that would soon pass and leave everyone refreshed and then the cool nights would return, and the dust, and the cycles of daily life.

I was still standing in front of my doorway when Neethu hobbled past on his way to the men's house. He greeted me cordially, because I had helped him the night before and he couldn't ignore me as he might have liked. He said, "It will cease. It is arriving too soon and will realize its error. It will stop." This sounded to me as though he had mustered the authority of his years and had commanded the rain to stop. I agreed, "Yes. It will be brief." Neethu grunted and turned his knobby back to me as he proceeded across the clearing. I made note of the way he had personalized the rain, had made of it a sentient, motivated thing. It was as Falatha had said -- even the rain had a spirit. I thought to return to my typewriter and record this observation. I turned, but then decided to gather a few more statements concerning the arrival of the rain and its apparent volition to stop, or not stop. Or perhaps I wanted further assurances that it would stop? I knew from my dream that it wouldn't, but I was denying that knowledge.

By evening, the rain had not stopped. Except for the small open space above the clearing, the trees were so thick that I could see the sky only in hints. I was ignorant about what the weather would do next. Was there one, immense cloud that covered all the sky? At this moment, it was raining, and it was all I could think of. Everyone was touchy and glum, and

Frederick was late and there was nothing I could do about it. Nothing at all. I imagined him involved only in the moment, forgetfully drunk on the local beer at the Urubus in Tuylo, and with a woman on each arm. He brandished the bottle with its gilded label of the two parrots with interlaced tails, waving the bottle about like a scepter. Perhaps it was not raining there.

Late in the morning, I stopped in to visit Falatha. She was only faintly courteous about my interruption. Her hearthfire blazed and clogged her hut with smoke that could find no escape except for the narrow slit in the roof, and so it bunched and roiled around up there filthily. When Falatha's husband saw me he snorted, gathered up his pipe and tobacco, and repaired to the men's house. I was both offended and relieved to see him go, because Falatha was likely to speak with me more freely if he wasn't present. Primarily, the men ignored me.

I fanned uselessly at the gathering smoke. Falatha glowered and said, "The bad luck continues. That is why it is raining now. It could be that someone has been improper and we are being punished." She didn't look at me as she said this, and we fell into silence. Falatha began busying herself with pointed haste, straightening objects, adding wood to the fire. I took her hint and went back out into the rain to my own house, squelching through mud that was already as high as my ankles. I wondered, did she blame me, somehow, for the rain? Surely I had made many mistakes, but how could I be blamed for breaking rules I didn't understand?

Mud was everywhere in my house. My clothes, when I washed them, didn't dry. They smelled of mold. This rain was not clean; it soiled and damaged everything it touched. That evening, alone in my house, I thought of my own appearance for the first time in weeks. I had only the small metal mirror into which I rarely gazed, but I took this out and looked at my reflection. In the village I was surrounded by people with glossy black hair, dark eyes, and brown skins. I had forgotten my difference from them. The face that looked back at me was an apparition. Skin as light as mine was vulnerable, revealing every blemish from insect bite or scratch. Below my eyes were bluish swellings where the skin was thin and the tiny veins were close to the surface. My eyes were reddened, and I wondered if I was becoming ill. The face staring back at me was so peculiar I didn't know how the Tekhla managed to tolerate me at all.

Evening had come with no fire in the central hearth and no common gathering. I had eaten my dinner alone. I wrote about the morning's encounter with Falatha as I sat on my bed in my little house. I angled the notebook on the rolled blanket I used as a pillow and noticed how the humidity caused my pen to smudge and streak the lines I was writing. The water was beginning to infiltrate my hut -- but not through the roof, which was turgid with moisture and didn't leak. The water sheeted down as if the thatch were duck feathers. The water was creeping in under the skirt of the wall. The hut was on a slight slope or mound, and the water followed the lowest, easiest path, around the periphery of the circle where a rivulet had dug a little channel. The collecting water outside my hut began to flow in and deepen this groove. The rain was eroding the ground upon which the village was planted.

I couldn't sleep. The rain was unlike any I had known in other places and times. Its coolness was an illusion. It was a teeming, smothering rain, and it brought heat with it. Steam rose everywhere. I was stunned by the noise of the rain as it slapped down. I wrote in my journal that surely this rain was a prelude to the rainy season that wasn't supposed to arrive for at least a month. The Tekhla would move camp then. Frederick must return immediately. He must.

When I thought about the missing Frederick, I became so terrified that my teeth chattered. Without him, I had lost my way home. Even if I could find my way to the river, it might have risen and might not be navigable. And then I told myself that I was alarmed for no reason. The Tekhla were the Tekhla, and I knew them. If the rain didn't stop very soon and if Frederick were not yet here, I would ask one or two of the Indians to guide me back to the river -- to the little dock. And once at the river, I would try to build a small shelter -- I thought I could do that -- and I would build a fire inside of the shelter. The smoke would be a signal for the boat, and the boat would stop for me. I could try to persuade one or two of the Indians to stay there with me. As incentive, I would offer to give them most of my belongings. I really needed to bring very little with me back to Tuylo. I could give them the camera. This seemed reasonable, and I slept and dreamed of nothing.

On the next day, it was still raining. It had brought an incredible heat along with it, a soup of heat, and all the smells were different, drawn from the earth's hot flesh. The minerals in the clay of the earth were tangy and pungent. The drowned vegetation gave off an outrageously fecund smell. There had been no campfires in the courtyard hearth since the rain began and the soggy ash stank like a wet goat. The rain was not slackening at all.

Rupaki and Falatha were cooking a stew in Rupaki's house. I had gone with them earlier to the gardens, where the vegetables were rotting on the ground. The bean pods, most of them, had blanched and split open, and the seedlings had been flattened and now were melting back into the earth. The corn was blackening on the stalks. I had not planted these seeds, but I could help with the gathering. We took the few vegetables that were still firm back to Rupaki's house, cut them into morsels, and now they were boiling in a pot.

The Tekhla rules that I had once studied now applied to me as well. Women had certain duties. To have food ready always when the men were hungry. To pretend that the secrets of the club house were unknown to them. To defer to the men and to the elder women in decisions of importance. To avert the eyes submissively when passing a man on a path -- any man. To prevent the children from crying in the night and disturbing everyone. I had learned these things, and was trying to comply with my attitude and actions. I couldn't afford to make mistakes.

Everywhere in the little house were unfinished projects. A hide half-scraped of fur. A beaded bracelet laid aside, the beads falling from the cords. The thatch and baskets and straw of the bed were all coated with mildew. And in my own house, my flour had been spoiled by weevils, and the dried beans had begun to sprout. My typewriter keys had been seized by rust, and my camera shutter had been immobilized.

Rupaki stirred at the stew, unnecessarily, while Falatha sat behind her and picked nits from Rupaki's hair. "It is the last of the gardens," Rupaki said. I noticed how severe and pinched her face looked, and how her ankles were spotted with weeping sores. Her usually serious expression had deepened, and her brows were drawn together dangerously. She said, "Tchilhu is already complaining about the sameness of the food."

"The men say that hunting is difficult in the rain," said Falatha.

"I think they just sit under the trees and smoke," said Rupaki. And then she said, "This all began with Luaka." Falatha nodded her head vigorously.

I dared to ask, "Do you really think that Luaka's death began the bad luck?"

"Oh, of course," said Falatha. "Her foolishness began it." And then she said, in nearly a whisper, "Namal did not accept it, you know."

I asked, "Who is Namal? Namal did not accept what?"

Rupaki answered, "Namal is Tadu's sister. Falatha means the baby. Namal did not take the baby."

"What! Luaka's baby? Then who took the baby in?"

Falatha said, so off-handedly that I wanted to slap her, "No one took the baby. There was no one else. Tadu did not take it with him because men do not care for children, and he was not likely to find another wife, at his age."

Rupaki added, "The baby was a girl, anyway."

"Then where is the baby?" I asked, although I already knew, then, and was already sickening with this knowledge.

"Namal has many children of her own. I think that she left it in the forest. That is all," said Rupaki. "The baby is gone." I saw that Falatha was putting the nits she picked from Rupaki's hair into her mouth.

Falatha chewed and said, "That is what happened. The baby was put down in the forest."

When I left Rupaki's house, I could only go to my own house and sit on the bed and rock and weep, although no one could have heard my weeping over the noise of the rain. I had held the baby in my arms -- I had held her close to my body and then I had let her go. I had felt such pleasure in the baby's warm, firm flesh, in the way she had clung to me, had searched my face with her damp fingers. I had let her slip away from me so easily and had scarcely thought of her since. I had assumed too much, and I had trusted. I had thought I was surrounded by human beings, but they were not human anymore to me. And I, also, was guilty. I had recorded everything I could about these people, but I had failed to arrange my facts with any sort of artistry. I *knew* that women were not as important as men. And I *knew* that girl infants were less important than women, or boy babies. And, I had understood that Luaka had not been liked. I had failed to comprehend consequences, and I had failed to intervene. I had not presumed or dared to tamper with a culture I felt I was not privileged to change. There had been no songs for Luaka, and there would be no songs for her daughter.

I could have taken the baby in. I would have managed, somehow, and then taken the baby with me when I left, or at the very least, found someone in Tuylo who would nurture it. Sparks' wife came to mind. I had not been asked. How much trouble could it have been to save a life? No one would wear this baby's bones as a necklace, and I wondered, would anyone wear mine?

I could imagine the baby, moistly rosy, fat as a grub, but with a fearful intelligence in her eyes as she was laid down on the earth – naked, intelligent, and inarticulate. Could these people not have been able to imagine what she must have felt when she was placed on the ground and not picked up again? There would have been fluttering leaves and hot sky high above her, insects beginning to crawl upon her skin. The pain of an animal's attack. The complete helplessness and fear. The abandonment -- the murder -- of Luaka's baby changed drastically my understanding of the Tekhla and I wanted -- I needed -- to go home.

The Tekhla now appeared soiled and mean to me, muddy in bodies and spirits, scabbed with scarcely healing sores, and with greasy hair. Dirty. Their children's pot-bellies were full of worms. Their huts were infested with fleas. The people ate spiders. It was their minds, in particular, that were soiled or polluted from having been confined by the rain to their fishy, smoky, houses. They quarreled and sniped, complained about one another ceaselessly. The culture itself was decadent, with every act caged by tradition.

And then I thought about the Indians' kindnesses. The friendship of Falatha. The food the women of the village shared with me, the secrets they told me. And if one person could be complicated to the point of incomprehension, how much more complicated an entire group or culture must be? It was too overwhelming for me, and my tools -- my notebook and pencils and facts -- were not sufficient for the task of understanding.

After I learned of the murder of Luaka's baby, I became shamelessly deferential to the Tekhla. I was ingratiating, gathering extra firewood close to the camp -- ever wary about snakes and sharpened, poisoned sticks -- and giving the firewood to Falatha. I shared great quantities of my salt, sugar, and oatmeal, to which some of the Indians had taken a liking. I only wished that I hadn't been so gluttonous in the early, careless days and had more of it to give. In the style of politicians everywhere, I was buying their friendship with things and favors.

My usefulness to the Tekhla was my future. I had been asked, three times since the rain began, to transcribe meetings. In that way, I found a small niche in a group of people who otherwise might have had no need of me. These meetings didn't occur in the men's house, because women were not allowed to enter that sacred domain. Instead, we all stood grumpily out in the rain and held banana leaves over our heads. I assumed the Indians blamed me for this discomfort. However, Neethu continued to require my services, probably so that he could dispatch grievances quickly. We all had been sitting inert, like mushrooms, in our molding houses, and the Indians spent much time quarreling. All looked to Neethu for resolutions. The weather had made Neethu's infirmities worse. He trembled, and he creaked audibly when he crossed or uncrossed his legs.

I recorded tedious and petty tales. Wayovi's wife hoarded feathers -- deprived him of feathers for his ornaments -- because he was an indifferent hunter and her hearth lacked fresh meat. Or, Piptcha and Dguu had married sisters and the sisters gossiped rudely about them as husbands. They revealed their husbands' weaknesses to anyone who would listen, which was, apparently, everyone, because there was no source of entertainment other than the telling of stories. The sisters were the tabloid rags of the village. And then, more significantly, it had been noticed that Tcheema's son resembled Piptcha more closely than his nominal father. Piptcha had protuberant ears, as did Tcheema's son. There was no privacy anywhere. Privacy assumed the importance of an object one could hold in one's hands and say, "I own this and I am free to share it or not share it."

I packed my things -- except for those few items I used on a daily basis -- because it seemed certain that we couldn't remain here much longer. I still held some, small hope that Frederick would arrive, rain streaking his foolish glasses and smearing his vision because he would be too proud to remove those unnecessary glasses and behave honestly, as a human being should. I would say, "So, there you are." I would say my good-byes, and we would go.

I even made grandiose plans to return someday with an army of anthropologists and graduate students and various technicians. If necessary, I would pay the Tekhla to perform their dances and to reveal everything to me until all of the information had been gathered. So much information would provide a lifetime of data. That is what I thought I would do, when I was in one of my more positive moods. My moods swung from optimism to abysmal despair, and I imagined the office I would have eventually, at some university or other, the electric hot-plate where I would make my tea, the substantial oak filing cabinets, and perhaps a few, luscious, candy-colored orchids under glass to remind me of the jungle. I would wear a human bone on a necklace. I would be a woman with a past, a person who had adventured.

I dreamed each night of the return of Frederick. I chastised him lightly for the worry his tardiness caused me, and for his boyish lack of good judgment. When I awakened, it was to the horrible vacancy that was the absence of Frederick. I thought it was quite possible that he had died. I recalled the fussy but evil pistol he wore like an ornament tucked into the waistband of his shorts. It was a weapon appropriate for interiors -- cantinas, or the houses of the women he visited. I imagined him as fiery tempered. A drunken brawl, a jealous husband. Anything could have happened. He could have been bitten by a snake and now was only a litter of bones on the overgrown trail, perhaps only a few hundred yards from where I waited in anguish. Frederick reached out to me in dreams and said, "Trust me," although I recalled that he had never specifically said those words.

The Tekhla also were making preparations for a journey. They said, "The rain will stop soon and if it does not stop, we will leave this place." To them, a premature rainy season was an inconvenience. It skewed the schedule of ceremonies -- initiations and marriages, for example, which were usually undertaken where we were, in the winter camp and out in the open. I knew that it was the cleared space in the forest and the fire it usually held, like a little guardian shard of the sun, that kept the animals of all sorts in their proper places. Without the Indians to keep the vegetation cleared away, it would grow more rapidly than I could hack it back. And the snakes -- at least on cleared ground the snakes could be seen and avoided. I had no idea whether or not the Indians would allow me to go with them, or would help me in any way. I was no one.

Chapter Twelve

The rain covered all of the other sounds of the village. I could no longer overhear the Tekhla conversations at night, and had no clear idea about what to expect from them or what they were planning. I dug a trench around my hut with a stick. The Tekhla also had done this. I stacked my firewood inside my house so that it could dry, more or less. All sorts of spiders, centipedes, and grubs crawled out of it. When lit, the wet wood hissed and spurted steam, and the insects that had harbored in the wood scurried out and then broiled and popped in the heat. My clothes had all soured and had blotched gray with mildew. My boots were rotting, and each day I scraped a fuzz of grayish-green mold from the leather. My straw mattress was muddy. Poor Frederick -- my rust-frozen camera would be only a sculpture of a functional camera.

I had by then asked the Indians, individually and shamelessly, to guide me back to the river to wait for the boat. I had offered to pay them all of my wealth, which I told them was at my own camp many miles away. Those wretched Indians regarded me curiously when I asked them to do that, or they laughed unpleasantly, or simply turned away. They had other, more pressing concerns. I could have been asking them, if it is not too much trouble, could they please take a stick and bat the moon down from the sky? If it is not too much trouble? Please bat it down.

The clearing where the Indians had built their houses was in a shallow depression, and when the ground had soaked in all it could of the water and the vegetation had bloated with all it could take up, the run-off water began to drain into the camp. The hearth was the lowest point, and the water first filled the ring of stones with a circle of water. The circle of water dimpled with the rain that was still falling, and concentric rings spread from each dimple and passed through one another in a complicated geometry. Sometimes I saw the pool as an eye -- a single, watery eye that reflected the face of whoever peered into it. Soon, however, the water rose and submerged the stones. Falatha had been right; this water was never blue -- it was the mineral color of ore. It shivered and wobbled like mercury.

The earth that sloped toward the hearth became netted with rivulets, and then these, too, sought one another and merged in deeper trenches that rushed with current. This water was running powerfully and carried silt in suspension so that it was nearly blood-red. It sought out the men's house and the men abandoned the place. It flowed through Neemba's house and she moved her family in with Hlisi's family. Then Hlisi's floor was skinned with water, and all these people moved out and joined Falatha's family, until her house bulged with all of them.

In my own house, I built a crude, slippery shelf of firewood logs and perched everything on it that wasn't hanging from the ceiling. The water covered my floor, as well. But that was manageable. It was. What was not tolerable were the snakes, because all manner of serpents had been washed from all those places where they hid themselves and bothered very few people. The snakes were everywhere -- they swam elegantly through the village in cursive strands and whatever they contacted that was dry and steep, they climbed, hefting themselves up with rhythmic muscularity. They infested the thatch and hung from the trees in heavy loops, like bicycle tires.

I couldn't sleep, but swept the walls and ceiling of my house ceaselessly with my flashlight beam. The black water of the floor swayed each time I shifted my position on the elevated mattress, which became a small boat that I clung to, alone in a liquid world. It was unendurable, and I gave up on Frederick. It was necessary to release that hope and replace it with others. There was the stream, which now raged and was close to breaching its channel. It was now a river that was entirely hostile and couldn't be crossed.

Eventually, I did sleep, the flashlight slipping from my relaxing grip and dropping to the floor of water and submerging. When I awakened at dawn, I saw the flashlight's faltering beam under the water, its light weakened to a trickle. It doused itself nearly at the same instant that I discovered it. The rain still hammered down. It was light enough by then for me to search the rafters and the walls for snakes, but there were none. There was only a tiny frog, cobalt blue, suckered onto the strut of a peeled sapling. Its eyes bulged and rotated independently of the bobbing of its narrow head. Its throat vibrated with pulse; the thin skin of its throat looked as fragile as the skin of a baby's fontanel. I felt privileged to see it there, because I had been told that the blue frogs were *owned* only by the men, who extracted their toxins in secrecy in the men's house. Ollie had seen the harvesting of their poison, but I hadn't been allowed. It was like a small, poisonous jewel of a sign, trapped by the flood just as I was. It was so small and frail.

It was obvious that the rainy season had arrived and expected to remain. The Indians hurried their preparations to leave. The village was flooding with the run-off from the rain. The stream wouldn't be contained within its banks for much longer. I sorted through my things again, calculating both the weight and relative importance of each item. My boots looked strange to me – stiff, thick, and coated with mold. They were club-like. I was the only person there who wore shoes, and they didn't seem to be designed for the flexibility of human feet. I had two pairs of boots, but knew that I couldn't carry the weight of both pairs. I would leave one pair behind.

I hung my ruined camera from the arch of my doorway as a sign that I had been there. Then I reversed that decision. If Frederick should make his way to the site of the camp, I wanted the incentive of the camera to motivate him to search for me. My metal box was heavy, but necessary, and I stowed it in my pack. It left not much room for anything else. In the pack I also put my pocket knife, some extra socks and underwear, two tee-shirts, and two pairs of shorts. I rolled up my sleeping bag and slung it from the straps of the pack. And then I removed it. It would absorb the rain and become impossibly heavy. I would leave it. I packed one can of insect spray. My dried meat had rotted in the humidity. The flour had turned gray and was infested with insects, and the coffee was unnecessary. I stuffed a can of beans into the pack, and then it was full.

That was in the morning, and the water continued to rise. At mid-day, Neethu convened a meeting and I was summoned. I took up my notebook and slogged through the silty water to a place where the ground was slightly higher, where the Indian men were gathering. Neethu cleared his throat and began. "We will go on the morning in front of this day. But we have something to decide." The men scowled, and curled and uncurled their toes in the mud. Neethu looked at me and commanded, "You will make the marks of what we say." Then he continued, "We must decide what to do about the ghost woman." The hair rose on the back of my neck. I was the problem they had gathered to discuss -- and they thought of me as a ghost! My hand was shaking as I wrote the words on the paper.

Neethu said, "I am not sure if she should travel with us. You see how pale she is. I think perhaps she is not well, and will be a burden."

"She is well enough," said Diama. "She helps Falatha on occasion, and she can carry firewood."

Rodomo snorted, and said, "She seems unwell to me."

"I think that is just her skin, " said Tchilhu.

I was horrified to discover that my paleness was seen as a liability. But then Wayovi offered that my clothing demonstrated that I was not completely witless. The fastenings of my clothing were clever -- the buttons and snaps and zippers, and I realized that Wayovi thought I had made them myself. Wayovi was a tiny, angular man whose presence I had scarcely noticed before, but now I was grateful for his observations.

"The rain is one thing among other bad-luck things," said Neethu. There were grunts of assent. "The ghost woman may be a bad-luck thing." There were a few more grunts. "But she has something she can do. Perhaps the ancestors have given her to us so that she can help with the meetings." Neethu scanned the faces of the assembled Indians carefully, and waited for their opinions.

"She cannot put the thatch on a house," said Rodomo.

I chafed at this, but dared not say, "I think I could thatch a house. I have watched how it is done." Instead, I continued writing.

"She cannot plant a garden," countered Rodomo.

This was answered by Tchilhu, who said, "I have seen her with the women bringing in harvest. She could learn to plant."

Wayovi asked, "Can she gather food in the forest? Does she know what we eat and where it grows?"

At this, I couldn't resist speaking and said, "I could learn this. I can find tubers and I can dig them. I could learn the other things, too." At the sound of my voice, Neethu's muscles twitched so that he actually jerked in my direction. I stepped back and shielded my face with my notebook. I thought he was about to strike me.

Neethu barked at me, "Only men may speak now! Do you understand? You are not to say anything unless asked." I lowered the notebook and nodded, poised the pen over the paper again. The Indians were glaring at me. And then, as if I

114

had not spoken, Neethu said, "She is like a child, but she is not a child."

"She is clumsy," Rodomo said. "And impolite. And her breasts are too small."

"But she could be stronger than we know," suggested Tchilhu.

I was too frightened to be embarrassed by Rodomo's remarks. I wrote the words on the paper. And then the conversation veered away from a scrutiny of my body and my personal failings. Frederick was mentioned, and the Tekhla's allegiance to him, if any, was questioned. Was anything owed to me because of my association with Frederick? The answer was a unanimous "no." I was right -- the Tekhla thought him an arrogant fool and a possible danger to their women, with whom he had flirted extravagantly. He was a Tuylo Indian, and there was no kinship with him.

We stood in the rain, our feet drowned to the ankles and our heads covered by banana-leaves from which the rain streamed mercilessly. My teeth chattered, but from fear of abandonment and not from cold, for the rain was warm as saliva. My future -- my very life -- was being decided. And then the meeting was nearly finished. Neethu asked me to read back what I had written. I strove for accuracy, of course, but I inflected the positive arguments with enthusiasm, and I diminished the negative points. My tongue had plumped thick as a tuber, and it was all I could do to speak around it.

When I had finished my recital, Neethu was silent a moment, eyes closed. When he opened his eyes again, he didn't look at me directly, but said, "She will go with us. But she will carry her own things. She will keep pace with us. She will behave as our women do." I felt again that the Tekhla were admirable among all the world's peoples, and that my fate had never truly been in question. They were righteous, good in their hearts. There would be but one more night to endure and we would go in the morning.

I had set the kerosene lantern on the pile of firewood in my house, wedging it in tightly, and its liquid reflection burned on the water that covered the floor. The water was running with a surf of small ripples that caught the one reflected spear of light and shattered it into many miniaturized, delinquent flames. I knew that outside my hut the ground was a welter of black water. I had no thought of sleeping. I would sit cross-legged on my bed until it was light enough to see and avoid the swimming snakes, and then the Tekhla and I would leave. In spite of the rain, it was unbearably hot. The hut was fetid and close, and rivulets of sweat wove down my forehead. I tasted brine on my upper lip, like tears I hadn't realized I had been shedding.

I had wedged my journal into my pack, which hung in readiness on its straps from the ceiling. I could take only what I could carry, and most of what I had would be left behind. It was a stunning thought. I sat on my mattress, hugged my knees, and listened to the many voices of the rain. As I listened, it seemed that the sound changed its pitch -- deeper, throatier, bolder. I thought at first that it was a wind that had sprung up and was dashing the rain into huts and trees. But no, the air inside my hut was perfectly still and ruffled nothing and the cloth covering the door hung quietly. Only the fiery water sheeting the floor was in motion. But yet there was that sound rising, growing stronger. It was a menacing sound, like an approaching army beating shields, stamping feet and roaring, a sound that became louder and wider. There was a confrontation welling up outside my hut, whether or not I could see it at that moment, or understand what it was.

The light from the lantern made the shadows important and keen-edged, and the containers strung from the ceiling threw shapes on the wall that were skull-like. The cloth covering the doorway had grown heavy, dragged down by the bulk of the water climbing up its fibers. Then, this cloth moved as if bumped by someone, or something, outside. The motion was more than shifting shadow, and my first thought was "animal." I thought an animal was blundering into the hut and I drew myself smaller, my arms wrapped around my legs protectively. My pocket-knife was in my pack and I had no weapons at hand. I watched helplessly as the cloth was drawn aside.

It was not an animal. It was the face of an Indian thrust into the one room that was my entire world at the moment. I saw immediately that he was not a Tekhla. His nose was refined, with nostrils that winged out sensitively. His skin was almost golden and was decorated with bluish lines, like a webbing of veins that had pushed close to the surface and had become ornamental. His hair was long and wet. He said to me, quite clearly, "You will go now. It is time for you to go." And then the face vanished. A Jukima. I felt he had not been a dream or apparition, because I had smelled the herbal warmth of his skin and had seen the concern in his eyes. I stepped down into the water, which was strangely cool despite the reflected flames of the lantern moving on its surface.

I took down the pack -- it seemed that I did this very slowly -- and shouldered it, and then I lifted the lantern from the shelf of logs and held it out before me. I carried no fuel for the lantern, because the fuel would be too bulky to carry, and too brief, but I remember hoping that the lantern-light would last long enough for this one night. And then I drew aside the soggy curtain and went out into the rain. The night was as black as heavy smoke, but the lantern spread an oval of light on the water that now covered all of the ground in the village. I was amazed to see that the village had been jumping with activity even as I had waited, dormant and solitary, in my hut. The Tekhla were rushing about, although at the edges of the lantern's light I could just see them as moving silhouettes.

Except where the lantern-light glinted off the water's surface, the water was black. It looked corrupted, like a black and boiling stew. I held my lantern higher and could see Neemba, a baby on her back and another in her arms, scrambling up the slight rise behind where the hearth had been. Not far from her, Neethu was slogging through the water and carrying what looked to be a heavy parcel. He looked at me directly. I knew he could see me clearly because of the lantern I held, but he seemed not to recognize me. I wondered, then, would they have left me there, after all? Would I have remained in my hut like a child who expects, with complete and unreasonable faith, to be fetched in time and delivered from disaster?

And there was that overwhelming noise, nearly upon us. I recognized the sound of thrashing water, like the roar of a cataract. It was the stream-turned river. It was my dream made real. The water had broken free of its channel and was bearing down on the village. I ran toward the higher ground. As I ran, waves spread away from the thrusts of my legs, and sticks and debris battered my shins. I stepped on bruising, unseen stones. I hadn't had time for my boots and I could picture, in detail, where they were, hanging dry and abandoned from the rafters of my house. Even as I remembered the boots, I realized that had I worn them they would have filled with water and would have slowed me dangerously. I thought that I would probably die there, and the crushing noise of the flood was the last sound I would hear.

I don't remember the rest of that night clearly. It was an attack of noise and rain and unreality. And yet, there are certain things that stay with me more acutely than the recollection of yesterday's ordinary events. Neethu's death. The loss of

Neemba's child, swept from her arms by the surge of dark water. The rain drilling through the wash of lantern light. The mud grasping at my bare feet. It was on the hill that Neethu died. We left him, snake-bitten and stoic, his chiseled arms folded serenely across his bony chest, the water lapping at his waist. He cried out once, considerately, to inform anyone listening that he had been fatally bitten, and then he sat straight down in the water, already beyond us. He looked Buddha-like, with a faintly rueful smile curving his lips. He had thrown his parcel up into the air as he crumpled, and it hit the water with a splash and sank heavily.

I remember thinking, so briefly, that someone should stay with Neethu now, and just as briefly that humanitarian impulse passed. There were children ahead of me, struggling up the small hill. We couldn't stop. I know that for awhile I gripped some child's arm and pulled him along, just as Falatha had supported me on that first day with the Tekhla that now seemed as far from me as a sun that shines in kindness. Neethu died there, but I pulled some unknown child along with me to the top of the slight hill where the water might not claim us.

There was lightning, now, with the rain. It was the rumble of thunder, along with the rising flood, that I had heard while I waited in my house. In the flares of lightning, I saw the dark mounds of the houses bobbing like corks on the water. Oddly, an ear of corn bumped against my leg, and then it slid past. We climbed the hill, and I know that some people were lost. The child whose arm I had grasped was not lost, but I released him when the water no longer buffeted us. The rush of water from the stream-gone-wild had not yet reached to the top of the low hump of ground, and we clustered there briefly. No one could know how far the river would rise, and we had to go on. In the flashes of lightning, the forest glowed lavender and then faded to gray, and then there was only the small circle of lantern light until the next strike of lightning. The noise was incredible. I hadn't known anything like it before.

I again gripped a child's arm, but whether or not it was the same child, I couldn't tell. In the darkness the unseen arm, braceleted with rolls of babyish fat, became the arm of Doreen and it was my sister -- my family -- that I dragged along with me. It was like an instinct, that somehow in the salvation of this one child was my own salvation. In one hand I brandished the lantern like a torch and the other hand was clamped around the child's arm. The touch of the child was fuel for my strength, and without it I might have been drawn in the opposite direction, to follow Neethu to wherever he had gone.

We went on, over the far slope of the little hill. We slogged through cluttered water that was waist-deep at times, but the farther we went into the forest, the less insistent the water became. Eventually the lightning strikes were more widely spaced. In the lantern light, I could see the stitching of the rain and the floundering forms of other people not far from me. A snake wrapped itself around my shin briefly, like a fat leather belt, and then it slithered loose before I had time to react.

During all of this, I had the strong sense that it was accidental that I was here. I had happened upon this monstrous night on my way to some other destination. And I had the credentials -- my passport, my plane tickets -- contained in a water-proof box in the pack on my back. I hadn't been born here, and my family was elsewhere. My mother had a harmless cardboard box in which she kept ribbons and buttons and the scraps from all the dresses she had made for me and my sisters. With such innocence as that for a legacy, surely it was unreal that I was here at all? This was someone else's disaster, but surely not mine?

In the lantern light, the entire world -- with myself at its center -- was an oval with melting edges that gave way to darkness. When the lantern light died, eventually and as I had known it would, the world contracted and was directionless and sounds reigned paramount. I was startled again by how huge the sound of rain could be, although the thunder was not quite so loud as it had been, beginning to move away from us. I could now hear the sloshing footsteps of the Indians struggling to move forward. I was still alive -- not yet drowned or struck by a snake -- and I was moving forward. I still gripped, or clung to, the arm of a child.

When my lantern gave out, we had begun to climb again. The water lapped at my ankles, and then, finally, there was only mud under my bare feet. The brunt of the storm had passed over us. The dawn, when it came, was ashen, but the rain was less fierce. It had lost interest in us. The encampment and the river that had drowned it were miles away by then. I felt the awakening of hunger in the deflated sack of my stomach, and I remembered the ear of corn I had seen floating past me. I wanted it, and scolded myself for not scooping it up. I saw that the child I had clung to and brought along with me was Hlisi's son, Yutta. The darkness continued to bleach, so gradually, and I could make out the faces of the survivors. I had the nonsensical thought that I wanted to make a list of who had survived and who had not, as if the making of a list would seal away the awful night in back of us into history.

Neethu was gone. Falatha, incredibly, was gone, and so was her husband, Diama. Neemba was gone, along with her two children. Her husband was nowhere that I could see. Rodomo was there, and Piptcha, and Dguu. Hlisi was there. When she took her son from me, her face was expressionless. For an instant, I expected gratitude, but there was nothing. She took the boy's arm roughly and when I looked upon her stony expression, I could see nothing in it that I recognized. We -- the Indians and I -- had come through the same space of time in one another's company, but their experience hadn't been mine. They had lost nearly everything in the way of possessions, but it didn't matter so much. Everything could be made again. But, they had lost so many people out of their small group. Was Hlisi angry that she hadn't been the one to drag the child along and save him? Or was she angry that I had survived and others had not? Or was she simply stunned out of her emotions as one can be knocked out of one's shoes? I didn't know, and I didn't know what would happen next, or where we would go.

The place where we had stopped was one of utter austerity, and the Indians themselves were stark and essential. My possessions were my greatest loss. I had not yet felt, fully, the loss of Falatha and the others. The tarps and food were gone, of course. The flashlight was gone, and the typewriter, the batteries, all left behind like so much nonsense, and the lantern was gone -- or its potential for light was gone, because I still held it, like a heavy souvenir. I set the lantern down on the muddy ground. It was metal, and I considered it thoughtfully. Something could be made from that, perhaps, if it was disassembled and rearranged. Fish hooks, perhaps, out of its thinner plates of metal? I nearly laughed at the absurdity of it. The empty lantern looked so crude yet mysterious.

The place where we had stopped was barren, even though it was full of shapes. In that first light squeezed out from the dark, all was gray. The tree trunks seemed to be hewn of stone. The vines and branches were iron-gray and heavy. The leaves glistened with droplets, hard and round as rivets. The stoic demeanors of the Indians were colorless. My feet were shod with gray mud. The grayness of the morning was a kind of equalizing non-color. I sank down slowly, squatting. I was beyond tiredness, and all I possessed was my dreamy, numb exhaustion, which also brought with it a kind of selective focus. Everything I saw took on a crisp singularity. The Indians, as they moved about, had the spare and grievous simplicity of poetry.

Rodomo very slowly and elegantly gathered materials for a fire and laid them out under the shelter of a tree that was so dense that almost no rain fell under it. He peeled the moist bark from twigs down to the dry wood. He shredded a twig patiently with his teeth until it was a dry fluff. He spun a stick. I watched, amazed, although I had seen this before in other times and in another place. A bud of flame sprouted and grew, and with its flourishing, its aroma was released and it was an aroma that stood at the very center of community, of logic. There was fire again.

Chapter Thirteen

The diminished group of us fit in a huddle under the tree -- a giant tree whose architecture was ribbed and vaulted and whose roots were set deeply into the earth. The day was already growing muggy and the fire was an anemic thing, but important. There was no food. I thought of the can of baked beans I had stowed in my pack, and brought it out. We all stared at this thoughtfully. On its wrapper was a color photograph of its contents: butterscotch colored syrup, with plump red beans floating in it.

"It is a tough husk," Hlisi said gravely.

"Yes," it was echoed, "a tough husk." I felt like a magician with my can-opener, which was one of many appliances that could be fanned out from my Swiss Army knife, but I had done nothing that anyone of my culture and having my supplies couldn't have done, and it was so little. We passed around the can and each of us took a modest portion on our fingertips. Yutta stuck his fingers into the can, and then thrust his slathered fingers into his mouth. He laughed at the unexpected clog of sugar. His laughter normalized the place where we were as nothing else could have. Yutta's laughter was infectious, and we all laughed until we were wracked with it. It was still raining, but the tree shed the rain and the fire crackled typically. The grayness of dawn had passed and a watery light was leaking through here and there in the forest's canopy. It was like the sort of healing that restores the warmth to a body.

And then Rodomo said, through tears of laughter, "Night in back of day, Neethu was sitting down -- plop -- like a bullfrog lands." "Yes, yes," Dguu said, and was convulsed by laughter. I was instantly appalled at the use of the dead Neethu as the butt of a joke, but yet, I couldn't help but laugh also. My laughter was forcing its way through guilt, through fatigue, through common sense. My muscles clenched and ached with sieges of laugher, and tears flowed down my face unchecked.

Dguu embellished, "Neethu was sitting down and his hands flew up, and pop, his bundle was up, out of his hands." I could see it clearly, but already the image was being rinsed clean by the laughter. I dared to add, "Neethu was sitting down -- plop -- but not with a very big splash." This was absorbed, and appreciated with more laughter. Hlisi was doubled over with laughter, but she reached up to put her hand on my shoulder and said, "Pressa is correct. Not a very big splash." Rodomo, who was not quick, added, "Because Neethu was very thin." This sparked a bit more laughter, and then the mirth faltered. The beans were gone, and the rain persisted and seemed as though it would always be falling in just that way.

Our laughter was also a parting gift Neethu had given us. A sacrifice. The beans were gone, but the sugar in their syrup had given us strength. We were ready to face the day and the hard memories that would dog us. Rodomo began it. He said, "On the night in back of this day, the dark was like the inside of a mouth, a screaming mouth." There were murmurs, "Yes a screaming mouth before words have come." Hlisi added, "And Pressa was taking Yutta and pulling him along and Yutta is still here." I was touched by this, but at nearly the moment I felt the thrill of having been acknowledged, even accepted to some extent, I felt the aching of my feet. I had no shoes.

My feet were naked, of shoes, of callouses, and they were bruised and torn from stumbling on the clutter on the ground: the roots, the sharp-edged stones and sticks that had been invisible under the black water. Almost shyly, I said, "I have no coverings for my feet." Rodomo considered this, and then said, "Pressa will have to walk like this, now," and he imitated the hobble of a disabled person. After the crude remarks about Neethu, this shouldn't have shocked me, but it did. My feet would have to toughen, or I would be unable to follow the Indians further and I could perish here. I was still reeling with exhaustion. We all were, and almost as one body, we lay down on the soft ground to rest, clustered under the tree onto whose branches the rain still fell and fell. The damp ground smelled of mushrooms, and yielded under my cheek like a cupping hand.

We gathered tubers, and I watched as the women rooted them out with their digging sticks. I imitated what they did with a stick I picked up off the ground. Imitation had become the visible edge of my nature. I decided to whittle my own digging stick that evening as we sat around the fire. I gathered broad leaves to sleep on. It was hot under the canopy, and the ceaseless green of it was monotonous, almost hurtful. The rain alternately pounded or sizzled in a fine spray. But strangely, there was no water in which to bathe and little to drink, except that which we tipped from leaves folded funnel-like. They gave up only droplets at a time. I worked very closely to Hlisi, so closely that I could feel the zone of warmth surrounding her skin. She seemed not to notice that I was there.

The men had been unable to kill any game, and there was no meat that night. I had only been able to discover and gather two small, wizened yam-like tubers, which I placed among the coals of the campfire. I watched them pensively as they shrank and oozed. Hlisi shared some of her food with me, but I had the sense that she begrudged its loss. She had Yutta to feed. The night was miserable and I barely slept, because I was fearful that the Indians would leave during the night and I wouldn't hear them going.

I thought about my own death, and wondered if there would be laughter at whichever way I was taken from life. If I died while among these Indians, would there be any sort of funeral for me, and would my bones nestle as beads, warm against someone's neck? There was thunder in the distance, and I wondered if the storm was continuing to lay siege to the village we had abandoned? I remembered my dream of water, of floods. I hadn't told anyone of the dream, and wondered if that had been a mistake. I was beginning to fear that I really was a foul stroke of luck to these people.

My feet began to heal as if by magic, and with their toughening I began to feel more hopeful. On the top of my foot, in the place where my high arch has always made shoes difficult to fit, there was a deep cut -- deep enough so that I could see the pale, striated meat of my flesh between the lips of the wound. I bathed this cut in the water gathered from cupped leaves, and slowly the wound shrank. It was true, that I applied some ointment from the small first-aid kit I had brought, but it was the same sort of ointment I had seen on television being applied to the scraped knee of a child. The child's face had brightened in a grin of relief that the ointment didn't sting the scrape. Of course, the child's scrape hadn't been real. It's strange what one remembers at odd moments? On the first day I applied a bandage of gauze, but the bandage sogged and grimed and was useless. It was fascinating how the edges of the cut dried in a crust that tore off several times a day, and each time the raw flesh bled less, was pinker, shinier. Finally, the scab tore off and there were no beads of blood at all and the flesh was pearly and firm. This gave me a small fund of confidence, that healing was my body's motivating goal.

Because there was no water close, I'd thought that we would leave soon and move on. However, on the third day, or perhaps it was the fourth, Pipchtka found a small stream. It was probably no more than the run-off of rain from the slightly sloping ground around us. Its water ran rusty with silt, but I drank from it as the Tekhla did. What else could I do? I had no privacy anymore in my life, except perhaps in my dreams. I often dreamed of Falatha. It was always as though she were on the verge of telling me some confidence that would repair the misunderstandings that had sometimes opened gaps in our friendship. I grieved for her in my dreams. The ground where I slept had no walls around it, and I felt it moving with insects. I took my medicine to prevent malaria, but secretly, lest the Tekhla think it was evil magic and distrust me. I didn't write in my journal and I lost track of the days, the schedule for taking the medicine, and the time that had elapsed since we fled the village. There were no edges except for the slow blinking of night and day and my bodily requirements, the rising and falling of hunger and thirst and the need to sleep, or to be wakeful and vigilant.

My journal was a notebook of stitched paper and the paper swelled until the pages became one solid, secret object. I would have to remember rather than write, and I had the thought that writing had blunted my capacity for recalling the events of my own life. I held out the hope that we would settle again and I would dry the notebook in the sun, pull apart its leaves, and resume my role as scribe. I did the best I could where I was. My feet toughened. I forgot to worry about modesty when bathing. I didn't think much beyond the moment.

We had been in our camp under the tree for a week, or perhaps much more than that, when I had an extraordinary dream. I dreamed of a white cliff, as steep and glittering as the buildings of Riolapa. There were birds of many colors, presented with their finest, most luxurious plumage against the screen of the white cliff. These birds were all energy and brief color -- with their flashes of turquoise, scarlet, yellow and the orange of tangerines, and an iridescent black. In this dream I was happy. It was a picture of a happiness that was possible. In the dream, my vision was enhanced and I saw each zippered feather singly and clearly, and simultaneously I saw the entire flock of birds in joyful motion. That was all, just that scene and the joy of it -- the birds darting, settling, lifting. I was watching them and was satisfied, as though I had painted the scene there and then had released the birds to their own natures.

On the day that would be my last day among the Tekhla, I had no premonition that it was the last, just as I had had no forewarning that I would not see Falatha or Neethu again. I was with the women and I had brought my emptied pack so that I could fill it with the fruit that Hlisi said she had found. My metal box, my medicines, my notebook, and camera -- all these things had been left under the dry shelter of the tree. We went farther than we had gone before, but I was becoming more confident in my surroundings. I could recognize individual trees with their vines that made graceful shapes. I didn't know what sort of fruit it would be, for I had no word for it and I imagined something dewy and fragrant -- kiwi fruit, perhaps, or bananas that tasted of pineapple or lemon.

The rain that had been so intractable before, was now falling only in smatterings as the trees shrugged off their moisture. Sometimes the rain would stop, briefly, and the sun would send poles of light through the foliage. Mbawa, a dignified older woman with pendulous flaps of breasts, said, perhaps to me, for I was closest to her, "If the men bring meat, what joy that will be!" I was surprised by her pushing aside of hardship, and I thought, "Life is made of such moments."

I was not as cautious as before. Each day I was more limber in my swinging arms and vigorous, economical strides. It was with this burgeoning confidence that I made a suggestion. It was nearing mid-day and we had eaten little that morning, and I said, "We could stop and make a small fire, because there are tubers here." I had seen their fronds and recognized them before any of the others.

My suggestion was taken and we stopped and built a small fire. The rain was an easy thing by then -- no more than a powdery mist. I was eager, taking each small triumph as a sign that I would prevail in this way, doing what the women did, learning from them, extending shy offerings such as the suggestion to dally and build a fire. Each success was a test that I had passed.

I had my digging stick and I was eager, squatting, sweating, and grunting, digging into the earth that was as crumbling as sweet, dense cake. Flushed with pride at my discovery of food in the forest, I was gripped by the urge to dig better, to dig more than the other women. I clawed at the ground, lifting free the clodded tubers and brushing them off with hands that had grown nearly as hard as workman's gloves. I would dig so many tubers that it might be mentioned, that evening, by the campfire. And then I saw yet another clump of sword-like fronds a short distance away. These were more luxurious than the ones I had seen at first. I moved toward them, and farther away from the women. I don't know if the Tekhla women saw me slip away or if they particularly cared that I did. The fronds were standing in a hollow that was more open than where I had been working. The leaves were a deep, blue-green and were spangled with dew-drops like little, domed lenses.

I descended into this slight hollow of ground. As I dug, I imagined the tune of a song, simple and round and comfortable. And then I heard it, and realized that there was another person there with me, a woman who was singing. I saw her profile, through the fronds and the powdery rain. Her hair, glossy and black, swung down over the side of her face in a sheaf like a wing. Her skin was golden brown, her nose narrow. She saw me and smiled. I thought, "Falatha," or "the ghost of Falatha," but of course she wasn't. She was smaller and younger, but the smile was the same. It struck me that Falatha had not been surly or suspicious. She had been tired, even as my mother had been exhausted, and sometimes I was too much for her. She couldn't always cope with me.

This woman smiled as if she knew me. I understood that she was a Jukima, and I ached for Ollieburton, that he hadn't been here to see her. The tubers slipped from my hands. The sight of this woman blotted out all other thoughts. This was why I had come here. One knows certain things if one attends to intuition. I stood upright and this woman who was so close to me stood also, and we faced one another. And then she moved off, away from me. I followed.

Chapter Fourteen

I can't really explain why I followed the woman. As I followed, I realized that she was not a woman at all, but had the simple, genderless form of a child. The forest became more and more open as we climbed. The landscape resembled, if only slightly, the terrain of my childhood in its wide harmlessness, and I welcomed it. The trees were more loosely spaced and did not seem so competitive. The ground sloped upward so there was the sense, if not the reality, of a reliable view down to the place where I had recently been. Each rock or the angles of particular tree branches were so full of personality that I felt sure that I could recognize them and return by the same route. Perhaps I even thought that I would see the thread of smoke from the Tekhla women's fire if I turned and searched for it?

The ground sloped upward and then it became steep, and there were boulders as large as the Tekhla houses. Some of these rocks were veined with quartz, and the patterns of these veins were like drawings of rivers branching into streams. Each pattern seemed as singular as a finger-print. As I climbed, the girl just ahead of me would wheel about occasionally, grin and toss her blue-black hair. I assumed that she intended for me to follow.

The boulders became larger and fewer, and between them were small meadows thick with grasses. The sun was hot on the top of my head. I realized that the rain had ended, or it had ended in patches, because up ahead there were places where sparkling fogs were rising, and where sunlight winked off blades of grass and glanced colorlessly off the rocks. I realized that I could see the sky. Seeing the sky again, the hugeness of it with its great, rolling white clouds, brought me back into myself with a sudden, sickening fear. I had been insanely foolish, almost trancelike in my following of this girl. Of course, I should not have left the little group of Tekhla women. I was following a child, and I didn't know her. This place was so different from where I had been. I had no idea how long I'd been gone.

I stood there on the path that was merely the trace of one girl passing through. I was shocked at my foolishness. The sky was huge above me, and the clarity of the textures of each shadowed thing was like a profound trickery. I turned and looked back the way I had come. I recognized nothing. Even the slight imprint of my own footsteps crushing down the blades of grass was fading as the limber grass unbent. There was a labyrinth of boulders, each identical to the other. The child had disappeared ahead of me and I couldn't hear her footfalls. The grasses were unfolding and resuming their upright growth.

I chose, then. I went on up the steep slope, following the slight difference of the trodden-upon grass even as it was erasing its marks. I hurried and felt the muscles of my calves burning. I don't know how long I hurried after the child who was the one, of the two of us, who knew how to flourish in this wilderness. I passed through patches of rainbowed fog and sears of brilliant sunlight until these changes became staccato. I was weeping, and then I willed myself to stop weeping because my vision blurred and I couldn't read the signs of the bent grasses. The reading of the trail was such a tenuous thing, with no margin for mistakes.

And then I saw her, insouciantly grinning at me, waiting, her woven sack of harvest slung from one shoulder rakishly, her hands on her hips like any modern teenager. She wore a skirt fashioned of leaves that were still green and moist, and she looked like an exotic flower sprung from a rosette of foliage. And something else -- when I saw her facing me, in full sunlight, it was clear that her body had been draped with a net of indigo decorations, in an intricate, floral design. I hadn't realized that her body was decorated in that way, with tattoos or painted with a fine brush, as elaborately as some Arab women's hands are painted with designs of Henna. The girl turned again and continued to climb. I understood that I must follow her and that my life had changed again without my rational intention.

I followed the girl. My pack was heavy and I shouldered it instead of swinging it from my hand. Carrying it was a chore. Perhaps as I climbed, the Tekhla women were roasting the tubers in the little fire they had made, and they were slightly but not terribly annoyed with me for vanishing, or at least for failing to return when I smelled the roasting food. They were already unreachable. The little I owned had been left behind, profoundly lost. The medicines, the money, the plane tickets, and my journal, all had been left in a little pile by the nest of leaves where I had slept in the Tekhla camp. My passport had been left behind. Why hadn't I worn it in a little pouch next to my heart, the way the tourists did?

My feet were bare, but I felt a twinge of pride at the way they had toughened. Sweat slathered my forehead and I was chilly in the fog, or warm in the sun. I hadn't felt the richness of the unfiltered sunlight for a long time. The girl remained just ahead of me like a leprechaun. I didn't always see her, but I could hear the sounds of her passage clearly enough so that I could follow without difficulty. Sometimes she hummed, and it was like a siren song. The shadows of the rocks grew and purpled. The fog was left behind. Had I turned around, I could have looked down on the tops of clouds. I hadn't realized that there were mountains so close to where I had lived with the Tekhla because I couldn't see them under the forest canopy, and the Tekhla had no desire to climb them. They had their ways of being and those ways included what they knew well. Novelty was not a virtue to them.

The rocks were now scabbed with lichens. The grasses brushed against my ankles and not my knees anymore. It grew cooler and the sunlight thinner. The shadows had stretched long -- it was already nearing twilight. The girl ahead of me fell silent. The distance between us closed, but it seemed that she had forgotten me. I watched the shadowed muscles of her calves pulling and pushing her upward, and I felt the same stresses in my own legs. And then we arrived. I smelled the smoke of the Jukima camp, and then I looked up and saw it.

Sparks snapped orange and leaped up from the campfire. The sight of the rising sparks made my throat constrict because of their loveliness against the curving shape of lavender sky. There was food cooking, and my mouth watered. The Jukima had made their camp on a level place that was but one summit of a string of mountains, and I felt the immensity of the lowered landscape behind me. I thought, when these people look up and see me, I would be to them like a stone thrown into moving water. The water will bend or crest up and make a different sound, and perhaps that small stone will be the final thing that causes the water to change direction.

The sun was sinking down quickly, flattening slightly as it bumped the horizon. The stars were already beginning to decorate the sky, and I must have been a silhouette as I stood there on the lip of the summit. When the Jukima saw me, there was no cry of alarm, and no particular greeting. They weren't alarmed, perhaps not surprised. If anything, there seemed to be a slight recognition, as though they said silently, collectively, "Oh, it's you," and then returned to what they had been doing. The girl I had followed didn't give me another glance, but strode up to the hearth, emptied her sack of tubers beside it and vanished into the small crowd of people as one of them.

These were the people of my dreams, but they were so specific as they did ordinary things. Stoked the fire. Conversed with one another. Turned and adjusted sticks on which bits of food were roasting, smiling at me shyly and then looking away. I went up to the fire and emptied my pack on the ground. That wasn't a grand gesture or a metaphor -- it was all that I had to bring them.

The flat space upon which the Jukima camped shrank to the limits of their campfire light as the night deepened. I saw that both the women and men wore wrappers of woven fabric, and the children were naked or wore leaves strung at their waists. All the people wore their hair long and loose, and some had adorned their hair casually with plumage. Their skins were decorated with indigo designs that were like a kind of essential clothing, the curves and angles of the designs accenting the curves and angles of their bodies. Some of these people had arm-bands of beads and feathers, but I couldn't see the fine details of these clearly in the growing darkness.

They served me food, graciously. I could discern no leader among them, although I realized that, as with the Tekhla, one could lead unassumingly. The Jukima spoke quietly among themselves, and not shrilly as the Tekhla did. I couldn't understand their language, although there were some sounds, some words that were like the Tekhla language and some that were like the sounds of other languages I had heard. I smiled, but not too much or too frequently. I didn't stare impolitely. I was aware of my posture and tried to stand or sit gracefully, because these people were graceful, as though the spaciousness of the place where they camped freed them from inhibitions of the body's placement.

I thought these Indians were glamorous in their innocence, or because of it, but I didn't know them. I couldn't understand the complexities of their language and didn't know if they were innocent, in the sense of being free of pettiness or meanness, although surely that wasn't so. Their innocence, at that moment, was something in which I chose to believe. They were impoverished in comparison to the Tekhla, or they had stopped there in a temporary camp and had carried little of their material world with them. I didn't know. I had no way to judge them. I was not self-deprecating or desperate, because they had offered me food, and they offered me a place to sleep. I was so stunned by the recent events of my life that I took pleasure in small comforts and didn't think of the future.

I was given a minimal, woven shelter, like a cocoon, and took my cue from the others around me and slipped into this shelter when the fire began to fade. I had no expectations at all about what would happen on the following day. In my sleep, I didn't feel alone. From their hospitality, I had the sense that these people wouldn't leave in the night without me. The morning opened a crack that I could see through the hemisphere that was my doorway, although the place where I had slept was no more than a bundle, slightly more accommodating than clothing. The dawn spilled out of this crack in the sky and it was the colors of ripe fruit.

In the days that followed, I felt welcomed, but I was as dependent upon the Jukima as I had been on the Tekhla. I wasn't frightened by this dependency. I'd lost everything, but I chose to trust them. I wasn't studying them as I'd studied the Tekhla -- with a self-consciousness that kept me separate from them. I had lost language. I had no notebook, and couldn't study their language as I had studied the Tekhla language from Ollieburton's notes. At first, I couldn't make myself understood except for simple things. I began to learn the people's names. Papeet was the girl I had followed up the mountain. Carogo was the one who was heavy and moved with a slow deliberation that was almost stately. Zhixo was a little like Neethu, I thought. He was thin to the point of emaciation; the way his bones were strung together was interestingly visible. He had long, tapering fingers, and deeply set eyes. And like Neethu, he rarely spoke. When he did speak, it was with a resonance that commanded authority. And Lajima seemed to me to be like Falatha in her concern for me. She took it upon herself to teach me to speak like a person. I thought my inability to speak must have seemed to her like a special kind of tragedy. She watched me cautiously, as a mother would watch a troubled child. I didn't know if she had been appointed to this task, or if she had taken it upon herself? It didn't matter. She was there. Her eyes were very dark, so dark that I couldn't know which was iris and which was pupil; in her eyes the sky was reflected.

On the second day, I realized that Lajima was narrating all that she did, and naming each thing as naturally as a mother teaches a child to speak. She wasn't impatient, but she was forceful and wouldn't allow me to rest. It was my work and I took up that task with total concentration. I elevated listening to a necessity. I followed Lajima everywhere she went, and I repeated after her each thing she wanted me to repeat. I was an earnest scholar again, and it was a role in which I was comfortable and by which I was driven. I listened to conversations and I would recognize a word, and then another, and with each word, my confidence and my yearning for understanding grew stronger. I didn't have the sense that these people would reject me if I made mistakes.

The Jukima had brought food with them and I knew from that, that they had gardens somewhere, and another place that was their home. This gave me confidence in their stability, their disinclination to move randomly across the landscape. I later discovered that I was both right and wrong about that. When I followed Papeet up the mountain, it had seemed like an arbitrary choice. But perhaps it wasn't. The Jukima had peopled my dreams and they hadn't harmed me, and the Tekhla had discarded a baby that was left in the forest to die.

During the time when I understood almost nothing of Jukima words, my mind became my habitat and that feeling hasn't left me. My thoughts and memories were my surroundings and my possessions. What I missed the most was the ability to explain myself -- my silence became a personal burden. I hastened toward that time when language would be restored to me. I followed Lajima everywhere, and she encouraged this.

In my desire to communicate, I found that I became more physically expressive. I animated my expressions to the point of cartoons. I drew pictures in the dust. I drew the Tekhla, their houses, their gardens, and I pointed back down the mountain. Then I recreated my climb up it in an exaggerated, high-stepping dance. And then, I recreated the flood by swishing my hand in a pot of water, pulling myself forward as if through deepening water, then putting my hands over my ears at the sound of thunder. I revisited the sorrow of the losses of that night until those sorrows -- of Neethu's loss, Falatha, the children who were gone -- shook me with a despair that was completely real. A small crowd of the Jukima gathered as I did this. I tried to become both the choreographer and the dancer of my thoughts.

I think I became more of a person to the Jukima because of my enactments, but it wasn't yet enough.

Chapter Fifteen

On my first morning with the Jukima, I looked down toward where the forest would be if it were not covered with clouds. I thought that from this height I might be able to see the Tesoura River -- where there were boats -- and even as far as the Bacaran Falls. However, I could see nothing but the sunlit tops of the clouds. Below them, I assumed it was still raining. My family, my friends at the university, my professors -- none of them would know yet that I had been stranded. No one would be looking for me, except possibly for Frederick, but if he looked for me I would be unfindable where I was now. If we were still here when the rainy season ended and the clouds lifted, I would be able to see, perhaps, the Tesoura and orient myself that way. And when I had learned enough words, I could explain myself and my situation and I hoped that the Jukima could be persuaded to guide me to the river. I would learn their language and I would wait for the clouds to lift.

The days blended together and were warm and pleasant. I knew this was a temporary campsite, but the Jukima seemed disinclined to move on. Now that my future was so uncertain, I had begun to miss my family almost intolerably. I thought about them often, and the composite that was my family assumed a firmer, simpler shape. When I was still living at home, we had almost always eaten meals together, and that's what I imagined most often. I thought about the mild conversations about ordinary matters, and the gracefulness of my sisters' hands as they passed the food or blotted their lips with cloth napkins. My father, sitting at the head of the table, wore a rueful but satisfied expression, surrounded as he was by his daughters. I thought about my family all together, or I thought about Doreen and her baby. I wondered how much Joel had grown in the time I'd been gone, how he had changed and what he could do now? When I left, he had just been beginning to babble, and I wondered, was he learning how to speak now, as I was?

I had been with the Jukima in their mountain-top campsite for about three weeks, when I became ill. This sickness began with a different quality in the light. The light granulated the surfaces of things into dazzling speckles. It was a seeded light that energized the edges of things until those edges seemed unstable. And there were distortions. I remember looking at my unshod foot with its little, bluish, pinkish scar and the shadowed tubes of veins covered thinly by my skin, and then the foot swelled into something monstrous as I studied it. I took a step and at the familiar sensation, the foot settled back into its normal contours. And then it would swell again and it seemed to detach from the gravity that had fastened it to the ground. Whatever complex mechanism it was that held me upright began to fail. All those unconscious adjustments of balance became deliberate. I couldn't manage the entirety of such a complicated process as standing up.

I crept back into my little, woven shelter, which became immediately a rough-edged casing for my suffering. I had been captured by a fever that rose and rose until my skin was scraped by the touch of the air. Each time I moved, even slightly, the air became rougher -- it became abrasive. I understood by then that the fever was altering my vision. I had never seen in this way before. I was inside a mirage, and the world was buckling and abnormal. I could see the components of things, but had no sense of how these things were assembled into something greater. For a time, there was an insect clinging to the weave above me -- a grasshopper, or a locust? I was horribly mesmerized by the hard, mechanical snag of the hinge of its leg-joint. I couldn't understand it, or its tarnished, coppery, color, a frightening color that I couldn't name.

All other senses were changed, as well. I lived in a distorted zone where sounds rushed toward me through a long tunnel and were hurtfully amplified. My sickness was growing rapidly worse. I remember thinking of the medicines I'd left behind and wondering if this was malaria or some undiscovered pestilence of the tropics that had sprung out of the busy-ness of the earth itself? I thought about the little finger or foot-bone I had been given that had once belonged to Luaka, and I sorrowed that it had been left behind with my other belongings. I didn't know what the Jukima did about their dead, and where they believed their dead went when they passed.

I have no idea how long it was that I was ill. The Jukima moved their camp during that time and took me with them, or they moved on because I was ill and it was necessary to take me elsewhere. They carried me with them, although I have little memory of that except that my suffering was like a small room of barbs or nails and I couldn't move within it without torment. I was carried on some sort of litter or hammock slung between two men, although I don't know if it was always the same two because all that mattered to me was my private struggle. As we traveled, the torment shifted and was no longer surrounding me. It *became* me. The totality of my identity was fanged and toothed.

My memories of this time are without sequence. I remember the sweating, sinewy back of the man who was carrying the front poles of the litter on which I rode. I watched the muscles of his back working and I was lucid enough, for an instant, to wish that his health were mine, to return to a time as automatic as that. Or, I glimpsed the spear points that were the tops of trees. They bounced and jittered until it became too painful to watch them. I couldn't remember a time when I had not been ill. I was too ill to be frightened, and the illness was so extreme, so powerful, that I thought that such a power as I housed could never die, and I couldn't die because the power that was pain wanted to live on and on and surely wouldn't destroy its host.

When there was not fever, there was the ache of coldness. Once, as a child, when I had taken a walk in the snow with my father we had walked too far. My coat was thinner than his coat, and although my mittens were wool, they were wet and of little use. I became so cold that I couldn't feel my lips and couldn't form words. All the while, my father was talking and talking, about what was wrong with the world today and how deceitfully beautiful snow was. He was saying that underneath the snow, there was still uncollected garbage because the trucks couldn't get through. I was so cold that the warm house where I lived had seemed so impossibly far that I felt I would never see it again.

I remember that on that walk with my father, my shivering stopped and the cold became like a shard of frozen metal that was chilling me from the inside out. My father eventually noticed that all was not right. My mother was very angry, later. I was bundled under blankets that were so heavy I could scarcely breathe, but they did nothing to warm me. I was made to drink hot tea, and eventually I warmed, but it was days before the shard of cold metal became memory.

The Jukima traveled for several days, and I sensed that our way grew steeper. On the journey to the village, I had seen fragments of mountains through half-closed eyelids, but I had been unable to look at them fully because of their sharpness, which was the same as the many, razored edges of suffering. And then we reached the village. I knew that it was high in the mountains. There was sometimes a little breeze, and the air was astringent, not cold, but carrying with it a purity like a scent of ice.

I was installed in a small house that was round, as the Tekhla dwellings were round, but more spacious and permanent in its materials of wood and stone. A fire burned peacefully in a hearth made of stones. I was made to drink a tea that was encouraging because of its bitter strength, a spoiled taste like sunless, basement earth. I gulped at this because it was a medicine, and it meant that something genuine was being done other than the doubtful effectiveness of the rattling of shells and bones. I gave myself over to the wisdom of the Jukima, which seemed profound, if only because of the foulness of their medicine. I was as selfish as an infant and the women who tended to me were all my mother, with her lavish haunches and invincibility. I gathered my resources into those things I could command. I swallowed, breathed, turned and turned, seeking cooler placements on the bed of mulchy leaves that were covered with a cloth that rapidly heated to the fever of my body.

The days and nights passed very slowly and without differentiation. And then I slid into another stage of illness -- the fever dropped, slightly, and the illness leveled. If the sickness were a terrain across which I traveled, this portion of it was flat and unembellished. My fever persisted, but lowered to coolness occasionally, and when it did, I began to hope that I would recover. I was never alone, and even in my dreams there was the comfortable presence of women. I didn't know if even my own sisters would tend to me so diligently.

The women tended to me and sat in my house and worked at the tasks of cooking food, minding babies, painting one another with blue dyes, or combing one another's long hair. I saw this in glimmers that lengthened until I was able to discover my curiosity again and watch them. And they talked, not particularly to me because I didn't have the strength to respond, but to each other and to their children. Sometimes they sang, in clear, darkly modulated voices or in high-pitched tones that sounded transparent and bright. I thought of what Ollie had told me, that these people sang like silver flutes being played.

Most of the time, I slept. My dreams at first were very local, snippets of what I had seen and heard recently. I dreamed of the various Jukima women whom I recognized but whose names I hadn't yet completely sorted out. Or I dreamed of the golden light that was strained by the texture of the sapling walls, and of the utensils that were placed on low shelves around the room and were strange to me. In my dreams I would touch these things, and the fibers of the baskets were warm and prickly; the clay bowls were cool and smooth. Or, I would dream a scent, no doubt inspired by whiffs of whatever the women were cooking, and the entirety of that dream would become the scent of roasting corn -- the blackened, milky, opulent yellow of it. I dwelled in my senses in a way that was unusual for dreams.

When my illness leveled, the dreams shifted and took on the overblown, anything-is-possible quality that is the usual, insubstantial material of dreams. I was dawdling through a field of flowers that were a hazy blue -- so many flowers that they appeared to be a lake of soft, blue water-- and then the flowers became birds with sugary wings. I didn't understand how I could have thought them flowers, at first, and then I realized, from within the dream, that it was a dream. Sleeping, dreaming, waking, began to take their proper places.

I also dreamed of floods, but they were floods that couldn't sweep me under. Those dreams were like a kind of work that I did, setting apart the possibility and angriness of floods, so that they could be safely investigated. And other dreams were of a type that I hadn't had before. In these dreams I was not myself, but was a Jukima. I was one of them, specifically, doing various things. I was a hunter stilled in a shadow, slowing the heartbeat deliberately, raising the bow so slowly it could have been only a thinning shadow of late afternoon. Or I was a mother bathing a child in a pool, swiping at its buttery limbs with a cupped hand through which the water leaked, laughing as the slippery child squirmed. I held the child with a looseness that was actually a complete guidance. I was these healthy people in my dreams, and in my dreams I spoke their language as naturally as if I had been born to it.

There was no, one, day when I was able to say that I was well. Recovery was a long, slow climb with many slippages. But I did recover, and it was when I was well that I realized that I could now speak like a Jukima. I didn't know how long I had been ill. It could have been weeks, or even months, but during that time I had been surrounded by language as surely as I was surrounded by the air. I had heard the women speaking to one another softly, or very occasionally, with hard blurts of annoyance or criticism. They spoke to their children differently than they did to each other, repeating the same, simplified phrases until they became a chant or the words to a favorite story. I heard no other language than the Jukima language, and in my dreams I was able to speak it. And then, when awake, I found that I could understand and I began slowly to form words, stumbling over those that sounded strangely like sucking on the teeth, or were guttural, explosive sounds, or nasal vibrations.   I hadn't   realized that the language was so complicated and subtle.

I heard the women speaking and I understood them. "Look, she is wakeful." "Yes, she sleeps for longer now, but with more rest to it."

And then, "I think I will make a different cape for Carogo's dowry. The one I made took so much time and is so beautiful that I think I will keep it."

And then laughter. "I will tell Carogo what you said." More laughter.

I said, in a rusty voice, "I think you should keep it. And tell yourself you will make one for Carogo that is better."

"You see, I thought she was wakeful."

"Yes. Perhaps tomorrow she will begin to walk around."

"I think that is true."

Someone said, "The dreams of flowers were beautiful." And another woman answered, "Yes, they were. She saw the flowers where we get our fibers for weaving."

I asked, "But how do you know that I saw flowers?"

The women giggled through their hands and didn't answer my question.

When I was able to walk about outside, I recognized very well the place where I was. I had been too ill to notice much of anything when we arrived there, but I had dreamed of this place many times, after. The village was situated on a wide, breezy ledge near to the mountain's summit. Under my feet were wiry grasses, and there were occasional wildflowers with succulent leaves and tissuey, veiny blossoms. The grass had been trampled by the Indians' footsteps, but considerate detours had been made around the flowers. The ledge was just wide enough to hold the Jukima houses -- several straw-roofed domes scattered about. There were fewer adults in this village than there had been in the Tekhla settlement, and not nearly as many children. The Tekhla children had been uncountable at first, but with the Jukima I quickly came to know the children individually. The children were few and precious. They were clean enough, bright, and mischievous

Above the ledge was a rocky, sparsely forested slope. Below, the trees were thicker and had dry, flaking bark. I couldn't see through the clouds to the forest far below us, but in the distance there were mountains with pointed peaks, part of a range that curved gradually to include the mountain, with its ledge, where we were. Whereas the forest had been many types of green, this place was blue. An enormous blue sky above, flaxen-blue mountains all around, the blue-gray bark of the trees, and the ashy blue of the rocks. The Jukima were a slim gathering of people in a place of immense solitude.

Lajima and Carogo walked with me, on either side. My surroundings were fresh and good, but I was not at peace. So much time had passed that my family must be concerned about me by now. I was sorry for the anguish this would cause, the terrible wondering about what had happened, or if I was alive at all. Perhaps someone was searching for me already? Someone, maybe my father, might travel as far as Tuylo, the last place I had been that was known and findable. He would make inquiries and would be shown my room, perhaps would discover the initials I had carved there. Would he press his fingers to the small marks and ask of anyone, what happened, after that? I wondered if Frederick would be there, and what he would say? I could imagine that he would lurk about and pretend ignorance of anything that had to do with me. I wondered if my father would be able to pay him enough for him to remember honesty and lead a party to the site of the Tekhla village?

I pointed down the slope in the direction I thought we had taken, and I asked Lajima, "When I am stronger, can someone take me down there? I think there may be a wide river I could see when the clouds are gone. I would like to go there."

Carogo looked away from me, her face coloring from embarrassment. She said, "We never go down there."

"But that is where I first saw Papeet. I followed her to your camp."

"Papeet was being naughty," Carogo said, "and she didn't go very far."

"Maybe she dreamed she would find Nweli there," said Lajima to Carogo, "and that is why she went?" Nweli was the name the Jukima had given me, more pronounceable to them than Noelle, and with its vowel ending it sounded more like common Jukima names. I liked the sound of it, and didn't correct them.

"But why would she want to find me?" I asked.

Carogo said, "I do not know. Sometimes we do things because of a feeling. We do not always know the reasons." And then she said, "We all had dreams. We knew someone like you would come. Surely you saw the Jukima in your dreams?"

I said, "Yes, I did see the Jukima. But how did that happen?"

Lajima asked, "How did what happen?"

"How did we dream of one another?"

Carogo laughed a little and said, "*How* is not important. It happens that way sometimes."

I didn't question her further about this, then. The idea that it was possible for people to dream the same dreams was not as frightening as it once had been. We had reached the trail that led to the gardens, which I had not yet seen. "We should go back now," said Lajima. And then to Carogo, "Perhaps we can take Nweli to the gardens tomorrow."

"It's higher there," I said, "and we should be able to see farther."

"Tomorrow," said Carogo.

We turned back and walked in silence for a bit. Then Carogo said, "Your own people are down there, by the river?"

I said, "No, they are much farther than that. But if I reach the river, that will be the beginning of my way back to them."

"We rarely go deeply into the forest. There are certain things we are afraid of. I am sorry," said Lajima.

"Perhaps the men go down there to hunt?"

"At times they do, but not often and not nearly as far as the wide river."

"But they know their way? They always know where they are?"

"Not completely, on the lower, wetter land. They know the high places well."

I dared to ask, "What are you afraid of in the forest?" There was a brief silence, and then Carogo said, "Xangu." And then she changed the subject, saying, "Here, with us, you will see Zhixo make shapes in the smoke."

"What are Xangu?" I asked, and Carogo simply said, "Enemies." I was too tired by then to ask what she meant by "shapes in the smoke."

When I was well, Zhixo came to see me to tell me that my house was finished. The Jukima had built a house for me close to theirs, and I was touched by their graciousness. I thanked Zhixo and said, "I want to learn things. I want to learn how to do things. Work in the gardens. Make things. I want to be useful."

He said, "Of course." As Neethu had been, Zhixo was the modest but incontrovertible leader of the group, although in the smaller things, the minor decisions, he was largely silent unless appealed to directly. He was not the oldest man, but possibly he was the most intelligent, and he was wisely reticent in his opinions. I studied Zhixo's face -- his golden-toned skin, broad cheekbones, the way a squiggle of vein flexed at his temple. It was as if his elegant carriage, with a straight-backed but limber strength, was summarized in the modest arrangement of his face. He was serene, but the burden of his responsibilities as leader of these people had bruised the flesh around his eyes and he looked weary. Although they had welcomed me, these were a wary, solitary people.

I asked, "Was it you who came to warn me on the night of the flood?" I was reasonably certain that his was the face I had seen in my doorway, his hair wet and lank with rain, on the night the stream burst loose.

Zhixo smiled, looked away from me and said, "I have never been to the village where you stayed."

Chapter Sixteen

The darkness in my house, of pre-dawn without moon, was made of shadows that separated gently until I could see the walls between them, and then objects such as the baskets I knew to be full of grain, dried fruit, or bracelets. The woven roof opened slits for the sunlight to come in. This light had the substance of golden flour and drew stripes of light on the floor and on my face. In this striped warmth, I awakened and stretched, combed out my hair, nudged the fire with a stick until it awakened, also. It could have been any and all mornings.

It was Lajima who had instructed me during the early days with the Jukima, but with Carogo I found the first, true friendship among these people. She was about my age but seemed much older, probably because she did everything with a stately calm that gentled everyone around her. Her hips were broad and substantial, and suggested the stability of her character. Her face was wide -- her nose, her forehead, her chin -- and this gave her an expression of being non-judgmental. Although Carogo was unmarried and had no children, she was maternal without being bossy. I felt safe with her.

Carogo took me to the gardens and named the things in them for me. The gardens were surprising in that they were terraced with large, rectangular stones that had been hewn by human hands. The stones had weathered and were crumbling in places, and the weight of the earth they held back had pushed some of the stones askew. A little stream ran through the place and spilled over each ledge in a fine spray. The stream was such a minor trickle, I didn't think it could become dangerous like the stream that had drowned the Tekhla village.

I asked Carogo, "Did the Jukima cut and place those rocks?" I was surprised when she said, "Yes," for I hadn't seen any tools among them that would be capable of such a thing. But then she said, "Our ancestors cut them. We return here again and again. There are other places like this."

Carogo taught me how to cook as she did. I have always been drawn to handling materials of various sorts. I enjoyed the touch of the vegetables we worked with -- their sun-warmed skins, their crinkled or papery or slippery textures. Carogo lifted up an odd-looking orange squash that seemed to have been dipped on one end in forest-green paint. She handed it to me and said, "This one is disappointing. The flavor is so mild it must be put in at just the end of the cooking or it will taste like nothing." The squash was surprisingly heavy in my hands, soggy with its dense flesh and seeds. I handed it back to her and watched as she began to cut the squash into rounds. The meat of it was gray and pulpy, and yes, disappointing. I watched for a time, and then I picked up a similar squash and began cutting it into pieces for the stew we were making. As we worked, I again asked her the question that had been on my mind for a long time, "How is it that we can dream the same dreams?"

I could have been asking her, "How do our eyes remember to blink?" Carogo thought a moment, and then said, "In dreams, we leave our bodies."

I said, "Yes, it seems that we do."

Carogo continued, "So where do we go, then?" I had no answer. She said, "We go to a different kind of place where our souls can talk. Without words. Or sometimes with words. But it is not the same as being awake."

"So we can communicate in the place of dreams?"

"Yes. Our thoughts can mingle."

"But how does that happen?"

"It is a mystery to us, but we think that the One who made everything guides our dreams. Isn't this what you were taught?"

I said, "I wasn't taught much of anything about that."

Carogo's eyes widened with surprise, and she said, "How is that possible? These are things everyone knows."

I shrugged, and said, "Ideas like that simply weren't mentioned much in my family, and where I come from not everyone believes the same things. Dreams aren't much discussed. I suppose we think they are not real."

Carogo said, "I will teach you, then." She pulled the pot to the side of the fire, where the coals had settled to a constant heat. She said, "The Creator made all things a long time ago. What I mean by that is that She started things, and then those things went on to discover the ways they should be. She made the sky and water and the land, and then She made the people -- the Jukima -- out of clay mixed with water. She shaped the people with her mind and then She touched them with a fingertip so that they became alive. Do you understand?"

I said, "Yes. But is the Creator female?"

Carogo was startled, then laughed. "Of course! What else could She be?" And then Carogo continued, "In dreams, our thoughts are not captured in our bodies. We sometimes are with loved-ones who have died. No one is ever really lost." Carogo was so certain, but to me this was like trying to understand a soul or the flicker that makes the heart beat. Carogo smiled and her face broadened slowly to show large, irregular white teeth. Her face was so homely that it inspired tenderness. There was honesty in such a face. She said, "I dream my mother and my grandmother, sometimes. And I dream places where the Jukima have been, before I was born." I nodded, but I didn't really understand how this could happen.

"And I dream you, also," Carogo said.

"You do?"

"I think it is you. Sometimes, I dream as if I were you before you came here. I see houses stacked up like the cliffs where birds live. There is noise -- so much noise. And terrible smells. I am unsettled because there is too much motion around me. I do not do any one thing well enough because of that feeling."

"I think I felt that way in Riolapa," I said.

"What is Riolapa?" she asked.

"Riolapa is a very, very big village. A place with many people."

"Oh. I see."

Carogo tossed her pieces of squash into the stew, and I added mine. She put a heated stone into the broth, which bubbled and a fragrance rose up from it. We worked just inside the doorway of Carogo's house; it was evening and the sun was so close to the peaked horizon that it painted the mountains with streaks of light. I was happy to be learning. It was possible that I would be with the Jukima for a long time.

The dreams I had among the Jukima were more vivid, consistently so, than at any other time in my previous life. Sometimes I would dream of the modern world, and it was as if I had discovered a new territory made of materials that were not exactly part of the earth. I saw cars, or small, domestic machines that were attached by cords to walls. With the Jukima, I had skills I couldn't use. I could drive a car, balance a checkbook, fit a key into a lock, and punch numbers in sequence on a telephone and insert the coins into the slot when I heard a sound on the piece of the mechanism that I held to my ear like a seashell. I began to learn to appreciate these things in ways I hadn't done before, when they seemed usual to me.

After the evening meal, the Jukima often sat around a common hearth as the Tekhla had done, using its light to work at crafts, or simply luxuriating and telling stories. In the evenings, the breezes slept. Carogo told me that as the breezes wandered, they gathered up conversations and carried them to other places, as gossip. From that I had acquired the habit of lowering my voice whenever a breeze was blowing. On this night, it was warmish, with a nearly full moon, and most of the village was there around the fire. Papeet said to Zhixo, "Could you please make shapes in the smoke tonight?" The children laughed in anticipation.

Zhixo said, "Then someone will have to go gather green branches." Papeet sprang up and said, "Tishaak, come with me." The two girls left the circle of firelight and returned in a short time with armfuls of bushy, needled branches gathered from trees a short way down the slope. When the branches were thrown onto the fire, the fire burst up so aggressively that I cringed away from it. The sparks showered down back down and then a pillar of white smoke climbed into the still air. I watched this raptly, but didn't see any particular shapes. Zhixo had not begun, yet.

One of the children asked, "Can you make a hawk?" Zhixo frowned and didn't answer. His head drooped forward slightly and his eyes became heavy-lidded. And then I saw it, at first vaguely, and then unmistakably. It was the narrow head of a hawk, in profile, with a tapering beak, slightly hooked on the tip. The shape's edges drifted and reformed. All the while Zhixo was frowning, his brows drawn so closely together that a shadow dug into the center of his forehead.

The children were delighted, but it was not over. Zhixo was still concentrating. The edges of the smoke in the shape of a hawk's-head solidified, and the body formed below it, not so much hardening out of the smoke as remaining still while all around it the smoke swirled and churned. The hawk became almost opaque. The wings extended in a stretching, testing movement and the hawk dipped its head.

I struggled not to cover my eyes with my hands. It was incredible, and terrifying. If these people could change matter with their minds, what else could they do? They seemed inhuman to me, then. This was not a dream. Carogo touched my shoulder and said, "You see!" And then to everyone, she said, "Nweli has not seen this before!" When she said this, the hawk-shape began to smudge, slightly.

Papeet said, "Hush, or it will go away." We watched in silence, and the hawk re-formed. Its wings were lifting, its body poised, its head turning this way and that way. And then it flew, and we all exclaimed "Ah!" as it beat at the column of smoke with muscular wings. It rose and scattered the smoke. It continued to rise until it was a dot and then we couldn't see it any more. The hawk vanished.

"Make another one," said Tihana -- Linari and Tamura's small son. Zhixo raised his head, blinked, and told Tihana, "No. I am tired now. You can try to make something?" Tihana clapped his hands and than glared into the smoke, which had reformed its column normally. Nothing happened. Linari reached out to scrub his son's hair with the palm of his hand. "When you are older, perhaps," he said.

That night in my house, I had the strangest thought, that I had died in the flood and was now a ghost of a woman in a territory that had slipped free of the laws I had taken as truth. That there was a shape of a hawk in the smoke was unacceptable. It was like a child's game, but with extraordinary implications. I had no way to understand it. It was a group-hallucination? It was some sort of hypnosis? But, I knew it was true. Zhixo could rearrange matter with his mind. I put more wood on my fire until it rooted out the shadows. I piled firewood in front of the door, so that if someone entered, the pile would tumble and awaken me. It didn't matter; I couldn't sleep.

The Jukima have a word for a cloud that resembles the form of an animal or bird or human. It is a "tylaya," but it is a discovered delight and they don't make them. I didn't *think* they made them? I wasn't certain of anything anymore. I decided to write down what I'd seen, to record the facts as I had once recorded facts about the Tekhla. I had begun writing again, in English. I wrote initially on thin slabs of wood, and then when I realized that they were too bulky, I wrote on pieces of peeled bark. I wrote with the tip of a sharpened bone engraving the marks to reveal a darker layer. My writing was as small as I could manage, as small as the secret notes a prisoner might write, although I was not exactly a prisoner. The facts I recorded were so extraordinary that I felt unsure now, about exactly what a *fact* was. Now I had seen a hawk in the smoke, and I could see the huntress in the moon. I wasn't certain that they weren't there, in fact. I was wavering on the edge where science and magic converse.

One night Zhixo told a beautiful story. He told it to the children, but I listened attentively, as well. He said that the huntress in the moon had been a young woman who took such pride in her physical body and the perfection of her skills -- at archery, at throwing a spear -- that she forgot to grieve at the deaths of her prey. She wore the limp, cooling bodies of animals strung around her neck like a necklace. In order to instruct her, the Creator fashioned, from clay, an animal designed to be savage and merciless. She touched it and brought it to life. The huntress became the hunted. The animal pursued her without ceasing, lagging just behind her as she fled from it, allowing her to know the desperation of the hunted. She understood the suffering she had brought to the animals, and was deeply ashamed.

The Creator allowed the huntress to choose her own punishment. She chose exile, and the Creator banished her to the moon, where she remains frozen as a portrait of herself. She is forever arrested in the pride of releasing a true arrow, but one that will never reach the mark. Her punishment was that she was stilled at one stage of her becoming. That she was now legend was her reward for prowess at her chosen occupation. I could see her there after hearing her story, and I thought she was an icon of great beauty, drawn from the mountains and valleys of the cold, marbled moon.

From the high place where I lived now, I could see the moon articulated with a clarity I hadn't seen before. There was the crater of a mouth, and the eyes gazing down, slightly askew. I knew that in the moon some peoples can see a rabbit or the figures of humans, and in it I could also see the huntress. The moon's features changed -- from face to huntress and back again -- much like the optical illusion of the vase that becomes the profiles of two faces, both types of images prepared to be seen.

I wrote about the hawk in the smoke, the huntress in the moon, and about the events of daily life. The bark sheaves accumulated into a small library and sometimes late at night I would light the oil lamp, take down these tablets and read them again. It was a pleasure. The simple act of reading had been denied to me for months and then restored, and was more luxurious for it. I also had begun to make a map on a sheaf of bark. The rainy season had ended and the clouds had lifted from the forest. I could see the landscape below me again, and how the earth heaped up or was hollowed, and how in the forest's darker folds, rivers and streams ran hidden.

I thought if I could recreate my journey on a map, I could find my way through the forest to the river, and even if I couldn't locate the flimsy dock, I could signal a boat from the river-bank somewhere. On the night of escape from the flood, I didn't know what direction we had taken, other than it had been away from the rampant stream. However, I recalled in what direction the sun had risen and set when I had been in the Tekhla village and compared that to the sun's location at the tree where the Tekhla had made their camp. From that I assumed that we had gone north, and west. And then the Jukima camp where I had stayed before I fell ill was still farther north. Between that camp and where I was now was a space of blankness. And who could say what the terrain was like beneath the uniform, green mantle of the jungle? There could be rivers that were not passable and detours would have to be made, or there could be villages that must be avoided because their people were unknown. There were many things that were not predictable.

When I had drawn everything I could remember, I showed my map to Carogo. I said, "It is a picture of the way the land below is arranged." Carogo said, "What does it matter? We don't go there." I sighed and hung my head. She embraced me, and said, "I know you want to return home. But I also know that often, you are happy with us." Even so, the map was what I had and it gave me some, slight, hope. I would work to perfect it, using the materials I had. I thought of all I had lost as support for my senses: my pens and pencils, my compass, camera, and my clock.

We looked down at the landscape together. I said, "It's beautiful." The sky was piled with fast-moving clouds and the sunlight lanced down from the spaces in between the cumulus shapes. The jungle was patched with shadows that were a negative image of the sky, opening, closing, changing so quickly that the jungle itself seemed to be in motion. The light and shade made it look like a sea that would be transparent if only it could be still.

One day as we worked in the gardens, Carogo had told me, "We look for the place to make our home, which will be of stone and terraces such as our ancestors made." I was very surprised at this. It hadn't seemed that the Jukima yearned for anything but a good harvest, abundant fishing and hunting, and good health.

I said, "But this is a good place, with enough of

everything."

"It is not far enough."

"Do you know where your ancestors built their stone houses?"

"Only that it was to the north, and in the mountains. And before that, they crossed oceans, began again."

I wondered if it was true, that the Jukima ancestors had migrated as far as that, or had been driven away from a homeland and now searched for something that had been lost, some place or way of being that was so obscured by the passage of time that they had no maps in their minds, anymore, of what they sought?

Chapter Seventeen

Of the Jukima women, I felt that I knew Tamura the least well. She was not particularly approachable and could be snide in her comments. Therefore, I was surprised when she asked me to go with her to gather blue clay from which dye was made. This clay was also used to make the small bowls for tea. But then she said, "The clay is heavy. You can help me carry it." I didn't mind -- I would learn how to dry it, grind it, and mix it with oils, and I would learn about the designs the Jukima painted on their skins. I followed Tamura up the well-used trail to the high place where there were gardens. Instead of continuing to the gardens, we turned left and passed through a squeeze in the rocks -- rocks that were bigger than the Jukima houses. This place was a darkly shadowed labyrinth. Only a few leathery plants grew in the higher clefts in the rocks, and only on their southern faces. I supposed that these plants were so well adapted that they grew nowhere else.

Tamura said, "Those plants there. Medicine comes from their juices." I wondered if these were the same ones that had provided the tea that I had drunk during my illness? I decided to collect some of these when I left the Jukima, and then I thought, "No. I'll protect them and these few people with my silence." And then I reversed myself, decided that these plants -- these medicines -- might be too important a discovery to hoard. It was a suggestive dilemma.

It was afternoon when we walked to the place where the blue clay could be found, and the sun lowered to the point where I could see its downward motion. And then we arrived, and there was a lake bounded on one side by a sheer, white cliff. On the opposite shore, there was a white-sand beach. I hadn't realized that there was a lake so close.

I asked Tamura, "Why is the village not here, instead?" In the village there were often fish to eat, but I had assumed that they had come from streams or pools that were lower, in the direction of the forest. Tamura said, "There is no fertile soil here. Only rock and sand." Of course. I saw some things, and not others. I hadn't planted a garden here.

The cliff was not precisely vertical, but nearly so. It was massive and glittered where the sun struck it. Low on the cliff's face were hollows where the rock had powdered and had mixed with the decaying roots and leaves. In these places, the alchemy of the mixture had formed veins and pockets of clay. The clay was the blue-gray color of a stormy sky. It was cold, faintly unpleasant to touch, and yet it was silken and left no grit when rubbed between the fingers. We collected some of this clay by digging it out with our hands, for it was soft enough and pulled away easily.

The small lake originated in a spring and was self-contained. It was like a pool held up on a white, marble pedestal, for the land dropped away steeply just beyond the flat beach. When we had finished our collecting and had turned away, there was a sound like many ribbons snapping in a breeze. When I looked back, I saw the birds. Parrot-like birds with wings of turquoise and flashes of crimson. They had massed against the cliff and hovered there, and appeared to be attacking the rock itself. I asked, "Tamura, what are they doing?"

She answered, "Eating the clay. The color of their wings comes from the color of the clay." I didn't think so, but I didn't contradict. The birds were brilliantly blue -- not the dull blue of the clay. I sighed. Tamura didn't know everything about her world. The birds were exquisite against the cliff, and when I saw them I was reminded of my dream of happiness. But these birds were not the many colors of the birds in my dream, and it was not quite the same.

As we returned, I worried some of this clay in my hand. I could mold it into shapes and show the Jukima the forms of cars or telephones, but I decided that I wouldn't. Instead, I would make bowls in which to store my rings or spices. Tamura and I walked single file on the trail. Her hips undulated in a way that was not efficient; she wore her bodily movement like fashion. Her hair was a little longer than the other Indians' hair, and she slicked it with oils until it looked artificial and gathered dust. Her eyes were so black they appeared always to be dilated with disbelief or on the threshold of anger. She had a barking, disparaging laugh. I didn't particularly like her.

Tamura had one child -- the boy, Tihana -- who was just past being a toddler. She was cursory with him, perhaps even cold in a distracted, irritable manner. Her ideas about motherhood seemed flimsy to me. It was troubling, and very unlike the usual kindliness with which the Jukima dealt with their children. I often felt the urge to gather her child up into my arms and warm him, but I resisted that urge because I didn't know how Tamura would react.

There was to be a dance to celebrate the coming of age of seven of the village's young people -- four boys and three girls. It seemed to me such a valuable few, and such a slender hope for the Jukima's future. After the celebration, Carogo told me, the seven young men and women would be free to marry. It was some days after the excursion to collect the clay, that we decorated ourselves for the dance. We sat in the burnishing light of oil-lamps and helped one another paint our skins. Tondi was decorating my arms with dye. The stroking of her brush was almost like the tingle of feathers beginning to sprout.

As she worked, Tondi said, to everyone present, "What about the dream of the dry river?" I had dreamed of it too. From the height of a mountaintop, I could see a gash cut down to the forest soil. It was mineral-red, and straighter than any natural river. I knew what the Jukima did not -- that it was a road. At first, in my dream, it was a road that was being constructed, and then the dream progressed. I was overjoyed to see cars moving on the road, and trucks, and jeeps. And then I was standing beside this road with a kind of enlightened trust, not minding that I had nothing -- no money, no tickets, no card that identified me by name. I knew that someone would stop for me. I didn't tell the women the details of this dream -- I didn't know how I would explain it to them. However, I said, "I think it is a road."

Tondi repeated, "road." Tamura said, "road," and batted her son away from the dye-pot. The child yelped and scrubbed at his arm where his mother had struck him. Lajima glared at Tamura, but was ignored. Carogo handed the boy a doll and he sniffed, and then began to dab at its limbs with ashes and saliva, imitating. It was a doll like the figure Ollie had photographed, and that Hlisi's little son, Yutta, had found. That was all it was. A child's toy, a miniature, winged human being who could be manipulated, dressed or undressed, or left behind in the ashes. When I had first seen these things played with in ordinary ways I had asked, "Why do they have wings?" The answer was, "We can fly in our dreams. Do you not fly, then?"

154

Carogo asked me, "What is a road?"

I said, "A road is a wide path, or it's like a river that can bring many people from different places up and down it. It makes distance shorter."

"Who makes it? Does someone make these things?" asked Tondi.

"People like the ones I come from make them," I said.

"I think it will bring our ancestors back to us," Lajima said. "They will walk out of a hole in the earth and walk along the surface of this thing, this wide path, and we will greet them."

At this, I wondered if, in days past, some of the Jukima had been enslaved and taken to the mines, as the Tekhla had? I dreamed sometimes of a hole in the ground that was sulfurous and ruined and seemed to be peopled by shades that I couldn't quite see clearly.

"It could bring the Xangu, instead," Carogo said.

'Yes. It could bring the Xangu. Or animals. It could bring many animals," said Lajima. "We could hunt them, or they could be dangerous. We don't know."

"If it brings the Xangu, then we will have to make weapons to defend ourselves," said Tamura. Her eyes burned so fiercely that I had to look away.

"We should remain here and watch what happens from this safe distance," said Carogo, who always seemed reasonable to me. And then she said, to me, "The Xangu burned our villages, once. They carried away all the women who did not hide in the cliffs."

"Yes, and so many of our men were killed," added Tamura.

"Did this happen recently?" I asked.

"Our mothers' mothers' mothers, I think," Tondi said. "Or before that."

Carogo said, "It is how our knives came to us. From those battles. They are Xangu knives that some of our ancestors took from the ground."

The Jukima had knives of a hard metal, but they didn't make them. So, then, the knives they used were antiques, not obtained by trading? The knives were similar in shape to Frederick's flat blade, but longer, and with carved wooden handles fitted to the blades. These handles were replaced when working hands rubbed and blurred the carvings and the blades grew loose in their fastenings. The men also used the knives for hunting, attaching them to long shafts for spears. I had been given one of the knives and used it as the other women did, to cut down the grasses when their tips grew heavy with seed-heads. These seeds were pounded into a flour and from this we made unleavened bread or thickened stews and sauces. The cut grasses were used for thatch and bedding. And, I also used my knife to harvest vegetables from the garden, to cut branches for firewood, or to peel the bark from which I made my writing tablets. I wondered, whose hands had used my knife for a different purpose, and what story could it tell?

I said, "I do not think the road will come this far." But I didn't really know, and I was conflicted about the road. The appearance of the road in our dreams made the Jukima seem somewhat like strangers, or I was a stranger myself, one who would reach the end of an elastic tether that would snap back my other life for me. The significance of these dreams was not knowable in ordinary ways. This road was, perhaps, something that was in our near future. We agreed, tentatively, upon that. It was important, we knew, because we had all dreamed it, although with varying details.

Tondi was finished with her decorations of my limbs and guided me up by the elbows until I stood. I was made to pivot in the dusky light. I turned slowly and listened to the comments. "Her arms are wrapped with fern shadows." "Are those the rosettes of panthers? They look more like flowers, to me." This was not a criticism of Tondi's artistry; it was simply a statement about the richness of the drawings on my body. I had no mirror, but from what I could see of them, the designs were much like those the other women wore, but on lighter skin. The designs were similar, but not identical. Some of the lines were more loosely wrapped, and some were pronged with angles, and some grew tendrils that coiled on their ends like the growing tips of vines. I had heard the story by then, that these were the same designs that the ancient Jukima had drawn, each for the other, and their thoughtful beauty and variety was what had begun to differentiate these people from the animals. I had been told, "The panther does not appreciate the colors of the sunrise."

Later that night when the moon rose, its cold illumination threw down the shapes of shadows that rippled across the ground. The Jukima were dancing, but unlike the aggressive dancing of the Tekhla, this dance was more improvised and graceful. The Jukima, both men and women, were dressed in mantles of plumage of a frosty white that matched the bird-cliffs in grandeur. They danced in a loose circle, and in the center of that circle were the seven young girls and boys, also dressed in white feathers -- feathers gathered from the aeries of birds. It took years to accumulate enough, and the feathers were precious. The moonlight sank into this whiteness and glowed it, as if the cloaks shone with their own light. I danced between Carogo and the old woman, Idisa, who was dancing with the suppleness of a girl, eyes half-shut and a smile curving her lips.

As the dancers moved, their feathered cloaks swung and settled and there were glimpses of color, for the linings of the cloaks were saturated with agate-blue, crimson, emerald, and a plush purple like the insignia of royalty. The colors, glimpsed through the covering-uncovering white, brought a thrilling pang, that they were so lovely and brief. The men wore slender quills through their noses, and these quills drew swaying arcs in the air.

Along with the dancing and inseparable from it was the playing of flute-like instruments made of hollow reeds, and there was singing. The Jukima used their voices like the instruments that they were. When Carogo added her voice to the chorus of voices, the others ceased for a moment, in deference, or pleasure at the sounds that flew like colors from her throat. Carogo's voice completely replaced the plainness of her face. I heard the deep emotion that had become Carogo, entirely. She sang, and gradually other voices joined hers until they blended. I was overwhelmed by the beauty of that evening.

I thought the dance would stop at dawn, but it did not stop. The sun, when it came, was rusty as though chafed by smoke. In daylight, the dance took on a more competitive character and most of the dancers dropped away, spent of their energy. Only a few of the men remained, including Zhixo, and some of the hardier women. The rest of us fell back to watch. There was drumming now, with a propulsive rhythm that seemed to reverberate off the mountains. The sunlight was hurtful to my tired eyes.

The Jukima danced until afternoon arranged their long shadows into moving silhouettes. I hadn't slept, and for a time the remaining dancers looked tawdry, their feathered cloaks soiled with dust. When dusk came, some of the beauty of the night before returned and the white cloaks were tinted violet -- briefly iridescent. When it grew dark, only a very few dancers remained, shuffling woodenly from fatigue, and stumbling occasionally. A fire was lit and its energy seemed to restore the dancer's ambitions. The dancers' shadows jumped wildly and their cloaks seemed to be blazing. The Jukima didn't wear paint on their faces as the Tekhla had done, but the leaping firelight exaggerated their expressions, made their faces strange, like those of mythical beings not completely human, or ghost.

During this time, many of those who were watching and not dancing, sang, played instruments, beat on drums, came and went from their houses, brought out food, and fed the children. When the moon rose, I could see that the faces of the dancers were lined with their exhaustion and their expressions were almost fierce with striving. The Jukima danced throughout most of that night as well, and I watched them until the accompanying songs dwindled, and ceased. I could hear the rasp of the dancers' breathing, the shuffle of their feet, and then they, too, stopped. It was over.

When I finally slept, I didn't dream anything at first. The darkness of this sleep sucked me into it and I had no sensations of a body and where it was in relation to the space that housed it, and I had no emotions. And then, I must have felt the warmth of the new day -- the bands of warm light moving across my face as they did every morning -- for I awakened briefly, my recollections tumbling about in images of dipping, floating plumage and a frozen moon hanging heavy in the sky. I slept again, and dreamed vividly. I saw the road again, but this time it was not a lifeless, fabricated thing, but was like another creature of the forest.

The road was growing longer and it was feeding on the forest. I didn't know why I hadn't seen it that way before? In this dream, I understood that I was dreaming as if I were Zhixo. I had climbed to a higher place to see the road without obstructions. There was fear in this dream, like the fear one experiences when hearing a sound in the night that is large and can't be identified. There was also curiosity, and the calculating thought that there was something to be gained here. Who could know what types of marvels could be found as a result of the road?

The dream shifted then, and whereas before I had dreamed of floods before the literal flood came, now I dreamed of fire. Many fires, and yellow smoke like pollen. This smoke settled among the trees, skirted the boulders with a yellow-grayness. It dulled the sun. The smoke rose up from these many fires as though an enormous village had been built and had many campfires made of green, smoky wood. And then I saw the fires at night and they were beautiful, in the way power can have a magnificence without conscience. I understood that they were not campfires -- there were too many of them, or they were all one fire that had separated into pieces and were roving like an army. This unseen army was carrying torches. They were Xangu with torches, catching the sun's fire for weapons.

The dream shifted yet again, and now it was a dream of complete terror, and of flight. At first I thought that the forest itself had grown monstrously large, but then I realized that it was made up of mushrooms as huge as trees, and the trees themselves were as unreachably tall as the stars or moon. In this dream I was running with the full velocity of panic. Beside me ran animals -- other animals -- for I had become a lesser animal of the forest, something small, with a tiny, rapidly clenching, unclenching knuckle of a heart. Beside me ran animals of prey that had the many shapes of death itself, the blank outlines of it. These animals were of no consequence to me beside the greater terror of the fire. I couldn't name this danger, but I knew it by the instinct that drove my flight. This dream was terrible in the totality of the fear that wrapped around it. The fear of immolation was worse than the fear of death. I awakened panting and my skin felt scorched, for I had spent all the previous day outside in the sun and I knew from how the skin was reddened that it would peel away like a shedding snake.

Zhixo came to see me the evening after the dancing. He accepted a bowl of tea and asked, "You have been to many different places?"

"Yes, many. But I didn't always understand them." Riolapa came to mind, and how I hadn't penetrated it at all, nor had I cared to. I remembered particular, trivial things. The traffic noise at night when I tried to sleep, all the grindings and the punctuation of horns blaring, all of it like the many sounds of a huge engine that was struggling to synchronize the notching of its parts. I remembered how some of the people I saw had interesting faces. I had imagined a quirky intelligence or an agile humor, but I hadn't had the time there to know anyone.

He asked, "Are the places you have seen better than here?"

I said, "I don't know if they are better." And then I laughed a little and said, "My father used to tell his children, 'Don't travel anywhere you couldn't stay forever. In case you have to?'" Zhixo didn't laugh at this. I knew he wanted me to tell him about the road, and what I knew of such things. As I spoke, I wondered, "Was this why the Jukima had dreamed of me? Was this why I was brought here? To explain these things to them?"

I said, "The road will bring your world and mine closer together. The road could bring diseases, and also the medicines that can cure them." I thought of the Tekhla and how they had beaten the metal of tin cans flat and had cut into them until they resembled the rayed suns that were the same as the ones they sometimes drew on their cheeks. They had forced conformity on this new material and it didn't break the web of their rules or change them very much. But, I didn't know how the road would change the Jukima.

I said, "The road won't come this far up into the mountains, but it will bring people closer, and some could come as far as this. It will bring many changes." I told Zhixo about how where I came from, people worked at different tasks, and made almost none of the things they used. They rarely grew or gathered or hunted their own food, and didn't really understand how these things were done. I told him what I could about crowdedness, and our differences from one another in opinions and beliefs. I told him what I could about machinery and how it was used. And I told him about travel, that we could go nearly anywhere, and quickly. I was afraid that what I said seemed condescending or childish? I knew that Zhixo was an intelligent man. I had already released whatever pride I might have had in the technologies that I'd used without the true mastery that comes of intimate contact and mutual dependencies. I hadn't maintained my machines, not even the simpler ones, to any extent more complicated than sharpening a pencil. I didn't feel that I could speak of them with any real authority, other than explaining the resonance they had throughout an entire, complicated, rapidly mutating culture that had no center or leader. I knew all that, but couldn't really describe my world, except to say that some qualities remained important and were increasingly difficult to hold close.

I felt that I was a failure as an ambassador. There were so many things for which I had no words, and my explanations were only part of the truth. I thought of the huntress in the moon and the face I sometimes saw there and how they couldn't be sustained together, except in a recounting of how both were there and both were true, and neither was real, nor true. The moon was a chunk of bombarded rock, and was like a Janus mask that conceals its other side. Zhixo considered what I had said, but I had the impression that he had already weighed his options and had decided on the discretion of a retreat to a prudent distance. He said, "I'm sorry that we cannot take you where you want to go." I forgave him, and said. "It doesn't matter. It's not your responsibility." At that he looked pained, as though it was exactly his responsibility, and he had failed it. He said, "We will wait for a time, and see what happens. Perhaps the road will not come this far?"

Chapter Eighteen

There was no road yet, and it was a happy season. There were many dances, and there was the celebration when Carogo was married. I liked her husband, Yktma, whose expression when he looked at my friend Carogo was one of complete adoration. I cooked for her wedding-feast; all the women did. For the dance I wore a cloak of feathers I had been given, that some of the women had made for me in secrecy. Carogo didn't sing at her own wedding as she had sung at others. She sat demurely, the designs drawn on her skin almost overcoming the ordinariness of her face, although I thought it was the energy of her voice, temporarily checked, that gave her her radiance. We all knew her capabilities.

During this season two babies were born, and one old woman died. Idisa's passing was peaceful. Lajima had been with her when she died, and told me that Idisa had said that when she closed her eyes she could still see the colors of things. Idisa had said, "Everything is so bright! Lajima, that cloth you are wearing has the colors of flowers. I can see colors in the metal of your rings. Your hair is shining with blue light!" And then she had died, surrendering to the soft ministrations of women, who made her passing a peaceful journey. I wondered, had she been dreaming, at the end, or was it a different world opening up to her at that moment?

My house became a library filled with wafers of thin bark and I took them down and read them again and again, hoping to write so much that one day I would read this writing and it would be fresh, as though another had written it. I wrote down my dreams. I wrote down the dreams of others. I wrote down the Jukima fables -- not necessarily as factual material, but as stories I could read again and again, late at night when others slept. And during the slack times when I wasn't working in the gardens or cooking or writing or reading, I labored over my map. In a layer drawn over my abstract sketch of the terrain I could see, I drew the landmarks that I remembered and tried to place them where I thought they should go, in relation to each other.

Tamura disturbed me, and she dampened any gathering where she was present . She didn't have a warm heart, or if she did, its was a puny glow. It seemed to me that she grew more mean-spirited as time passed. Her son, Tihana, was sometimes dirty, because she couldn't always be bothered to take him to the stream to wash him. The best pieces of food were not for him. Her son became more quiet as he grew, and not livelier. I sometimes dreamed Tamura's dreams, as I did those of the other Jukima on occasion. In these dreams I was both myself and another, and was aware of the difference. I can't explain it more fully than that, or how it happened, but it was true.

When I dreamed Tamura's dreams, I knew that the touch of Tihana's skin and hair didn't bring her joy as it should. She didn't exult in his scent. The child exhausted and irritated her. His talking -- his questions and ideas -- were a buzzing in her ears. When people spoke, sometimes it sounded to her like monkeys chattering in the trees, but she couldn't follow the sense of what was said, and it was a kind of pain, like the persecution of a relentless noise. Hers was a generalized malaise. She would pick up one thing to do and then put it down, almost immediately unhappy with it, and she would cast about for another thing. She yearned for something she couldn't identify. To hold some new, extravagant object in her hands and to be the first one to display such a prize? To accomplish some feat that had not yet been invented? I didn't know what she wanted. I felt sorrow for Tamura because she was so dissatisfied. The dreams of the road had fueled Tamura's restlessness, and she desired for something to come toward her that she would recognize, and she would be able to say, "Yes, this will fill my life." She had a feeling of volatile temporariness to her.

I wished I had something to give Tamura's son, perhaps candy, as I had given the Tekhla children -- something that would delight him. I made ornaments out of grasses for his arms and ankles, and he wore them until they fell away and I replaced them. He was thin, and his thinness seemed to be a condition of his spirit. He was not nourished. Zhixo told me that he was concerned for the boy. He sometimes took Tihana

162

on his knee and told him stories in a whisper that included the child in a kind of privileged exchange.

Tamura's husband, Linari, was a good hunter and often brought more meat to her hearth than anyone brought to any other, but Tamura shared little. I knew from what the women told their husbands that Linari thought Tamura was almost frighteningly seductive. He enjoyed the tilt of her eyes and her opulent hips, but he was anxious about losing her to someone, perhaps to Kaanu, Zhixo's brother.

There was no road that any of us could see, and Zhixo didn't say anything about moving on. I didn't know what month it was anymore, or exactly how long I had been gone. I wasn't unhappy where I was, but I worried greatly about what my family would think of my absence. I didn't want them to grieve. To leave the Jukima and trek alone through the forest was impossible -- I hadn't the wisdom to avoid the pitfalls. The map I had drawn was unfinished, but I had no more information and couldn't complete it.

I had been given seeds, and I was excited by the way they sprouted, like anyone's seeds. I hadn't planted a garden before, anywhere, and I was heartened by the inevitability of the swelling seeds pushing back out of the earth, the leaves bursting through their sheaths and unfolding like strong, new wings. I nurtured the delicate plants, and was gratified that I would be able to provide more for myself and not depend so much on the charity of the Jukima. I was nearly mesmerized by my work in the gardens, by the rhythm of its repetitions. The Jukima nearly always sang or hummed while they worked, and I was surrounded by music as I never had been before.

I was as surprised as anyone when the day came that there was a thick smoke in the air. The yellow of the sun was soiled by haze until it shone a glassy orange and one could nearly look upon its face. There was a dimness, like the almost sickening, metallic light of an eclipse. I smelled the bitter smoke. That same night it rained. The sound of this rain was heavy, as though it were a rain full of particles. It hadn't rained for a long time, and Carogo said that this rain must be a cloud come to earth for companionship, to touch the earth again.

During the day it was dry, but the following night the rain returned. I knew what the rain meant. If it was to be a not-stopping rain, it was a sign that it had been an entire year since the flight from the Tekhla village. Surely someone had searched for me, and I wondered if anyone had come as far as the place where the Tekhla village had been washed away by the flood? If so, then it was likely that it was thought I had perished. And, if it was thought that I was no longer alive, then the searching had stopped. The evening after the rain, I sent prayers up with the camp-fire cinders, but not to a Creator. I sent the prayers to my mother, my father, my sisters, in the hope that they were not suffering because I was lost. I hoped they knew in their hearts that I was alive and thinking of them. I wondered if they dreamed of me?

I asked Yktma if it would be a not-stopping-rain? We sat in the house he shared with Carogo, and were full with a meal. Yktma smoked his pipe, and Carogo sat and worked at her loom. The cloth she was making lengthened so slowly it was like a tree growing, at a pace below the level of delectability, but persistently. The light was dim, but her fingers counted the threads as she worked. Yktma said, "I think it is a hint of the not-stopping rain. We are mostly above it, here."

Carogo said, not looking up from the motions of her fingers, "We are above where clouds are born. The forest is like a hot animal that makes clouds as it cools." I wanted to say, "The forest is the engine that makes the weather below us," but I had no Jukima word for engine. It was too complicated to explain, and I was satisfied with the food I had just eaten, and I was lazy. I listened to the evening rain beginning again. It would be gone by morning, and the roofs of the houses, the rocks, and the grasses, would sparkle until the sun dried them.

"What about the smoke?" I asked. Every afternoon the smoke lifted from the canopy below us and masked the sun and stained the clouds a dull ocher. I expected the rain to be soiled by its falling from such a grimy cloud, but the rain was clear.

Carogo's hands stilled, and Yktma took his pipe from his mouth and studied it thoughtfully. The moment gaped open. I had been indiscreet to have mentioned the smoke, because we all knew that the smoke had to do with the road. We had all begun dreaming again, intensely, each in our own way. I didn't want to return to my house yet because my fire wasn't lit and because Yktma and Carogo shed the comfortable glow of a family, but now there was a somber mood.

Carogo finally said, "In my dreams, I see men who are like you. I mean, with your colors, with light hair and eyes. But no women, yet. Or I see the Xangu and their knives." She shuddered.

I had dreamed of the Xangu also, and when I saw them they were always coming up over the ridge of rock to the west of the village. At first, I couldn't see their faces -- only the tips of

164

their knives held aloft, growing longer as they ascended the ridge. When they crested the ridge, I witnessed the blankness of their eyes that held no compassion for us, only a terrible and unthinking loyalty to their own people and to themselves, as individuals. The dream was so frightening that I always awakened panting.

The noise of the rain rose until it sounded like animals stampeding through grasses. Each night the rain had been stronger. Carogo added sticks to the fire and it flared, and we watched it moodily until it sank back and was rosy again.

I changed the subject, saying to Yktma, "This fire in your house is full of itself. I think it doesn't appreciate how you made the roof that keeps the rain away from it. The roof keeps it *alive*." Yktma smiled at the compliment to his skill at building a house. The fire contained in the center of the house was a piece of the same fire that was burning in the forest, clearing the trees away to make a passage for the road, but it had a different name. It was a fire that had been taught to keep to its proper place. Its flames jostled themselves slightly in their confinement. The melancholy mood had broken, and I looked fondly at my friends.

The rain stopped, and the memory of it took on the aspect of a premonition. With the stopping of the rain, the smoke burgeoned, as did the fires that made it. The sky at the horizon was sooty and brown. At night now we could see glow of the fires to the south, like a rime of lava at the base of the mountains that were the far rim of the bowl that held the forest. Zhixo said, as we sat around the common fire in the center of our village, "Those fires that eat at the mountains and forest were made by people, not by a lightning strike." He was staring at me as though he had just recognized me as a criminal. I was chilled by his stare.

I said, "People use fire to clear away the forest. I think they are clearing away trees for the road, and perhaps they are clearing land for . . . " I hesitated, not knowing the word for "farm." And then I added, "For very large gardens."

Zhixo glared at me and didn't say anything. I protested, "I didn't make the fires."

"And she can't stop them," added Carogo.

I said, "The fires were made by people, and the people who made them are there with them. I know the things they use, but I don't know those people.'"

"Do you want to travel in the direction of the fires? Will you leave us, now? And if you find the people who are making the road, will you tell them of us?" Zhixo's voice had a coldness I hadn't heard him use before, to anyone.

I said, "The men tending those fires would likely be rough men. Perhaps like the Xangu. I don't think we speak the same language." And then I added, "I wouldn't be able to find the fires from the level of the forest. I wouldn't be able to see them from under the forest canopy." At this ambiguous answer, Zhixo spat into the fire and soiled it.

The days passed and I loathed the evenings, because then we could see how the fire had bored deeper into the forest. Drawn out along the night-dark forest, it was obvious to me that there now was the undeviating shape of a road. Zhixo watched me carefully. He knew my conflicted heart. After evenings about the common hearth-fire, where we spoke desultorily or not at all, I retreated alone to my house and was restless on my bed. When I finally slept, it was uneasily. There was one night when I was awakened by a sound, the thin, tremulous wail of a child crying. I waited anxiously to hear the soothing murmur of its mother, but the comfort didn't come. I thought, "Tamura," and fell into a dreamless sleep.

The evenness of the days and nights ended, because the time came when the Jukima burned all that they had except for what they could carry with them: a few utensils for hunting, fishing, and cooking, the cloth and ornaments they wore daily, some food for the journey, and the seeds to begin again. Their pyre seemed to me to be a sacrifice they made because of what could not be challenged or changed.

Zhixo said, "The Xangu plundered our village once, and now we will be certain they will take nothing from us or find us when we have left this place." The Jukima would leave no relics, no artifacts that could be deciphered, nothing that would reveal these people to anyone who was not them. They broke their pottery into tiny shards and threw them onto the blaze. Their woven cloth and the looms that once held the cloth, their ornaments, the very substance of their houses were thrown onto this fire and the fire ate all of this and grew tall and wide until I was sure it could be seen from a great distance. The finality of it was appalling to me. Once again, I was to be bereft of all that I had accumulated and had gathered around me pridefully. After only a slight hesitation, I threw my belongings onto the fire, including the scrolls of writing, but not the map. I wanted to preserve where I had been. The words of my writing were cleansed as they took on the shapes of the fire. In the fire, I thought I could see the shape of the great tree where I had sheltered with the Tekhla, and I could see the faces of Neethu and Falatha. I saw Luaka's face and I closed my eyes; when I looked back, the faces were gone.

We burned nearly everything. I thought that perhaps the souls of these people burned more brightly when they had nothing material to define them, and then I rejected this idea. We were all impoverished by this divesting. I was comforted by the thought that our friendships -- our relationships -- still held us together. The tears ran down my face at the enormity of the sacrifice, but Zhixo put a hand on my shoulder and said, "No matter. We can make other things." I said, and it was selfish, I know, "I can't remember all the words I put on my tablets. They are lost." Zhixo looked at me incredulously. "Of course you'll remember. If the words were like songs, you will remember."

As the thatch of the houses was thrown on the flames, an obscene ball of fire raised up like a fist. Tamura was not philosophical about the burning, as Zhixo was. She seemed crazed, and pulled at her hair and screamed as she threw each thing in. "I made this with my own hands!" she said as she tossed a cloak of white feathers into the fire. The cloak rose a moment on the heated drafts and opened out its multi-colored lining. I saw it for a moment as a magnificent bird ignited by the sun and immolating itself in glory. I decided that this was the most beautiful thing I had ever seen -- that moment when the plumage hung suspended against the twilight and was on the threshold of igniting and flying away into memory.

The moon was full, and we traveled by night. We didn't linger to see the ashes of the morning and the circles that were the footprints of where our houses had been; they were footprints that would be erased by rain and wind. As we walked, it was as though I could feel the heat of the flames at my back, but each time I turned to look, the fire was smaller until finally it was so small that it seemed unimportant. It was almost morning when I slept on the bare ground and dreamed of the sorrow of a child who had seen the stability of its world transformed into smoke.

The trek with the Jukima became a time of hunger because Zhixo kept us at the pace of a forced march. There was little time to find and prepare food. At first, we kept to the high ridge of the mountain top, or just below it, so that we couldn't be seen as silhouettes by anyone looking up. We traveled north, and west. We talked among ourselves very little as we moved along the rocky ground. The dust that rose up under our feet was as white and sterile as chalk. Sometimes, we descended lower and found valleys and the streams that had made them. We knelt at these streams and drank until our throats were numb with the icy water. We wove cocoons out of the long grass and waited for night to pass and for it to be time to begin again. These things assumed a permanence that blocked the memory of comfort and of ways to be in the world other than toiling painfully across its surface.

The farther west we went, the more sparse the vegetation became. We passed ribbons of quartz layered in the rocks, and sometimes the quartz held flecks of golden minerals frozen within it. I thought that to be safe from the strangers they feared, the Jukima must go to a place that had nothing anyone would want to claim, a place that was nearly as far and barren as the moon. At one place on our trek there were images of birds and animals carved into a cliff, and marks that seemed to be hieroglyphics, but the markings on the cliff held no interest for me. I was so oppressed by exhaustion that I had only the resources to lift up my feet and set them down again. The fires in the forest vanished behind a ridge of mountain on the first day of the journey, but I could smell their corrupt breath for five days more.

On our march we found very little that we could eat, because Zhixo was loathe to go farther down the slopes. At times we stopped and harvested seed-heads and ground them to make unleavened bread to roast and eat on the journey, and this took some time. I was grateful for the pauses. I stayed near to Carogo and Ytkma. Carogo was pregnant by then, and her face became drawn when she was tired. I wondered where we would be when her baby came? We all began to grow thin.

I didn't know where the Jukima were going or where we would settle. I sometimes dreamed the Jukima dreams of a beautiful village with terraces laid in stone, and solid, stone houses. It had the feeling of being a place where leisure was a kind of wealth and the mind would be free to invent. The people who lived there had a serene complexity to them. This settled place felt like a worthy goal to have.

As we walked, we all toughened. Although we were usually hungry, we burned with the chemistry of our bodies using themselves to capacity, refining them for the task of placing one foot in front of another smoothly and strongly, tiring less soon each day. The faces I saw around me took on a lean intensity of purpose – that of migration and survival. I sometimes walked near Zhixo, who had no wife to speak with -- his wife had died many years before, and there were no unattached women of his age among us.

Zhixo and I walked in silence for a bit, and I marveled at how my calloused feet had become like shoes to me, insensitive to the rough gravel that I trod upon. I asked Zhixo, "Do you know where we are going?" And then I thought I was being rude, or asking him to betray an inability. But no, he was like Frederick in that way. He simply said, "I haven't been this way before." He had an idea of the direction that was necessary, and was looking for signs of the familiar. And sometimes he chose this way or that way because choice was necessary.

My footsteps were hypnotic, and my thoughts roamed freely. I fell into a morose silence, trying to recall with exactness the texts of the writing I had thrown into the fire. The ideas that had inspired the writing were still in my mind. The rest of that day I spent silently repeating the words I'd written, until they were as unvarying as the stories the Jukima told their children.

We spent the night on rocky ground and there was little to eat. My bones ached, and the stars were as cold and sharp as the pointed gravel. And then I dreamed. In this dream, I was hiking over rough ground – terrain that was familiar to me from the trek we had already endured. In this dream I was aware of pacing myself until my beating heart and the pumping of my legs was a synchronized rhythm, and I felt nothing but that and my strength. I passed boulders similar to those I had passed on my climb to the Jukima camp on my first day among them. These boulders had rolled themselves into place and had attached there, like monuments to endurance.

In the dream, the trail divided. It was bisected by a boulder that was blackened with lichens, its profile stern against the bright sky. The path to the right seemed correct, and it was this path that I chose. And when the decision was made, I awakened to hard ground and the weak light of dawn. The night had been so cold that there was frost on the ground, and when I stood, clumsily, I saw that my reclining body had left its impression on the grass. As we walked that day, I told Zhixo, "If we had a road to walk upon, we would be there by now." I was immediately sorry for what I'd said, but Zhixo said nothing. He didn't say, "If we had a road to walk upon, we wouldn't be the same people."

We walked for hours, and then Zhixo stopped. I saw a boulder bisecting the trail. It was scabbed with lichens, and it had a stern profile. We took the trail to the right. As we walked, the effort became less -- this was a place where the slope was more gentle. The mountain ahead of us would look like a saddle, or the groove worn in a stone stair-step by thousands of rubbing feet. Zhixo led us up and over this peak-rubbed-to-a-curve. Before us we saw a shallow valley, concealed by the elevation of the land we had just traversed. The grass in the valley was long and pale and heavy with seeds, and there was water – a spring that didn't exactly flow, but rather leaked into a marshy pool. This water went nowhere, but soaked back into the softened ground and didn't spill over to make its way to larger streams, to rivers, or to a sea.

When Zhixo said, "We will stop here," I sank down gratefully. I thought that we would stay here for awhile. We were all so hungry and exhausted that the little valley already had a look of familiarity to it. By evening, we had built our temporary shelters and had placed stones on the ground in rings, as the foundations for our new habitation. Our hearth-fire that night added its slight texture of smoke to the clouds that had begun to assemble so that the sun could paint them with its evening colors. We were tired. We had no dinner that night – only water.

When we abandoned our mountain village, we destroyed everything, but the gardens still remained. The species of plants that could survive without our nurturing would spread, and others, the fragile, coddled ones, would vanish in only a season or two. What I regarded at our new settlement was the remainder of a garden – the grasses loaded with grain were too concentrated, too plentiful, to have arrived in this spot randomly. It was a garden gone wild, and I wondered, "whose?"

I asked Zhixo, "Have you been to this place before?"

He said, "Never."

I corrected myself, and asked, "Have the *Jukima* been to this place before?"

He answered, "Who can say?"

We did what was necessary to do and soon the houses were constructed and the gardens planted, but this time the gardens were closer to our houses, and close to the pool fed by the small spring. We cut armfuls of the tall grass and bundled them for thatch. The houses were warm and strong. It was necessary for the women to go down nearly to the forest to cut the saplings for the poles for the houses, but we didn't yet venture into the thickness of the lower land. The men made forays into the forest to hunt, and there was fresh meat to eat, and meat to dry over the fire. The Indians were as always: wary, good-natured, competent, and uncomplaining. It was a good place -- perhaps not so good as the home we had left -- but good enough.

The next piece of my life with the Jukima marked the beginning of drastic changes. In thinking back, I know I had come to associate these sorts of changes with the dank, jungled places. The changes began harmlessly enough. After we had been in the small valley for a period of weeks, I had gone with a party of women down past the forest's edge and into its murkiness. Our gardens had only then begun to sprout, and we needed fresher food than we could gather from the slopes of the mountains. We were a small group, and had left the children behind. As we descended, we could see below us the textured forest with its curvaceous clefts where water ran, and the cloud-shadows that wandered, unattached, on the mass of green. The tree tops looked as neat and round as the tufts of lichens that grew on the rocks. But it was not that way under the trees, and I knew from experience the forest's complexities.

On the first two nights, we camped on the slope of the mountain. On the third day, we began to descend into the forest where there would be fruits to gather. We moved very slowly, ever vigilant for snakes. The foliage drooped and moisture pattered from it. We pushed the leaves away from us carefully. As we descended, the day warmed and then grew hot and airless. The warming of the air made me anxious. The trees pressed close to us, and seemed to give off a heat like the heat of beasts. The vistas were near and opaque, and anything or anyone could be concealed.

The Xangu were real to me by then, and were any people whose hands were filled with weapons and whose hearts had no place for those not of their group. They were dangerous because of their certainty. They were the bureaucrats of war -- heartlessly rulebound to whatever restrictions and permissions that formed the structure of their lives. I imagined that the Xangu were there in every forest pocket that I sensed, but couldn't see.

It was afternoon when we came unexpectedly upon a village of Indians who were unknown to us. Lajima was with us, and Meeri, Idisa's daughter, and a few others were there. We were quiet as we went, carrying our woven bags that we used to gather food. We discovered some bushes of the berries that leave coolness in the mouth, but there were few berries on the twigs when there should have been many, and so we looked at one another, not understanding. It was then that we smelled the heavy aromas of human habitation. It was a thick smell of smoke and roasting meat, and the decay of refuse, and animal waste. We looked at one another in wonderment and with some alarm. As one body, we ducked low, breathing softly, collapsing quietly close to the ground.

Tishaak, who was young and impetuous, raised her eyebrows in a question and we decided without saying the reasons why we did, to go closer. We moved silently, invisibly – with stealth -- creeping through the forest with-not-sounding-feet. We saw the sharp peaks of the dwellings first, unlike any shapes around us, for these Indians grew houses that were round and pointed on their tips -- conical roofs extending to the ground. The smoke from the cooking fires hung around them, blue and ribboning slowly in the still air. That there had been little breeze this day had confused our senses, and had caused us to go so near without realizing that there were other humans close. We crouched low and peered through the foliage. Tishaak pinched my arm, not unkindly, and I saw the people, then, dense and muscular, with bronze skins and caps of shining hair. I didn't know them. They were not Tekhla.

"What if they have dogs?" Meeri whispered.

I said, "I don't think they have dogs or they would have sensed us by now and raised an alarm."

"Well, I don't know about that," said Meeri, suspiciously.

"Maybe they have lazy dogs?" I said, thinking about the indolent yellow mongrels the Tekhla kept.

"They have pigs," Lajima said. "I smell them." And I smelled them, too, an oily, rotten smell.

We watched the people moving about between their houses and I thought that they were sluggish, in the way that jungle-life makes the warm-blooded creatures cautious about squandering their energy. These people had stout, short, legs and they plodded when they moved about on their errands among the houses, between which they had hung hammocks of vines. Each hammock had the lumpy form of a sleeping person held within its webbing, and I thought of the living bundles of insects that spiders store in their webs. There was a trash of bones and shells and greasy leaves littering the ground. It made me uneasy, that these people might be as careless of each other as they were of their surroundings. I didn't wish to know them, and so I was surprised when Tishaak said, "I wonder if their men are kind?" The Jukima had few options among the opposite sex, and to Tishaak, perhaps the difference of these people was appealing? I thought that a party of Jukima men wouldn't be so curious or trusting as these women, but by then, I had come to believe that Zhixo was over-cautious. Zhixo's fears were not necessarily those of all the Jukima people. The sleepiness of the scene, the absence of dogs, the drone of insects that had not paused to acknowledge us, perhaps gave us confidence. Tishaak licked her lips and whispered, "Shall we leave them something?"

"We don't know if they know of us," said Lajima carefully, "and Zhixo would not allow it."

I said, "They don't look adventurous to me. I doubt if they ever leave this lower land."

Papeet said, "These people aren't the ones building a road. And perhaps they dream of us, already?"

Lajima said, "All right. We'll leave them something. Some small gift."

Tishaak took off a bracelet made of shell and colored stones and hung it from a twig, then said, "Should we go closer?"

"They could have brutal ways," said Meeri. "I think that they may eat monkeys." I didn't know why she had this idea, but it was a chilling thought. Monkeys were like nervously delicate people to the Jukima -- or like babies -- and eating them was unthinkable. I didn't know if cannibals existed in this forest.

I said, "I think we should leave, now. They could have sleeping dogs." Sleeping but nearly feral dogs, poisoned darts, spears, and quick tempers spawned from the squalor in which they lived. I didn't like them, because they were dirty. Although I was curious about these people, the risks of their differences were overwhelming. Without knowing exactly when it had happened, I had begun to think like a Jukima. With a worried glance at the bracelet that declared our presence here, I began to retreat. The other women followed this example.

We slid away from this unknown Indian settlement, and when we were far enough, Papeet said, "We don't have to speak of this in our village. Do we?" I knew instantly what she meant. Papeet was lively and impulsive, and occasionally impertinent to her elders. I didn't think that these people were Xangu -- they hadn't looked specifically dangerous. Zhixo would be alarmed, regardless, and I didn't want to have to move again so quickly.

Tishaak said, "I don't see why we have to speak of this. I'm certain they never travel to the higher places. They have what they need where they are."

I said, "Well, they don't look ambitious to me." This provoked a sharp look from Lajima, but then she relented. She said, "All right. We will agree not to speak of this." No dogs had barked at our presence, and except for the bracelet left on the twig, those Indians had no knowledge of us and surely there was no harm in this small gift? They would wonder about it, but it was a simple thing. On the next day, we found some fruits to gather near the forest's edge. Then we climbed the mountain again.

Our village took shape; our gardens were growing, and we had begun to make ornaments again. Life took on something of the texture of what it had been before we fled our other home. But there was a division now between the women and the men – a division caused by what we had seen in the forest and had not spoken about. The men were uneasy, for I knew they had begun to dream of a strangely disorderly people who seemed to mill about in a gloomy, shaded place. I dreamed of them as well, and my dream explained something to me that I hadn't understood at first. These people didn't laugh, or if they did, I hadn't heard any laughter as we watched them. The children didn't laugh as they played in the dirt and in the mud that fouled the doorways of the houses. The banter of women had not reached our ears. These people had been quiet, and this quietness had the feeling of oppression or suppressed anger. No one had laughed, and no dogs had barked. This worried me, but I couldn't say just why it did, or what it meant. However, the younger Jukima women were still curious. At the first opportunity, the same group of us traveled down the mountain again.

The Indians of the forest hadn't moved their village. We found it easily, approached quietly. This time as we watched, it seemed that no men were there. "The men are hunting," Papeet said, disappointed. This time, I observed these people more critically. Some of the women reclined in the hammocks, and others worked at grinding tubers into paste. We went closer, and could see everything clearly. There was no laughter among the children as they played their simple games. They arranged piles of leaves or stones, or threw sharpened sticks at targets. I watched as a heavy-browed woman spat into the porridge she was making. Lajima recoiled in disgust. I said, "It's all right. The Tekhla do that too. It softens the mixture." Lajima looked at me incredulously. "Do your people do that?" she whispered, and I said, "No. They never do." She turned again to watch, but her face tightened into a frown.

"The men must be industrious hunters?" Tishaak said hopefully. Papeet said, "The men looked strong, to me." I reminded myself that these were teen-agers; the Jukima men were few, and so I said nothing. I saw that some of the houses had pigs tied to them with ropes. I was startled when I realized that they were ropes from modern culture, not made of vines. I began to notice other things. A dented, blackened coffee pot near a hearth-fire. Although most of the people were nearly naked, incredibly, one woman wore a modern brassiere. Some of the litter on the ground was modern, as well. Rusted cans. Bits of plastic. I saw a discarded flashlight. Seeing those things gave me a pang of hope. It was garbage, but it was partly modern garbage, and perhaps there was direct contact between these people and modern life? Some sort of regular schedule of trade? Someone I could speak with, and who could lead me home? This thought made me love the women I was with all the more. I loved the open gaze with which each woman regarded me when we spoke. It was like the unconditional love of a treasured friend. I began to ache with the thought of leaving them, someday.

Our group stayed in the jungle for three days gathering fruit to dry. Each day, late in the afternoon, we approached the village to watch. On the third day, the men returned. It was terrible, what we saw. We heard their noisy approach for a long distance before they appeared. We were frightened, but frozen in our places because any movement might bring discovery. We remained where we were and watched. The men seemed to be drunk or addled by strong emotion. Each man had a bow slung across his shoulders, and a quiver of arrows at the hip. Their arms were full, but not with game. They carried masses of objects before them like soiled laundry. It was plunder of some modern type; I recognized this by the colors and metallic sheen of some things. One man wore on his shoulders a modern back-pack on a metal frame, and another was helmeted with a saucepan, and another held a shovel before him like a scepter, blood and hair gobbing its sharpened edge.

We heard laughter, but it was bawdy and crude. Horror traveled with these men, for the last Indians in the group carried two dead bodies. I thought from the way the bundles sagged and flopped that they had been carrying sacks of flour or grain, but then I realized that they were the lifeless bodies of men, with light hair and modern clothes. The dead men had beards on their faces. I was shocked to see that – the Jukima, and also these Indians that we saw, plucked their facial hair and their faces were smooth. The coarse hair sprouting from cheeks and chins made these dead men appear vulgar -- almost sub-human. Even less than that, they appeared to be carrion. Lifeless, hairy creatures divested of their spirits.

I dared not move even so much as to turn my head, but Lajima was crouched close to me and I hissed to her, "Xangu?" And she hissed back, "Yes. These people are Xangu. We have been so stupid." But yet, we couldn't move, so compelling was the terrible sight of this afternoon. It was so terrible that it seemed impossible. It may have seemed impossible, but I knew we were at mortal risk. The women had rolled from their hammocks or put down their stirring-sticks, and they clustered around the men. The women pinched the cloth of the dead men's clothes in their fingers, knocked on their boots with their knuckles, exclaimed over the contents of the pack as it was spilled out onto the ground for their inspection. I saw binoculars, canned goods, foil packets of dried foods, and a first aid kit with a chunky red cross emblem painted on it, and there were small bundles of clothes. I was ashamed of the way my mouth watered to see the cans of soup rolling about on the ground as the women nudged them with their bare feet. The Jukima women and I squatted, unmoving as tree roots.

From the Jukima I had learned that death is to be honored as a passage that continues a heroic journey. Each life is a fable that is carried forward. The shell that is the body is honored with washing, decorations, and respectful touch, as though it could still feel and appreciate. Its spirit presses close to it until the preparations are completed, and then the body is burned on a pyre. We breathe the smoke of the funeral fire like a spirit we make complete again, in all of us. The smoke is the vapor of our dreams, connecting us through generations. This way is correct and commemorative. The body that was the spirit's container is blessed for the worthiness of what it once housed.

What I saw before me was the nightmare of complete disrespect. It was appalling, as though somehow these Indians had no sense of the similarities between them and other human beings. I had not been confronted with such depravity before, and so near to me that I could smell it. These people pulled off the boots of the dead men, and I thought I could hear the dry snap of bones. The bodies flopped in a macabre animation at the pushing and pulling as their clothes were stripped off. The dead men looked more vulnerable in their pink nakedness than anything I had ever seen, as pitiful as the dimpled skins of birds plucked bald. The children poked fingers into the opaque orbits of eyes, squealed, and poked again. They stretched back the dead men's lips to look at the fillings in their teeth, tapping on the teeth with their nails. They pulled hanks of hair from the men's heads.

The grotesque laughter of these Indians was like a growl to me, a threatening rumble that went on and on. Who would be there to hear us women if we were discovered, attacked, and cried out for help? Who would hear us? These people had been here all along, in this forest if not in this exact place, and who knew how many others there were like them? I stole a glance at Lajima and her mouth was opened as if a scream were being pushed back -- pushed back until her eyes bulged from the strain of her silence. We retreated then, not daring to breathe or to stand upright until we were a long way away.

Chapter Nineteen

Our small group of women returned to the Jukima village as rapidly as we were able. We didn't stop to build campfires at night. We slept on the bare earth, beginning again when it was light enough to see our way. We had decided that the Xangu we had seen in the forest were cannibals. They were depraved. Corrupted. It was a culture in ruins. When we were far enough away from the forest to speak freely again, Lajima had said, "Zhixo was right. I didn't want to move from our last place, but he was right to keep us far away from anyone." I couldn't disagree.

When we arrived at our village, we told Zhixo about everything we had seen. We apologized for our duplicity in not telling him immediately about the village we had found, and we apologized for leaving the little gift on the bush. We were weeping as we told him these things; we were so ashamed of our mistake. However, Zhixo said he was not sorry we had seen the Xangu and the dead white men, because it was better to know of this danger than to be ignorant. He forgave us. That evening, he called a meeting of everyone and said that we must scatter the thatch of our houses, uproot the gardens and scatter everything in them. We must strew the stones of our houses' foundations until they seemed to be naturally placed. And then we were to pack what little we had, and we would begin to journey again.

We would follow Zhixo away from this village -- this piece of land that was too close to the Xangu who most likely ate the flesh of monkeys and of human beings. We did as Zhixo asked us to do. When the houses and gardens were scattered and the belongings packed for the journey, we slept on the open ground and built no fire that could have been seen from below. Before I slept, I watched the moon roll across the dark sky, stiff-cheeked and horrible with its silent, open mouth.

In the morning, we began our trek and traversed the mountain's flank, going farther north than where the monstrous village lay below us. The little food we brought soon was gone. We walked for many days and carried our hunger with us, heavier each day. We built no fires, and didn't alter the land we traversed. The children understood not to cry or laugh loudly, although there seemed to be no immediate danger because the Xangu were no doubt occupied with their spoils. The Jukima kept no dogs, and I understood now why the village we had seen had no dogs in it. The Indians below were hiding from retribution, and we were hiding from *them*, or from those like them. The noise of dogs would have given away location. The crying or laughter of children would have given them away. The Xangu were predators. I thought of us more and more as prey.

This was a time when hardship was heaped upon hardship, a trend that seemed unstoppable. It was necessary, eventually, for us to descend into the forest for food, although when we did so we were many sun's revolutions away from the Xangu village. The forest was a seethe of sounds that competed for attention, and the heat was damp and sickening. However, there was comfort in the closeness of my companions, and it seemed that when I traveled with these people, I was in a childlike state of invincibility. I had felt this way sometimes as a child when riding in a car driven by my father. I would doze and the slats of light that shone redly under my closed eyelids as we passed through sun and shade were like a kind of motionlessness. My father's hands were so firm and steady on the wheel of the car and his concentration was so complete that no harm could come to me. This was not a reasonable thought, but these people around me were all that I had to call home.

We stopped at what seemed to be a sullen place, but we had gone as far as we could travel that day and didn't want night to drop down upon us before we could explore where we were, and discover what our location offered. There was a slow stream of brown water that widened, not to a beach, but to a marshy smudge where water and land confused one another. The water had a musky odor. We would spend the night there, and we would fish and see what there was to be gathered. The fish we didn't eat that night, we would smoke over the fire we would build, and we would carry the smoked fish with us on our journey. There was no sign that other people had passed this way. The air was stale and swarms of gnats bothered us. It was the kind of brackish place where diseases are born.

It was distressing not to be able to see the sky except in complex-edged fragments. Even so, I was anticipating the roasted fish I would eat, and I hurried as I helped to clear away the vegetation with my knife to make a place where we could sleep on bare ground. I had my knife raised to chop at the slender pole of a young tree when I heard a woman scream! It was Tamura. At the moment she screamed, sunlight glanced off the flat of my blade, so it seemed that the flash and the scream were made of the same substance.

I later discovered that Tamura had reached into a clump of reeds; she had been reaching for what she thought was a small, colorful frog. She was as thoughtless as a child reaching for a shining object. But it was not a frog -- it was a snake, and it had bitten her hand. The flash of light on the blade of my knife and the scream occupied an instant that was peeled of its tiny concerns to reveal a deeper layer of the irrevocable. I turned, and the flash of light echoed my turning, shaping a perfect arc like the arc of a rainbow, When I turned, I saw the triangular head of the snake flicking back, striking once more at Tamura's still outstretched hand, and then vanishing into the reeds.

It happened so quickly. Tamura fell or jumped back, and her scream stretched to one, continuous wail. The coming together of the scream, the light, my turning toward and not away from the fusion of these things were like a jolt into awareness. In that instant, I became wholly myself again – not a Jukima woman, or a woman who traveled with the Jukima, or whoever I had become in the time that had passed since I had left Tuylo. I was prepared for this, without knowing how my preparedness had come to be.

I saw myself as if observed by another, and yet I was oddly conscious of this self-protective state of mind. I reached Tamura in two strides, two heartbeats, and pulled her farther from the clump of reeds. I cut away a strip of cloth from my clothes. I grasped her arm and tied the cloth tightly around it. I picked up a stick from the ground and laid it over the knot I had made in the cloth, looped the two ends of the cloth around it and tied them together, pulled it tight and twisted the stick until I heard the cloth creak. Then I tied the stick in place with another knot. The poison of the snake was now trapped in Tamura's hand and was not traveling to her heart. The pull and squeeze of her veins could not move the blood past the tourniquet I had made -- I knew that much. And then I turned to Zhixo, as a child might turn to a father to make something right that was impossible.

180

Zhixo did nothing and offered no advice, because there was nothing to do and no advice to give. The snake-bite had been mortal, and he knew that. Many things happened simultaneously, in what I remembered later as a series of stilled images. I saw Linari, Tamura's husband, drive his knife blade into the ground as though he were swearing a pledge. He squeezed his eyes shut. Tamura was quiet now, staring vacantly. Lajima dropped her bundle of leaves and said, "Ah," as one might exclaim at the surprise of a dropped and broken cooking pot.

No Jukima said anything. Tamura's hand had begun to look like bluish wax. How long had it been? Only a few minutes? If the tourniquet were not loosened, the hand would die and she would lose it, and if the tourniquet were loosened, the toxins would flow to her heart and she would lose her life. I thought of Sparks at the telegraph office in Tuylo and his missing thumb. I raised my knife and brought it down and cut off the hand. Tamura's body loosened in a faint. The hand lay upon the ground, obscene and absolutely loathsome. At that moment Baalu emerged from the reeds bearing a limp and headless serpent upon the flat of his knife, which was held out straight and distastefully away from his body.

Tamura did not die that night. The snake-bite would have killed her quickly, if I hadn't done what I did. I knew that, but still I doubted the rightness of what I had done. "This is witchcraft," said, Kaanu, Zhixo's brother. He said this with the immense certainty of an inquisitor. He squatted on the ground and watched me as though he had never seen me before.

"No, not witchcraft," Zhixo pronounced. "Witchcraft is a harmful power."

"And you think what she did was not harmful?" spat out Kaanu. Zhixo said, "I think that is how they treat snake-bite in the place she comes from." And then a pause, before he said, "Hers may be a brutal people. We do not know them." I didn't contradict him. I sat on the ground with my hands clasped around my knees and rocked like a fool.

Baalu said, "I think Tamura would be dead now, if she hadn't done it. No snake bit her arm, the part that is left. It has no marks of the snake-bite on it."

There was a murmuring of assent.

Zhixo said, "She is quick. She could be quick because she is confident, or because her people are sudden that way?"

And then Tondi said, almost as an idle comment, "She never liked her, I think."

That was true. I didn't particularly like Tamura. I thought her moody and sly, and unkind to her son. However, that dislike hadn't influenced my actions. I had done what I did because I had had the knowledge to act decisively, and I hadn't shirked. Whether or not the Jukima would understand my reasoning, I didn't know for certain. They had slight knowledge of the hidden aspects of human physiology, and I didn't have the strength to explain what little I knew about this.

"It's all the same. Tamura will be dead by morning," said Linari. At that he began to moan with an unrestrained, animal-like sound. Zhixo allowed this for a few moments, and then silenced him with a sharp word, lest his noise attract the Xangu. The afternoon was a terrible, elongated time. Drifts of mosquitoes whined over the nearly motionless water, and the mud stank. When Tamura tried to speak, once or twice, her voice smeared into meaninglessness.

Before night came, the men speared some fish, for that had to be done regardless, and there were some bitter, nut-like fruits on the ground that we gathered. Peeling their tough skins was a welcome distraction. However, I re-lived those few, singular moments of the afternoon again and again. The horrible sound of that instant was trapped within the caverns of my ears and had no escape.

There had been very little blood, for the tourniquet had been tight enough. If any poison had seeped through, it must be nothing compared to the assault upon the nerves that were now exposed. Tamura was strangely, absently, quiet. I made the women boil water to bathe Tamura's wound. They followed my instructions meticulously and without argument. A fire had been built, and they dipped brackish water into a cooking pot and dropped hot stones into the water until it boiled.

The women bathed Tamura's wound when the water cooled, and dressed it with medicinal leaves. Linari hung back and twisted his hands together in grief. I didn't go near Tamura, out of concern that I might frighten her with my presence. I doubted myself, berated myself in an interior dialogue that lacked hope of resolution, like the hoop of a snake with its tail in its mouth. I was a hasty, foolish woman and I had caused senseless and undue suffering, and I was ashamed. But still, Tamura hadn't died. And there was her child to consider. Tihana had seen all of this, and at first he had been neglected in the extremity of the moment. But now, Carogo tried to distract him with a little game that involved tossing pebbles into the air and clapping before they fell. Tihana was watching Carogo incredulously, his eyes wide but filmed, as though he had been stricken by fever. He hadn't spoken since his mother was bitten by the snake. I didn't know then, that he wouldn't speak again for weeks.

Every rustle in the leaves was a malevolent slithering. The few stars that were visible through gaps in the canopy were diffused by haze and very far away. We sat vigil with Tamura throughout the night. Some of the women sang songs that had the deep colors of grief, and we all scanned the darkness for dangers -- for the Xangu to come crashing through the bushes with flickering, forked tongues and bearing shovels clotted with blood and hair. The Jukima and I sat awake and waited for anything that might come. The morning seeped in, finally, with its pale light growing fully and rapidly into a withering heat. Tamura remained alive. Her face was leached of color, but her breathing was regular and strong. One of the women said, "I think she will live." I thought so, too. I ventured to sit next to her and take my turn at waving the flies away from her face.

Baalu asked me, "Is this how snake-bite is treated in the place you come from?"

I had to say, "No, it's not. We have our medicines. But I have none of that with me."

Then Baalu pronounced, "I think the people she comes from are a sudden people, but that's not always a bad thing, on some occasions?"

Zhixo asked, "Did you dream of this and not tell anyone what you dreamed?" It was an accusation -- that I had withheld critical knowledge.

I said, "No, I've never dreamed anything like this. The poison was in the hand and now the hand is gone. I did what I thought was best."

Zhixo said, "I believe you."

And Baalu said, "I believe you did what you thought was best." These words began to rebuild the fallen bridge between myself and the Jukima.

We stayed in that place for four days, and then carried Tamura up the mountain. I suspected that we wouldn't go down into the forest again for a long time. Linari walked beside his wife. Tondi walked at Tamura's other side and shaded her face, and Carogo and I walked behind them, side by side. Tamura's face was nearly blank, except for an anger that was beginning to narrow her eyes at bumps in the path.

Linari said, as though Tamura were not present, "She could be just now beginning to think of the things she cannot do.

Carry things with two hands. The normal ways of cooking and making things. I think that she will not be able to tend to our child." He said this almost as a question.

Carogo touched my arm tentatively. She said, "Tamura hasn't much liked mothering."

I said, "I know that. We *all* know that, but I've not heard it said before, until now."

Carogo looked momentarily guilty, and then said, "But it's the way she feels, in her heart." For some reason, because of some omission in her character, like a deformity of her spirit, Tamura couldn't give herself to her child. I sensed no aspect of blame in what Carogo had said. It was fact, and would have to be accommodated.

Linari had overheard and glanced back at Carogo, and then at me. He pursed his lips. "She is my wife," he said. Tamura was Linari's unconventional, irritable, beautiful wife. I waited. Linari looked at me with a strange expression of hopefulness, and said, "She is my wife and I will need to take care of her. But the boy is unhappy. You have seen that? So -- Tihana is *your* son now. You will take him into your house."

I was shocked at his words, and said, "But why? He's your son! You can care for him."

"I will need to care for Tamura," Linari said. "It will be all I can do. He is your son now," he repeated, with finality. And then, abruptly, Tamura began to laugh, a peculiar, gulping laugh. Her husband shook her gently by the shoulder, but Tamura continued laughing, and so he released her.

Zhixo had been listening, and turned to me and said, "You see how it is with her? I think it's the best thing, for you to claim the boy."

There was a logic to this idea that I understood. I said then, to Linari, "I will take Tihana as my son, but you are still the father."

"Yes, I am the father, " Linari said, "but the boy will live with you."

I didn't yet fully comprehend what I had taken on, but I understood that this was somehow the correct thing. I thought of the Tekhla infant I had failed to save. This could be a reparation for that failure, and I would do what Linari asked. The group of us had been rearranged. Baalu carried Tihana, who had fallen asleep, his face flushed and moist. He hadn't heard what was to become of him. The air began to smell sweet again, and a breeze lifted my hair.

With my acceptance of Tihana, the mood lightened, nearly

as much as it did when there was a birth in the village. I decided that I would teach Tihana English, and that it would be our secret language. Slowly, we began to talk of other things as we climbed back up the mountain, Tamura carried in a litter as the Jukima had once carried me.

Lajima said, "We will make her some broth, from the fish we have."

"Yes, we will feed her," I said.

Chapter Twenty

We carried Tamura up the slope. Once we had reached a higher elevation, we traveled so quickly and far that I became dizzy. We were hungry. We stopped long enough to boil some fish into a broth for Tamura. Tondi tipped the bowl toward Tamura's mouth, and she drank it tentatively at first, and then avidly. That was good, and we continued, climbing higher up the face of the mountain at an angle so gradual that we felt the height primarily by the tang in the air -- its freshness and coolness against our skins. This aroma and texture was familiar to me, and I knew that we would find a new place to settle, and it would be a place of tingling air, and these people all around me.

It was several days after Tamura was bitten by the snake that Zhixo led us to a small valley that was higher than the first mountain home where I had lived with the Jukima. It was a concealed place, and we had to pass into the valley through a funnel-shaped opening between cliffs where the wind formed itself into a wedge until we had to lean against its force. The valley was held by two strong arms of the mountain, and there were trees that were dwarfed by the altitude and wind, and there were mountain goats that moved on suckered hooves over the crags with a lively clatter. From this cradled valley, we couldn't see the forest or the weather moving toward us. I thought it would be cold there sometimes, but it was a good place and we would build houses again. It was on the way to nowhere else, and I thought that no road could come this far.

When we settled in the valley Zhixo had found for us, we had just enough time to dig the gardens and plant the seeds before the not-stopping rains began, although at such an altitude the rain was scarcely ripe in the clouds and it misted down. The earth of this valley was black and fragrant, and it sparkled with claret-red stones that I hoped were garnets and not rubies. The Jukima gathered them to fashion into beads, but I did not, in the event that they were indeed precious stones, and would be seen at some future time by those who would be drawn to this location by the desire for wealth. I didn't know how long we would stay, or what the future held. The stones didn't seem like wealth to me, because they were common in this valley. I have never understood how the rarity of a thing was in itself a sign of its value -- a chunk of naturally faceted quartz holds much more fascination for me that did those red-colored stones.

On some days, the rains relented and the clouds opened enough to allow the sun to pull the shoots from the earth and firm them. We placed stones in a circle for a common hearth, and arranged our houses around this hub. We were hungry until the first harvest, but we survived. There was sometimes meat to eat, and we boiled the roots of the broad-leafed, rough plants that grew there, to make a broth. We fabricated again those tools we used to make the stuff of our lives. Tihana's father built a loom for me, and Carogo showed me how to weave. Our lives subsided into normalcy.

Linari was as solicitous of me and my new son as a bachelor uncle would have been, one who was immersed in the busy-ness of his own life and who was respectful but somewhat mystified by women. Linari tended to his wife with a gentle wariness, because she often stubbornly refused to do simple things that she was capable of doing, or perhaps it was that she had grown even less attached to her surroundings? It seemed that whatever unknown opportunities she had hoped for had outdistanced her. Her arm healed. I didn't know if she blamed me, but if she did, she wouldn't say. I didn't know if she was grateful to be alive. She moved among all of us nervously, as though a suspicion had been justified. We appreciated her as one might appreciate a beautiful flower that has no use except for pleasure for our eyes. We didn't criticize her for what she couldn't accomplish. We accepted her as a family might, in the sense of accepting her importance to us.

My house in the valley was a hemisphere made of limber saplings brought up from below where the trees grew more thickly. Linari built its frame and he was meticulous, making it with pride because it would hold me and his son. He said, "The wind will hump over this house and not uproot it." He was right. The wind pushed it closer to the earth. Its covering was plain on the exterior, a thatch of silvered-yellow grasses that reached nearly to the ground, but inside it was rich with detail and color. From the outside, the Jukima houses and mine were identical. However, I wove mats and padded the walls with them, curving them around warmly in an intricate and kindly landscape. The landscape outside was drawn with monochromatic roughness -- stark and narrow in its colors: gray, brown, muted yellow, and the iron-dark, severe tones of the mountains' faces that rose up on all sides. Inside, I surrounded myself with shifts of color and layers of patterns. This was what I wanted now. The mats were woven as I had learned by watching the Tekhla make them, and so I brought a little bit of that history forward.

I didn't want to walk upon the bare earth of the floor, and so I covered the floor with rushes that were replaced and freshened often. I made a nest for Tihana. I was free to create my surroundings, discovering what was pleasing to me now. The Jukima's unspoken rules had to do with deference to one another, but not so much with stylized restrictions. I was amused when Carogo copied my example by piling the floor of her house with rushes until it smelled like a stable in which sweet-breathed animals are comfortable. She said, "This will be good for my child, too." Carogo's child would be born in that valley.

I laced braided cords from the sapling struts and hung baskets from them, and I used my knife to make two plain chairs and a table that were unlike anything the Jukima had ever seen, except in dreams. The process was laboriously slow, but when I was finished, I would sit on a chair and eat my meals from the table. This was such a simple and obvious idea that I nearly wept when I realized that I could have done that before. I taught Tihana to sit on a chair, and I instructed him as best I could in the social graces of my culture, as well as the Jukima ways as I understood them. When we were alone together, we took our meals seated upon the chairs, and we spoke English. As a mother, I couldn't allow the obliteration of the self that I was. I examined what I still believed, so that I could impart this to my son in what I did and said. In this way, Tihana began to give my personality back to me.

The rainy season kept us in our houses for long periods of time and was a peaceful setting where I could begin to know my son, and could begin to teach him my personal language. It was a wonderment to speak my own language again. I had understood in a conceptual way that language, with its permissions and limitations, was linked to how the world was perceived. Now, I saw that my very thoughts had changed. I

188

continued to think of night as being in back of day, and of the night of the flooding as a mouth with a scream caught inside it. A falling star would make me think of the seed of an ancestor returning to colonize the earth. I apologized to the food I ate, for taking its portion of sunlight into myself. I no longer thought of situations as having resolutions that were opposites -- many dilemmas were unclear and strange, and required inventive thought and compromise.

We had food and shelter and we had our routines, and could think again of other things than the provision of essentials. I could see that the faces of the people around me had become round again as their bones retreated, but I had no mirror in which to inspect my own face. I sometimes saw the webbing of jet-trails in the sky, lacing the world smaller and tighter. I wondered about the people in those planes, eating and drinking, conversing, dozing, and accepting their luxuries as common.

It was winter, and the moon was a rind or paring, tipped and supporting a curve of dark sky. Tihana was sleeping heavily, dropped into the portion of sleep where there are no dreams, and his body, if I picked him up, would be limp with sleep and would not adjust itself to my arms. He smelled like torn grass or the faint sweetness of clean fur. I had become a good mother. At first, I worried about the austerity of Tihana's quietness. What he had witnessed had been unspeakable, as the imprints upon the mind of a child of war are unspeakable. I thought for a time that he had forgotten how to speak and that he might be afraid of me for what I had done to his mother.

In a genuine sense, Tihana had lost his mother, however flawed she had been in that role. I saw it as not so much an abandonment as an inability. She was still among us, and she greeted Tihana pleasantly when she saw him, although she didn't ask me if she could take him into her house, and she didn't go out of her way to encounter him. The event of the snake-bite and the loss of her hand had sent her so deeply within her own mind that she laughed, sometimes for a long time, when there was no reason, or she sat in her house and did nothing. I had flowed into the void that was left by her absence and had taken up the work of nurturing a child.

I was depending upon the resilience of the very young. Tihana was just a little boy. His curiosity began to unfold, and he began to speak again. He began to comment on his surroundings. "Look how the centipede tickles the ground with its many legs." Or, "Does it hurt the fish, when the hunters spear them?" And finally, he asked, "Can snakes get into this house?"

I said, "No, the hearth-fire keeps them away," although I didn't know if this was true.

Tihana once brought me a rock with a fossil print pressed into it. He handed it to me, and my thumb exactly fit its ribbed hollow. I asked, "What do you think that is?" He shrugged. "It came from an ocean," I said, and then I explained. "An ocean is like a land of water, and if one is far out on it, it is flat all around the horizon."

Tihana said, "There would be nothing to hang onto." On the occasions where we had found small lakes, Tihana had remained prudently in the shallows. He couldn't swim, because he had had little opportunity to learn that skill. He reached for the rock with the fossil print and studied it. "It's a shell," he said. "Or, where a shell has been."

Tihana looked back at the mountains. "Are there mountains under the ocean water?" he asked.

"Yes, there are," I told him. "And valleys. I think there are even rivers, of hotter or colder water, faster or slower than what is around them."

"That's strange," Tihana said. "Rivers of water in the water." We looked at the fossil together. Its ribs fanned out in rays from the small tuck that folded them in and fastened them. Tihana blew on the rock and a fine grit flew up. "This is like a ghost," he said. He asked, "Did it take a long time?"

"Did what take a long time?" I asked him.

"For the ocean to rise and the water to drain away?"

"Yes. A very long time."

He cocked his head, was quiet a moment. He said, "We'll keep this," and handed the bit of rock back to me. The mountains seemed different, then -- not permanent, but caught by the instability of all things. I noticed that black shadows moved over the stony crags of the mountains until the rock seemed to buckle or stretch. I took the piece of rock and later made it into a bead, which I wore on a cord around my neck.

This village suggested a security that I hadn't felt in the other places where I'd lived with the Jukima. I learned much about the little boy through my dreams, because often we would dream the same things. He dreamed boyishly of accomplishing the simple but grandiose feats of running and climbing. I enjoyed these dreams, and during the days sometimes I would run with him. I shortened my pace to match his steps.

Sometimes Tihana dreamed a nightmare of reed-stalks seen in bright sunlight. They were sharply shadowed, glistening and pointed. The sky sizzled with heat. I don't think he ever saw the snake that had bitten his mother, although it had been explained to him. There were no snakes in our valley, or none that I ever saw. Tihana was about four years old when we came to our mountain home, and I enjoyed his steady glow of warmth as I carried him on my hip. It was as though he was a part of my own body and had always been there.

Tihana took such pleasure in visual things. The shifting glow of a sunset was like an orchestration to him. His coming upon a back-lit, veiny leaf would cause him to exclaim with happiness. He would summon me, quickly, quickly, to share his discovery before it faded. He enjoyed watching the birds that spiraled on the winds above us. He stalked the birds that perched on the rocks, and was disappointed that each time he came close, they lifted up and flew away from him. He meant no harm. I told him, "Be invisible, and they will let you approach them." I meant it as a game, but he believed me and said, "If I concentrate enough on this idea, I will be invisible to them." He tried and tried, but they always saw him and flew away. I admired his perseverance.

I brought small gifts to Tihana for his contemplation: a leaf-turned-to-lace, reduced to its structure, a stone with a mossy patch that looked like the head of a wolf, and the precious, ivoried skull of a mouse. Our valley had its moments of desolation, when the steely shadows insinuated themselves down the crags just before the sky dimmed to evening, but to Tihana it was a place full to saturation with experiences.

Because of Tihana, I discovered my differences from my own mother. How could she have noticed as much about any of her many children as I did about Tihana? She must have been so weary, trying to keep up with all of us. My mother's competence had been like a hard sheen that both allowed her to function, and was a constriction to her personality. I thought that she had given too much, and had been unreasonably impoverished because of it. I began to see her as a person, and as I did so, I became an adult.

My environment during the time in the high valley was shaped by weather -- by the subtle changing of seasons. And, my world was shaped by its songs. The Jukima sang often – spontaneously -- or they sang songs at celebrations. I came to associate music with births and deaths and weddings, and with work, and leisure, and with a drumming rain. I could identify the song of each thing and person, and condition.

I didn't write anything in this valley home. There was no bark for my tablets, and I had seen how fragile my scratchings of words were, how easily discarded. However, committing my thoughts to memory came more easily as time passed. I found it increasingly difficult to imagine the person I would be if I were to leave the Jukima. And who knew what changes, what inventions or knowledge had happened even in the relatively short time I had been away from my former life?

Shortly after we came to the valley, I began to work on my map again. Eventually, I put the map away and concentrated on where I was. The valley was like a room that held our tiny lives. I didn't know that it would be the last place where I would make my home with the Jukima, because I still dreamed of their terraced home-land with them, and thought that I would be with them when they found it. Although our home was higher than the village we had left, it had a humbling feeling of "below-ness" to it, and the wind that came at us from many directions was shaped and tuned by the angles of the mountains, in extrusions of sound and force. When this wind was blowing aggressively I felt like a spindly interruption walking against it.

Chapter Twenty-one

Carogo had her baby after we became settled in the valley, and by then I had come to know Tihana as a son. We were new mothers together. I had seen other births, but I was fearful for my friend because she was the closest person to me other than Tihana. I had my ideas about medicines and devices that would preserve her and her baby if the birth were complicated, and I was troubled by the absence of these things.

As Carogo climbed the slope of her labor, the women attending her spoke of other births. Tondi said, "Remember how Tishaak was born?" Tishaak smiled with a guilty pride. Tondi said, "Her feet came first, as though she was testing the coldness of water before entering it."

Lajima said, "When Tareeth gave birth, it was never so long as this." I asked, "Is Tareeth an ancestor?" for there was no one of that name among us. "We all know of Tareeth," Tishaak said. Even Carogo smiled at the mention of Tareeth. Tishaak said, "She had very many children and each birth was easier than the last. Each child was born pink and loud." For this one quality, Tareeth's life had been worthy of recording in a fable. She gave the Jukima women hope.

As Carogo's labor grew more serious and demanding, she squatted on the ground, supported upright by the elbows by the women. I petted her hair and gave her small sips of water, although I don't think that she noticed. Between contractions, her face took on a quizzically introspective, listening expression. If women's months are measured by the tidal pull, there was nothing of that sort of measurement in the convulsion that was childbirth. It was like a geological upheaval -- profoundly wounding and generative, although at its conclusion, there would be only a small infant and a few modest women to see how it came.

When a new contraction grabbed her, Carogo's face would harden like the distorted face of a Mayan sculpture of a woman locked into the struggle of childbirth. Her expression was like a scream turned to stone. I asked Tondi, the midwife among us, "Is there nothing you can do to help her?" She said, "See how she helps herself? She pushes gigantically, and that shortens the time."

Carogo's baby came in the false dawn when the birds began to sing the sun out of its hiding place. It was very quick, then, and liquid, the baby dropping down into the waiting hands. There was silence, and then the baby's outraged bellow, and the efficient scurrying to clear her gummy mouth and wash away her waxy coating and rub her skin to pinkness. The baby's limbs were firm, her arms thrusting out in jitters, her legs drawn up protectively. I said, nonsensically, "That's good. She weighs about seven pounds." The women ignored this, eased Carogo down, and placed the infant upon her hollowed belly.

Carogo said, "I would like some tea," and then gazed for the first time at the face of her daughter. Her eyes took on an almost drunken expression of joy mixed with exhaustion. At the stroking of the mother's finger against the baby's cheek, the baby's mouth slid toward the touch and her lips smacked impatiently. Carogo laughed and said, "She already knows what she wants." And then she turned to me and said, "Nweli, my friend, I would like you to name her." I saw the other women glance at one another quickly, and then Lajima said, "Yes, Nweli should name her." This was so unexpected that I was uncertain, and then the name came to me. I said, "You could name her 'Falatha.'"

"That is not one of our names!" said Papeet, but Carogo said, "Falatha. It has a good sound." That evening I watched Tihana as he slept, and the haze of his sweet breath was like a cloud around him. I thought that both Carogo and her baby had survived a terrible and splendid journey, but I wondered, could there not be another, gentler scheme for how a life begins? The birth of Carogo's daughter was an event that gathered celebrations around it. We all enjoyed this new presence in our group. It made our valley seem more like a place where we could stay for a long time.

The seasons passed in quiet transitions, and Carogo's daughter thrived and grew. Carogo and Lajima and I sat on the floor of rushes and drank strong, bitter tea and watched Tihana playing with the child. Lajima asked me, "What of your family, now?" and then, considerately, "What of your 'other' family?"

I said, "They must think I'm dead by now."

"They must grieve for you very much," Carogo said.

"Yes -- I'm sure they do, but there are so many of us. We were very crowded, in our house."

"Perhaps they dream of you here?" said Lajima.

I said, "They may, but I don't know what they would think about that. They seem so far away from me now."

"Sometimes I think we are the farthest people," Carogo said, and pulled her cloak close around her shoulders. This was on the first night of the snow. It had snowed on the mountains that day. We could see it, not its individual flakes, but its effects, smoothing out the wrinkles of the peaks, like white cloth thrown over them. It made the valley seem farther from everything, somehow, and closer to the sky. The presence of the snow drew us closer together in our houses.

Tihana had a string of chunky beads and was showing them to Carogo's child, each of them singly, for they were of different colors and designs. I don't know how the little girl saw them. They must have been like new planets to her.

I asked Carogo, "If we could climb those mountains, do you think there might be other, higher mountains behind them?"

"If we climbed the mountain with snow, it could be the top of the world," she answered.

"And would we see, do you think, if there is a road, or if no road has come this far?"

Carogo considered this soberly, and said, "Perhaps we should climb it." Tihana, who had been listening, said, "I could climb that high. I am certain of it." I stroked his cheek and said, "My little mountain goat." He shrugged my touch away, affronted. "I could climb it," he said.

I thought that the snow wouldn't come as low as the valley. We felt safe where we were and didn't climb the mountain that season, but it remained a tantalizing goal. These were the best times, when my house was full of people and there were children there. I said, "Perhaps my sisters are all married now. There could be many children."

Papeet looked at me shyly and said, "I will marry in a few seasons." She was the only girl of her age who remained unmarried, and she had no prospects. The future of these people was so fragile. A world without the Jukima in it was not one I could imagine. I asked, "But who will you marry?" Papeet said, "When we join with other Jukima for the betrothing, I will meet my husband."

"What do you mean when you join with other Jukima?" I

couldn't believe what I was hearing. I had thought these people were the only ones!

Carogo said, "After the Xangu came, we never gathered in large groups again. The ones of our ancestors who remained, split apart, with just a few in each group. They went different ways. That's what we think."

"And these few, these groups, made other villages?"

"Or they wander," Lajima said.

"Yes, they wander," Carogo said. "They have crossed a desert, and they stayed for a time beside a wide river. Or, they lived in the caves. They are somewhere."

Lajima added, "We have unmarried women among us here, and so we will travel one day to find others of the Jukima." And she raised her eyebrows at me, including me in their company.

"But when the Xangu came, that was generations ago," I said.

"Yes, generations," Carogo said.

Lajima fingered the cloth of her cloak and distractedly watched the child as she searched for a bead that had rolled down into the rushes. The child's squatty fingers probed and she poked out her lower lip. I said, "Tihana, find it for her please." Tihana had been listening, and I wondered what the implications were for him, as well? I had seen in dreams arid landscapes, with their buff-colored sand, and spires of weathered rock like the devastated columns of temples, and I didn't know what to make of them. I had seen the caves, muddied with the smoke of torches and campfires and with drawings of animals on their walls -- some of them animals that no one recognized anymore. And there was a river, too, very wide and whose water ran white as though with a slurry of chalk. I hoped that Lajima was right, but I didn't think so. These could have been images of long ago.

When the nights were clear and warm, we gathered around the common hearth and told stories. Most of these stories were like gossip about people who were no longer with us. I could trace my lineage -- my genealogy -- back only a few generations, and none of these people had names with any meaning for the Jukima. I didn't know the stories of my own ancestors' lives as I should. Whatever they might have learned in their lives was lost to me. The Jukima didn't disapprove of my not knowing, but they didn't understand how it could be. For them, the connections made among people and among all things, were glimpses of a system, an ordering, that was fluid and exquisitely responsive.

Tihana, at this stage of his life, had the temporarily blurred, awkward form of a boy growing through phases so rapidly that his body seemed disjointed. Soon, he would wear a cloak of white feathers that I would make for him and he would become an acknowledged hunter, apologizing always to the creatures he killed for food. As a son, he was more than sufficient.

I didn't know exactly how long I had been with the Jukima, but I tried to compute the number of times the rainy season had come. I could remember eleven times, which amounted to twelve if one included the rain that had flooded the Tekhla village. Twelve years. I thought that Tihana was about sixteen or seventeen -- on the brink of becoming an adult. I was restless, without knowing exactly when that restlessness had begun to push to the surface. Perhaps it was because Tihana would soon have the dance that would mark his coming-of-age, and then he would move into his own house. The end of Tihana's childhood was to be framed in that way -- it would be finished.

There was a spring of cold water near the cleft that was the valley's entrance. On the day of the dance for Tihana and the other boys who would come-of-age, Lajima and I had gone to fetch water. We carried the water in sacks made of skins, and the water in each sack was as heavy as a stone of similar size would be. If one has water close at hand, one cannot comprehend how essential water is and what a task it is to fetch it. We carried back the water that would be used for drinking and cooking and washing. Dark birds wheeled above us, and the sky was filled with rapidly moving clouds. I said, "This day is exciting."

Lajima snorted and said, "Carrying water is not exciting." And then she agreed with me and said, "This day makes me feel like dancing." There was a tingling in the air, a coldness coming, a change of pressure or a storm of the kind where lightning jumps from peak to peak. We could see the smoke rising from the Jukima houses, and the smoke was rushing away in imitation of the clouds.

Later on that day, snow began to fall on the higher peaks and a scattering of wet, clinging flakes fell upon the village, although at first they melted when they touched the ground. I showed Carogo's daughter, Falatha, how to catch snow-flakes on her tongue and this thrilled her, but she complained when they vanished quickly from her warm hands. Tihana was not there when the snow began. For the first time, he had gone hunting with the men, along with three other boys of roughly his own age. As the snow began to fall earnestly, the hunting party returned. When I looked up and saw Tihana, surrounded by the others, it was as if a circle had closed. I felt such relief to see him. We all clustered around the returning men, who had gone down into the forest and had returned with game. We exclaimed politely over what they had brought to us -- a modest collection of small animals that were of good-hearted, plant-eating species and generous in their sacrifices to us.

Tihana displayed to me what he had killed -- just one small animal, already cold and stiff. A swipe of blood had stiffened on the fur. Its eyes were closed. Tihana wouldn't look at me directly, but presented me with his trophy and asked, "Do you know how to prepare this for eating?" I said that I did, and I took it from him. The tufted ears of the creature were flattened against its head and its lips were drawn back to show tiny, rounded teeth. Its last, defiant gesture had been too harmless to frighten anyone.

The celebration for Tihana and the other boys-turned-men was held that night. The snow had melted from the ground, but in the moonlight I could see that the mountain peaks were white. Carogo had helped me make a cloak of feathers for myself and one for Tihana -- his first. My cloak was light on my shoulders. Each small movement was exaggerated in sweeping drifts that had their own momentum. The feathers swayed as a ripple in water continues until replaced by one that has had a stronger or more recent push. Although we wore feathers, we couldn't fly, at least not in the ordinary manner. It was more that we were suspended in a levitation of spirit.

I danced with the Jukima, but I felt I would never dance as well as they did. I tried to place myself within the rhythm in the fullest, most connected sense. We danced for hours, and some of the Jukima, Tihana included, danced for two days. My bones ached and I knew them this way as the delicate framework that held me upright in the flawed position of a human being. My muscles quivered, and from this I knew their strength and possibilities.   My vision blurred as my eyes watered from fatigue, and so I looked inward.

When I couldn't continue, I sat with the others who had dropped away. I watched Tihana as he danced with the other boys in the center of the circle. The cloak he wore gave him an attitude of self-possessed grandeur, and yet I knew he was only a boy. In my own culture, he might be thought of as a child, still.

When the last of the Jukima had surrendered to exhaustion, the dance was finished. It was nearing evening again, and the air again held a hint of snow. The fire had been built up, and it was warm enough around it. I clung to the emotions of the celebration, savoring them.

We were all sitting quietly and watching the fire when Zhixo said, "I will try to do something, now." We turned to him expectantly. During our years in the valley, Zhixo had more and more isolated himself, and often when one spoke to him, he didn't respond. I worried for him, for he had no wife and no children. I had asked him many times to have food with us in our house, but he simply said, "It isn't necessary. I enjoy being alone." He still smiled at the children and told stories, but his mind seemed to be roaming to places that had nothing to do with where we were at the moment. He had grown older, obviously. His face was more angular -- his eyes seemed to be set more deeply and sometimes appeared to be filmed with a milky cast. His hair and his eyebrows had begun to silver. If questioned about his withdrawal from us, he simply said, "I am learning many things. Considering, and learning."

Zhixo said, "Look up at the clouds." We looked up at them, and saw that the clouds were dark and almost boiling in the sky, the way it is before a storm. Zhixo then said to Tihana, "Come and sit next to me. Now that you are a man, I will begin to teach you this. Watch what I do, and try to feel what is possible." I glanced at Zhixo and saw that his eyes closed. His head drooped forward, slightly. He relaxed his hands, which had been placed, palms up, on his thighs. There was a gasp and I looked up again. A cloud had begun to detach from the others. It dropped lower and seemed to be rotating slowly in a private, conjured wind. Its edges darkened and began to unravel, and then these frayed edges separated and grew pointed until they had become the feathers of wings. When I saw this, I was afraid. It was much, much more than making shapes in the smoke. A wedge-shaped beak congealed from the cloud-substance, and then the head and body refined themselves unmistakably. Someone said, "Eagle!" And then we were quiet again. Lightning had begun to flash from peak to peak, and I wondered, had Zhixo made the lightning also? The great wings spread open until, from tip to tip, they nearly spanned our valley. Carogo's daughter began crying and Carogo said, "Hush!"

I glanced back at Zhixo. His body was trembling. He looked very old to me -- frail and weary. When I looked up again, the bird had begun to lift, although its wide wings were nearly motionless. The bird lifted and passed through the clouds above it, which parted momentarily for its passage. For an instant there was a hole in the clouds -- an eagle-shaped opening of blue sky. And then the clouds rushed in and the sky was as it had been before the eagle appeared. Zhixo raised his head, opened his eyes. He smiled wanly and asked, "Was it there?"

"Yes," we said, "it was there."

When night came, Tihana and I returned to our house. When we were alone, Tihana said, "Zhixo said he would teach me that. Do you think I can learn?"

I said, "I'm not certain. But you will try."

And then Tihana smiled and said, "Will I have to be very old before I can do that?"

I said, "I don't know."

The walls of the house seemed close and snug, and I was relieved that the roof shielded our view of the sky. What I had seen there had been too strange for comprehension, and certainly too strange for comfort. I didn't know where that sort of power might lead. I asked Tihana, "How do you think it happened? How could one man's mind rearrange a cloud? Was it only a waking dream?"

Tihana said, "It was there. We all saw it."

I answered, "Yes, we did." And I wondered, what else could Zhixo do?

The mood of the evening had broken. Tihana and I sat on our chairs and had some tea, placing the bowls carefully on the table between sips. Tihana drummed his fingers in that way he had when he had something to say. He and I had not spoken privately since his return with the hunters. He asked me, "Did you enjoy the cuaynel I brought back?" A cuaynel was a small, furred, rabbit-like animal, and we had all shared in the ritual of eating morsels of its roasted meat during the celebration. I said, "Yes, of course." I was surprised to see that Tihana had tears moistening his eyes.

Tihana said, "I killed it with a spear, and when I speared it, it screamed. It was a woman-like sound. Only one, short woman-like sound, and then it was quiet." He paused, and I waited. Then he said, "I wanted to make it un-happen. The flight of the spear. The scream. The ending of a small life. We didn't need its meat that badly. We are not starving."

I said, "No, we are not starving."

"Its body was warm and loose when I picked it up," he

said.

"I'm sorry," I told him.

"I think it was terribly afraid, before it died," he said.

"But only for an instant."

Tihana looked at me sharply, and I nodded. I understood. I said, "Then perhaps you should only hunt if we are starving?"

He smiled when I said that, because he had been unburdened. "Yes. That's what I'll do. I can practice throwing a spear toward a target, and hunt only if we are starving." His hands uncurled, and I realized that they had been squeezed into fists. I thought of a baby whose hands clench into small, ineffectual fists, and when it learns to relax those hands, then they are ready for holding the things, the implements, that will help the child begin to master its world. I looked at Tihana's relaxing hands and thought of all the things he could hold with them, even though he had had no opportunity. A violin, a camera, a microscope's focusing wheel, or the hand of his own infant.

Chapter Twenty-two

Tihana had his own house now, and when I was alone I began to miss my family intolerably. It was as though they were the ones who were absent rather than myself. I was contented where I was, but it had become a question of responsibility and where it was placed. My family had no idea what had become of me, and I still wanted to go home. That desire had not left me. I wondered how my family had changed, and if anyone had died? I knew I must have nieces and nephews I'd never met. I felt that seeing my family again wouldn't alter the memories of them I carried with me, which were elegant in their resolution. My mother in summers, her clothes damp and soft with a generous heat, her hair escaping from its clasp. My father as we walked through the snow, the frost-blossoms of our breaths mingling and drifting. I thought of my father as oblivious to such things as cold, or impossibility.

I remembered my sisters, in their uniqueness. Gretta standing before a mirror and frowning suspiciously at her own image. The brief kiss that Vernelle would sometimes bestow on my forehead as she went out the door to somewhere, in an unconscious imitation of our mother's hurried affection for us all. Amanda and Martha I visualized as always together, finishing one another's sentences and passing secrets in glances. I wondered if Amanda had children by now, and if Martha had ever married? Doreen, I thought of as wearing a wry, humorous expression and shabby, ill-fitting clothes. We had passed down clothes one to the other until Doreen, as the last among us, must have felt herself gifted with a dubious wealth -- clothing saturated with the scent of all those others. All these people formed a pattern that divided, converged, or sent tendrils away.

On that first night without Tihana in my house, I had a dream that was rich and specific. I saw the long-ago Frederick, comfortable upon an iron bed and a straw-tick mattress in a room like my room at Tuylo. I appeared to him and scolded him sharply for his disappearance, even though I had been the one to send him away. He tossed and muttered in his sleep as though he dreamed of me also. I hoped that he saw me as a frightful, plumed ghost with blazing eyes, quite unlike the negligible woman he had abandoned. I saw, not Sparks, but his Indian wife and to her I said, "I remember you as a kindly soul." She looked up startled, swiveled her head, searching for who had spoken. Next I saw my mother, and she seemed so real. She was dressed to go out of her house, in a coat and a hat I remembered. She paused at the doorway and seemed to shiver, slightly, although she was warmly dressed. "I will come back to you," I said, and watched as she frowned thoughtfully and picked up her gloves from a table, went out the door. I didn't think that she had seen me there, but there was something of my presence that she sensed: a warmth, a scent, a subliminal motion? I awakened satisfied, as though I had somehow caught up with myself and had made a small difference in the world. I understood that Zhixo had come to me in this way on the night of the flood, and I was grateful that he had.

I often dreamed my private dreams, but also, we had all begun to dream of the road again, like a nemesis intruding. That dream didn't leave us again as long as we were together. It pestered us with worry at the times we felt the most satisfied with our isolation. It appeared first as a worm-like thing tunneling into the borders of other dreams. It was like a place where a rubbing finger had blurred a track on a drawing or a map -- a blank space or lesion.

One evening when some of the women were gathered in my house, I asked Carogo, "Have you seen it?" and she said, "There is a place that is wiped clean and something is coming in there." I knew what she meant.

I said, "It's like looking through an eye where there's a spot of nothing and there should be normal things. Continuations of things."

Lajima added, "It is like a headache is coming in there. The kind of headache that makes bright, wavy lines. But in my dreams, it isn't a wavy line. It's straight, and each day it comes closer."

I said, "I think it's our dream of the road. The road we can't see from here." For me, although I didn't say this, the image of the road brought a mingling of fear and desire. A road. A conduit for the travels of human beings.

I asked Lajima, "Do you think it has to be a bad thing that's coming?" She rocked back on her heels, considering my question.

It brings people," I offered.

"Is that a bad thing?" Lajima asked me.

"I don't know," I said. "It depends."

Meeri said, "It could mean the Xangu coming up out of the earth, or the ancestors returning to us." I thought of those ancestors, haggard and traumatized by the horror of a tin mine. The road would carry jeeps and trucks at first, and then, when it was hardened with some sort of pavement it would carry cars, and tour buses filled with every sort of person. It could bring armies, but I didn't think so. There would be stores one day along its route where one could buy fuel, batteries for a flashlight or radio, and a can of soda from a machine. Ordinary things.

The dreams of the road had made us fearful. We couldn't see from our valley how far the road had advanced, and we became overwhelmed by the anxiety of not knowing. To see if the road was coming, we had to climb the mountains and look down on the land. The cliffs that cinched our valley were inflexibly steep, and so we left the valley to find an easier route. There were only a few of us who climbed. Carogo was pregnant again and didn't go. Zhixo felt that he had grown too old. But Lajima was in our group, and Baalu, and Linari, Tihana's father. There were a few others. And because he was no longer a child, Tihana went with us. We passed through the gap that was the valley's entrance, and I felt that this opening was a mouth with each one of us a single word passing through it. We were a collection of words that all together, had meaning. When I passed over this threshold, I was both exhilarated and fearful. Life in the valley had become predictable, and whatever awaited us outside was not.

We skirted the mountain that was just one vertebra in a spine of peaks that arched up out of the mass of the forest. We walked to the north and west, far enough down on the slopes so that the land was agreeably pitched. We didn't find a suitable place for our ascent on the first day, and we camped in a meadow where we could see again the great march of the clouds from horizon to horizon. The clouds were puffy and white and moved slowly toward the east. At dusk, the clouds purpled and the wind rose and then leveled itself to a gentle tug.

We spoke lightly, of average things. "A tea made from these grasses would be good."

"We brought no cooking pot."

"We could collect the seeds for the gardens."

I said, "I think where we live, it would be too cold for them to grow." We didn't build a fire, for the night was almost balmy there. I slept on my cloak laid flat on the ground and the grasses bent under it and made of themselves a cushion.

We awakened at dawn and continued our trek. It was only late morning when we found the correct route up to the summit. We recognized it at once as a landmark from our dreams. There was a boulder upon which a stunted tree grew, and the roots of this tree had exerted an insidious but relentless pressure until the boulder had opened a split that would someday send it crashing, the pieces of it skidding down the slope. I wondered at the whimsical humor of the passing bird that must have dropped the seed precisely in that place. The mountain relaxed its flank just there, and we began to climb. The grasses grew shorter, and the trees had stiffened and gnarled their limbs against the wind. We all put on the cloaks that we had brought. As we rose higher, the grade became steeper and was littered with a rubble of rock that clattered dryly under our feet. The incline then grew almost impossibly steep. We began to use our hands and feet to search for notches and then lifted our bodies upward.

The cold now had a painful edge to it, and the crags were so chilled that they burned our hands. The cloaks we wore were not of feathers, but of coarsely woven fabrics that were of dull colors, like a kind of camouflage for when we were moving about in our valley. We would have been invisible to any watcher as we toiled up the face of the mountain. We reached the snow-line at mid-day, and the steepness eased, then. The snowy slope was not so difficult as the rocks had been, and I marveled at how our footprints left glowing, blue holes in the snow.

Baalu said, as our breathing smoothed and our ascent became more gradual, "It will not be there. It hasn't come this far." The snow squeaked and rubbed like corn-starch as our feet pressed it down.

Tihana said, "I think it's there, and we will see it." It was a pointless disagreement, for the answer was very close. The summit was not exactly an arrival, for when we reached it we saw bands of mountains to the east, many of them higher than where we stood. To the north were valleys of forest and then other bands of mountains like folds in the same cloth. We could go no farther because before us was a sheer drop, nearly vertical, where the snow fingered down onto the verdant land. When we crested the slope the wind clapped its hands over our ears and pushed at us so that we had to lean against its force. We turned as one, and looked to the west.

I saw something below that I hadn't known was there -- there was a large lake that had opened a space in the forest. The lake was longer than it was wide, like the kind of lake that is formed when a river is dammed, with serpentine curves to its edges -- bays, inlets, and peninsulas. Tihana saw it and asked, "Is that the ocean?" I said, "No. It's just a lake, but a large one." I didn't recognize it from any of the maps I'd seen long ago, and I wondered if it were named? I didn't even know what country this was, where we were now. Thin steam hung over the forest, shimmering the edge where sky and forest canopy met. It was disorienting to be so cold and yet look down on the distortions made by heat rising.

At first, we didn't see it and were relieved. And then when we looked to the south, we saw it. Baalu said, "I haven't seen a river as straight as that one." We looked along the trajectory of his pointing finger. It was a shadowed cut where the trees parted in a straight line. Seeing that perfect line on the landscape made me think of crystals, as though beneath the clutter that lay on the surfaces of things, there resided a deeper order, like the strict, fertile mechanics that were the stuff of stars. However, what we saw was not a crystal or a celestial pattern, but the genesis of a road. Ahead of it, the forest was as always, but if one followed the road back along its track one could see it until it vanished at the place where the mountains began to rise. If the construction of the road continued as it seemed to have been planned, it wouldn't climb push through our valley, but it would pass very close to the feet of the mountains. A person departing from that road could reach us in one day's march. The inevitability of this was infinitely disillusioning. The wind howled at us like spirits.

We came down from the peak and camped just at the tree-line. We built a fire. I thought I could see faces in the flames, and birds, animals, and cumulous clouds that had been torched. The fire had the instability of liquid.

Baalu said, "We must plan to leave our valley, now."

"Yes," I said.

"But we'll go more slowly, and take more with us," Tihana offered. "And there will be no burning." This seemed reasonable, that it would be more of a migration than an abandonment. Baalu agreed with him. With his agreement, all of us looked at Tihana, and I knew that was how it would be when Zhixo was too old to lead us. Even though he was so young, Tihana had a dignified authority that we respected.

Baalu said, then, "In the valley, when the fogs come, it's clammy and some of us cough."

I smiled and said, "Now we'll find fault with our home and it'll be easier to leave it." Baalu produced a counterfeit cough, and we laughed.

One part of my life had closed -- the part where Tihana had lived in my house with me. I was proud of him -- I'd done the best I could. I wasn't sorry to leave the valley -- I felt that there would always be other places that we would discover. I didn't think we would be hungry. The not-stopping-rains had just passed, and there would be time for us to search, and then to settle somewhere and plant gardens again. We took apart our houses and spread the materials we had borrowed back onto the land. We carried the rocks of the common hearth back to where other rocks lay in a rubble, and we placed our hearthstones among them. When we left, we passed through the squeeze of cliffs at our valley's entrance, and I had the thought, "Jukima will never live here again."

We went very low on the mountains, because there was more food to be gathered. Although we carried heavy parcels, we traveled faster than the road grew -- we knew this, even though we couldn't see the road's progress. There was no sign that other people had passed this way. I often walked next to Carogo. As we walked, I asked her to sing, but she said, "Now is not the right time. But when we settle again we will plant our gardens, and when the harvest comes we will have a great feast and I will sing, then." We had descended into the forest and were passing through a place where there were thick-trunked trees and orchids in their branches. The air here smelled of vanilla and ginger. Tihana plucked some orchids and put them in Falatha's hands and the girl laughed at how surprising the flowers were, with their dustings of spots and marvelous colors. She hadn't been in the forest before.

I said, "Carogo, what do you hope for?" She laughed.

I asked, "Why are you laughing?"

She said, "I hope for not much more than this." I saw her daughter holding so many flowers that it seemed there would always be more, and even if they were dropped carelessly by the path, they would be replaced by others. The flowers were so abundant here, it seemed as if they could be found in all places.

I asked again, "But in the future, what do you hope for?"

She paused, and said, "I suppose it would be for my child, for all of my children that will come, to be happy and kind and not to fear. For them to have courage, if there ever is the need for courage." I was satisfied with that, and plucked an orchid for my hair. I had desired to speak further with Carogo, but I was tired and the bundles I carried were heavy. Now and always, I wish I'd spoken more, but one never knows for certain what the next instant will bring. I had thought to compliment the fierce intelligence I saw in Falatha's face as she examined the small treasures that Tihana gave to her. However, I didn't say anything because the sack I carried was grooving sore marks onto my arm where the strap looped over it. My concentration on that small discomfort prevented me from speaking. There are many things I wish I'd said, but that time cannot be retrieved and it had seemed like any other day.

We camped that night in a clearing close to a stream, and the stream sang a pleasant song. The night was hazy and soft with moisture. In the morning, we resumed our journey. We were careful, as always, but not overly cautious because the road we had seen had been at some distance and we didn't think that any of its builders had come this far. We were *wrong*. We smelled the men before we saw them. At first their smell was only a hint of a memory to me. I then recalled the stink of the cantina at Tuylo. A beery, burnt scent, like the odor of clothing saturated with dried urine. The men's bodies stank like those of carrion-eaters, and when I smelled them, I shrank away from the implications of such a noxious odor. At first, I thought it was a large animal I was detecting, or the den of carnivores. I don't know if it affected the Indians in quite the same way -- they had never smelled the cantina at Tuylo and its dirty sawdust floor, and stale, spilled beer. I stopped, lifted my head, nostrils probably flaring. I remembered the rotten, candy colors of Tuylo, and next I thought, "men – Xangu." These thoughts happened almost instantaneously. The Indians stopped, heads raised, sniffing the air.

Soon after we smelled the men, we heard them. I couldn't understand their language, but they were making no effort at concealment. The men were drunk – I'd been right to think of the cantina at Tuylo. I didn't know what these men were or why they were there. They could have been prospectors, or surveyors for the road. I didn't think they were scientists of any sort, or scholars, but I didn't know that for certain.

We all crouched, easing ourselves down so silently that we could have been plants sinking back toward the earth. No one spoke. I parted the foliage slightly with my hands, and then I could see the men. There were more than a few; I couldn't tell how many, because some were moving about and it was confusing. Some of them reclined or lounged on uncleared earth, apparently oblivious to the dangers of snakes, and others walked about hitting at the foliage with sticks. At first I thought they carried sticks, but then I understood that they carried guns. I hadn't forgotten what guns were for.

The men wore flapping, khaki shorts and loose, once-white shirts now soiled with the reddish dust. They had beards, which I found shockingly unclean. Leaning against logs and tree trunks were their packs, and when I saw the efficiency and modernity of the aluminum frames, I changed my opinion somewhat about the character of these men. They might not be Xangu? The packs looked expensive and well-designed. It could be some sort of harmless expedition? I think the Jukima sensed my wavering; perhaps I leaned forward, or my breathing eased toward a normal rhythm.

Baalu touched my arm and mouthed, "Do you know them?" I was insulted.

"How could I know them?" I whispered. "I don't come from these people." And then I said, "They aren't speaking my language."

But he said, "Perhaps they could take you to the place where you were born?" He was right, of course, but I felt betrayed by this bald statement, as though my years with the Jukima had accounted for nothing and my life among them could be erased by a simple act – that of my standing up and announcing my presence and allowing those men to deal with me as they would. So many things were cluttering my mind at that moment. To reveal myself to these men would be to surrender to their mercy, or not mercy. Perhaps I could follow the white men silently as they went along, never alerting them to my presence? At the end of their particular trek, there could be a crossroads village. I would walk into it like the conscience of the wilderness and someone would take me in and feed me and clothe me in modern clothes. There could be a telephone, and I would call my parents as if the miles between us did not exist and we would exclaim and cry. I would return to my family. My original family. I would gather myself in, define myself yet again. But then, there was Tihana. There would be no time to explain, and I didn't know if he would go with me, or if he should? I didn't know what would happen to him, or what was right. In a modern setting, he would be disoriented and afraid.

All these thoughts passed quickly, in a dream-like but acute silence.

We were all crouching down, scarcely breathing. And then at a signal from Zhixo we began our retreat, very cautiously, crab-walking backward with the intent of vanishing into the forest like shadows. But there were so many of us this time. It was the entirety of our group, and because of that we moved more slowly, aware that the motions of our limbs could set in motion eddies and spirals in the thick air that could move the foliage, although no wind had stirred it. We could allow no twigs or dried leaves to crunch under our feet. We wanted only to reach a reasonable distance where we were undetectable and could converse in peace about what we had seen. We wanted only to leave this place behind and move on.

All was well, until Tamura laughed loudly. She laughed! Her foolish spurt of laughter swelled to a cataract of noise. At this unleashing of noise, many things happened at once. Tamura's head was tipped back in a laughter that streamed out and out. Linari's hand clamped her mouth and she clawed his hand away and bellowed louder. All of us stood, then, and each of us gathered up the nearest child and fled. I lifted up Baalu's daughter because I was closest to her. She was just a small child, and couldn't run with any speed. We were unprepared for this, and we were in a panic. Tamura would not be silent, and no matter how quietly we retreated, she burned our presence into the still air. I thought, for an instant, that Linari should kill her and silence her that way, and even though I was ashamed, later, of this thought, I still don't know that it was incorrect. She risked us all.

We fled, but we were carrying heavy parcels and at first didn't think to drop them. I heard Zhixo saying , "Xangu!" And then, "Drop what you carry, except for the children and the spears." We dropped the bundles containing our cloaks of feathers, our cooking pots, our beads, and bowls, and sacks of seeds. I saw Tihana helping Zhixo, nearly dragging him along by the elbows. Baalu's daughter wrapped herself around me and clung like a monkey-child. We heard a crashing behind us, and there were sharp, cracking sounds. For an instant, these sounds had form for me -- they were the cracking thuds of the wings of a huge bird beating holes in the air with its wings. Lajima had been running beside me and then she was gone, dropped like a small animal speared by a hunter. It was the guns. I had no time to explain to my companions what they were.

210

Our men carried spears, but I knew it was futile. These people hadn't fought anyone in battle for generations. They wouldn't understand the ferocity of guns, and they would hesitate and would be lost. I almost turned, thinking to face the men that were crashing toward us. If I could only tell them we were harmless, they would understand and it would be over? But it wasn't possible for me to turn and face the men without risking the life of the child I carried. I realized by then that they would see me at first as an Indian. My hair was long; I wore Indian clothes, and there were blue decorations painted on my limbs. There would be no time for words. We ran as far as the place where we had camped on the previous night, where there was cleared ground and where the stream ran. The men overtook us there.

Tihana and the other men turned to face the Xangu, giving some of us the gift of a chance to escape. The roar of the guns was like the thunder of the night I had fled the Tekhla village. It was such a primitive sound. The egg of the earth cracking open couldn't have been more devastating than this assault of noise. We milled about in confusion, and the blood soon flowed like silted water toward the stream. I saw the blood running like water and I didn't know where to go, which path to take. Then I chose the way down the stream.

Now Carogo ran beside me, her face cast in terror and determination. Her daughter, Falatha, ran with us. I held Baalu's child tightly as I stumbled through the foliage. The cracking of the guns retreated. And then I could scarcely hear the guns anymore. There was only the rending of branches as they gave way to our churning limbs. The noise of the battle was pushed back until it became a buzzing in the ears -- not real at all, but something we had imagined. Noise caught up with us again in the roaring of our breaths – the air we dragged in seemed corrosive -- and there was the snapping of fern-fronds and twigs, and even the branches breaking as we trampled through them. We went so rapidly that no snakes had time to strike at our legs, even though we didn't notice where we placed our feet. We followed the little stream, curving beside it when it curved, bending to whatever direction it had chosen for itself. As we followed the stream, the ground became boggy. There was a steamy heat, and the earth clung to our feet and ankles and slowed us, the way it is in a nightmare.

We realized that the sounds behind us now were gone. The insects droned heartlessly, as though there had been no disturbance and nothing had changed. We went more carefully, began to think to cover the traces of our passage. The group of us was so small, and we carried nothing with us but the children. All the men of hunting age had stayed behind. Carogo was with us, and Tondi was there, but Lajima was gone, and Tishaak and Papeet were not with us. Of the older men, Zhixo was not among us, and Njwe, the old man who had been Idisa's husband, was not present. I hoped that these people had gone another way and hadn't been brought down by the Xangu's guns, but I wasn't certain of anything.

At first, Tamura wasn't with us, and then she caught up with us, running with frantic energy, then slowing as she joined us. Tamura was quiet now, and had a blank expression on her face, an expression of profound withdrawal. The ragged jerking forward of time and space smoothed. A sequence began to form. A history.

In the open places along the stream we followed, the sunlight that leaked through the forest canopy was turning the foliage sharp and hard as glass. We finally sensed that we had gone far enough, and we sat down to rest for awhile. The children's eyes were as huge as the eyes of the starving. The children were silent, as the children of the Xangu village had been silent. I thought, then, that we had been mistaken for those others or some like them, but that didn't matter now.

We were afraid to wait in that place, or in any place, for very long, and so we went on when we had regained some slight composure. The stream had torn a channel through the soft earth and was below us. In this place the water ran clear, and was mild. We left off following the stream when we smelled the wide water. It had a fragrance of clouds, and ice, and clay. Then we saw hints of the water through gaps in the trees. Bright candle-flames of water glowed through the trees, and its shine made it seem like a promise of something untarnished soon to come. We were so heartsick and weary. We arrived at a place where the forest opened out, and a lake was there. It had a polished sheen and was floated by reflected clouds, and was very broad. The opposite bank was so distant that it was only a smudge. When we went closer and saw the water unobstructed by forest, it was like the relief of taking a pure breath after inhaling flames. Terror was beginning to dissolve into a numb bewilderment that was not the same thing as healing.

I didn't think the Xangu would be able to track us this far - - they had not the skills. I didn't know what had happened at the place where the blood had run like water, but I hoped that some who had stayed behind would return to us. The space in the forest, the openness of the lake, gave us all room to hope. There were no footprints to show us that people had passed this way before us, and it seemed to be a good-enough place to stay and wait for whomever among us had escaped. I didn't know if Tihana had survived. My not knowing made my heart icy.

Except for the children we had carried, our hands were empty. I looked around for someone to say what we should do, but no one stepped forward to speak. I ventured, "We could stay here and wait for who comes?" We waited. We dared to build a fire, because although the fire could attract the Xangu, the aroma of its smoke would be a signal to the absent others, and it would keep the animals at a distance in the night. The fire we built was not close to the shore, but was still within sight of the lake, which gleamed whether or not we were deserving of its beauty.

Chapter Twenty-three

In our place of pausing by the lake, a rosy sunset came and was ignored. Its beauty seemed like a falsehood to me, and its colors vulgar. I watched the quiet choreography of my companions as we gathered firewood. Carogo was stooped over her swollen belly -- she was close to giving birth again. She poked at a fallen branch, her expression grim. She said, "This wood is wet and will burn badly. The smoke of it could be seen for a long way." I didn't answer her, for she was right, of course, but we had no choice. The fire could be like a signal to the Xangu, but it also could lead the Jukima men back to us.

The people around me had scratches on their arms, legs, and faces from our flight through the forest, and their hair was tangled. I felt the stings of my own cuts and there were burrs in my hair. I saw my companions as I had not quite seen them before. They were average people, and could be quarrelsome or placid or tediously excitable, just like any people anywhere. These were my neighbors, friends, and family and they were completely familiar. They had lost their glamour, and because of that, they were more dear to me in their shabby vulnerability. Even Tamura was dear to me then, although she seemingly had no understanding of what she had brought down on our heads. She was whispering to herself as she pointlessly rolled a twig back and forth with her bare toe. Around me, these people were doing normal things with stoic, repressed sadness. I knew them as well as it was possible to know anyone.

We did the customary things. We cleared the ground. We built a fire, which became indispensable as the daylight withdrew. When night came, I felt that the forest was crowding us -- that the mass of it could smother our little group if we were not alert. No one slept, and none of the babies or children laughed or cried. The fire burned down to its radiant coals and clung to life through the night.

At dawn, I heard the sounds I had hoped for -- from the forest there came the reassuring whispers in our language. Some of the Jukima men had survived, and they took recognizable shapes as they stepped out of the shadows and were among us again. Our group had shriveled to these few. Tihana was there, and when I saw him, the moment swelled and filled with the past up until this time – all of the past selves we had been at other ages were like ghosts standing with us. Even as I was thinking this, I could see that Tihana was changed. His face and arms and legs had been scratched by the brush of the forest as he fled through it. He was not badly injured, but he was different now. His eyes were stripped of childhood; they were no longer penetrable. His expression was so unearthly that I had to veer away. I didn't know yet what had happened in the clearing when the men stayed behind.

Some of the other men were there and came to stand among us, but some were gone. Linari, Tihana's father, was not with them. Neemara, one of the boys who had gone on the hunt with Tihana was there, but the other two were not. Zhixo was not there. Ytkma, Carogo's husband, thankfully, was there. Baalu was there. Many of those who returned to us carried the packages that we had dropped in our flight, and we had again some of our utensils so that we could fetch water and cook. All of our dreaming of the Xangu with knives in their teeth and dull stones for eyes hadn't prepared me for this -- none of us had been prepared. Our collective spirit was clothed in rags, but we would find ways to continue. I wished we were in a higher place, because the forest had a way of swallowing its tragedies.

A word in English filled my mouth and nearly snapped out. "Regret." Although regret for what or whom, I couldn't say exactly. Tihana began to tell us what had happened. He said, "I was invisible. I became invisible. The concentration came over me -- the ability -- and it was like a flow that I hooked into. And I tried to help the others. Some of them became invisible, too. I was like a phantom with my spear." It was the only explanation he had for his survival and the seemingly arbitrary fates of some of the others. His hands were still trembling. The spear remained in his grasp, tipped in gore. For us, he had killed three men, he said. He seemed taller as he spoke, and his voice grew resonant with righteousness as he went on. For us he had done these things. "I killed three Xangu – they were *not* men. I could see that they were not men." And what must the Xangu have seen – those Xangu who were not men? We had been diabolical creatures to them, and less worthy, even, than vipers? We must have seemed violent in our paint and feathers? Stealthy and probably clothed in an alien reek, and then revealing ourselves with maniacal laughter. I was certain it had been a terrible misunderstanding. We had misunderstood, and so had the white men we had identified only as Xangu -- the enemies. I said nothing. Tihana was still speaking.

"Some of us became invisible," Tihana said, "untouchable. And others did not." He spread his hands, blameless and open, and the spear tumbled down. It was unclean, but he would later wash it in the lake.

Tihana spoke of the loathsome, faintly resistant jolt of flesh yielding to the spear, of blood running into the water. Of Linari placing himself between Tamura and the guns. Although Linari couldn't have known exactly what guns were or how they worked, he surely knew them from their effects. He had done this, and Tamura was still with us. Tihana said, "I saw my father struck down. And that's when the magic came to me -- the invisibility." I know he believed what he said. I wasn't sure if it were true, or not true.

Tihana continued. A blossom of blood had appeared on Zhixo's forehead, his hand traveling upward to staunch it, then pausing while he stared at his hand incredulously. He stared at his hand and then dropped to the ground in an inelegant pile of limbs. His legs were crooked and undignified, his toes scuffling with the earth energetically for a short time, his face grinding into the dirt, dirt filling his open mouth as some peoples fill the mouths of their dead with clay. And then he didn't move again.

Linari had fallen, his spear held before him like a slender shield. Tamura, not laughing then, blundered away, a demented woman who once had hoped for something that she would recognize when it came to her. And Tihana – Tihana had been invisible, and the bullets didn't touch him. He had killed the man who had shot Linari, and then he had killed two others. There was a snarl of blue smoke fouling that place. The mud was squashy with the blood that seeped away. There had been shouting in a non-language that all, nonetheless, understood in its elemental pouring out.

As Tihana spoke, I thought that perhaps the Xangu hadn't expected resistance, or they had expected nothing at all? Many of them were befuddled by drink, and they had streamed out of the forest into the open place in a messy crowd, firing their guns at anything and everything. It might have seemed to them to be almost a game or contest? Some of the Jukima had been killed in this game, and some of the Xangu had been killed by the Jukima spears before there was any comprehension, by anyone, of finality.

It had been a random convergence, or that is how it had seemed to Tihana at first, he said. Tihana said that he had wanted to apologize, because of the mistakenness of it all. He had thought to extend open hands and to quell the carnage through this plain gesture. But the noise had been incredible, and then Linari had fallen. And Zhixo's churning the bloodied earth with his bare toes was such an insane and irreversible condition, that whatever apologies and explanations there might have been, were impossible. Tihana had killed the man who had killed Linari, and did we understand what a necessary thing that had been? And having killed one Xangu, he had to kill others. Tihana had killed these men to protect us. He wanted us to understand how necessary it had been?

As Tihana spoke, these events placed themselves beside the things we assumed were true and right, even though Tihana wouldn't look at me directly. As he was speaking, I imagined that Carogo was inventing a song in her mind that would omit the drunkenness, confusion, blunders and the crazed laughter. It would be a song that would arrow toward myth. We were a nomadic people, justified in our severe isolation, our suspicions. We were loyal to one another; we were courageous, and some of us had capacities that no one quite understood. I thought it might be possible that Tihana literally had become invisible.

It was morning. Tihana went to the lake and washed himself, and washed the spear that was an ancient Xangu knife attached to a pole. Then he crouched and polished the blade with a stone. When he returned, he said, "We should make more of these spears so that if some are lost in battles, we will have others. We can take some of the knives used by the women and they can share the ones that remain." Neemara looked thoughtfully at his spear, and then said, "We will teach the younger children how to use these weapons and we will never be un-ready again."

I could see Carogo twisting a strand of her hair furiously, and she said, "But what would Zhixo do?"

"It is because Zhixo is gone that we must think of these things," said Tihana. His eyes shone with a hard light and he said, "Yes, we could teach the smaller ones what they need to know. And I have a thought. The Xangu have the knives that we need to make more spears. Perhaps some of us, in the future, could find their camps and take some of their knives."

"Yes," said Neemara, "we could do that." His eyes, too, glittered.

Then Tihana turned to me and said, "Do you know about those weapons they used?"

I said, "Yes. They used guns."

"Could we learn about those?" Tihana asked.

"I don't know," I said.

Tihana continued. "Perhaps there are not so many of these Xangu? We could eliminate them so that they could not harm any more of the Jukima? We are few, but we could surprise them -- attack them before they have time to react." Tihana was breathless, and I had the sense that he was still stunned by the battle and was not thinking clearly. Without pausing or asking for our opinions, he said, "First, we must learn more about the invisibility, and the other things like that. Zhixo entertained us, when we should have been studying the power of it."

I was appalled at Tihana's criticism of Zhixo, but I said, "Tihana, there are many more of the Xangu. Many more of them than the ones we saw."

He frowned then, and said, "We will think about all of this."

I said, "Yes, we should think about all of this carefully."

We couldn't stay where we were, or anywhere, for very long, and so we covered the fire with earth, and put leaves and rubble over the clearing we had made. We followed the shore of the lake, away from where the tragedy had befallen us. The events that had just passed seemed not to be real. I comforted myself by imagining that Zhixo and the other absent ones were already back in our valley as though they had not left it. I knew this wasn't true, but everything had happened so suddenly that I was unable to accept the truth just then. I would speak with Tihana about all of this, and our words could construct some sort of balance, and allow us to survive.

There were soft reeds at the edge of the water, stepping down into it. We walked beside these reeds, blending into them. We followed the shore-line until late afternoon, and although there was no warning, suddenly there was a white cliff with colorful birds swirling against it. It was exactly the scene I had dreamed about, many years before -- so long ago now that I'd almost forgotten it. The birds of many colors swooped against the cliff, so unexpectedly that they took my breath away. The flashes of color that were birds of mingling species were like thoughts of joy as they swooped, settled, and lifted again. They soared and paused and lifted like spots of light. There was a beach of granular white sand that sparkled with mica and chips of quartz that had fallen away from the cliff. There were larger stones with which we could build a hearth if we chose. Below the cliff were drifts of feathers of blue and green and yellow and scarlet, and raven-black.

I said, "Look, Tihana, it's the place of joy in my dreams! I'm seeing it now, like a gift." He said, almost irritably, "I'm happy for you, then," and I could see that he was considering other things. His inattention was a brushing away of something that was important to me. I understood that my dream had not been his. I both knew him, and didn't know him, anymore. I looked away from Tihana and watched the birds.

The minds of children can be resilient and forgetful, and already the terror that was so recent was passing from them. There was laughter again from the children when they saw the cliff and the birds, and they began to gather the fallen feathers with a kind of frenzied hoarding. They had never seen anything like this before. The children were giddy as they gathered handfuls of feathers and threaded feathers through their hair, and tied them with grasses at their wrists and ankles. They were accumulating these treasures, and some were beginning to quarrel and others shared what they had, depending on their natures. The children looked like vivid fledglings.

I asked Carogo, "What about the dead we left behind? What do you think they will do with our dead?"

"We can't change what's happened," Carogo said. "We will grieve properly when we are far away from here, and commemorate our dead as best we can."

"I hope that a jaguar will come for Zhixo," I said, but Carogo looked at me with eyebrows arched, and I didn't explain. We would speak of all of this when we could, or that's what I assumed.

We camped there by common agreement. We would post sentries to watch over us in the night. When the fire was built and was steaming and popping as it fed on the green wood, it was time to fetch the water for the cooking pots that had been retrieved along our path of retreat. I started off for the lake with a bowl for water. Carogo put a hand on my arm and said, "What of the little, vicious fish that could be in the lake?"

"That's true." I said, "We don't know if they are there in the lake." I believed, however, that this lake was untroubled by the little fish with teeth. I didn't know how I knew this, and then I realized and said, "The shore birds are wading with confidence.

Their legs are in the water and they are not being attacked by the little fish."

Carogo sighed and said, "Then it must be all right." I was amazed at my intuition, which was not an intuition at all, but a subliminal reading of the clues in my surroundings. "Have I been capable of this for a long time?" I wondered. Able to read the expressions of my surroundings with fluency? The lake was safe, but it was not intuition that had informed me, but a kind of literacy that I had learned.

I waded into the water, which closed around my ankles and then my shins. I dipped water into a bowl and stood there in the water, the bowl brimming, the seam where water and air met tickling my legs. I watched the birds swooping against the cliff. I thought, "the leaves of autumn," although I hadn't seen an autumn and its many colors for years. I thought, then, "I will remember this," for the scene had the acuteness of a memory being secured. Carogo, who had come to fill her bowl beside me, clucked critically at my slowness, and so I brought the bowl back to the campfire and poured it into a cooking pot. Carogo put wild onions into the water, and some pieces of smoked meat that had been recovered from one of the dropped parcels. I took a blackened cooking spoon and lifted a hot stone from the hearth and dropped it into the pot. The water began to simmer. The scent of cooking food rose up and began to renew the bonds we felt for each other. I stirred the broth. When I looked up from this work, a mist had begun to rise from the surface of the lake, and then the one, climbing shaft of smoke from our fire didn't matter very much. We were concealed from the lake's eye by the mist, and by fronds and shadows.

The coals of the fire crumbled back into themselves and glowed in a heap. They were a center for all of us to look to as the last thing we saw that night. I slept like a ghost who had only the slimmest recollection of her body. In the morning, I awakened sorely, bruised from lumps on the ground, and I thought, "Oh, am I getting older? Is that why?" And then I remembered those who were no longer with us. I didn't know what we all would do without Zhixo. All around us was a gloomy fog that moved in eddies, pushed about by the slight motions of the air, as a breath would push feathers. The pale circle of sun could not yet burn through this fog.

A baby began to cry, and there was the murmur of its mother and it became quiet again. My companions, huddled on the bare ground, were blurred, slipping in and out of their outlines. "Another morning," I thought, and then, "I'll wait for someone to make the tea." I could almost taste it -- the hot tea that I hoped would warm me from within. I could have made it myself as a gift to my companions, but I didn't. Later, I regretted not having made the tea. It would have been such a small but significant thing to do for these people. Gradually the fog rolled away and the morning began.

We lingered in that place throughout the morning. Soon, we would move on, climb higher again. But first, we would gather some plumage from beneath the cliff, and we would catch fish. Perhaps there would be good hunting, and we would dare to stay a day more and smoke the meat the hunters would bring, and the fish that we caught. And then we would move on to higher ground, perhaps to regions that were more protected by their desolation. I thought that despite what Tihana had said, we would not come down to the forest again for a very long time.

I went to the lake to drink, and the water was cool around my ankles. Surges of tiny, harmless fish whisked across my feet, fish that were packed closely together as one, flickering, sensitive shape. I called to Tihana, "Come and see the fish!" but when he came near, the fish had gone. I said, "No matter. They were there." But they had gone, and Tihana went off down the shore to look for birds' nests with eggs. I watched him going and thought about how tall he had grown and how gracefully he moved, and how like an adult he had become. I looked away from him, then, and bent and picked up some water in my hands. I watched, meditating almost absently, on how the water's color drained away as it slipped through my fingers.

It was at about mid-day, just moments after Tihana went away from me to look for the eggs in the nests. There was a sound like a humming caught in the throat, but it was not a human voice. It was something alien and unstoppable -- a devised, calibrated throbbing. This sound grew louder. It was a noise not made by a body nor any sort of living thing. I saw the source of it, then, but didn't understand it at first. It was like a hallucination, but shedding noise. There was a boat where there had been nothing but lake shining in its skin of blue. The boat, I knew, was made of thick metal and rectangular compartments, designed cleverly and with exacting purpose. I almost said aloud, "You see, the things that people can make!" At first, I didn't understand even that there would be people contained within it and upon its decks. I wasn't thinking in those terms.

It was so sudden, so unexpected – the second sudden thing to happen in a short time. Above the noise of the engines, there was a thin, tinkling music, and it was surrounding the boat like a scent. Then I smelled literal perfume, more assertively seductive than any flower, drifting from the boat, and I thought, "Women!" The women were there on the canopied deck, and I could see them, in frothy dresses of pale colors -- colors not often seen in the forest. These clothes looked so strange and perishable to me that I almost didn't understand them. When I saw the women and their delicate dresses, I thought, "There are no Xangu on this boat," although I couldn't know that for certain. I couldn't quite see, but imagined, the jewels at the women's throats and wrists and on their fingers. I was entranced to a kind of stupidity by what I was seeing.

Then I noticed the men. They were dressed in black, and at first I thought, "soldiers," for their clothing was uniform-like. Very strict. Did the Xangu wear such armor? The hair of these people was of different hues. I was mesmerized by this, by the various colors of their hair and the flimsy styles of the clothes, and the different appearance, one from the other, of the people on the boat. How strange, to notice that? And I smelled food, with the oddly robust odors that I remembered from long ago. The vision of the boat seemed insubstantial because of its suddenness, and yet it was complete in its details. The boat had a row of windows with rounded corners. The flanks of the boat were of metal plates held together with rivets, each placed a measured distance from the next. There was a shapely brass bell mounted at the stern of the boat. The canopy over the deck was striped, red and white, and was scalloped on its edge.

And then I looked back and saw the Jukima positioned as tensely as startled animals. Tihana had just cupped his hands to drink from the lake; the water was leaking through his fingers and joining with the other water that was the lake. The engine sounds had became an already familiar drone, and the water falling back into the lake joined with the music that radiated from the boat and surrounded us. Tihana was half-stooping, his eyes frightened -- not glazed with his new, adult expression -- and I thought, how perfect he is, at just this time, and I collected that image like a snapshot.

The others, the people on the shore, were not moving. No one spoke. I didn't speak. There wasn't much time, but it seemed that time had slowed, or stopped. This isn't a road, I realized, in a kind of panic. It's a lake, and I've been tricked. I didn't know this lake and how it connected with other water, with the rivers that were also roads. The boat was large, and it had come from somewhere. From a village where there were tourists? From a river, and all that it could bring? I hadn't understood that a literal road was but one of many possibilities.

With this stunning comprehension, I flung myself into the water and began to swim toward the boat. It all came together in an inevitable moment -- the lake, the cliff of birds, the boat, the modern tourists, the decimated band of Jukima startled on the shore, and myself centered within that mixture. It was a moment that wouldn't arrive again, and I knew that. The water had weight as I pulled against it, but each scoop of my hands was like a discovery of strength. It was almost as if I pulled the boat slowly toward me as I swam. The cloth wrapper I wore dragged at my legs, but I didn't pause to discard it. My muscles were burning with my striving. The boat was moving on very slowly and wrinkling the water. My splashing seemed to me as loud and forceful as breakers striking at a shore. Surely the people on the boat would hear me, but I didn't call out to them. I didn't know in what language I would call out, or if I would only make inarticulate sounds, and so I swam silently, except for the splashing of my hands as they struck the water.

The features of the people began to clarify themselves as the distance narrowed. Some of these people were dancing to the music, and some were holding up slim glasses in which there must be champagne. The music had the sound of many, precious bubbles rising a little way and then bursting in showers of sound. There was melodious laughter that sounded stylized to me, as if those people were acting in a ceremony and exaggerating normal, human sounds.

The white cliff was opposite the boat now, and I realized it was the cliff with its welter of birds they had come to see. That was why the boat moved so slowly; the cliff was a display for a sight-seeing excursion. I looked back. Tihana was still standing in the water; he had waded into the water up to his waist. There were no others that I could see, now, on the shore. I paddled in a half-circle and called out to him, "Tihana, swim to me! Do it now!" Tihana stood with his arms upraised in what could have been a defensive posture, or a surrender. At that distance, I couldn't see the features of his face and I was unable to stop his vanishing.

"Tihana!" I called out. He didn't answer, but simply stood there in the water, arms upraised, his features blanked by the distance. Surely he understood, but he didn't move toward me, didn't try to swim. I called out, "Tihana, wait there for me and I'll come back for you," but even as I said those words I sensed it would not be possible, that he would be too fearful and wouldn't understand. And, if he left with me, what would the Jukima do without him, now that Zhixo was gone? It was not for me to decide.

I called out toward the boat. I shouted something in English. I don't remember what I said. Perhaps, "Over here! I'm over here!" But they didn't hear me over the conversations, the music, and the squawking of the birds. I swam again, even more strongly.

The music stopped for a moment, and all I heard was the chugging of the engine, the calls of the birds, and the rhythmical splashing made by my arms and legs. The boat was continuing to move on, and I was so tired. I cried out again, and then they heard me. There were fingers pointing in my direction, connecting me to the people in the boat. At first, they must have thought I was one of their own that had fallen over the railing? But my straggled, long hair, and the lace of indigo drawn on my face and arms so lovingly by the Jukima women several nights before, were very foreign to them.

There was kindness in the people on the boat, of course, as there can be kindness in any people, and there was an understandable confusion about who or what I was. I could see that they took a kind of excitable pleasure in this event. I could appreciate how they would cherish the small adventure they'd come upon. They would condense and elevate this experience, as one needs to elevate a confrontation with the ambiguous -- simplifying it, making it acceptable. I saw myself simultaneously as a woman in near-to-absolute disarray, and as a self-assured creature comfortable in my own skin.

While I was being lifted onto the boat, I was already remembering shame at certain things and not others. I folded my arms across my chest because my clothing was wet and transparent. I moved into shame as one would step into a dance that one remembers from childhood. I must have shouted at the people there, my voice rising in pitch as it had rarely done among the Jukima. I shouted, "My son is back there. We must put down a boat for him!"

"Your son?" It was the captain looming over me, glittering white and tan and impossibly clean. He was saying, "Your son is there in the forest? Back there? But there is no one." The shore was dangerously elemental already, vacant of human presence. It was a place in which I couldn't, just then, completely believe.

"My son is there. He is frightened of this boat and of you. But he's there, hidden behind the trees. He can't swim." I said again, "He can't swim," as though that explained everything.

"You lost your way? You and your son?"

"Yes. No. We weren't lost. We didn't expect you. It's been such
a long time."

The captain didn't say anything for a moment. He was looking at my feet, considering them with his nose elevated as though he found what he was seeing repugnant. I looked down as well. My naked feet were monstrous. Wide and scarred, and calloused with pads like the pads of an animal. I looked at the feet of the women, who also leaned in toward me, suffocatingly close. Their feet were propped at angles by their shoes, and covered with unstained, delicate cloth. Diminutive, stylized feet, nearly useless, I thought.

"It's been years," I said.

"Ah, years. You've been lost for years?"

"Not really lost. I didn't intend -- I was lost -- it was years ago that it happened."

"You and your son were lost?" The captain seemed like an idiot to me, repeating and repeating what he couldn't understand, as though if he repeated it enough the quandary would vanish.

"No, it wasn't that way. . ." And then I understood how it might seem. "Yes, of course. My son and I were lost. There was an expedition and the guide was lost, and then there was a flood that washed away everything, and we must go back for him. For my son." I thought I sounded intelligent and reasonable enough as I condensed the span of the years that had passed.

There was pity on the captain's face, and then his expression seemed to move through a series of conflicting emotions. He may have thought I was deliberately deceiving him in some crafty way? I was speaking English, but there were vines, spirals, birds, and clouds drawn on my skin. I didn't know how my own face, my own expression, appeared to him, or to anyone? I must have been a water-woman to them, rising up out of the lake like a displaced spirit who was possibly even dangerous, if one believed that such a thing were possible.

The captain jerked his wrist in a gesture that I knew to be the reflex of a glance at his watch. Then he suppressed the impulse out of courtesy, sighed, and said, "I'll put down a boat. You can show us." The Jukima had gone, as I had known that they would. I was sure they were talking of me even as I searched the shore with my eyes and other senses, and they were beginning to speak of what it had all meant. They must have been sorrowing, angry, betrayed, and resolved. I was already to them another person who had been lost. The captain was disinclined to put to shore, and said, "A few steps away from the lake, into that jungle, and we'd lose our way." He was right, of course, and the Jukima would not be findable if they didn't want to be found. It was over. I knew that Tihana would grieve that I was no longer with him, but he carried me in his mind already as his conscience and security. There would be new songs, and I would inhabit those songs. The distance between myself and the people who sang them would be insurmountable, as if I were an ancestor who returned but could not touch the people.

We reboarded the boat, and the engines began their thrumming again. We moved slowly away from the cliff with the birds. I watched it until I couldn't see it anymore. The boat slid away from the shore and into deeper water. The captain stood beside me at the railing and said, "Look down there, at the water." At first, I didn't understand what he meant, and then I saw the trees. The boat was gliding over the tops of trees that had been drowned so recently by the lake that foliage still clung in rags to their branches. The captain said, "This lake was made by a dam, not so long ago." I said nothing, and he hesitated and then said. "But surely you knew that?" I said, "No. I didn't know it." At first I thought it was a deathly place we moved across. I thought of the deaths of all those things that needed the air to live, including all those animals in their burrows and the ones who were too slow to flee the rising water. But the birds could fly away, and the winged insects, and the jaguars and hoofed animals might have escaped. I watched the forest as we passed over it. It was like a kind of flying, to look down on the treetops that way.

I was shown to a cabin -- a small, hollow room that was hard everywhere with resistant, glossy surfaces, cool to the touch. Up through my bare feet I could feel the floor shaking with the engine's vibration, and it seemed as though the fluttering rhythm would change the very way my heart was beating and the pace of my breaths. From inside the body of the boat there was no sensation of movement, except for that vibrating tickle. I crossed over to the window, nearly pressing my face to its surface, and I tried to see the forest as it retreated, perhaps to capture its image in a final impression. However, the window was crosshatched with fine scratches and everything seen through it was indistinct. The forest was only a quaint scene painted on the surface of the window. It was already bluing with distance, and cast bruise-colored shadows on the

226

water. I turned away, then. It didn't matter; already I was separated from that place and the people I'd known there.

I took a deep breath, and then another, and smelled nothing familiar. The smells of the little cabin stung my nose -- the diesel fuel, the chorine bleach, and a fungusy, damp and unwholesome essence that chemicals couldn't quite mask. I crossed again to the window, but it was sealed closed -- a lozenge-shaped wafer of marred plastic, with a gray rubber edge dividing the outside air from the inside. I wondered how one could breathe one's own recycled breaths -- how long it would be possible to do that? No snakes or poisonous frogs could enter through these windows, and my breaths could not escape. I had nothing -- only the damp cloth wrapper I wore and a necklace that was a cord with the little fossil attached, the one I had shown to Tihana. I squeezed this bit of stone in my hand like a talisman. I sat down on the bed, holding this small stone at my throat.

I sat quietly. The window was purpling with the night when I was startled by a rapping at my door. The Jukima cleared their throats obviously to announce themselves, but this was a hammering that sounded hostile. I was instantly dry-mouthed, palms upraised, then, and pushing back at nothing. My heart was racing, even after I identified the sounds as the courtesy of someone knocking on my door. There was so much to remember.

I opened the door to a diminutive woman holding a bundle of clothes. I remember her clearly, even now, because she was so different from my companions of the last years. She had a feeling of "yellow-ness" to her -- her buttery dress, her short, wheat-colored hair, and her bright expression. She wore a wide, inclusive smile. Her eyes were so light and tinny that at first I thought she couldn't see. The woman extended the bundle of clothing toward me as she said, "I think these will fit you." And then she pushed past me and sat uninvited on my bed, and asked the most intrusive questions. "The captain said that you have a son. That is why we put down the boat. So, how old is your son?"

I hesitated, and then said, "He is seventeen. Or perhaps sixteen."

She nodded thoughtfully, and then asked, "And is he an Indian
boy?"

I said, "Yes. He is." And then I said, "He's a hunter."

The metal-eyed woman continued to smile generously,

and asked, "Do you have a husband?"

I said, "No. My son was given to me." I didn't know where to look, or how to deflect her questions and it was a kind of pain that came over me -- the explanations I would make, the explanations that I knew would go on and on. I closed my expression, as the Jukima did. I looked inward and endured until the questions ended.

And finally, the woman asked, "Are you hungry?" At first I said, "I don't know," and then I said, "Yes, I suppose I am." The woman said, "Good. I'll come back for you soon," and she stood and patted the bundle of clothing she had put on the bed. I sensed that she was kind-hearted, but she had exhausted me.

In the cabin's bathroom, I turned the faucets on and off, and took a long time in a kind of private play with this. And then, I stood in a spray of luxuriously warm water, the warmest I had felt for a very long time. The designs on my face and limbs didn't scrub away, regardless of how vigorously I rasped at my skin with a rough-textured cloth. The designs remained, but were lighter, and would dim more each day. I combed the tangles from my hair. I put on my new clothes. I looked in the mirror and saw that I had grown older and that my face was more interesting than I had remembered. This didn't disappoint me. By my eyes were the lines drawn by smiles.

Shoes were found for me. Toothpaste. A tube of lipstick. Except for the designs on my skin, it wasn't difficult to make myself presentable. I had the thought that I should write this all down -- record these customs -- and that my recording would have a unique freshness. The woman with the gray eyes returned, and led me to where I had a meal in a common room with the other people on the boat. It was not too terrible. I remembered how to eat with a fork and not injure my mouth, and how not to wipe away grease from my lips with the back of my hand. The captain sat beside me, and said, "I think I remember reading something about you. There was a search." I nodded and said, "Yes, there would have been."

On that first night, my skin was rough against the sheets, but it would smooth. The food would not sicken me, soon. I would feel the cold again, and would take it into my body and shiver as though cold were an invasion and not something that could be ignored. I would receive my original culture back into my life and would synchronize with it as best I could. I knew I was not the same person as the woman who boarded the boat at Tuylo.

I dreamed of snow that first night on the boat, of walking

228

through a blue-shadowed snow-field to the base of a cliff. I knew that the top of this cliff was the highest place. I began to climb, and as I did so, I could see myself as if from a height. At the same time, I could feel the grit, the hardness, the painfully alive coldness of the rock under the strong contact of my hands. I was small as I climbed -- insignificant, but persistent. There were no other people with me in this dream.

I climbed through a thick fog, but was oriented in it as long as I climbed upward. And then the fog was gone, burned away, and the sun was an eye into whose gaze I could not look. Everywhere the mountain peaks were penetrating the cloud banks that bundled the land as a blanket covers a body. I saw the mountain range as a human body. And with that recognition, it began to take form as something to which I could relate. This mountain range was a body at rest, and also it was only one part of a continuous earth. It was a body curved into the position of a child not yet born. This was a dream, and in the dream, the land was still, as the huntress in the moon is stilled in her moment of becoming. When I awakened, I was strangely calm, despite my unfamiliar surroundings. My time with the Jukima, and the dream, were already taking the simpler shapes of memory.

Chapter Twenty-four
Epilogue

When I left the Jukima, it was with tangled emotions that were a mixture of sorrow and relief, and the relinquishing of self to a momentum toward whatever forms my life would take next. I've grown older, and, paradoxically, I feel that I'm a child who is thrilled by the novelty of things. There are no artifacts from my time with the Jukima, no proofs, and no resolutions. I don't have explanations.

In my last home with the Jukima, the mountains had loomed over us and endured in a spread of time so colossal that their events were not ours. From their vantage point our scramblings were meaningless, as the droplets in a downpour are meaningless to the mountains, yet change them. The valley had been a hidden place, or a hiding place, for although the Jukima had achieved an imperfect but functional harmony within their group, no one was affected by them except themselves, alone. Sometimes now, I look up to see a cloud that detaches from the others and takes on a form that would be the yearning of clouds if clouds could choose their own shapes and I wonder, "Is that magic?" I have my opinions -- that some people have capacities that they don't have the wisdom to use effectively or honorably, and some have good-hearted desires, but not the tools to change very much. It's not easy being human.

If Ollie had still been alive, I perhaps could have spoken with him about so many things -- but perhaps not. He had been satiated with his own ideas, and his head must have echoed with his own voice. There might even have been jealously that my experiences had not been his. I discovered that Ollie had died only a few months after I had left, probably even before I had joined the Jukima. So, I don't know what he would have thought or said, and I released him to the past. He had inspired me, and that was enough. Of Frederick, I have heard nothing, but that doesn't matter. I sense that he's still living, and I imagine that his has been a disreputable life. There is a rightness to honor and responsibility that has come to seem to me like a natural law.

That the boat trip took a dawdling four days was a mercy, because it allowed me the time to collect myself, and to look forward. Arrangements had been made by the captain, by radio, and my mother and Doreen had traveled to Riolapa to meet me. They were there when I arrived. I know that the trip summoned all the reserves of fortitude they had, and from their perspective, Riolapa must have seemed dangerously exotic – treacherous in ways they couldn't imagine. They wanted only to retrieve me and bring me home. When I saw my mother and sister, they both were hugging their purses as though they suspected thievery at every turn, and perhaps they were correct in their caution? When we embraced, all three of us at once, I realized that what I'd missed most about my family was their touch. Mostly that. A warm and solid embrace, a casual stroking of my hair as they placed stray strands in more modest arrangements. And their aromas -- so foreign at first -- became the strongest reminder that I had come home.

My mother embraced me and then held me at arm's length, studying the daughter she had rediscovered. She said, "The way you carry yourself is different. You're straighter." And then she looked at something imaginary over my shoulder, embarrassed perhaps, by the intrusion of inspecting me so intensely. Doreen said, "I dreamed of you often. Not of where you might be -- I didn't know about that -- but simply your face. Usually, you were smiling." There were questions. Was I well? How had I survived? Had I tried, and failed, to return? Was I the same person, now, as the young woman who had left? The explanations took a long time to unwind. Much has been omitted, still.

Riolapa was not a sterile place to me, despite the earth sealed and airless beneath the pavement. In the two days we had together there before the return flight, we strolled around the city -- I think that Doreen and my mother assumed that now that I was with them, we were all more secure. The guidebook my mother had acquired in the hotel lobby said that some of Riolapa's crooked streets had been paths worn by cattle in other times. These streets were paved with rounded stones and lined by vendors' stalls where fruit was sold, and candles, and flowers, and roughly painted plaster statues of saints, almost sordid in their colors. Those wandering little streets were clogged with children in motion, and I wondered, did they have homes, anywhere? They were all elbows and knees and wise expressions, and they seemed ravenous beyond the need for food. Children squatted around brief fires made of cardboard, or they clung like monkeys to the backs of buses, or they were caught up in our wake as we walked.

The traffic noise and stink on the thoroughfares were incredible, but Riolapa's cathedrals seemed unaffected by the hectic pace. They gathered quaint, cobbled plazas around them. The cathedrals were gloriously embellished. Garlands of stone gentled their facades. Spires, turrets, towers, and domes were uplifted from the ground. Tucked into alcoves under the roofs of the cathedrals were demons with elephantine ears, bulging eyes, and stretched lips, awaiting the rainwater that would spew in arcs from their mouths. Pigeons stepped in jerks in the plazas, mumbling nonsense and jostling one another. At night from my hotel room's window, the city lights were stunning, as strangely beautiful as anything I had ever seen. In this city, the earth had fractured and within it, Riolapa glittered like a geode's crystal.

Of all the disjointed things that happened during the process of my repatriation, I suppose that the speed of the return journey was the most unsettling. It took so little time. Hours, only. The plane crossed over the threshold where land became ocean in an instant. This edge was hemmed by yellowed suds and then we were over only water, where sandy fingers of land probed toward the deeper channels. The rim of the continent was busy with changes. It looked unstable. And then the sea ledged abruptly, darkening to a rich, royal blue, a fertile color that hid the mountains below -- the undersea ranges that surely were rising. Far out over the ocean, the ruffles of breakers appeared to be still, although I knew they were relentlessly proceeding toward a shore where they would roll over and release their small treasures of shells and bones onto the land.

I dozed on the plane, and each time I awakened, many miles had passed without my effort. Soon there was another coastline, although by then it was night and I could only assume that the ocean was behind us by the nets of lights that replaced the blankness of the water. Lights were below me and ahead of me. It was abrupt, and yet the blue designs were scarcely faded from my skin.

In the last place I lived with the Jukima, my surroundings were so stark that my dreams were richly varied, in contrast. In my dreams, a recurring image was that of my childhood house. The straightness of its outlines was in counter-point to the foggy air around and the mushy grass at the foundation of the house. My family would come out on the porch to greet me and they posed there, like a tableau. It must have seemed to them that had I walked out of a hole in the ground. In this dream, my family hadn't changed with the passage of time -- they were the ages they had been when I had left them. My sisters smelled of interior spaces, like warmed dust and plain food, and the aroma of the starch of their clothes clung to them, an essence that was industrious and severe. I was gathered in by them all, as if these people related to me by biology and a common history would have to accept me, no matter how far I'd gone from them. When I saw them all again, in the flesh, these impressions merged with the ways they had changed and became one thing, one complicated truth.

I have changed in essential ways that I can't always identify. It's difficult to penetrate the masks that cover the emotions of people. The Jukima had been a small group within which trust had been earned and had flourished, but here, instant judgments seem to prevail. Avoidances. Deceptions. Attractions. Evaluations of someone's usefulness or not usefulness, in various ways. The faces flicker open or closed. It's confusing, and one must be cautious. The lines between the people and the Xangu are not clearly drawn, or perhaps I'm not astute enough yet in deciphering the facial language of my recovered culture? Does a smile indicate candid affirmation, or is it a baring of teeth? I compare these mysterious expressions to Carogo's eloquent, unguarded face.

The first time my family shared a meal with all of us together again, there was a display of foods from many places and all seasons before us. We ate at two tables pushed side-by-side, with another table set for the children. The tables and chairs and people strained the room to capacity. All my sisters but Martha had married, and their husbands were with us -- some of them innocently gregarious, like our father, and some sat uncomfortably and with wintry expressions. And there were so many children. Doreen's three, Gretta's four from her three marriages. Amanda's son and daughter, and Vernelle had an infant. It was difficult, at first, to learn all the names. Doreen's eldest son, Joel, was the only one of these children I had seen before. His adolescence was not graceful, but he had a kindness about the eyes and he was gentle with the younger ones. We could start a tribe from all of the children and the partners they would choose, when they came of age.

Vernelle's baby was fastened with straps into a high-chair next to her own straight-backed chair. She wiped orange muck - - was it squash? -- from his chin with her finger, then laughed when the baby sucked her finger clean. That evening, my father was telling a complicated story, about how our neighbors across the street were feuding with the family next-door to them. One family had built a "hate-fence" of solid planks, high and tightly clenched together, and entirely shading their neighbor's south-facing windows. And these people had retaliated by planting a row of quick-growing pine trees that soon outstripped the fence and shed a litter of thatch and cones on their neighbor's driveway. Then, the neighbors had installed a flood-light at the entrance to their garage that was so bright that the other feuding family had to cover their bedroom windows with thick draperies. And so it continued, to my father's amusement, although he found the floodlight irritating, as well.

I watched Vernelle's infant opening his mouth for the food like a baby bird. His eyes, lush and purely blue, had an intensity that was both imperious and needy. He smacked his lips, opened his mouth, and Vernelle inserted the spoon. I didn't know him yet, and I thought, "Love has many, specific, faces."

When I decided on the place I would live, I recognized it immediately -- it was like an instinctively correct arrival. With the help of my family, I bought the property on that same day. A little, square house, its clapboards rounded by layers of creamy paint. A river-rock chimney, with stones that were stacked round and solid, growing upward from a wide base. There was a scrap of lawn in the front, and a pyracantha bush loud with scarlet berries. The small bush sheltered tiny birds in its cage of thorns. However, it wasn't the house or its frontyard that pleased me. It was the yard in back of the house, which was bordered all around with a dense hedge of hemlock, buffering this small square of earth from the noise of the street. This backyard garden stepped down in levels, and on its east side, cushioned by the hemlock hedge, were stone planter-boxes, wadded with the stalks and spent foliage of a garden gone wild. I lifted up a pad of moss with my toe, and saw just enough of a stone walkway to be intrigued. There were paths laid in stone under the grass and moss, and restoring this garden would be satisfying work.

When I had been a student at the university, I didn't particularly care about my surroundings. That is one way I am different, now. Now I'm always aware of the way the light changes in various weathers and in different seasons, and how the shadows shrink or extend. I always awaken with the first light, and I'm brimmed with hope. In my little house, the walls are starkly white, as a neutral field for the drama of shadows. There are only a few things that I have -- a few calming things. I have some containers of thick, bubbled glass into which I put twigs with berries or black, twisted branches that project interesting designs onto the white walls. I have a rectangular mat of jute that smells like a mown hayfield. I like to feel the prickling texture of it under my bare feet. Shoes will always be an imposition that I tolerate when not at home. I wear the bit of fossil-rock on a cord around my neck – it's my only material connection with the Jukima. Although I still think of myself as a kind of scholar, for my work I write stories for children and illustrate them with fabulous creatures. The stories are as solid and yet fanciful as myths that can be told again and again without growing stale. This work brings me great contentment.

My house has a fireplace that's set into a gray stone niche. There are twin kerosene lanterns on the mantle over the fireplace, and on some evenings, their dusky illumination is something I choose. My house is so drafty that when I build a fire, currents of air pull at the flames and make them leap crazily. Sometimes when I look into the fire, I can see the faces of people I've known and lost. Even now, it pains me when I think of Tihana. I regret that he had come so easily to ideas of war, and that those ideas had been waiting for him to discover them. He had not had the perspective that comes from exposure to challenging dilemmas, and he hadn't studied the choices made by those who came before him.

It's night outside the windows and I've opened the shades and invited the darkness to enter. There is no illumination except for the fire in the fireplace, and I am seated cross-legged before it. I'm sitting quietly and meditating upon the quandary of how wonder can exist in the illusion that all is explainable by those things that can be proven -- tiny, bounded facts that have been reduced to manageable simplicity. How can wonder exist within that illusion of certainties? And then I take a deep breath and send my words away with my exhaling. I rest my hands, palms up, on my thighs and I think of nothing, in any language. I restrain nothing with definitions. Inside my eyelids it is entirely dark -- but that's where I look -- upon that darkness, until a pulse-beat appears, a reddish-purple circle, dilating, contracting, flaring again, and I say to myself, "It's the throbbing of pulse in the capillaries of my eyes," and with that the vision

vanishes and I must begin again, must think of *nothing*. A
ruddy-purpling glow returns, and pulses. And then an image –
a bird-shape -- but I must not say a word -- any word. I let my
eyes drift open. The room is dim and there is only the fire in its
stone niche. The heat of the flames agitates the molecules in the
room and the air quivers. The flames toss like surf, and I look
upon them and then into them, and my vision opens. A shape
appears in the flames, a bird-shape, but I do not say its name. It
is not separate from who I am and it is not contained in my
mind. The bird rises.

***